PONY CLUB SECRETS

TWO BOOKS IN ONE!

Destiny and Stardust

The Pony Club Secrets series:

Also available...

Coming soon...

Pony Club Secrets

Destiny and Stardust

Destiny and the Wild Horses

and

Stardust and the Daredevil Ponies

STACY GREGG

HarperCollins *Children's Books*

www.stacygregg.co.uk

Destiny and the Wild Horses first published in paperback in Great Britain by HarperCollins *Children's Books* in 2008. *Stardust and the Daredevil Ponies* first published in paperback in Great Britain by HarperCollins *Children's Books* in 2008. First published as a two-in-one edition as *Destiny and Stardust* in Great Britain by HarperCollins *Children's Books* in 2010.
HarperCollins *Children's Books* is a division of HarperCollins *Publishers* Ltd, 77-85 Fulham Palace Road, Hammersmith, London W6 8JB.

Visit our website at: www.harpercollins.co.uk

1 3 5 7 9 10 8 6 4 2

Text copyright © Stacy Gregg 2008

ISBN: 978-0-00-734609-7

Stacy Gregg asserts the moral right to be identified as the author of the work.

Printed and bound in England by Clays Ltd, St Ives plc

Destiny and the Wild Horses

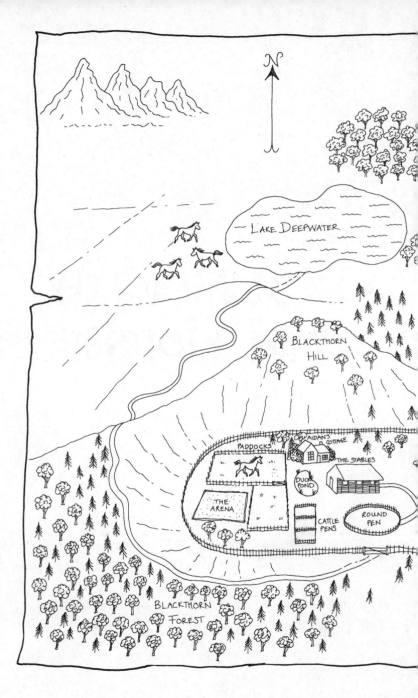

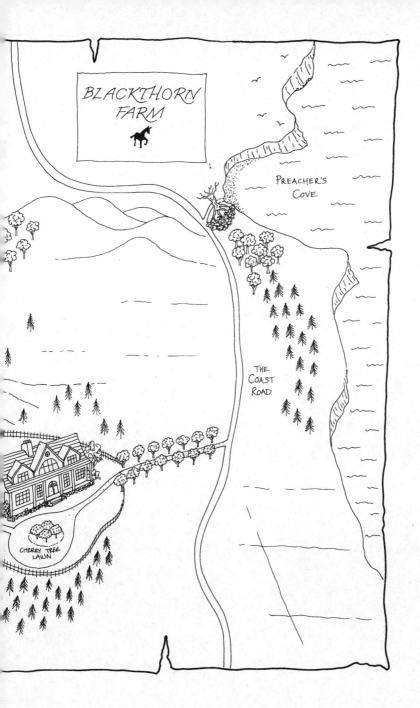

For my mum, who never liked horses at all, but loved her two horse-mad daughters. Thanks for everything.

Chapter 1

One of the best feelings in the world is waking up and thinking, *Ohmygod, I'm late for school!* That isn't the good bit obviously. The good bit comes in a sudden rush a few seconds later when you realise that you don't have to go to school after all because today isn't an ordinary Monday – it's the first day of the summer holidays!

Issie was savouring that exact moment right now as she lay snuggled up in bed. She gave her legs a big, wriggly stretch underneath the duvet. There was something so luxurious about lying there, knowing that she didn't have to hurry up and put her uniform on and pack her book bag. No school for two whole months. And this summer promised to be the best ever.

Issie had big plans for the holidays. And most of those

plans involved Blaze, her chestnut Anglo-Arab mare. Summer meant pony-club season. There would be gymkhanas, ribbon days and one-day events to ride, and Issie had Blaze in perfect condition ready for competition.

Her pony had been schooling beautifully ever since Issie got her back from Francoise D'arth. They had been having regular dressage lessons with Tom Avery and she was amazed at how responsive and clever her horse was. Now that Issie and Tom knew Blaze's real background – that she had once been part of a famous troupe of dancing Arabians – they had begun to try new things with her. Under Avery's tutelage, Blaze and Issie had easily mastered fancy moves like shoulder-ins and piaffes.

"That mare is the perfect school mistress for you," Avery told her. "We're going to make huge strides in your training this summer, Issie."

Avery was confident that Blaze was ready to compete in the summer series dressage competitions at the Chevalier Point Pony Club which began that weekend. "You'll only be in the novice section so there certainly wouldn't be any piaffes in your dressage test," he said.

Still, Issie was nervous. She had never done dressage on Blaze before. What if the mare got all heated up and panicked in the arena? What if she forgot the test and got lost halfway through?

"Don't be ridiculous!" Stella had told Issie when she blabbed her fears. "You and Blaze have practised your test, like, at least twenty times! I still don't know it and Coco is being so stubborn lately she won't even lead on the correct leg when she canters. She's being a total nightmare!"

With the competition looming, Stella, Issie and Kate all agreed that they needed more dressage practice, so Tom Avery had arranged a training session for the Chevalier Point riders at the pony club that morning.

Issie gave one last squirm under the duvet. It was so warm and comfy she still didn't want to get up. "One, two, three!" she counted herself out of bed, jumping up on three and making a dash across the bedroom to the pile of washing on the floor. She pulled on her jodhpurs and grabbed a hair band off her dresser, sweeping her long, straight, dark hair back in a ponytail as she headed down the stairs.

Her mother had left for work early that morning but she had left Issie a note on the kitchen table.

11

Gone to work (obviously!). Have to pick up groceries on the way home so won't be back until six. We need to talk about the holidays — make sure you are home by seven for dinner. Mum x

Issie read the note, popped two slices of wholegrain bread in the toaster and poured herself a glass of orange juice from the fridge.

What did her mum mean "We need to talk about the holidays"? Her holidays were already decided – she planned to spend every minute at pony club with Stella, Kate, Dan and Ben. What else was there to talk about?

After a second round of toast she finished getting dressed, grabbed her bike out of the garage and cycled off to pony club.

When Issie arrived at the club she found her two best friends Stella and Kate staring at an expensive-looking silver and blue horse truck that had just pulled up at the club grounds.

"Wow! Very flashy," said Kate.

"I've never seen that truck before. It doesn't belong to any of the Chevalier Point riders, does it?" Stella asked. Her question was answered instantly as a girl with a sour expression and two ramrod-straight shiny blonde plaits emerged from the truck to open the gates.

"I should have known! Stuck-up Tucker's mummy has bought her a brand new horse truck," Stella sighed.

They watched as Natasha stood sulking beside the truck, refusing to move until her mum asked her for a third time to help lower the ramp. Issie had been expecting to see Natasha's palomino mare Goldrush coming down the ramp. Instead the girl led out a very refined-looking rose-grey with a white heart shape on his forehead and a steel-grey mane and tail. He wore a dark navy wool rug and matching floating boots to protect his delicate legs. As Natasha removed the boots the girls saw that his hind legs had two pretty white socks.

"Check out Natasha's new horse!" Stella gave a low whistle of admiration.

"Issie! You have to go and ask her about it!" Kate demanded.

"What? Why me?" Issie groaned. "Natasha can't stand me!"

"At least she speaks to you! She won't even bother

to talk to me or Kate," Stella countered. "Go on! Go and ask her."

"All right, all right…" Issie muttered as she walked off across the paddock. The truth was, she didn't need much coaxing. She was dying to know about the new horse too.

"Hi, Natasha, I didn't know you were riding with us today," Issie said.

"Hmmph? Oh hello, Isabella," Natasha said.

"It's Isadora," Issie replied flatly. One of Natasha's favourite games was to accidentally-on-purpose forget Issie's name.

"What-ever," Natasha sniffed. "How's your little circus pony?"

Ever since Issie had beaten Natasha Tucker at the pony-club one-day event, the bratty blonde had been spiteful towards Issie and her chestnut mare. Natasha had called Blaze a "scruffy pit pony with no papers" until the truth about Blaze was discovered: she had once been one of the El Caballo Danza Magnifico mares, the famous Anglo-Arabs with immaculate bloodlines dating back to the great desert-bred Arabians.

Of course even this news didn't stop Natasha. Now that everyone knew just how valuable Blaze's breeding really was, Natasha had taken to teasing Issie about having a "circus pony", even though everyone knew that the El Caballo Danza Magnifico wasn't a circus at all – it was a *haute ècole* riding school that travelled the world performing fantastic dressage movements to music. Blaze had once been the star of the school. But now, thanks to a mysterious benefactor, the chestnut mare belonged to Issie.

"Blaze is fine thanks, Natasha," Issie said. She turned her attention to the beautiful rose-grey gelding. "Is this your new horse? What happened to Goldrush?"

"I told Mummy that Goldrush simply wasn't up to my level any more so we got rid of her," Natasha said coolly. "This is Fabergé. He's a sport horse, bred by Iggy Dalrymple, so you can just imagine how much he cost us. Mummy says it's vulgar to talk about money but she did tell me that he cost more than all of her Prada handbags put together."

"He's really beautiful," Issie said as she ran her hand gently down the crest of Fabergé's neck. "Are you going to enter him in the summer dressage series?"

"Uh-huh. I'd say we're bound to win it actually." Natasha smirked. "Fabergé has been off at Ginty McLintoch's stables for two weeks being schooled up. Ginty herself has put in hours of work on him – Mummy paid her an absolute bomb to do it." Natasha wrinkled up her nose. "I couldn't be bothered with doing all that training myself! Anyway, now he is positively a push-button ride apparently. I can just sit there and Fabergé knows exactly what to do. It should be a piece of cake to win the novice ring this season."

"Well, I guess we'll see you at the dressage test on Saturday," Issie said. "Blaze and I are in the novice ring too." Issie was sure she saw the smug look on Natasha's face fade for a moment. And then the blonde regained her haughty composure.

"They don't give you points for doing circus tricks in proper dressage, you know."

"That's a pity because Blaze can balance a ball on her nose while doing a dance on her hind legs," said a voice behind them.

Issie turned round to see Stella on top of Coco, smiling brightly at her. Kate, who was with her on Toby, was trying to suppress her giggles. Natasha's scowl deepened.

"You always have your little gang with you to stick up for you, don't you?" Natasha snapped. "I wonder how cool you'd be if you were all on your own with no one else to look after you."

They were interrupted at that moment by Tom Avery's booming voice.

"Riders into the arena now, please!" he instructed.

Issie gave the rose-grey gelding a pat. "Anyway, it was nice to meet you, Fabergé," she said. Natasha continued to glare at her. "Bye, Natasha." Issie shrugged and began to run back across the paddock to the tethering rail where Blaze was waiting for her.

"Can we all line up, please?" Tom Avery said.

The riders had been warming up their ponies. Dan and Ben had arrived a little late, but had quickly tacked up Kismit and Max and joined the others. Now the six riders all stood in the centre of the arena awaiting Avery's instructions.

Avery slapped his riding crop against his long brown leather boots to get their attention. "With the dressage test approaching this weekend, I think you're all ready for some more advanced schooling," he said. "Does anyone here know how to do a flying change?"

Without hesitation a hand shot up amongst the riders.

"Ah, Natasha. Of course. Please come forward for a moment," Avery said. Natasha cast a glance at Issie as she rode Fabergé past her to stand at the front of the ride.

"Now Natasha here is going to demonstrate a flying change," Avery said. As you all know, a flying change is when we ask our horse to canter with a leading leg, and then we ask with our aids and make the horse change legs in midair." Avery paused. "You might have seen this on your Olympic dressage videos at home. It looks a bit like the horse is skipping, doesn't it?"

"Anky makes it look really easy when she does it on Bonfire," Stella said.

"Well then, let's see how easy it really is, shall we?" Avery said. "Natasha, why don't you work your horse around the arena at a canter and then ride a flying change through the middle of the school to show us how it's done?"

Natasha set off on Fabergé with a look of grim determination on her face. She cantered the rose-grey around the arena and then turned him down the centre of the school to begin her flying change. In the middle of the school Natasha gave Fabergé a big kick with her heels. Nothing happened. She looked exasperated. Poor Fabergé looked confused.

"Try again, this time with nice, clear aids. You don't need to kick your horse! Just put that right leg forward on the girth," Avery instructed. Natasha rode around and down the centre line again. This time, though, she ignored Avery's advice and gave Fabergé an almighty boot with her right leg. Fabergé shot up like a rocket, putting in a vigorous buck. Natasha gave a yelp of horror as she flew over Fabergé's head and sailed through the air, coming down in a heap on the sandy surface of the arena. Fabergé gave a terrified snort and cantered off. Dan and Ben quickly clucked their horses and rode after him while Natasha stood up grumpily and dusted herself down.

"Are you all right?" Avery asked her. Natasha, who was bright red in the face, nodded quietly.

"He's a very sensitive horse. If I were you I'd master the basics on him before you try a flying change again," Avery said kindly. Then he gestured to Issie. "Isadora, why don't you give it a try on Blaze? Remember, you need to move your right leg to the girth."

"Good girl, c'mon," Issie clucked to Blaze as she set off around the perimeter of the arena. As she rode down the centre line in a canter she sat tall in the saddle and tried to think about arranging her legs into the correct position. Right in the middle of the arena Issie did exactly as Avery had instructed – she moved one leg forward and the other leg back and squeezed hard. Beneath her she felt Blaze rise up and throw out her front legs like a schoolgirl skipping down the street – a flying change!

"Textbook stuff! A very nicely executed flying

change." Avery was pleased. "Excellent. Now, who's going to give it a go next? Dan? How about you?"

Issie slowed Blaze down to a walk and gave her a big slappy pat on the neck as she took her place back in the line. "Not bad for a circus pony!" she whispered to her pony.

In the end, Issie was the only rider that day to master the flying change. "It's not as easy as it looks," Stella had grumbled as they untacked the ponies. Issie had nodded in agreement with her friend, but the truth was that to her it had been easy. It was as if she only had to think about what she wanted to do and Blaze would respond. OK, so there weren't any fancy flying changes in their dressage test this weekend. Still, Issie felt certain for the first time ever that she and Blaze stood a really good chance. They might even win.

"Mum! I'm home! I did a flying change today!" Issie charged in through the front door without pausing to take off her riding boots.

"Isadora! You'd better not still have your muddy boots on!" her mother yelled back from the kitchen.

Issie stopped dead and ran back to the laundry, stripping off her boots and socks before running back to the kitchen to find her mother.

"You can tell me all about it while you eat your dinner," Mrs Brown said. And so, between mouthfuls of potato salad, Issie told her mum about Natasha and the flying changes and the dressage series that was starting on Saturday.

"Blaze is going so perfectly. This is going to be the best summer I've ever had!" Issie said.

Mrs Brown didn't say anything. She just looked down at her plate and gave her quiche a distracted poke with her fork.

"Mum? What's wrong? You've hardly said anything since I got home," Issie said.

Mrs Brown pushed her plate aside. She looked serious, but still she didn't speak.

"Mum?"

"Issie, I am afraid I've got some, well, it's not bad news really. I mean it's good but it's not good…" Mrs Brown hesitated. "I've been invited away on a conference for work. They're going to fly me there and pay for accommodation – the whole thing. I'll be gone for two weeks."

"That's great!" Issie said. "When?"

"We leave on Friday," Mrs Brown said. "That's why I wanted to talk to you tonight about the holidays. I've made plans for you."

"What do you mean?" Issie said.

"Sweetie, I can't leave you here by yourself. If I'm away for two weeks then who would look after you? You're only thirteen. You're not old enough to be by yourself."

"Cool. I can go stay with Stella!" Issie said.

Mrs Brown shook her head. "There's something else, Issie. I got a phone call last night from your Aunt Hester. It turns out she's had a bad fall off one of her silly horses and broken her leg."

"Aunty Hess? That's terrible! Is she OK?"

"She's fine," Mrs Brown sighed, "but she can't possibly look after that farm of hers. She has Aidan to help her but it's not enough…" Mrs Brown paused "…and so I suggested that you could go and stay with her until she gets better again."

"Me?" Issie squawked.

"Sweetie – it's perfect! You can stay with Hester while I'm away, and she needs your help so it suits her," Mrs Brown explained. "Besides, you've never been to the farm before and I know you will just love it. Hester has loads of ponies and all those other animals that she trains. You'll adore it there."

"But, Mum! Blaze and I have been working so hard for the dressage competition," Issie said.

"I know, honey. But I can't see any other way." Mrs Brown sighed. "I've already asked Aidan if he can drive through to get you. He's going to be here on Wednesday morning."

"But it's Monday now! When were you going to tell me this? What about Stella and Kate? What about my holidays? What about Blaze?"

"I'm sorry, Issie. It's the only option. Really, you'll see. You're going to love it at the farm... Issie? Issie!"

But Issie didn't hear her. She had already left the kitchen in tears, run up the stairs to her bedroom and slammed the door shut behind her.

Chapter 2

How could the school holidays go so wrong so fast? Issie flung herself down on her bed and buried her face deep in the duvet. She couldn't believe her mum would ruin her summer like this!

"Issie? Come on. Let me in and let's talk about this," Mrs Brown's voice echoed softly outside Issie's bedroom door.

Issie stood up and walked over to let her mother in, before flopping back down, rather over-dramatically, with her face in the duvet again.

"It's not fair. Why do I have to go to Aunty Hester's?" She gave a muffled groan from beneath the blankets.

"Sweetie, I really do think it's the best idea for everyone – especially Aunty Hess," Mrs Brown said.

"It would be a huge favour to her if you helped out until her leg is better. Hess has a big movie coming up. They start filming in a couple of months and she has dozens of animals that need to be trained. She has so much work to do she could really use an extra pair of hands…"

"But *I* had plans!" Issie said. "The dressage series is on and Blaze is going so well. I can't just leave her and go away to the farm."

Mrs Brown suddenly perked up. "Hey! I tell you what – how about if you could take Blaze with you?"

"What do you mean?"

"You could take Blaze to Aunty Hester's. I could call Aidan and ask him to bring the horse truck when he comes to pick you up on Wednesday and then you can take Blaze with you. I'm sure Hess won't mind. One more horse on that enormous farm of hers won't make the slightest difference."

Issie sat up. "Do you mean it? Could Blaze really come too?"

"I don't see why not," Mrs Brown said. She was clearly very pleased with herself for coming up with the idea. "You know what? I'm going to give Hess a call now and ask her!"

Mrs Brown trotted off down the stairs and a moment

later Issie could hear her on the phone chatting and laughing happily with her sister.

If I could take Blaze with me, Issie thought, *maybe it wouldn't be so bad.*

Issie really liked her aunt. For starters, Hester was horsy through and through. Issie always thought it was so unfair that her own mother hated horses while her Aunt Hess adored them. If Aunt Hester had been her mother then she would have got a pony straight away. Instead she had to beg for years before her mum finally gave in and bought Mystic.

Mrs Brown couldn't understand why Issie loved horses so much. "It must be genetic. Your aunt was exactly the same when she was your age," Mrs Brown had told Issie on more than one occasion. "Hess was totally horse-mad! And now look at her – she has seven horses, a trained pig, a goat, several sheep, those nuisance blasted dogs and heaven knows what else on that crazy farm of hers!"

Hester worked as an animal trainer for the movies. Three years ago she decided to set up her own business, and so she bought Blackthorn Farm, where she kept and trained her menagerie of four-legged movie stars.

Blackthorn Farm was a rambling old country manor, high up in the hills near Gisborne. The manor and grounds had once been quite grand, apparently, but Hester had got the place for very little because it had become quite rundown.

Blackthorn Manor was huge – it had eleven bedrooms – but Hester lived there alone. She had been married three times – "All of them wonderful weddings!" she told Issie – but she had never had any children of her own. She called Issie her "favourite niece" which was a bit of a joke between the two of them since Issie was in fact her only niece.

Hester ran the farm herself with help from her young stable manager, Aidan. With her leg in plaster and all those animals to look after, she was bound to need some extra help.

Issie listened to her mum hang up the receiver and head back up the stairs. When she entered Issie's room she had an enormous smile on her face.

"Good news! Hess says she'd love to meet your horse, Issie. It all sounds perfect. There's a spare stall for Blaze in the stable complex and she's getting it ready for your arrival and Aidan will be here to pick you both up first thing on Wednesday morning with the truck. It's a long drive. It will probably take you most of the day to get there."

"Really? So Blaze can come with me? And we're actually going?" Issie said.

Mrs Brown looked at her daughter's uncertain expression. "Issie? I thought that would make you happy. You can take Blaze with you – there's lots of land to ride there – that farm is positively huge – you could ride all day without leaving the property."

"I know… I mean, yes, it's great, Mum. Honestly. And I want to go and help out Aunty Hess and everything…" Issie sighed. "It's just that Stella and Kate and me had the whole summer planned out and now I'm not going to be here. And what about Tom? He was expecting me to ride the dressage series and—"

"I'm sure Stella and Kate will understand. I know you three are pretty hard to separate but maybe it will be nice to have some time on your own for once," Mrs Brown said. "As for Tom, you leave him to me. I'm sure he'll agree with me that a few weeks out of your training schedule isn't going to ruin your chances of riding at Badminton!"

"Mum! As if!" Issie laughed.

"Aha! I knew I could get you smiling again." Mrs Brown grinned back at her daughter. "Now, I'll dig out your suitcase and let's make sure you actually have some clean clothes to pack, shall we? Hand me that pile of washing over there and we'll get started!"

The news that Issie was going to Blackthorn Farm left Stella speechless – for a moment anyway. "Stella?" Issie said. There was silence at the other end of the phone and then a torrent of words came pouring out.

"I can't believe your mum is doing this! We had plans, Issie! Big plans! What about the dressage series? What about the summer holidays? It's not fair! How long will you be gone for?"

"I don't know. I suppose I'll stay there until Aunt Hester's leg is better and she can manage on her own again." Issie sighed. "You know, I am her favourite niece and everything."

"Very funny, Issie! Your mum's ruined our whole summer! Have you told Kate yet?"

"No," Issie said, "I thought I'd tell you first because I knew you'd take it so well!"

Stella gave a giggle at this. "You're right, I am overreacting, aren't I? You might only be gone for a couple of weeks. I suppose we can always email each other while you're away."

"Actually I don't even know if Aunty Hess has email.

Blackthorn Farm is in the middle of nowhere. Aidan is coming to pick me up first thing on Wednesday morning and it will take us pretty much all day to drive there."

"Who's Aidan?" Stella said.

"He works for Aunty Hess. He runs her stables and he's driving the horse truck down from the farm to pick up me and Blaze."

"Oooh! How old is Aidan? What does he look like?"

"What? Oh, Stella! I think he's, like, maybe seventeen. I have no idea what he looks like. I've never been to the farm so I've never met him, OK?" Issie snapped. Stella had gone a bit boy-mad lately, which Issie found very annoying. She hadn't even thought about what Aidan might be like – but now she realised he would be here tomorrow and they would have to spend the whole day together driving to the farm.

"I'd better tell Dan. I'm sure that will make him jealous," Stella laughed.

"Stella! Don't!" Issie said.

Dan had asked Issie out once – at least she thought he'd asked her out – but things got all confused because it turned out he'd asked Natasha too and maybe it had never been a date. Anyway it was all a big mess and nothing had ever happened after that.

Issie sighed. "Oh, go on then. Tell Dan and Ben that I've gone away and tell Natasha too while you're at it; I'm sure she'll be thrilled that I won't be competing against her in the dressage."

Stella groaned. "Ohmygod! Natasha. I'd forgotten about that. She's going to be unbearable if she wins. Issie! How can you leave me? Don't go!"

"I'm hanging up now, Stella," Issie said. "I have to go pack and then I have to clean Blaze's tack and get her floating boots out and make sure that all her gear is ready to go…"

"OK, OK." Stella sighed. "But you'd better email me. And if they have no email then send a carrier pigeon or whatever they've got up there."

"Knowing Aunty Hess, I wouldn't be surprised if she hasn't trained up a pigeon or two," Issie giggled. "It's a deal – I'll send you a letter by pigeon post."

Aidan was due to arrive at seven a.m. on Wednesday morning to pick Issie up. But when Issie opened her curtains at six a.m. to check the weather, she saw the horse truck was already parked outside.

"Mum?" she called out as she padded downstairs, still in her pyjamas. "The horse truck is here already."

"I know," her mother replied from the kitchen. "Come in and meet Aidan!"

Issie walked through to find her mother making coffee for a young boy in a plaid shirt and jeans who was sitting at the table. The boy, who looked not that much older than Issie, had black hair that fell over his face in a long, floppy fringe almost covering his eyes. He stood up as Issie sat down next to him and stuck out his hand for her to shake.

"Hi," he said, "I'm Aidan."

"Hello Issie! I mean… hello, I'm Issie!" Issie said, flustered. She shook Aidan's hand. "Sorry, I'm not ready to go yet obviously," she said, looking down at her pyjamas, which she now realised were the ones with pink kittens all over them. "I didn't expect you to get here so early."

"I got here late last night and slept in the horse truck," Aidan said.

"Was that uncomfortable?" Mrs Brown asked.

"It's better than my bed back at the farm!" Aidan grinned. "It might look like a horse truck on the outside, but the inside is pure luxury. Hester's got it rigged up with two beds and a shower so we can travel with the horses. There's a kitchen too," he added, "but I never use it. I'm not a very good cook."

"Well, don't you worry about that, I'll make you breakfast." Mrs Brown smiled.

"Thanks, that would be great." Aidan grinned.

He looked over at Issie, who was fidgeting and looking down at the table, clearly embarrassed to be meeting a boy for the first time dressed in her pussycat pyjamas. Mrs Brown noticed her daughter shifting uncomfortably in her chair. "Issie, it will take a few minutes to get breakfast sorted. Why don't you go and have a shower and get dressed and I'll call you when it's ready?" she suggested.

"Thanks, Mum!" Issie said gratefully.

When she came downstairs for the second time that morning, Issie was ready to go. She was wearing her favourite jeans, a pair of brown leather boots and her favourite T-shirt. Her long dark hair was now neatly combed and tied back in a thick ponytail. She carried a big overnight bag thrown over one shoulder and was dragging a suitcase with her right hand.

"Let me help you." Aidan smiled, taking the bags off her. "I'll put these in the truck." He went out the front door with Issie's bags and she sat down at the table as her mum dished up her bacon and eggs.

"Aidan's already eaten. You finish up and then you can get going," Mrs Brown said as she poured herself a coffee from the plunger and sat down next to Issie. "Aidan will help you load Blaze at the pony club and then you can set off straight from there. Aunt Hess is expecting you in time for tea. I've packed you a banana cake to take with you; Hess is terrible at baking. In fact, all her cooking is terrible! You'll probably come back as skinny as a rake!" Mrs Brown said. She gave Issie a big hug.

"I've packed you a big bag of carrots for Blaze too in case she gets hungry during the trip."

Issie smiled. "Thanks, Mum!" she said.

"Take care, honey. Call me every night, OK?" Mrs Brown was still hugging Issie.

"Mum, you have to let go of me now, I need to leave." Issie laughed.

"Are we ready to go?" Aidan stuck his head around the kitchen door. "The truck is all packed. Let's go get this horse of yours."

It was only a five minute drive to the pony club, and Issie said nothing all the way. She was quiet even as she velcroed on Blaze's floating boots and loaded the dainty chestnut mare into the truck stall, tying her up with a hay net for the journey.

Issie hopped back into the cab, Aidan raised the ramp and they drove out through the pony-club gates. Issie took one last look over her shoulder at the horses who were left behind grazing happily. "Bye, Toby. Bye, Coco," she murmured. She felt a strange sensation in her tummy, like the butterfly nerves she usually got before a showjumping competition. She looked back through the window of the cab. Blaze was chewing contentedly on her hay net. Issie pressed her nose up against the glass and gazed at her pony, taking in the delicate dish of her nose and the deep, dark eyes fringed by her flaxen forelock.

"She's beautiful, isn't she?" Aidan said.

"What?"

"Your mare." Aidan smiled at Issie. "An Anglo-Arab, right? Half Arab and half Thoroughbred?"

"Uh-huh," Issie said.

"She looks like a very special horse. Where did you get her?" Aidan asked.

"It's a long story," Issie said.

"It's a long drive too," Aidan smiled, "so why don't you start now and maybe you'll be finished by the time we get there."

Issie laughed. "OK," she said. And so she told Aidan the story of Blaze. She started right at the very beginning, from the awful tragedy of Mystic's death. When she had lost her lovely grey gelding she thought she could never love another horse again. And then Avery had turned up with Blaze. She had been rescued by the International League for the Protection of Horses and was in a desperate state, terrified and half-starved. It had taken every last ounce of love that Issie had in her to win Blaze's trust and bring her back again. She nearly lost Blaze once more when Francoise D'Arth arrived in Chevalier Point and told her that Blaze was actually one of the famed El Caballo Danza Magnifico Arabians.

"She must be worth a fortune!" Aidan said.

Issie nodded. "I guess so. I don't really know. When Francoise brought Blaze back to me she told me that someone had paid for Blaze and wanted to give her to me. Now she's mine to keep for ever. I never found out who it was or how much they paid for her – and since I'll never, ever sell her I guess it doesn't really matter how much she is worth."

Aidan looked at Issie. "You've been through a lot with this mare, haven't you? I can see why you didn't want to leave her behind."

"She's my best friend." Issie smiled.

Aidan was right: it was a long drive to the farm. They made their way out of the city into the open countryside, and it was late in the afternoon when they drove up to the crest of a very high hill and Aidan finally turned the truck down the driveway that led to the farm. The limestone driveway seemed to almost burrow a tunnel through the dense native woods that surrounded them. The trees blocked out the light above them and Issie could hear scraping and rustling as the enormous branches that hung overhead began to brush against the roof of the horse truck. She pushed her nose up against the passenger window and stared out at the lush ferns, bright vermillion fuchsias, brilliant yellow kowhai flowers and boughs of crab apples laden with blood-red fruit. When the truck finally emerged into the golden afternoon light she found herself in front of an enormous two-storey white mansion, with latticed Victorian verandas and broad balconies on the second floor. There were cherry trees in full bloom covering the vast circular lawn in front of the house.

Standing in the middle of the lawn under the cherry trees was Aunty Hess. She wore a long, white, cotton dress and her hair, which was very blonde and tightly curled, tumbled over her shoulders. There was a loud baying as three dogs came bounding out of the house to join her. One was a smiling golden retriever, the other was an enormous black shaggy Newfoundland and the third was a whippet-thin black and white hound.

As they drove up towards the manor the dogs all leapt up dangerously, bouncing up to put their paws on the side of the horse truck as it pulled to a stop in front of the cherry trees. Then they dashed off again at a mad run and sat obediently on either side of the woman in the white cotton dress.

"Lie down, stay," Hess instructed the dogs. All three of them put their heads on their paws and lay perfectly still as she walked towards the horse truck and opened Issie's passenger door.

"Aunty Hess!" Issie beamed down at her aunt.

"Isadora! My favourite niece!" Hess held her arms up to help her down from the truck cab. "Welcome to Blackthorn Farm."

Chapter 3

Aunt Hester led Issie through the cherry trees and up the wide path that led to the grand entrance of Blackthorn Manor.

"You must be starving after driving all day!" she said. "Don't worry about your pony; Aidan will take the truck down and settle her in at the stables. You come with me. I've made you dinner."

Dinner, it turned out, was three burnt fish fingers with runny mashed potato and peas. "Your mother probably told you that my cooking isn't up to much," Hester smiled, "and I can tell you that she's quite right and it really hasn't improved!"

While Issie ate, Hester sat down next to her with her leg propped up on a chair. Issie hadn't noticed at first, but under that white cotton dress Hester was sporting a brilliant pink plaster cast that ran from her toes to her knee.

"Wow!' Issie said.

"Pretty, isn't it?" Hester smiled, knocking on the plaster with her knuckles. "They let me choose the colour, you know. Schiaparelli pink is so chic, don't you think? I'm still supposed to use crutches but I can't be bothered so I use a walking stick or I sometimes just hop," Hester continued. "It's a very long driveway down to the stables when you're hopping on one foot, I can tell you. And feeding out the farm animals takes me for ever."

"How did it happen, Aunty Hess?"

"Oh, I was training one of the horses, Diablo. I was teaching him to lie down dead as if he had been shot, you see, like in a cowboy movie. Well, he lay down dead all right, but he did it right on top of me! Not his fault, of course; he was only doing what I asked him to do. But it broke my leg in two places, and there you go!" Aunt Hester smiled. "I must say it is lovely to have my favourite niece and her mystery mare here to help me out."

"Blaze! I should go and check on her." Issie suddenly panicked. "She's not used to being stabled and she doesn't know any of your horses. I should—"

"Don't worry about Blaze," Aunt Hester reassured her.

"Aidan will take excellent care of her. He used to work at a fancy stable in Ireland when he wasn't much older than you are now – looking after racehorses for some high and mighty Arab Sultan. It was all rather grand. Frightfully expensive horses too! I'm sure looking after your pony is well within his capabilities. We'll go down there in just a moment and you can check on her. But first…" Aunt Hester swept her hand dramatically towards the doorway that led to the main hall "…the grand tour!"

"Downstairs to start with, I think," Hester said. "Yes, yes. Follow me." She led Issie through a maze of vast wood-panelled rooms, each one more fantastic than the last, all of them with high ceilings, well-worn parquet floors and enormous, sparkling crystal chandeliers. The walls, which were papered in faded flock wallpaper, were adorned with antlers and wild boar heads. There were paintings everywhere of elegant racehorses and black and white photographs of grand old ladies looking out at you regally from the frame.

"Not my taste, you understand," Hester giggled. "I'm a little more shabby chic, aren't I, darling? Most of this lot was already here when I arrived. They sold the place to me lock, stock and barrel," she said, sweeping through the billiard room, where a game of pool was set up under the watchful gaze of two large stuffed pheasants.

Hester set a cracking pace through the manor. Issie had thought the plaster cast would have slowed her aunt down, but she grasped herself a walking cane out of the wicker basket in the hallway, propped herself up on one leg and skipped along very quickly indeed. Her progress wasn't aided by the three dogs, Strudel the retriever, Nanook the enormous black Newfoundland and Taxi, the skinny black and white cattle dog. The dogs all darted constantly around Hester's ankles, getting underfoot and almost tripping her up as she hopped from one room to the next.

"…and this is the ballroom, and the servants quarters – not that we have any servants!"

"What about Aidan?" Issie said.

"Oh, he's got his own place down the hill, next to the stables. Farm manager's cottage – very sweet. Right next to the duck pond," Hester said. "I'll show you when we do our outdoor tour. Now follow me up the stairs."

The grand, wooden staircase stood proudly at the centre of the manor. "There are seven bedrooms upstairs," Aunt Hester explained as she reached the top of the landing. "This one is your room."

Hester swung open the door and beckoned for Issie

to step inside. The room was enormous, but it felt cosy. The walls were papered with the most beautiful wallpaper Issie had ever seen, illustrated with old-fashioned drawings of exquisite Thoroughbreds standing with their jockeys dressed up in racing silks. Above the grand fireplace was a large oil painting of a beautiful grey horse with a long, silky mane. The horse was captured in action, cantering with his neck arched, and his proud head held high.

"Isn't he beautiful?" Hester smiled. "That's Avignon. He was my very favourite horse – a Swedish Warmblood stallion. I just adored him! Oh, I could look at this painting for ever…" Her voice trailed off as she stared at the painting. Then she picked up Issie's luggage, throwing the bags on the four-poster bed.

"Come on," she smiled at Issie, "that's the tour over and done with. Let's get out of here and go and see that horse of yours, shall we?"

If Hester had bounded swiftly around the manor, the long walk down to the stables seemed to take the spring out of her step. The driveway wound along the side of the manor then down past the garden, bordered by a stand of enormous puriri trees. Beneath the trees were gardens filled with magnolias, camellias and ferns, bordering a green lawn covered in daisies. At the far end of the lawn was a tennis court which looked as if it had seen better days. There were weeds springing up everywhere and the dilapidated old tennis net sagged in the middle.

"As you can imagine, tennis is not my priority right now." Hester said, tapping her cast. "Still, if you want play, I'm sure I've got racquets somewhere."

They continued their walk to the stables. Hester had to pause for a rest several times on the way, propping herself up against the huge boulders that lined the driveway to catch her breath. The three dogs all lay down obediently at her side each time she stopped, waiting until she instructed them to move again.

"This is why I need your help, Isadora darling," Hester said. "I simply can't get about to manage the animals. And Aidan couldn't possibly do everything on his own. Besides, Butch cannot abide Aidan, so that would never do."

"Who's Butch?" Issie asked. Just as she said this, round the corner from behind the stables lumbered a massive, black, hairy boar.

"Butch!" Hester cried. "Come and meet Isadora!"

The pig grunted happily and broke into a jog as he came towards them. His tiny little trotters looked like they might not be able to support the enormous bulk of the beast for much longer as he wobbled along.

"Butch is one of my superstars," Hester cooed as she reached down to feed the pig a carrot and give him a vigorous scratch behind the ears with a stick. "Do you know he's been in three TV commercials already this year? He's the pig in that bank ad – you know, the one with the piggy banks? He's rather famous, aren't you, Butchy? Shall we show Isadora some of your tricks?"

Hester put down her scratching stick, stood up from the boulder and produced another carrot which she held high above her head. "Beg, Butch!" she commanded. The pig grunted and then shifted his enormous weight, slumping back to sit on his haunches. Slowly he adjusted his position and lifted one front trotter and then the other off the ground so that he was balanced back on his hind legs. He looked just like a begging dog.

"Good lad!" Hester praised him and tossed the carrot up in the air. Butch opened his mouth and snapped at the carrot as it fell, crunching it up eagerly in his vast jaws.

Hester produced a second carrot. This time she held it directly in front of her like a magician brandishing a wand. "Play dead!" she commanded the pig. Butch gave a grunt and then fell dramatically, landing on the ground with a leaden thud. He lay perfectly still, even when Hester gave him a gentle prod with her foot. "Nice and dead," she cooed. "What a good pig! Now, Butch, up!" Butch grunted again and lifted his head, then braced himself with his front trotters and rather ungracefully pushed himself up again so that he was standing facing Aunt Hester.

"Well done, good Butch," she said as she fed him one more carrot.

"How did you teach him the tricks?" Issie asked.

"Oh, pigs are very easy to train; they're smarter than dogs," Hester said. "I've had Butch since he was a little piglet and I always knew he was clever. When he was a piglet Aidan caught him in the veggie garden and pelted him with an acorn. Butch has never forgiven him. That's why you'll have to look after him and keep his training up while you're here."

"But I don't know anything about pig training!" Issie spluttered.

"Don't worry, I'll explain everything. It's all quite simple," Hester said. "I've figured out a roster. Aidan will take care of the chickens and ducks. They've got a big role in this movie and they all need to learn their cues. One of the ducks needs to open a door – you can imagine the fuss he's made learning that… You're in charge of the rabbits," Hester continued. "There are seven of them and they're quite a funny bunch, I can tell you. You'll look after Butch too, of course, and then there's Meadow and Blossom."

"More pigs?" Issie asked.

"No, dear, a calf and a goat. Both of them are frightfully naughty and I'm afraid I've fallen quite behind in their training. You'll have to be rather firm with them."

"What exactly am I going to teach them?" Issie asked, feeling nervous.

"Oh, the usual. When to stop and go, nodding and shaking their heads… all the standard stuff," Hester said. "It's such bad timing to break my leg just when all my little stars are needed for such a big movie. *Tenderfoot Farm,* that's what it's called. It's an American crew. They're coming here next month to start filming. They need barnyard animals that can act on cue – and that's where I come in. My darlings are the best in the business." Hester gave Butch one last scratch behind the ears with the stick and then began to walk again towards the stables. The pig now joined them, trotting alongside with the dogs.

"The horses are my first love, of course," Hester said

as they approached the stables. "Other animals are lovely, but there is something truly magical about horses, don't you think?" She gave Issie a strange look as she said this and Issie didn't know what to say. Even Aunty Hess would be shocked if she knew about Mystic.

Issie's grey gelding had been such a special horse. She had loved him so deeply; it felt like her world had been torn apart the day he died. But since then, well, maybe *magical* was exactly the word for it. Issie had missed her horse so much that at first she couldn't believe it when Mystic had come back to her. He would appear just when she needed him most – and not like some ghost or anything, but a real horse. He had saved Issie and Blaze on more than one occasion. If anyone believed in the magic that horses held within them, it was Issie. But Issie knew somehow instinctively that Mystic was her secret now – and anyway, how could she possibly explain it all to Aunt Hester?

The stable was a large building, just a single storey with wide weatherboard planks painted a clean, crisp apple-white. Next to the stable block was a covered arena, not like a dressage arena, but a round pen with high walls and tiered seating. "That's where I do all of my stunt training." Hester gestured to it as she breezed past the pen towards the enormous sliding barn doors that led into the stable complex.

"It's so beautiful in here!" Issie was amazed. The stable doors were pale, honey-coloured wood. Each stall had a horse's head carved ornately on the door and a horse's nameplate hanging from a hook.

"We have seven horses of our own here so there is plenty of room for Blaze," Hester said as they walked. "We've put her right here, in the nearest stall to your right. Why don't we check on her first and then you can meet the others?"

Issie walked up to the stall. She ran her hand over the carved head on the door. There was no nameplate on the hook, but she could hear her horse nickering softly on the other side of the door.

"Blaze? Hey, girl, it's me." Issie said.

The mare went quiet for a moment, listening to Issie's voice. Then she nickered back, louder this time. Issie could hear her shifting about anxiously in the stall. She opened the top half of the Dutch door and bolted it back. There was Blaze, standing in the far corner of the stall next to her hay net. She nickered happily and came over immediately to Issie, nuzzling her soft muzzle against Issie's hands, taking a carrot from her palm. Issie raised her hand up and stroked just behind Blaze's ears, her fingers tangling in the mare's long flaxen mane.

"Well, isn't she something!" Aunt Hester said. "Your mother told me the whole story," she added, "so I knew your Blaze would be a beauty. But she's more than that, isn't she? She's a very special horse indeed."

Issie nodded silently.

"I know a thing or two about special horses myself," Hester said. "Come on. I want you to meet them." Hester walked over to the next stall and unbolted the door. "Come and say hello to Titan," she said.

Issie walked over and looked into the stall. It was completely empty. "Umm, Aunty Hess? There's no horse in here." Issie was confused. She stared at the unoccupied stall and back at her aunt, who had an amused smile on her face. And then she heard a noise, just a faint sound, the sound of a pony's hooves on the straw. Issie stuck her head right over the top of the Dutch door and there, hidden from view on the other side, was the smallest pony she had ever seen!

"Titan is a Falabella – a miniature horse," her Aunt said. "Nine hands tall. But such a big little horse, so much character! And quite the bossy-boots too! She keeps the big horses in line, I can tell you. Don't you, Titan?"

The tiny pony looked up at Issie and Hester. Her eyes were barely visible beneath her shaggy brown mane as she gratefully accepted Hester's offer of a carrot.

Hester left the top half of the Dutch door open and moved on to the next stall. "This is Dolomite," she said. Issie looked down, expecting to meet another miniature, but in fact Dolomite was just the reverse; he was an enormous bay Clydesdale with a broad white stripe running down his nose.

"Dolly is eighteen hands," Hester said. "You'd need a step ladder to get up on him, wouldn't you?"

Issie reached her hand up to pat Dolomite's nose. The gelding was so huge she had to stretch to reach him.

"He's a big softie. And very good for vaulting tricks," Hester said as she bustled along to the next stall.

"This is Diablo, the silly boy that broke my ankle," she said merrily. Diablo, a very handsome black and white piebald Quarter Horse, stuck his two-toned face over the stall. "Diablo loves doing cowboy tricks. He's a bit of show-off but I do love him," Hester said. "Diablo! Count to ten!" Hester barked at the horse.

The handsome piebald began to tap against the floor of the stall with his hoof, "one… two… three… four… five… six… seven… eight… nine… ten!"

Issie was amazed, but Aunt Hester just shrugged. "It's not so clever. A simple trick. I'll show you how it's done."

She moved across now to the other side of the stable and worked her way along the row, opening the doors to another two stalls. To Issie's surprise, each stall contained a palomino. The horses were so alike they were almost identical. "Meet the girls," Hester said. "That's Paris Hilton and this one is Nicole Ritchie." Hester stood there in front of the golden mares. "They're as pretty as their namesakes but much smarter." She grinned.

Hester opened the doors to the last two stalls now. "This is Scott," she said, patting the nose of a large skewbald gelding with a white face. "He's not the star, you understand, hasn't got that look-at-me quality in front of the cameras. But he's a good solid bet as a horse to play supporting roles."

Issie fed Scott a carrot while Hester walked on to the last stall and gave a soft cluck. In the final stall was a handsome bay gelding. "Tornado is the bad boy of the stable," Hester sighed. "But he will do absolutely anything you ask if you bribe him with peppermints. He used to be my eventing mount years ago. I still hunt on him occasionally. At least I did until this season." She tapped her plaster cast and shrugged. "I have tried to teach Tornado tricks like the others but frankly he doesn't want to know! He's very bright; I guess he thinks it's beneath him." She pulled a mint from her pocket and slipped it to the bay horse, who snuffled it down happily and poked his head over the stall looking for more.

"Well!" Hester put her arm around her niece's shoulder and gave Issie a squeeze as she looked about contentedly. "Now you've met just about everyone. What do you think?"

Issie gave her aunt a hug back. "I think this place is totally mad!" She grinned. "And I think this could be my best holiday ever!"

Chapter 4

Issie could feel the waves lapping at her feet. Her toes wriggled in the delicious warm sea. Suddenly a sharp nip on her big toe woke her up and she sat bolt upright in bed. Her feet, which were sticking out from under the duvet, were being vigorously licked by Strudel the golden retriever.

"Ewww! Gross! Strudel, get out!" Issie shrieked, throwing a pillow at the dog, who loped happily off through the door.

Issie jumped out of bed and picked the pillow up off the floor. The alarm clock said it was only six a.m. Bleary-eyed, she changed into her jeans and a navy v-neck jersey before heading downstairs. She wasn't getting caught by Aidan in her pink pussycat pyjamas in the kitchen a second time.

"Ah-ha! I sent Strudel up to wake you. I see she did her job nicely." Aunt Hester smiled as Issie walked into the kitchen. "Did you sleep well?"

"Uh-huh," Issie replied.

"Sit down. I've made us some breakfast," Hester said. She began to dish up some rather strange-looking lumpy objects out of a frying pan.

"Pancakes!" Hester said brightly. Then she frowned and looked at them again, "Or are they griddle scones? I can't quite remember what I put in the recipe and I got confused halfway through... anyway, here's some maple syrup, If you pour enough of this on them I'm sure they'll taste fine!"

Issie ate a mouthful of pancake and discovered that they tasted just as odd as they looked.

"Now," Hester said as she watched her niece slowly eating, "the weather promises to be just beautiful today. Why don't you take Blaze and go explore the farm? It goes for miles, you know. I was just about to find you a map and then I got sidetracked with the pancakes..." Aunt Hester put down the pan and began rummaging through the kitchen draws. She pulled out a piece of dog-eared paper. "Here we are – a map of Blackthorn Farm." Hester spread the pale parchment out on the kitchen table.

"Our land stretches from Blackthorn Forest here at the rear of the property," her finger traced along the dotted red line, "all the way to the east along the edge of the forest to Lake Deepwater, and then up along the ridge of the hills to the Coast Road until you reach the sea."

Issie looked at the map and hesitated for a moment. "But Aunty Hess, shouldn't I be helping Aidan with the animals?"

"Oh, there's plenty of time for that!" Hester smiled. "Aidan will manage for now, I'm sure. You need to get your bearings first before you start work. It's such a lovely day; it doesn't do horses or girls any good to be cooped up inside."

The dogs bounded along beside Issie as she walked down the limestone driveway and through the heavy wooden stable doors.

"It's me, girl!" Issie called to her horse as she hurriedly unbolted the top half of the Dutch door. Blaze immediately thrust her head over the door, nuzzling Issie and nickering happily.

"Hey, Blaze," Issie said, "did you miss me? Were you

lonely here all by yourself in the stable?" She fed the mare a carrot and felt the tickle of her velvet muzzle on her fingers. "C'mon, we're going for a ride."

As Issie led Blaze through the stable block towards the back door the other horses nickered out friendly greetings to her. Diablo put his pretty black and white patchy head over the top of his stable door and gave her a vigorous whinny.

"Good morning to you too, Diablo!" Issie grinned. Blaze skipped along lightly at Issie's side, her hooves chiming out a delicate trip-trap against the concrete floor of the stables.

Issie led Blaze through the cattle pens at the rear of the stables and used the fence rails to mount up. Then she pulled the map out of the pocket of her shirt. To her right was the duck pond and a small cottage surrounded by magnolia trees, which Issie figured must be Aidan's house. To the left was a five-bar wooden gate and on the other side of the gate was a dirt track, bordered on the far side by dense forest. Issie looked at the map. There was a gate and then a red dotted boundary line marked: CATTLE TRACK.

"This must be it, Blaze," Issie said to her horse. "According to the map, this track takes us all the way along the edge of the forest and then down through the farm to Lake Deepwater."

Issie clucked Blaze through the gate, doing the latch back up after herself. Ahead of her the red clay path ran all the way along the ridge next to the trees.

Blaze jogged nervously along the track, her ears pricked forward, nostrils flared. The mare was keyed up after spending the day in the truck and then being kept stabled last night. All she wanted to do was run.

"Easy, Blaze, easy," Issie steadied the mare, keeping a firm grip on the reins. She knew she shouldn't give Blaze her head so soon, especially in a new environment. Then again, Issie had been cooped up too and she couldn't bear the thought of a quiet walk any more than her horse could.

"OK, OK, you win." Issie smiled. She readied herself, standing up in her stirrups in two-point position, and slackened her grip on Blaze's reins.

Issie felt her stomach lurch suddenly as Blaze lunged forward and she got left behind. She quickly regained her balance and crouched low over Blaze's neck as the mare stretched out into a gallop. The red clay soil was hard from the summer sun and Blaze's hooves beat out a clean rhythm as she ran. Issie sat very still, barely moving in the saddle. She didn't need to urge her forward, Blaze was running for the love of it.

To the right of the ridge track the land dropped dramatically away down a steep grassy slope which was dotted with surefooted, grazing sheep. To the left was the forest, a dense blur of trees and shadows flashing black and green as they galloped past.

Suddenly Blaze let out a snort and swerved hard, away from the trees. Issie shrieked as she felt the pony's centre of gravity shift out from beneath her. For a moment Blaze teetered sickeningly close to the edge of the track and Issie was terrified that they would plunge down the slopes of the steep bank.

"No!" Issie shouted, thinking fast and pushing Blaze back on to the track with her legs, yanking at the mare's mouth with the left rein. Blaze responded instantly, correcting herself, and Issie regained her seat and gathered up the reins again.

Why had Blaze spooked like that? Maybe Issie had been wrong to let her gallop too soon. She had just decided it would be best to pull the mare up and trot for the rest of the track, when she heard a noise in the forest that changed her mind.

From the dark blur of the trees right beside them

came the sound of an animal crashing through the undergrowth. Even though Blaze was in full gallop the creature was keeping pace with them. It was now so close it was running alongside them. Issie felt a chill of horror. Whatever it was, it was big. And it was after them.

Now Issie understood why Blaze had bolted. She wasn't misbehaving after all. She was terrified!

Issie tried to look into the woods to see what was chasing them, but Blaze was moving so quickly and the woods were so thick and impenetrable, it was impossible. She couldn't see a thing. One thing was certain: she wasn't waiting around to see what it was!

"C'mon, girl," Issie clucked the mare on now, asking her for more speed. Blaze immediately responded, her stride lengthening, her neck stretched out. Issie felt the pony surge forward underneath her and she bent down low over her mane. The wind whipped against her face, stinging her eyes and whistling around her ears. She strained to listen, trying to hear if the creature was still following them, but any sound was drowned out by the blur of Blaze's speed.

It was only when they had reached the ridge of the hill that Issie sensed she and Blaze were alone once more. Whatever was in the woods, they had outrun it.

"Easy, girl, steady. It's OK." Issie pulled the mare

back. Blaze's flanks were heaving, and her neck was wet and frothy with sweat. "It's all right, girl. I don't know what that was, but it's gone now," Issie said, giving Blaze a comforting pat on the neck. She knew that she was trying to reassure herself as much as her horse. She listened, but there was still no sound of anything following them. Issie turned her head slowly and looked back up the track behind her. There was nothing there.

Ahead of them, the red dirt path ran close to the forest for another mile or so, then the trail cut down through the paddocks towards the lake. *Good*, Issie thought, *the sooner we get away from the trees the better.* She coaxed Blaze into a trot. They needed to keep moving, keep up the pace until they were away from the trees.

When the track finally veered away from the forest and down into farmland again Issie heaved a sigh of relief and let Blaze walk for a while. She still couldn't believe it. What was that creature in the forest? It must have been almost as big as Blaze – and almost as fast. One thing was certain: she wasn't taking the same way home!

Issie took out her map again. Lake Deepwater was maybe an hour away. Once they reached the lake they could loop around on to the Coast Road and go back to the manor that way. Then they wouldn't have to ride back past the forest again.

Issie had the feeling they were still being followed. "Trust your horse, Issie," she reminded herself. Horses have strong instincts for danger and if Blaze was calm now, that meant they had nothing to fear. Besides, they were in open grassy pasture so if anything was following them Issie would be able to see it coming.

They had been riding on for about an hour when they reached the brow of a hill and looked down at Lake Deepwater. The lake, which was smaller than Issie had expected, sat in a natural basin. The area around the banks was grassy pasture, dotted with a few willow trees by the water's edge and on the far side next to the water there was a thick grove of blackthorn trees.

Issie looked at her map again. It looked like the Coast Road lay just over the ridge beyond those blackthorn trees. Once she was on the road it wouldn't take her long to get back to the farm again.

Issie was about to ride Blaze towards the trees when she heard a crashing noise from over the ridge that made her freeze. *Not again!* Issie thought.

She began to gather up Blaze's reins, looking around, trying to decide which way they should run. The noise was getting louder now. It sounded like thunder; Issie could feel the rumble shaking the ground beneath her.

With relief, she realised that this sound was nothing like the one coming from the trees earlier that morning. No, this was a sound she had heard many times before and it was unmistakeable. It was the sound of hoofbeats.

From behind the blackthorn trees the horses came into view. Issie watched in amazement as the herd rounded the edge of the lake at a gallop, bucking and swerving wildly as they ran. At the head of the herd was a thick-set buckskin with a bushy black mane and fiery eyes. The buckskin was followed by a stocky strawberry roan, a black and brown skewbald and a motley assortment of buckskins and bays. At the rear of the herd was a grey mare and a chestnut skewbald with a white face, both of them with foals running at their feet. The foals stuck close to their mother's side. The grey mare's foal was jet black. The skewbald's foal was the spitting image of its mother with chestnut and white patches all over its body and a broad blaze down its face.

The horses pulled up on the other side of the lake and stared at Issie and Blaze. They were stocky and broad, Issie noticed, and not really horses at all. Most of them were ponies, not much bigger than thirteen hands high.

Their manes and tails were ragged and sunbleached. Their coats were dusty and mud-caked. These were wild ponies, totally unbroken. Maybe they had never even seen a human before.

Blaze, who had been pacing nervously beneath Issie this whole time, suddenly let out a shrill whinny. To Issie's surprise the mare's call was immediately returned as a horse rose up before them over the brow of the hill.

This horse's whinny was brutal and fierce. It sounded to Issie like a battle cry. There was something defiant and challenging about the call and Issie realised what it was. It was the cry of a stallion.

The stallion who stood on the ridge was nothing like the rest of the herd. Those wild ponies were no bigger than Blaze. The stallion, on the other hand, was huge. He must have been at least sixteen hands high and his coat, which was jet black, shone in the sun. He had no markings, except for a slender white stripe which ran down his forehead.

The black horse held himself so proudly with his neck arched and his tail held erect. He had the noble bearing that comes with fine breeding – his face handsome and aquiline, his body large and powerful. It was as if he was sculpted from granite. Issie was possessed with the feeling she had seen this horse somewhere before. But where? Then she realised. He looked just like the painting on her bedroom wall, the portrait of Avignon, Aunt Hester's great grey stallion.

For a moment the stallion and Issie stood staring directly at each other. Then the big, black horse gave an arrogant snort and began to canter down the hill after his herd, rounding on his mares and threatening them back into formation with his ears flat back. With his teeth bared and his magnificent neck arched, the stallion nipped and squealed at his mares as he cantered. The grumpy buckskin mare nipped defiantly back at him, but even she obeyed eventually, and within a few minutes the stallion had gathered the whole herd together and was standing between Issie and his mares.

With the herd corralled safely behind him, the stallion seemed uncertain what to do next. He cantered back and forth and then stopped, pawing the ground restlessly as if he was considering his next move. Then he raised his head and let out a war cry that was filled with fury, like the bellow of a wild boar.

Issie's face went pale with fear. Beneath her she felt Blaze stiffen in terror.

I'm so stupid, Issie thought, furious with herself. *He's a stallion and we're a threat to his herd and now he's going to attack. We should have run the moment I saw him. Why didn't we run?*

The black stallion was close now – too close for Issie and Blaze to turn and run. His eyes were black with anger. His teeth were bared, ready to fight.

Issie tried to steady Blaze, but the chesnut mare trembled with fear and rage. What would Blaze do if the black horse attacked? She was no match for a stallion! No. They had to make a run for it. What else could they do? After all, there was no one here to save them.

And then Issie realised. Mystic! The little grey gelding always seemed to know when they needed help. Well, she was certainly in trouble right now. Surely Mystic would appear? Issie's eyes scanned the crest of the hill. Nothing. Maybe she should call for him?

"Mystic!" Issie yelled. Her voice came out reedy and shrill, strangled by her fear.

Mystic had died trying to save Issie. Since then he had saved Issie and Blaze so many times. He was always there when she really needed him. So where was her grey pony now?

The shrill whinny of a horse shook Issie back to reality. Not Mystic's whinny, but the piercing call of the stallion. In that split second Issie made up her mind.

She couldn't do nothing and rely on Mystic to come and fight her battles; there wasn't time for that. She would have to find her own way out of this.

OK, so they needed to run – but where? Issie looked around for a way to escape. To her left were the grassy slopes of the hill. Should she try to outrun the black horse? Could they make it up the hill? She looked now to the right of her at the still, deep waters of the lake. *No way out*, Issie thought. *What now?*

As the black horse began to gallop towards them Issie felt her pulse race and she realised she knew what to do. They weren't going to run away from this horse. They were going to run straight for him.

"C'mon, girl!" Issie said to her pony. And with an almighty kick she drove Blaze on straight at the stallion in a hard gallop. Blaze was only too willing. The mare's eyes were fixed on the black stallion. She was ready to fight.

Issie held her path as the two horses bore down on each other. *Keep your head,* she told herself, *keep going. Just a bit closer…*

Suddenly, just as the horses were moments away from colliding, Issie hauled desperately on Blaze's right rein. "Go, Blaze!" Issie yelled at her horse. Shocked, the mare leapt forward at Issie's command, up into the air and down again into the murky waters of the lake.

There was an awful moment when Blaze hit the water, lost her footing and stumbled forward. Issie managed to pull the mare's nose up and ride her on, keeping her at a canter as she regained her feet. Then they ploughed on through the mud and the reeds, the water splashing up Issie's jodhpurs, seeping into the leather of her boots. Blaze snorted in fear as she cantered in deeper; the water was up to her chest now. Issie looked back over her shoulder. The stallion was behind them. He had followed them into the lake, but he was hesitating. Instead of cantering after them he was weaving backwards and forwards, as if uncertain whether to go any deeper into the water.

"Come on, girl!" Issie gave Blaze a sharp kick in the ribs. "Come on, girl! Let's go!" The kick made Blaze leap forward again. Issie looked around her and realised that they were already in the middle of the lake. Then they were past the middle and heading back out the other side – and the water hadn't so much as gone over Issie's boots!

So much for Lake Deepwater, she thought with relief. *More like Lake Shallowmud.*

Issie looked back again over her shoulder. The stallion had given up on them and turned around now, trotting out of the lake and back towards his herd.

"We've lost him, Blaze! Not much further to go, girl!" Issie gave her mare a slappy pat on her neck. Once they reached the other side, Issie was pretty sure that just over the ridge they'd find the Coast Road that would lead them home to Blackthorn Manor.

"Good girl, Blaze!" Issie gave the mare another big pat on her neck as Blaze leapt up the muddy slopes of the bank and on to the green grass that bordered the lake.

She had been worried that Blaze might have been exhausted from the chase that morning, but the mare still seemed to have plenty of speed left in her. As they rode up the grassy slope and hit the dirt track that led them along the Coast Road back to the farm, Blaze stretched out at full gallop.

The black horse hadn't followed them. They were safe. All the same, Issie stayed low over Blaze's neck and let her run. She didn't stop galloping until they were another two miles down the road. And she didn't stop checking over her shoulder until they were safely home at Blackthorn Manor.

Chapter 5

Aunt Hester sat on the front veranda of Blackthorn Manor with a mug of piping hot tea and a copy of the *Times*. As Issie and Blaze trotted down the long, leafy avenue of the limestone driveway towards her she looked up and gave them a cheery wave. Then suddenly she stopped waving. Her face turned dark with concern and she propped herself up with her walking stick and hobbled down the steps that led from the veranda and across the cherry-tree lawn to meet the horse and rider.

"What on earth happened to you two?" Hester said as she took Blaze's reins. Issie dismounted and promptly flopped down, lying spread-eagled on the cool, green lawn next to her horse. She was completely exhausted. Blaze, who was caked with dried sweat and mud from her marathon galloping efforts, looked even more wretched than her rider.

"We got into a bit of trouble – well, two bits of trouble actually," Issie said.

"I can see that!" Aunt Hester said. "Isadora, how did you end up in this state? Are you all right?"

"I'm fine, Aunty Hess. Honest. I just need a minute to get back up..." Issie took a deep breath and forced herself to stand up again, reaching out to take Blaze's reins. Aunt Hester reluctantly handed them to her.

"Her stable is all ready for her. Aidan mucked it out this morning. I'll come with you and help you untack. And on the way you're going to tell me what in the blazes you two have been getting up to out there!"

As they walked slowly down the driveway to the stables Issie told her aunt about the animal in the woods that had stalked them along the ridge track.

"So you didn't see this creature at all?" Hester asked. "Not even a glimpse?"

"It was too dark in the trees and we were moving so fast that I couldn't see," Issie said. "All I know is that it was big. Really big. It could keep up with Blaze even when she was galloping."

"Could it have been one of the dogs? Did they follow you out?" Aunt Hester asked.

"It was far too big to be Taxi or Strudel," Issie said, "but I suppose it could have been Nanook." The enormous black Newfoundland was large enough to have made the crashing noises she had heard.

"Oh, I doubt it. Nanook never goes for a walk without me. She's bone idle and as slow as a wet week." Hester dismissed the idea. Then she paused for a moment. "Could it, well, could it have been a cat?"

Issie looked at her aunt. "What do you mean?"

"Oh, I don't mean like a common moggy, dear," Aunt Hester said. "No. I mean a big cat, a mountain cat. There's a myth in these parts, you know, about a black cat that lives wild in the hills. They say it escaped from a zoo, and I suppose it's possible since there was once a wildlife park not far from here. They had antelope and lions and all sorts. When the wildlife park closed down all the animals were shipped off, but this particular black cat escaped and they never found it again. I've always thought the whole story sounded rather ridiculous. You hear a lot of tall tales about that sort of thing when you live out this way. Still, people do believe the myth. The Grimalkin they call him. The witch's cat.

Although I can't imagine that even a witch would be too pleased if she came across an enormous great panther! Old Bill Stokes who lives down on the Coast Road farm claims he saw it one night. He said a great black cat the size of a bear came out of the undergrowth and attacked one of his sheep, dragged it off right in front of his eyes. Of course they never found any sign of the sheep – and old Bill Stokes does like a drink so his accounts cannot always be relied upon..."

"Well, whatever it was, Blaze was terrified of it," Issie said.

"I haven't heard any reports of lost stock or anything unusual lately," Hester mused. "I think the best thing we can do is to let Cameron know about it. He's the local ranger with the Blackthorn Hills Conservation Trust. He's coming out to see me tomorrow and this is exactly the sort of thing he deals with. If there's a wild beastie in the woods he'll soon see to it."

"Do you think he'll believe me?" Issie said.

"Why?" her Aunt said briskly. "Do you often go making up stories about being stalked by phantom creatures and coming home covered in mud? Of course he'll believe you! He's a good man, Cameron. If there's something out there he'll find it."

They had reached the stables now and Issie undid the girth and slipped off Blaze's saddle while Aunt Hester hobbled across the stable to fetch the mare some hard feed. Issie took Blaze out to the rear of the stables and hosed her down in the wash bay to get rid of the sweat and dirt, using a sweat scraper to dry the mare off before letting her loose in the stall. Hester gave Blaze the tub full of chaff and pony nuts and they stood there together watching as she ate.

"Now," Hester said, "you said you had two bits of trouble? What else did you find out there?" Issie told her about the herd of horses she had seen down at Lake Deepwater.

"Now this is a mystery that I can solve," Hester said brightly. "Those are Blackthorn Ponies you're talking about. I'm surprised you've never heard of them before."

"Blackthorn Ponies?" Issie said.

"A breed unique to this area. There's been a herd roaming the high country here for over twenty years," Hester said. "They're wild horses, descendants of a few local riding ponies that got loose and then refused to be caught again. The herd has survived somehow over the years; they are very hardy little specimens I must say. There must be at least twenty of them by now?"

"Closer to thirty, I think," Issie said. "Aunty Hess, there was a stallion with them. He was at least sixteen hands, much taller than the rest of them, and jet black."

"Really?" Hester looked interested at this. "No, I don't recall a stallion, but then I haven't seen the herd in quite some time."

"It was the stallion that attacked us – me and Blaze," Issie continued. "It was my fault. He was so beautiful and I was so busy watching him, I didn't think. Then when I realised we were in danger and we needed to run it was too late. He was going crazy trying to protect his herd. We had to swim the lake to get away."

"Ah, so that's where all the mud has come from!" Hester nodded. "Well, you were lucky, my dear. A stallion can be as ferocious as a tiger when he thinks he's protecting his herd. If it actually was his herd. You say this horse didn't look like the others?"

"Well, there were two foals – the black one looked just like him. But none of the others… There was something about him, Aunty Hess. He was so handsome, he reminded me of that painting on my bedroom wall."

Aunt Hester raised an eyebrow at this. "Avignon? He reminded you of my darling Avignon? Well, I suppose anything is possible. Avignon was a great jumper, you know. Fences could never hold him and he frequently made his escape into the hills. I suppose on one of his great adventures he might have found the wild herd and bred with one of the Blackthorn mares." Hester smiled. "Wouldn't that be a treat? If my great grey stallion had sired a son – and a few grandsons by the sound of it – and now they're running about the countryside following in his footsteps. You say the little black foal looked just like him?"

"Uh-huh." Issie nodded.

"Well, this is very exciting news!" Aunt Hester said. Her smile suddenly faded. "Oh no. I've left lunch in the oven! It will be burnt to a crisp by now – if it hasn't set fire to the kitchen!" She turned towards the stable door and began to hop off briskly with her walking stick.

"Aunty Hess, don't be ridiculous. You can't run in a plaster cast. I'll dash back and turn off the oven," Issie said.

"If it's burnt on the outside don't throw it away. Just cut the black bits off. That's what I usually do," Aunt Hester called after her as Issie ran out of the stable doors.

When she arrived at the house Issie found what looked like the remains of a cottage pie burnt to a crisp on the top and promptly put it in the pig's bin before Aunt Hester could try to salvage it.

Issie stood there for a moment and stared at the charred remains on top of the bucket of pig slops. *Another narrow escape in my first day at Blackthorn Farm.* She smiled to herself. Avoiding Aunt Hester's cooking efforts was one thing, but wild stallions and black panthers were another matter entirely. Issie knew they had been lucky to escape with their lives today.

When Issie checked in on her horse at the stables later that afternoon Blaze seemed none the worse for wear after her adventures. She fed Blaze her chaff and pony nuts for dinner and hung up a hay net for the mare to munch through overnight. Then she checked on the other horses in their stalls.

Issie was adjusting Diablo's stable rug when she heard a noise behind her. "Miaow!" The sound made her jump and she turned around to see Aidan leaning over the stable door, smiling at her.

"Ohmygod, Aidan! You scared me!"

Aidan pushed his long dark hair back out of his eyes. "It wasn't me – it was the Grimalkin, the witch's cat of Blackthorn Ridge!" He grinned at her.

Issie threw a sponge out of Diablo's grooming kit at the stall door and Aidan ducked as it flew past his ear.

"I'm not imagining it, Aidan. I was chased by something today in the woods. I'm not saying it was some imaginary cat. I don't know what it was, but it followed me and Blaze and it was fast and it was huge." Issie stood her ground.

"Hey," Aidan raised both his palms up as if surrendering the conversation to her, "I believe you. There's a big kitty out there who wants a saucer of milk and a pony."

"Aidan!"

"No, seriously, Issie, I do believe you. The horses have all been very spooky lately and last week we lost two chickens from the henhouse. I thought it was probably a stoat, but maybe it was whatever was chasing you and Blaze." Aidan cast his eyes over Diablo. The piebald was shifting restlessly in his stall. "Horses can sense things, you know," Aidan said quietly. "They know when there's trouble about."

"So can pigs," Issie added.

"What?" Aidan said.

"Well, I hear that Butch doesn't like you much, so I guess he knows trouble when he sees it too." Issie grinned.

"Yes," said Aidan, "yes, I guess he does."

After she'd helped Aidan feed all the horses and lock

the stalls for the night, Issie took the leftover scraps of burnt lunch, potato peelings and last night's supper and went to visit Butch.

"Don't worry, Butch, it's just me. Aidan isn't here," she reassured the big, black pig. Then she tipped the scraps into his trough and, while he ate, gave him a firm scratch behind the ears with his favourite scratching stick.

Once Butch was fed she headed down past the stables to the cattle pens where Blossom and Meadow were kept. Blossom looked at Issie gratefully with her scary yellow goat eyes as she filled the feed bin with carrots and apple slices.

Issie pulled a carrot out of her pocket. "Count to five, Blossom!" Issie instructed, holding the carrot over the goat's head just as Aunt Hester had done with Butch the other day. "Count, Blossom!" Issie commanded again.

Blossom looked up, snatched the carrot out of Issie's hand and then carried on eating.

"Ummm, well, I guess I'll start training you properly tomorrow," Issie said.

In the pen next to Blossom, Meadow, a patchy chestnut and white Hereford calf, was pacing up and down waiting for her supper. She gave Issie a friendly lick with her coarse sandpaper tongue as she entered her pen. Issie had heated a bottle full of milk for the young calf and, as she produced the teat, Meadow suctioned on immediately and began to drink, pushing and nudging at Issie as the bottle began to empty.

"Wow! You have a big appetite for a little cow," Issie said. Meadow had emptied the bottle now and was sucking on Issie's fingers instead. "Stop it!" she giggled, edging backwards out of Meadow's pen and locking the gate after herself.

Before she left the stables Issie stopped in once more at Blaze's stall to say goodnight. "Sleep tight, Blaze," she said, patting the mare's velvet-soft nose. Blaze nickered softly in return and Issie gave her one last carrot before she locked the stall doors behind her.

The first day at Blackthorn Farm had given Issie more than enough news to tell her friends. Luckily Aunt Hester did have the Internet so she didn't need to use carrier pigeons after all. "But what an excellent idea!" Hester had laughed when Issie suggested this as a joke. "Carrier pigeons! I shall have to train some up just in case. We are always having problems with the phone lines here after the autumn storms. A pigeon might come in handy!"

Issie wasn't sure if her aunt was joking or not. **After all**, she told Stella in her email, **this is a place where it is considered perfectly normal for ducks to open doors, and tomorrow I'm supposed to be teaching the goat how to bow. Aunt Hester says it's time I filled her shoes and began animal training. Yikes! It's like I'm Dr Doolittle or something. I can't believe I am missing the summer dressage series. Say hi to Coco and to Kate and Toby. Miss you. BFF XXX Issie.**

Issie only had to wait a few minutes after she'd sent her email before she heard the ping of an email coming back in return.

You think you've got it tough? Stella wrote back. **I wish I was teaching goats to bark or whatever you're doing. Meanwhile, I'm stuck here doing the summer dressage series and guess who is winning by, like, a million-kazillion points with her new pony and won't let any of us forget it? I'll give you a clue and that clue is STUCK-UP TUCKER! Oh I wish I was at the farm instead**

with all those animals - it sounds cool.
Apart from the bit where you got chased by
the thing in the forest and nearly killed
by the wild stallion. You're lucky that
Blaze is so fast - if it had been me on old
slow-poke Coco we'd have been eaten by the
Grimalkin already! BFF Stella XXX

Issie knew Stella didn't mean to make fun of her, and neither did Aidan really. Still, she wished she had never told anyone about the animal that had chased her and Blaze on the ridge that morning. Now that Issie was safely tucked up in bed at Blackthorn Manor she was beginning to wonder if there really *was* an animal in the woods or if her mind had been playing tricks on her. It was only natural that Blaze would be a bit spooky in her new home. Perhaps the mare had shied at her own shadow and then bolted? Maybe there wasn't any animal chasing them. After all, Issie hadn't actually seen anything, had she?

No, she thought. *I didn't see anything – but I did hear something.*

Blaze had heard it too. The mare hadn't just been spooked – she had been terrified. She wasn't imagining things. Something was out there; she was sure of it.

Issie fell asleep in her four-poster bed that night thinking about the creature in the woods. The moon was full in the sky outside and she could see the inky crest of the ridge outlined through her bedroom curtains as she dozed off.

When she woke again she guessed it must have been about midnight. The moon was still high in the sky, illuminating the view outside. Issie lay in bed and listened. In the hush of the night she could hear a scratching noise. It was coming from her door. She got up and quietly padded across the floor to open it, and there was Strudel, waiting patiently for her.

"Hello, Strudel. I suppose you want to come in?" Issie said.

The dog began to pad into the bedroom, but then suddenly she stopped. Her ears perked up and she froze. Then she turned tail and raced off again straight down the stairs. Issie grabbed her dressing gown and followed after her. A noise outside made the hairs on the back of her neck bristle as if someone had just walked over her grave. She could have sworn she had just heard the growl of a cat. A very big cat.

Outside on the back veranda Issie found Strudel standing alert. The dog was growling a low, rumbly growl.

"What is it, girl?" Issie said, putting her arm around the golden retriever. "Can you hear something?"

Suddenly a cacophony of squawking and flapping came from the henhouse. Strudel took off in the direction of the noise, her bark raising the alarm for the rest of the farm. Issie paused for a moment, peering blindly into the darkness and wondering what was out there waiting for her. Then she pulled on her boots and ran after Strudel down the driveway. Behind her she heard the barks of Taxi and Nanook, who had both heard Strudel's cry and were joining in the chase.

Down at the henhouse feathers were flying. The bantams were in a total state of terror, and Issie wished she had brought a torch with her so she could see what was going on. She opened the door to the henhouse and stepped inside, relying on the moonlight to guide her, trying to calm the frantic chickens so that she could check that they were all OK. She was just in the process of counting the chickens in the dark when she heard a squeal coming from the paddocks next to the stables. Strudel, Nanook and Taxi immediately bounded off in the direction of the sound, with Issie following.

The dog's cries were bloodcurdling and growing more frantic by the time Issie arrived at the stables. She ran past the horses' stalls to the back door that led out to the duck pond and the cattle pens, pushing the enormous stable door open, and cast her eyes around the pens. The three dogs were barking wildly now.

"What is it, Strudel?" Issie asked. And then she saw the shape looming in front of her. Enormous and black, silhouetted against the night sky. The creature was sleek and huge – bigger than Nanook even – and it was moving fast, padding silently across the top of the fence-line, balanced on the wooden frame of the cattle pens.

The black shape of the Grimalkin disappeared into the darkness. The dogs were going crazy now, barking and wailing so loudly that Issie didn't hear the footsteps behind her. A hand on her shoulder made her jump.

"Shhh, it's me!" Aidan's voice calmed her down. "Just a second – let me find the torch – I've got one here somewhere..."

Aidan shone the torch beam on to the cattle pens. Issie peered at fence where she had seen the shadow of the Grimalkin just a moment before. There was nothing there now except the black night sky. Worried that Aidan would think she was silly, Issie couldn't decide whether to tell him that she'd seen the Grimalkin again. She didn't need to say anything, though, because Aidan spoke first.

"Go back to the house now, Issie," he said.

"Why, Aidan, what's wrong?" Issie moved closer.

"I said go back *now*!" Aidan shouted at her.

And then Issie saw why he was sending her away. The body of an animal lay covered in blood in the cattle pen at Aidan's feet. Issie rushed forward to help, and as she came closer she realised that it was Meadow. The chestnut and white calf was lying very still as Aidan bent down to examine her.

"Aidan! Ohmygod! I'll get the first-aid kit out of the tack room and…"

Aidan looked up at Issie. There were tears in his eyes. "It's no use," he said softly. "Issie, she's dead."

Chapter 6

Issie looked down at Meadow. The little calf's rust and white fur was smeared with blood and there were two deep gashes that looked like claw marks at her shoulder and throat. Aidan was right. There was no doubt that she was dead.

Aidan looked up at Issie. There were tears streaming down her face. "Honestly, Issie, I think she must have died instantly. Whatever did this was quick and deadly; she didn't suffer." He stood up and put his arm around Issie as she wiped the tears off her cheek with the sleeve of her pyjamas.

Aidan picked Meadow up and carried her inside the stables into one of the empty horse stalls, bolting the doors shut. Then he walked Issie back up the driveway to the manor, with the three dogs following noiselessly at their heels.

"What do you think it was, Aidan?" Issie asked.

"I don't know." Aidan shook his head. "Could have been the same thing that stalked you and Blaze."

"Poor Meadow," Issie said. "Can we give her a proper burial tomorrow under the magnolia trees?"

Aidan nodded. "Cameron will want to see her first. He'll need to figure out what it was that killed her. But yeah, of course we can."

As they reached the veranda, the lights came on inside the manor. "Aidan! Isadora! What's happening out here?" Aunt Hester emerged, wrapping her dressing gown around her.

"It's Meadow. She's been attacked," Aidan said. Hester turned quite pale.

"Is she all right?"

"She's dead," Aidan confirmed. "I've moved her into one of the stalls in the stables. I figured Cameron could check her over in the morning."

"Poor little Meadow!" Hester shook her head.

"I saw it, Aunty Hess!" Issie said. "The Grimalkin. At least I think I did. It was on top of the cattle pens and then it was gone... If we'd only got there sooner..."

Hester put her arm around Issie. "Isadora, thank heavens you didn't get attacked by that thing. If you two and the dogs hadn't turned up and scared the Grimalkin off when you did, it may have hurt even more of the animals. Aidan, are all the animals safe for the night?"

"I've checked all the horses," Aidan told her. "They're all OK. I'm going to take one last check around the farm now and make sure everything is secure before I go back to bed. You two go inside and I'll see you both in the morning."

Hester nodded. "I'll report this to Cameron first thing. Come on, sweetie, it's two o'clock. Let's get you inside and back into bed. I'll make you a hot milk to help you sleep."

The hot milk did help. Issie didn't wake up again until nine a.m. When she finally came downstairs to breakfast Aidan was waiting for her at the kitchen table.

"How are you feeling?" he asked.

"Ummm, OK, I guess," Issie replied.

"I checked all the animals again this morning," Aidan said. "They're all fine. Whatever it was that killed Meadow is hopefully long gone…"

"If we'd only got there in time to save her…" Issie's voice was wobbly. She felt like she might cry and fought hard to hold back the tears.

"I still can't imagine what kind of animal would make those wounds." Aidan shook his head. "When Cameron arrives you can tell him what you saw and he can take a look at Meadow – maybe he'll have some ideas." Aidan picked up his riding gloves from the kitchen table and stood up.

"Meanwhile, we've got training to do." He smiled at her.

"We? You mean you and me?" Issie squeaked.

"Sure," Aidan said. "Didn't Hester tell you?" He looked at Issie's shocked face. "I guess she didn't. OK. Well, I'll head down to the stables and get the horses ready. You have some breakfast and then meet me at the round pen. We're doing some trick training."

"Really?" Issie felt a shiver of excitement run up her spine.

"See you there in fifteen!" Aidan said, already disappearing out the door, heading for the stables.

Issie felt almost too nervous to eat. Trick riding! It was just like in the movies. She managed to calm her butterflies enough to cram down a piece of toast and jam and then ran all the way down the driveway to the stable block where Aidan already had Diablo, Blaze and Paris saddled up and waiting at the side of the round pen.

"This is where we do most of the stunt training," Aidan explained. "I've been working on this stunt lately, I call it a 'Flying Angel'. I've been training Paris to do it with Diablo, and she's pretty good, but it's important that she can do the same trick with other horses and riders too. So I thought maybe today you could try it with her and Blaze?"

Issie nodded. "Umm, Aidan?" she asked.

"Yeah."

"What exactly is a 'Flying Angel'?"

Aidan grinned. "It's hard to explain. It's probably easier if you let me show you."

Aidan tied Blaze up outside the round pen and then he rode Diablo into the arena, leading Paris beside him. The wood-lined walls of the round pen were about two metres high and above them, circling the arena, were two rows of wooden bench seats. Issie climbed the stairs and sat down in a front row seat, watching silently as Aidan worked the horses in. He trotted back and forth in the middle of the arena on Diablo, keeping an eye on Paris, who was also wearing a saddle and bridle as she cantered riderless around the arena.

"Do you see how she's cantering in a circle like that?" Aidan called out to Issie. "She's been trained to do that. It makes it easier to do the trick if she's got a steady stride." As he said this he clucked Diablo forward and the black and white Quarter Horse began to canter behind the palomino.

Issie watched as Aidan cantered Diablo right up next to Paris so that he was riding neck and neck with the palomino mare. The two horses fell into step together, matching each other stride for stride.

Aidan smiled up at her. "Here we go!" he called out. And with that, he let go of Diablo's reins and sat bolt upright in the saddle with his arms spread out to either side for balance. Aidan rode one more lap around the round pen with his arms out. Issie could see him counting the beat in his head, figuring out his moment. Issie noticed that he was edging Diablo closer to Paris now, so that the piebald gelding was almost touching the palomino. Suddenly Aidan slipped his feet out of the stirrups and pivoted in the saddle, turning his body to face the wall. He cast one last look up at Issie, gave her a wave and then leapt.

Issie couldn't believe it! There was a split-second when Aidan was in midair that she imagined the worst.

He was going to fall and get trampled beneath Paris and Diablo's hooves. Then she saw Aidan grasp Paris' saddle with both hands and deftly swing his leg over the mare's back. Before she knew it, Aidan was in the saddle on Paris with the reins, which had been knotted around the palomino's neck, in his hands. By the time he rode around the arena to where Issie was seated he had a grin on his face and was waving to her as he went by.

Issie stood up, clapping wildly. "That was amazing!" she called out to him.

Aidan pulled Paris up in the centre of the arena and saluted to Issie, while Paris dropped to one knee underneath her rider, bowing theatrically.

"That," Aidan said, "is a Flying Angel."

He dismounted from Paris and walked over to Diablo, who was standing waiting for him. Then he led both horses up to the side of the arena and looked up at Issie. "Come on then – it's your turn. Why don't you bring Blaze into the arena and have a go?"

"But I don't know how…" Issie began.

"The only way to learn is to do it," Aidan said. "It's all about timing. You need to get Blaze into a rhythm next to Paris, then move them close, drop your stirrups and jump."

"You make it sound so simple," Issie said. She could

feel the butterflies in her tummy going berserk now.

"Yeah, well, it is simple once you've done it a few times. But the first time I made the jump was pretty hairy," Aidan admitted. "Are you ready to give it a go?"

Issie untied Blaze from the hitching post and led the mare in through the sliding wooden doors on to the sawdust floor of the round pen. As she put her foot in the stirrup, Blaze danced nervously.

"Easy, girl, it's OK," Issie cooed.

"I'm going up there to watch," Aidan said, gesturing to the stands above the arena. "Paris knows what to do – she'll just keep cantering around the arena. All you need to do is ride Blaze up next to her and make the jump." Issie nodded silently and as Aidan rode out on Diablo she turned Blaze around to face the palomino.

"Gee-up, Paris!" she called, waving her arms to get the mare moving on to the perimeter of the arena. Paris instantly reacted just as Aidan had said she would, high-stepping into a graceful canter, staying close to the wooden walls of the round pen.

As soon as Paris had cantered twice around the ring and settled into a steady stride, Issie clucked Blaze on and rode the liver chestnut mare out to join her. At first Blaze flinched a little as she edged closer to the palomino.

Then she seemed to understand what Issie wanted her to do and fell into a brisk canter next to Paris, running neck and neck alongside the pretty palomino.

"Steady, girl, that's it…" Issie said. She knotted Blaze's reins now, and then, very carefully, she let go. She was riding now without any hands, her arms floating up and up, helping her to balance so that eventually she was sitting straight up in the saddle with her arms spread out like angel wings.

"Now, turn your body to face Paris and drop your stirrups!" Aidan shouted at her from the side of the arena.

Issie looked up at him and gave him a quick nod. She did as he said, slipping her feet out of the stirrups so that she was now riding with the irons dangling at her feet. She turned her torso to face the wall and looked at the rise and fall of the palomino's empty saddle. She had to jump into that saddle. All she needed to do was reach out her hands and make that leap from Blaze's back on to Paris. Issie took a deep breath and counted down – ah-one, ah-two, ah—

She froze. She couldn't do this! It was crazy. She looked down and saw the horses' hooves churning beneath her on the sawdust floor of the arena. What if she fell? She would get trampled beneath Paris' hooves for sure!

"Come on, Issie! What are you waiting for?" Aidan called out. Issie felt her skin turning clammy, her tummy was churning with butterflies.

"Calm down," she told herself. "You can do this!"

She put her hands back out again and focused on getting back into position. Then she edged Blaze closer to Paris once more and waited until the two mares were matching each other stride for stride. Ah-one, ah-two, ah… noooo!

Issie pulled Blaze up to a halt. She could feel her heart beating like crazy, her palms were wet with sweat and she was trembling.

"Issie, Issie are you OK?" Aidan ran into the arena, his face grave with concern. "What happened? Why didn't you jump?"

Issie shook her head. "I don't know, Aidan. I thought I'd be able to do it but then I looked down and…"

"It's OK. Honest." Aidan smiled at her. "It's a pretty advanced stunt. It was probably too soon to ask you to try something like this. Don't worry about it. Really. We can try again some other time."

Aidan reached out to take Blaze's reins as Issie dismounted, but she was still holding them and instead of grasping the reins he found himself holding Issie's hand instead. There was a moment when Aidan and Issie were locked together, holding hands. Then the pair of them jumped back from each other and stood there looking embarrassed.

"Sorry, I mean, I didn't mean to…" Aidan stammered.

"No! I mean, that's fine…" Issie replied, looking at her feet. "I umm… I'd better put Blaze away now." She hurriedly led the chestnut mare out of the arena and back to the stable block, leaving Aidan standing there with Diablo and Paris.

"Ohmygod, could that have been any more embarrassing?" Issie murmured to Blaze, burying her head deep into her pony's mane as they stood together in Blaze's stall. Not only had she chickened out on doing the Flying Angel stunt, she had held hands with Aidan! This was just the worst!

Untacking Blaze quickly, Issie slipped out the back door of the stable, hoping she stood less chance of running into Aidan again if she went out that way. Then she ran across the lawn, up on to the porch and in through the back door of the manor.

As she walked towards the kitchen she thought for a moment that Aidan had somehow got back there before her. She could hear a man's voice in the kitchen talking with Aunt Hester. When she got nearer, though, she realised the voice didn't belong to Aidan.

"Isadora! Is that you? Come and meet Cameron," Aunt Hester said. "Cameron is the head ranger for the Blackthorn Hills Conservation Trust." Her Aunt smiled at the sandy-haired man in the khaki jacket sitting next to her at the table. "Cameron, I'd like you to meet Isadora, my favourite niece. She's the one who first sighted the Grimalkin up on Blackthorn Ridge yesterday."

"Is that so?" The ranger looked at Issie.

"Well, kind of..." Issie said. "Something was there and it chased me and my horse, but it was hidden by the trees so I never actually saw it. I just heard it."

The ranger cocked a suspicious eyebrow at this.

"But I did see it last night!" Issie added hastily. "It was right there on top of the cattle pens just before we found Meadow. It was balancing on the top of the wooden railings, running along them like a cat."

"Could it have been a cat?" Hester wondered.

"Ohmygod no! Not a normal cat. It was enormous. I mean, really huge," Issie said. "Bigger than Nanook even."

"Did you see what sort of an animal it was?" Cameron asked.

"Umm, not really. There was a full moon but it was

still very dark. It was black, I think, and it had a long thick tail, but I couldn't really see much more than that. It disappeared pretty fast and then Aidan found Meadow and…" Issie's voice trailed off as she remembered the awful events of the night before and the gruesome discovery of poor Meadow.

"Could have been a stray dog," the ranger assessed. "We've had a couple of reports of stock loss lately. Once a dog gets the taste for blood, they're trouble."

"It wasn't a dog," Issie said firmly.

The ranger looked at her again. "Well, whatever it was, we'll find it. I'm going to take a couple of men up to the ridge today and we'll try and track it."

"What will you do if you find it?" Issie asked.

"We've got long-range rifles. Our men are trained sharp-shooters," he said coolly.

"Would you like more coffee, Cameron?" Aunt Hester offered the ranger. "Issie, why don't you join us?"

Issie sat down reluctantly next to the ranger as Aunt Hester poured more coffee from the pot for herself and their guest.

"Anyway, I didn't come here just to look for your… what did you call it? A 'Grimalkin'?" the ranger told Hester as she sat down again. "You know the Conservation

Trust has been concerned for some time now about the damage the Blackthorn Ponies are causing to the native wildlife."

Hester nodded.

"We've been discussing the problem for months now. The Blackthorn Hills district is rich with rare native flora. There are species of lichen and moss here that simply don't exist anywhere else in the world. It's our job as the Conservation Trust to protect the land," the ranger continued.

"But the ponies have been here for years, Cameron. Why is the problem suddenly so urgent now?" Hester asked.

"Numbers, mostly. The cold winters have usually kept the herd numbers down but the Blackthorn Ponies have been thriving for the past couple of years. There's twice as many as there used to be. It looks like we have no alternative but to undertake the cull immediately."

Aunt Hester looked shocked. "You realise that as the chairwoman of the Save The Blackthorn Ponies Group I'll be fighting any action you plan to take at the highest level—"

Cameron cut her off. "Hester, we've been through all this a million times already and you know it. I'm not here to ask your permission. This cull has been debated and now it's been officially rubber-stamped. There's nothing you can do any more. Telling you today was only a formality. I thought you'd want to know since the herd often run on your land. We'll have our men up here next week to get the job done."

"What are you talking about?" Issie squeaked. "What do you mean by a cull?"

The ranger looked up at Issie. His face was grave. "You have to understand that these Blackthorn Ponies are hard to catch and almost impossible to manage even if we could get our hands on them, Isadora. We need to get them off the land, and as far as the Conservation Trust is concerned, that leaves us with just one solution. We'll have to shoot them."

There was silence in the kitchen for a moment. Issie looked at the ranger to see whether he was joking, but his eyes met her with a deadly serious gaze.

"Aunty Hess!" Issie gasped. "You can't let them! This is your land! They can't shoot all those beautiful horses! You can't let him kill them! You just can't!"

Hester looked distressed. "Do you think I haven't fought this tooth and nail, Issie? I know how upset you must be; I'm upset too. This debate has been raging a long time now and our action group have fought this all the way, but now it seems like this may be the only solution. Cameron is right. These ponies are destroying rare wildlife – species that may not survive for much longer. If we can't stop them – if we can't catch them – then this may be the only solution."

"But what about the ponies? What about *their* survival?" Issie said.

"I know. I know. I wish there were a way to save them," Hester said. "Cameron has tried in the past, you know. They are fiendishly difficult to catch and it takes an expert horseman to manage them. They're wild, Isadora, not at all like your typical riding ponies. And even if we could save the herd, what on earth would we do with them all?"

"Still, there must be something we can do, Aunty Hess!" Issie insisted. "What about the black stallion? What if he really *is* Avignon's son?"

Aunt Hester went quiet at this. When she finally spoke she seemed enormously sad, "He's a wild stallion, Isadora. The last time you went out there he tried to kill you. I simply don't see what we can do to save him. It's too risky. Someone might get hurt."

"Honestly, Isadora, we wouldn't be doing this if we hadn't exhausted our options," Cameron said. "It's a very humane—"

"Humane? It's murder! These are ponies we're talking about! Beautiful ponies! Some of them are just foals! I can't believe you're doing this!" Issie turned to her aunt. "And I can't believe you won't stop him!"

And with that she stormed out of the kitchen, charged up the wide wooden stairs and ran into her room, slamming the door shut behind her.

Issie lay on her bed for a long time staring at the portrait of Avignon that hung above the fireplace, wondering what she should do. She couldn't believe her Aunt was actually agreeing with the ranger. I mean, maybe they couldn't save all the ponies, but they had to try, didn't they?

Issie stood up from her bed and walked over to the sash window that looked out over the back veranda down to the stables. Aunt Hester was right. The stallion was dangerous. The last time Issie and Blaze had faced the black horse he had tried to attack them. But really, that had been Issie's fault. She hadn't been ready for him. This time, though, she would be. She could take a spare halter, some carrots to tempt the ponies…

Issie paused for a moment. Then she walked across the room to her wardrobe and got out her jodhpurs and boots. She pulled on a light jersey over her T-shirt in case the weather turned and grabbed her backpack. She climbed out of the sash window on to the veranda of her room and was about to shimmy her way down the fire escape to the lawn when she heard voices below her.

Aunt Hester and the ranger were out on the driveway. Issie lay down on the veranda out of sight and watched as the ranger got into his Jeep and said goodbye to Aunt Hester.

Issie watched the Jeep drive away and then she waited until she was sure that Aunt Hester had gone back into the house. She couldn't risk being caught and she knew she had to hurry. If Aunt Hester knew what she was about to do she would try and stop her. It was better if Issie just left now without saying anything. By the time Hester noticed that she was gone, Issie and Blaze would be on their way. With a little luck they'd capture a pony or two and be back home again in time for dinner, and Aunt Hester would be so amazed she wouldn't have the chance to be mad at her.

Issie climbed silently down the fire escape ladder, then hid against the wall of the manor until she was sure that no one was around before making the dash across the manor lawn down to the stables.

The big wooden stable doors made such a loud screech when she opened them that Issie was sure Aunt Hester could hear them all the way back up the driveway at the house. In the gloom of the stables she checked to see if Aidan was there. Luckily he wasn't. She raced straight to the tack room, grabbing her helmet, Blaze's saddle and bridle and a spare halter off the racks that lined the wall.

"Hey, girl, it's me," she said as she unbolted the door to Blaze's stall. The chestnut mare nickered when she saw her. Issie opened the stall door and slipped inside. She gave Blaze a carrot and ran her eyes over her pony's legs. She seemed none the worse for her galloping efforts yesterday.

Issie was about to start tacking up and then she stopped. What was she doing? This was crazy. She was all alone and there were at least thirty ponies out there. She didn't even have a plan. But then, what other chance did the Blackthorn Ponies have without her? She couldn't just stand by and do nothing.

"Come on, Blaze," she said to the mare as she threw the saddle blanket across her back. "We're going for a ride."

Chapter 7

A shiver ran down Issie's spine as she led Blaze up through the five-bar gate on to the forest ridge track. The last time they rode the ridge track they had been forced to run for their lives. Now Issie listened keenly, alert for even the slightest sound from the trees. Apart from a few bird calls, the woods were totally silent. "There's nothing in there," Issie told herself out loud. She stepped up on to the rungs of the gate and leapt lightly into the saddle, gripping the reins to steady Blaze, who was pacing nervously underneath her.

"What is it, girl?" Issie asked. She held her breath for a moment, trying to listen again, but still she heard nothing. Her eyes scanned the woods in front of her. "It's nothing," she told herself firmly. "You're just imagining things."

Issie pushed Blaze into a trot, deciding that the mare would settle down once she began to move. "Easy girl, there's nothing there to worry about," Issie reassured her. All the same, she found herself keeping one eye on the woods beside them as they rode on.

Eventually they reached the point where the track finally veered away from the forest and travelled down into the farmland and Issie breathed a sigh of relief. "See, Blaze? No big, bad kitty chasing us this time," she said, giving her pony a pat on the neck.

As the track into the farmland flattened out, Issie pushed the mare into a canter and stood up in her stirrups as Blaze fell into a steady, swift stride. They cantered on like this for a long time and by the time they slowed back down to walk again Issie could see the peak of the green hills that surrounded Lake Deepwater in the distance.

On the lake ridge Issie pulled Blaze to a halt. The Blackthorn Ponies were there, just where she had seen them last time, grazing peacefully. Issie held Blaze back for a moment, uncertain what to do next. She didn't want to startle the herd and risk a stampede. Perhaps if she rode around to the far side of the lake where the blackthorn thicket grew she could sneak up on them under the cover of the trees.

She turned Blaze around now and rode back out of sight of the herd, down the slopes away from the lake, circling around the ridge. As they reached the point where Issie figured the blackthorn trees must be she rode Blaze back up over the crest of the hill so that they were looking down on the lake once more. The herd were still grazing happily. They had no idea that Issie was stalking them. Issie held Blaze still as she counted the horses – the buckskins and bays, pintos and greys – "…twenty-five, twenty-six, twenty-seven…" She smiled at the two foals frisking along beside their mothers. "…and the foals make twenty-nine, thirty!"

Suddenly the peaceful scene was disturbed by the shrill whinny of a horse. Issie looked up along the ridge. The stallion! Issie had been wondering where he was. She held her breath and tried to keep a grip on the reins as Blaze danced and pulled beneath her. The mare wanted to run. Issie knew how she felt. She was scared too. And there was time to run now, before the stallion came too close. This time, though, something told Issie that she should hold her ground.

The stallion's stride ate up the ground as he cantered swiftly towards them. He was just a few metres away – closer than the last time they had met – when he stopped dead in front of them. He was so close that Issie could see his flanks quivering with nerves. The stallion let out a deep snort and shook his head, but instead of charging at them as he had done last time he stepped backwards, as if uncertain what to do next.

Issie realised now that it was fear, not hatred, that had driven him to attack them when they met last time. As far as the black horse was concerned, they were strangers – they were a threat. Even now, the stallion was deciding if it was safe to be this close or if he should gather his herd and run.

Issie ran a hand down Blaze's neck. The mare was shaking with tension. Issie murmured softly to her horse now, trying to soothe her. "Easy, girl, be nice, let's see if we can make friends, eh?"

The stallion took another step forward then stretched out his strong, elegant neck and greeted Blaze nose-to-nose. But Blaze wasn't so sure she wanted to make friends. She gave a tempestuous squeal and lashed out viciously at the black horse with her front leg.

"Hey, hey, girl, it's OK," Issie kept speaking gently to her horse.

Blaze seemed to listen to Issie's soothing tone because she let the stallion touch noses with her again and this time she didn't strike out.

And then the penny dropped. Issie had ridden out here on a whim to save these ponies, and here she was, so close to the stallion. *Wouldn't Aunty Hess be thrilled?* she thought to herself, *if Blaze and I could bring him home to her?* After all, hadn't Aunty Hess been convinced that the black horse was the son of Avignon, her own beloved Swedish Warmblood? If Issie was going to save just one horse from this herd, if that was all she could do, then it had to be this horse. She knew that now.

As the big black drew in close again, trying to touch noses with Blaze once more, Issie saw her chance. She unhooked the rope attached to the halter on her saddle and leant over to slip it gently, carefully over his neck. Nearly there, nearly... Issie held her breath as she leant in closer to the black horse. The stallion kept a wary eye on Issie but he didn't flinch.

"Steady, boy, it's OK," Issie said. Suddenly the stallion felt the rope against his neck and realised what was happening. He startled backwards and Issie, who had been intent on her mission, found herself losing her balance. As she made a grab for Blaze's mane to keep herself from falling she felt herself lose her hold on the halter and it slipped out of her hands and fell to the ground.

"Damn," she cursed under her breath. She had

no choice but to dismount and get it back.

Carefully, slowly, Issie climbed off Blaze's back, trying not to spook the black horse with any sudden movements as she dismounted and edged over to pick up the halter lying in the grass. All the while as she moved, she kept talking to the stallion, her voice steady and low. For a moment, the horse stood there calmly, his ears swivelling as he listened to her. Then, suddenly, he decided that he had had enough. He backed away from Issie and Blaze, wheeled about and set off at a gallop towards the herd.

At the same moment Issie, who had been preoccupied with trying to reach the halter, realised she was no longer holding on to Blaze's reins.

"Blaze!" Issie leapt forward and made a grasp at the reins, but Blaze was spooked now. She backed away from her, confused and panic-stricken. Issie lunged once more in a last desperate attempt to catch her horse as Blaze snorted in surprise and then turned and broke into a canter, following the stallion across the tussock grass, heading towards the herd.

"Blaze! No!" Issie's voice was a rasp in her throat as she shouted desperately after the mare.

Issie began to run after her, but the sudden movement of the two horses had frightened the rest of the wild herd and now they too began to scatter. As Issie sprinted across the tussock grass she found herself surrounded by Blackthorn Ponies, all of them in a blind panic. The herd were on the move and none of them wanted to be left behind.

Issie had been worried about Blaze but now she found herself fighting for her own life as she was forced to duck and weave her way through the panicky herd. The ponies seemed to be all around her now and they were in a frenzy, not knowing or caring that they might run over the girl who was in their path. Issie let out a shriek as a little bay pony narrowly missed colliding with her and she had to make a leap to get out of the way in time. As she did so she lost her footing and stumbled on a rock. She crouched down, instinctively curling into a tight ball, and managed somehow to wedge herself into the small hollow beside a large rock. The next thing she knew there was a rush of air and noise overhead and the sky above her became a thrashing, boiling mess of hooves as the herd came right over the top of her. Issie squealed and put her hands over her head. The noise around her was deafening.

By the time Issie was sure it was safe to stand up again the ponies were miles away and running up the ridge that led away from the lake. She had lost sight of Blaze completely. Where was she?

Issie held her breath and scanned the horizon, her heart beating like a drum in her chest. Where was her horse?

There! Blaze was running right near the front of the herd. Issie could see her flaxen mane and tail streaming out in the wind, her head held high as she galloped. Suddenly Blaze stopped, wheeled about and looked back towards the lake. She seemed to be searching anxiously, as if she knew she was lost and she was trying to find Issie again.

"Blaze!" Issie called out. "I'm over here! Blaze!" She cupped her hands to her mouth and whistled, but she was drowned out by the shrill call of the black stallion as he galloped up the ridge behind the mares, driving his herd on, forcing them over the crest of the hill.

"Blaze!" Issie called out desperately again. It was no good. Blaze had turned away already. Issie watched helplessly as the horses disappeared over the rise of the hill.

"Blaze!" she cried out again, but she knew it was futile. The sound of hoofbeats was so distant now she could barely hear them. The wild ponies were gone – and Blaze had gone with them.

Issie stared at the ridge for a long time after that, unable to believe what had just happened. Then she walked back across the grass, shaking and sniffling, until she found the spot where she had dropped the halter. She reached down to pick it up and then found herself collapsing in tears on the ground next to it instead. She was in big trouble this time and she knew it. She had no way of getting her horse back. Not only that, she was stranded hours from home and no one even knew where she was.

Issie lay there in the long grass thinking about what she should do next. *Should I wait here?* she wondered. Maybe Blaze would come back again. She couldn't just leave Blaze out here with the herd. Blaze wasn't a wild horse – she had no idea how to survive in the wild. And she was still wearing her saddle and bridle. What if she got tangled in a tree or something? Besides, the black stallion was so protective of his herd he might turn on Blaze and hurt her. After all, she was an outsider. There was no way Blaze would be strong enough to fight a stallion like that. She had to follow the herd and try to get her horse back.

Issie looked at the halter lying next to her. She picked it up and stood up, surveying the ridge in front of her. Then she threw it down on the grass and flopped down next to it once more. What was she thinking? Blaze was probably miles away by now. Issie had no chance on foot. The only logical thing to do was to try to get home and get help. If she set off now, Issie figured she might reach Blackthorn Manor before nightfall.

There were two ways to get home from Lake Deepwater. She could go home the same way that she had come, along the northern ridge past the forest, but somehow taking the same route home again didn't seem like such a good idea. She might be able to outrun the Grimalkin on Blaze, but on foot it would be a different story. Besides, the woods would creep her out too much. Better to go around the loop of the Coast Road. It would be slower by an hour or so, but at least it was open countryside.

Issie consulted her map. The Coast Road ran right through the length of Aunt Hester's property, starting at the sea and travelling past Lake Deepwater and through acres of rolling farmland all the way back to Blackthorn Manor. To the left she could see a peek of blue ocean on the horizon. She turned to the right – it was going to be a long walk back to Aunt Hester's.

The word "road" was actually a bit grand, Issie decided as she walked along. In fact, the Coast Road was not much more than a broad dirt and gravel track. It was wide enough for a car or a truck, but it wasn't a real road. This was private land and the only people who ever drove down here would be Aidan or Hester. There was no chance of Issie hitching a lift.

After she had been walking for a couple of hours the road swerved back inland and cut a broad ribbon through lush green pasture. The sun was shining overhead, but a cool breeze stopped the day from getting too hot. Issie stopped for a moment and took off her jersey and put it in the backpack along with her helmet and the halter.

She was just hauling the pack back on to her back when she heard a noise. She looked around but she couldn't see anything. For a moment she held her breath, not moving. There it was again! It sounded like a low, rumbling growl. She scanned the horizon. The land to her right was open green pasture, but to her left there was a dense, tangled thicket of blackthorn trees, not far from the road. Issie looked at the blackthorn trees. She couldn't see anything, but she was sure she heard something. She started walking again but she had only gone a little way further down the road when she heard it once more. This time she was certain. It was a low, rumbling feline growl. The Grimalkin was in the blackthorn bushes and it was stalking her.

Looking back later, Issie realised that what she did next was dumb. But panic had gripped her. She kept walking for a moment as she tightened the straps on her backpack and then, without even daring to look back, she broke into a run and began to sprint as fast as she could.

As soon as she started running the noise behind her became louder. She could hear the Grimalkin thrashing through the undergrowth beneath the blackthorn trees, the deep, feline growl growing nearer and nearer. It was chasing her. She should never have run, she realised. She couldn't outrun it. Maybe she should try to climb a tree? But then the Grimalkin would probably just climb after her. Besides, there weren't any trees to climb! Issie could feel the pounding of her heart in her chest. She couldn't keep running like this for much longer.

Behind her now she heard the Grimalkin, getting even closer. And then she heard another noise, a noise that made her heart soar. It was the sound of hoofbeats. Too scared to slow down, Issie tried to keep running and look behind her at the same time. The sun was glaring overhead and as she squinted into the brightness it was hard to see. Was that a horse approaching her down the dirt road? Yes! It was a horse. She could see the dapple-grey coat shining like armour in the light of the afternoon sun. It was Mystic!

As the little grey gelding got nearer Issie thought fast. She stopped running and jumped on to a nearby tree stump. "Mystic!" she called out.

The grey pony swerved to follow her and as he drew close she made a flying leap for his back and scrambled quickly onboard. Mystic slowed down just for a moment while Issie regained her balance, and then he surged on again at a gallop, with Issie clinging on desperately, her hands wrapped tightly into his long, flowing mane.

"Go, Mystic!" Issie urged the horse on. She needn't have bothered though; Mystic was already stretched out running, his legs flying over the ground beneath him, his hooves striking out a frantic rhythm on the rock-hard dirt of the road.

When the dapple-grey finally slowed his stride they had left the blackthorn bushes way behind them and Issie knew that they had outrun the Grimalkin. It wasn't until Mystic began to walk and she could untangle her hands from his mane that Issie realised how much she was shaking.

"Mystic! Ohmygod! What was that thing?" Issie murmured to the little grey. She realised now, she had been so terrified of the Grimalkin that she had barely had a chance to think about the fact that her Mystic, her own special, special Mystic was back. He hadn't forgotten about her. He was still here watching over her.

Issie ran her hands down the silvery dappled neck of the little grey. The pony shook his mane and snorted. Mystic was back. Whatever the creature was in those blackthorn trees, he had saved her from it. Issie looked back up the road behind them. There was nothing there. But she knew now that the Grimalkin was still out there somewhere. And so was Blaze.

Chapter 8

Issie arrived back home to find the entire manor in a state of high drama. The dogs were all racing around madly on the cherry-tree lawn and Aunt Hester was standing on the veranda with Aidan and a group of men dressed in ranger's uniforms. Hester, who was doing most of the talking while the men listened and nodded, seemed to be very upset.

Issie walked across the lawn towards them. She had let Mystic go as soon as she had reached the Blackthorn Farm driveway, since she didn't want to risk him being seen by anyone. Now, as she came into view of the manor, the dogs began barking furiously and bounded up to meet her. Aidan saw her too and came running after them.

"Where have you been?" Aidan panted as he reached Issie's side. "Hester has been mad with worry. She called in the rangers. We were just about to set out with a search party."

"I know, I'm so sorry," Issie said. "I didn't mean to worry anyone. I thought I would be back home way before now."

"Back from where?" Aidan asked.

"The lake," Issie said. "I went down to the lake to look for the horses..."

"You did what?" Aidan was stunned.

"Aidan, I found the stallion and I nearly caught him! If the rest of the herd hadn't spooked him and I hadn't dropped the halter it would have all been OK, but then Blaze got scared too and she bolted and I was stuck out there in the middle of nowhere and Blaze is gone and..."

Aidan shook his head in disbelief. He looked up to see Aunt Hester approaching them, hopping along briskly on her walking cane across the lawn.

"Listen," he hissed at Issie, "don't tell her any of this! You'll never be allowed out of the manor again if she thinks you've been off hunting wild stallions. Just keep quiet and leave it to me."

"Isadora! Thank heavens you're all right!" Hester

dropped her walking stick and grabbed Issie, smothering her in a Chanel-scented bear hug. "Where on earth have you been? We've all been so worried!"

"I… umm… I …"

"Issie went for a hack on Blaze and got thrown," Aidan said quickly.

"Really?" Aunt Hester raised an eyebrow in surprise. "You seemed pretty upset this morning. I thought perhaps you had dashed off to do something rash?"

Issie looked sideways at Aidan. "Ummm…well, I guess I was upset. So I thought I'd go for a ride to calm down. I know I should have told you that I was going out but I thought you might not let me because of the Grimalkin, so I decided to sneak out. I'm really sorry I caused so much trouble. I thought I'd be back before anyone noticed I was gone—"

"So you're back safe and sound I see!" Cameron's voice booming across the lawn interrupted her. The ranger didn't look pleased to see Issie at all. "Well that was a complete waste of our time then, wasn't it, Hester? We'll be packing up and leaving you now." The ranger glared at Issie. "You gave your aunt quite the scare young lady and wasted valuable time. I hope it won't happen again." Cameron nodded to the other rangers, who set about packing away their backpacks and walkie talkies before piling into their Jeeps and setting off down the driveway.

"Don't worry about Cameron," Hester said as she waved them goodbye. "A good search and rescue mission is what those men thrive on. They're just cross that we found you so quickly and ruined their fun!" She turned to her niece now with a serious expression. "Now, are you going to tell me what's really going on? Where is Blaze?"

"I… I went to find the wild horses and I… Blaze got spooked by the stallion and she took off. I lost her and I had to walk home again…" Issie sighed.

"Are you OK?" Hester asked, her face grave with concern.

"I'm fine, Aunty Hess. But Blaze is still out there. She's probably terrified by now. Aunty Hess, we have to go and get her!"

"She's a horse, Isadora," Hester said firmly. "She can cope with one night of freedom out there in the wild. Besides, it's too late in the day; you don't want to be out there in the dark horse-hunting. You and Aidan can take Diablo and Paris out together tomorrow morning at first light and look for her." Hester looked sternly at

Issie. "And don't you go disobeying me on this matter. No more racing off again half-cocked to rescue wild horses, OK? I know that Cameron's news about the cull must have come as a shock to you and I love that you want to save the ponies, but we must be sensible and think this through – together." She smiled at Issie. "Now let's get you inside. You need a long hot soak with some Epsom salts in the bath. You must be aching from walking all the way home."

"I guess so," Issie replied.

Issie took one last longing look up the driveway.

"Don't worry," Aidan's voice was reassuring. "We'll find her tomorrow. We'll saddle up and set off as soon as it's light. I'll meet you down at the stables at around six a.m. OK?"

"Oh, Aidan…" Issie began, "it's all my fault. Blaze is out there all by herself and the Grimalkin is out there too…" She shivered at the thought. The Grimalkin had killed Meadow. What if it hurt Blaze?

"We'll get her back. I promise," Aidan said softly. "I'll see you at six."

"Aren't you going to come into the manor now and have dinner with us?" Issie asked.

"No thanks," Aidan said. "I've still got to feed the

horses. Besides, Hester is doing a roast." He pulled a face. "I've had one of her roasts before and once was enough." He smiled at Issie. "I'm really glad you're OK, Issie. I was… I mean, your aunt was worried about you." And with that, Aidan waved a hasty goodbye as he turned and set off down the driveway.

When Issie arrived at the stables the next morning Aidan already had both horses tacked up and ready to go. "I'm taking Diablo, you're on Paris," he said, handing Issie the mare's reins. Aidan looked at his watch. "Ten to six," he said. "We should be at the lake in a couple of hours if we make good time along the ridge track. Come on, let's mount up."

"Stand still, Paris," Issie said as she popped one foot in the stirrup and bounced up neatly into the saddle. It felt strange to be on a horse that wasn't Mystic or Blaze. Paris felt new and totally different. She was stockier than Blaze – a Quarter Horse like Diablo, with a short neck and broad shoulders. Issie's legs wrapped around the barrel of the mare's wide belly. She looked down at the golden palomino and hesitated for a moment.

"She's a lovely ride; you'll have no trouble with her. She's Hester's favourite." Aidan smiled.

The dawn light was turning the sky pink on the horizon as Aidan led the way through the gate on to the ridge track. "Are you ready?" Aidan asked. He was having trouble holding Diablo back; the piebald wanted to go.

Issie nodded and clucked Paris on, settling the mare into a steady pace beside Diablo, the two horses matching each other stride for stride.

They cantered on in silence all the way along the ridge. Occasionally Issie cast a wary eye at the forest next to them, but it was quiet. There was no sign of the Grimalkin. Issie stood up in her stirrups and leant low over the Paris's neck as she cantered. The sun had risen now and the palomino looked even more beautiful bathed in golden morning light.

It wasn't until they were past the forest and heading down into the farmland that Aidan finally slowed Diablo to a trot and they were able to talk.

"Thanks for coming with me to find Blaze," Issie said to him.

Aidan shrugged. "That's OK. I don't think Hester would have let you ride back out again on your own and anyway, it's kind of fun. I don't get to do much hacking out these days; I have too much farm work to do."

"Oh," Issie said, "I see. I'm really sorry. I know you have loads of work and better things to do than go looking for my horse—"

"That wasn't what I meant," Aidan stopped her. "I just meant… I'm having a really good time."

"Me too." Issie smiled. "But you have a big movie coming up, don't you? Aunty Hess says you're really busy with trick-training the horses."

Aidan smiled. "Hester worries too much. Most of her horses are totally ready – they don't need any more training. Take Diablo here," Aidan said, "he knows every trick in the book. He can climb stairs, count to ten, dance a waltz and take a bow at the end. Hester taught him all of that and I guess she's trained me too," he laughed. "She knows a few things about convincing animals and people to do whatever she wants."

Aidan gave Diablo a pat on his neck. "Hey, do you want to see one of his tricks?" Issie nodded.

"Here we go then!" Aidan suddenly pushed Diablo on into a canter. Issie pulled Paris up to a halt to watch as the piebald cantered a circle in front of her. Aidan waved over his shoulder to Issie.

"Watch this!" He grinned. While Diablo was still

cantering, Aidan quickly swung one leg over the back of the saddle so that he was standing up in the stirrup, balancing on one side of the horse and clinging to the saddle with both hands. Diablo kept cantering smoothly as if there was nothing at all unusual about having his rider hanging off the saddle like a performing monkey. As they circled once more, Aidan crouched down. Now Issie couldn't even see him as he rode past her on the circle. He was hanging on so low he was hidden behind Diablo, and the horse looked totally riderless as he cantered by. Then she saw Aidan appear, hanging upside down now, dangling underneath the horse's belly. He cantered around once more, clinging on with just one hand. With the other hand he reached all the way down to the ground and as he raced past he snatched up a wild daisy. He swung himself gracefully back up into the saddle and pulled hard on Diablo's reins. The gelding reared up dramatically, thrashing the air with his front legs. Then he came down to the ground again, snorting and prancing, clearly pleased with his performance. Aidan rode up to Issie and handed her the daisy.

"Wow!" Issie grinned, taking the flower from Aidan and reaching forward to tuck it into Paris' bridle behind the horse's ears. "That was incredible!"

"Cowboy tricks!" Aidan smiled. "It's just like in those Western movies. You know, when the cowboy hides by riding low on the side of the horse so the other cowboys don't even know he's there to shoot? Diablo is great at all the cowboy tricks. Hester even taught him to play dead when a gun is fired; that's how she broke her leg. He dropped to the ground and she got pinned underneath him by mistake."

"I know, she told me," Issie said.

"So, Hester says that Blaze knows a few tricks too?" Aidan asked.

"She can't do anything as fancy as Diablo, but she can bow. She learnt that when she was in the El Caballo Danza Magnifico," Issie said. "And she always comes when I whistle."

"Well, that trick may come in handy," Aidan said. "There's a whole lot of land out here. You may have to do a fair bit of whistling before we find your horse."

Issie looked up ahead of her. Aidan was right. Blackthorn Farm went for hundreds of miles in every direction. How on earth were they ever going to find her horse? It was like looking for a needle in a haystack. Issie was about to say as much when she heard a shrill whinny carrying clear and sharp in the morning air. Could it be Blaze? She looked up to where the sound was coming from. Ahead of her, on the horizon to the far left of the valley, she saw the grey shape of a pony, his dapples flashing in the brilliant sunshine. She squinted hard and tried to look again. The horse had disappeared, but she knew she wasn't seeing things. It was Mystic. He was trying to tell her to follow him. He was leading her to Blaze.

"This way!" she said confidently to Aidan. "I heard a horse; we need to go this way."

As they cantered on through green pasture, Issie kept checking the horizon for the little grey gelding. Sometimes she would see Mystic just up ahead of her, as if he were waiting for her to join him. But as soon as she got close enough the little dapple-grey would run again, always staying ahead of her, guiding her on.

They had ridden for several miles like this when Issie finally rode up to the brow of the hill and looked down the other side. When she saw a horse in the valley below at first she assumed it was Mystic. Then she realised it was one of the grey mares, the one with the little black foal at her feet. Next to the grey mare grazed the chestnut skewbald, the buckskin and a couple of bays.

"Aidan!" Issie called back excitedly over her shoulder. "Aidan, we've found the herd!"

As Aidan drew Diablo up next to her, Issie scanned the horses, looking frantically for Blaze. The chestnut mare and the black stallion were nowhere to be seen.

"Aidan. She's not here!" Panic rose in Issie's voice. Where was Blaze? Had something happened to her beloved pony?

"She'll be here. Stay calm," Aidan said.

Just as he said this, over the brow of the hill came Blaze.

Issie was relieved to see that Tom Avery's much-loved cross-country saddle was still on her back. The saddle had slipped a bit to the left and Blaze's reins were broken and dangling loose around her legs, but otherwise everything looked OK. As for Blaze, she looked just fine. She cantered along with her head held high and called out once more, a high shrill whinny. This time another horse answered her call.

Now the black stallion came into view. His enormous strides swallowed up the ground as he caught up to Blaze. Issie was struck once more by the beauty of the black horse.

"Isn't he beautiful?" Issie said to Aidan.

"I can't believe it. He's just like Avignon – except he's jet black!" Aidan said.

"Do you think so?" Issie said.

"Absolutely. Hester will go wild when she sees him," Aidan said. He was transfixed by the big black horse and couldn't take his eyes off him.

"What do you mean?" Issie said.

"Come on, Issie. You said yourself that you nearly caught him the other day. And now he's made friends with Blaze it should be easy. You said you wanted to save him, Issie. Well this is your chance. We can do this together. We can bring the black back home. What do you say?"

Issie looked at Aidan. "Do you really mean it?" She said.

Aidan grinned. "Uh-huh!"

Issie grinned back. "Then let's do it!" She felt a tingle of excitement run down her spine. This time they were going to catch the black horse, and she knew it. She had a plan.

Chapter 9

There was no time to lose. The horses still hadn't seen them, but to keep the element of surprise on their side they would have to move fast.

"Over there, behind those trees!" Issie instructed Aidan. To their right was a small copse of blackthorn bushes, perfect for hiding out of the stallion's line of sight. Issie and Aidan clucked Diablo and Paris into a canter and within a few strides the horses were behind the trees.

"What now?" Aidan asked.

"Now it's time to get my horse back," Issie said. She jumped down off Paris and peered through the trees, handing Aidan the reins. Then she cupped her hands around her mouth and blew – a shrill, high-pitched whistle.

Issie and Aidan waited in silence. Nothing.

"Try again," Aidan said. But before Issie could raise her hands to her mouth, they heard the sound of hoofbeats.

"Blaze," Issie whispered hoarsely. Her heart was thumping in her chest. She couldn't see a thing from behind these trees. Was Blaze coming to her? She didn't dare stick her head out to look now in case the stallion saw her and spooked again. She cupped her hands once more and gave another low whistle. There was a nicker in reply this time, and then there was Blaze! The mare popped her head tentatively around the corner of the trees and Issie couldn't help but giggle.

"Well, hi there!" She grinned. She dug around in her backpack for a carrot as Blaze came all the way behind the trees to join them, nickering happily as she was reunited with her girl.

"Hey, Blaze, are you OK? I missed you!" Issie hugged her pony tight around the neck, feeding her the carrot and grasping on to the broken reins. She wasn't letting go of those again in a hurry.

Issie stood back for a moment and ran her eyes over the mare. Blaze seemed fine. She ran her hands over her body. There was hardly a mark on her.

"Good girl, I'm so glad you're OK," Issie cooed. She

led her horse back over to where Aidan was holding on to Paris and waiting for them.

Issie quickly undid Blaze's girth and slipped off her cross-country saddle. Then, still holding Blaze's reins with one hand, she reached over and undid Paris' girth and slipped the saddle off the palomino. Compared to Blaze's lightweight saddle, Paris' saddle seemed enormous. It was a stock saddle, big and bulky enough to hold the weight of a rider hanging off the side, perfect for stunt riding. She swung the saddle up into the air, throwing it on to Blaze's back.

"Steady, girl," Issie said to Blaze as she did up the girth.

"Why are you swapping the saddles over?" Aidan asked as Issie yanked the girth up and checked it one last time.

"Because I need the stock saddle to do the trick of course!" Issie said matter-of-factly to Aidan. "Now I need you to stay here and hold on to Paris. You can put Blaze's saddle on her while I'm gone. Stay hidden unless I call out for you. OK?"

"No. It's not OK!" Aidan said. "First you'd better tell me what's going on. What exactly is this plan of yours?"

"Actually, it's kind of your plan," Issie said. "I got the idea from watching you do that trick on Diablo on the way here." She turned to face Aidan. "The black stallion really likes Blaze, right? She's a part of his herd now so she can get right up close to him. But he doesn't trust me just yet. If he sees me on top of her he just might freak out and bolt." Issie paused. "But what if he didn't see me?"

"I don't understand," Aidan said. "How can you get near him without him seeing you?"

Issie put her foot in the stirrup now and mounted Blaze. She swung one leg back over the saddle, balancing like a gymnast on one side of the horse, with all her weight in one stirrup. From here, she practised crouching down and hanging off one side of the saddle, just as Aidan had done on Diablo.

"Like this," she said to Aidan. "I'm going to ride the same trick that you did on Diablo. I can do it on Blaze."

Issie practised the crouch again, then she swung her leg back up and over so she was sitting in the saddle properly once more.

"Aidan, this will work! If I hang on to the side of the saddle and stay crouched down low, I can ride Blaze up towards the stallion. He won't even know I'm there until we're right up close. Then I can slip a rope around his neck and tether him to Blaze's saddle so he can't get away."

Aidan said nothing.

"Well? What do you think?"

Issie held her breath as Aidan mulled over the idea. Finally, after a long pause, he said, "I think it sounds like the best plan we've got. You and Blaze have more chance of catching him on your own. If we all charge in there he'll just bolt. Now, let me show you how to hang off the side of your saddle properly. We don't want you getting dragged under Blaze's belly."

After a quick lesson from Aidan, who also helped fashion a lasso for her to slip over the stallion's neck, Issie mounted up again and got into position.

"Steady, Blaze," Issie said as she dropped down into a crouch against the mare's left side.

"Are you ready?" Aidan asked.

Issie nodded. She had only been in position for a couple of minutes now but already her arms ached from supporting her body weight. She could feel her fingers cramping from gripping on to the front end of the saddle with one hand and the back end with the other. She needed to do this fast before her arms gave out.

"Trot on, Blaze!" Issie whispered quietly to the mare. Blaze responded instantly to her voice aids, breaking into trot as Issie tugged on the left rein, turning the mare in the direction of the stallion.

As Blaze's trot quickened the ride got bumpier. *Just*

hang on, not much longer now... Issie told herself. Her arms really ached. She could feel the fingers of her left hand cramping painfully as she gripped on to the pommel. Her right hand, which was wet with sweat, was beginning to slip off the cantle...

Just as Issie felt like she was losing her grip, Blaze began to slow down and pulled up to a halt. The mare gave a keen nicker and Issie heard the sound of the stallion talking back to her. He was close. Very close. Issie couldn't see where he was, and she was too nervous to lift her head up above the saddle in case he saw her and spooked. She didn't know what to do next. She held her breath, too scared to move at all. This was crazy! She couldn't catch the stallion if she couldn't see him!

Then she realised that she could pull the same trick Aidan had done when he had picked her that flower. If she hung low enough under Blaze's belly then she'd be able to look through the mare's legs and see the stallion on the other side.

As she lowered herself down head first she felt her face flush from the rush of blood. Then, there she was, swinging upside down, dangling with her face precariously close to the ground, with just her right hand gripping the stirrup leather to keep her from falling.

Now that she was down low she could look through Blaze's legs and see the stallion. She was right. He was very close. In fact he was standing right next to Blaze. If she suddenly appeared, the stallion would be spooked for sure. How could she get close enough to slip the rope around his neck without him seeing her? She had to think fast.

Steeling her nerve, Issie unhooked the rope from the saddle and slipped her foot out of the stirrup, dropping silently to the ground. She was still hidden from the stallion's view by Blaze's body. She leant her back against Blaze's belly and took a deep breath. Stay low, that was the way to do it. She dropped into a low crouch on the ground next to Blaze, then crawled under her belly and crouched between her legs. It was a risky place to be and Issie knew it. If Blaze lashed out suddenly or even moved a hoof Issie would get kicked. She had to put her faith in her pony. Blaze knew that Issie was there; she wouldn't hurt her. Blaze didn't move a muscle as Issie edged further under her belly and got into position.

The stallion was right above her now. He was so close that Issie could reach out her hand and touch him. The big black horse lowered his head over the chestnut mare and nibbled affectionately at her shoulder. There wouldn't be a better time to do this. She had to move now!

In one swift motion Issie slipped out from underneath Blaze's belly, quickly throwing the rope around the stallion's neck, grasping the end and looping it back through the lasso.

The black horse felt the rope against his neck and suddenly noticed Issie. Startled, he reared back, taking up the slack. As he did so, Issie hurriedly tied the rope to the pommel of Blaze's saddle. Then she swiftly jammed her foot into the stirrup and threw herself desperately back up on to Blaze's back.

As the stallion reared back and pulled against her, Issie reined Blaze backwards too, asking the mare to hold her ground against the big, black horse. The stallion strained against the rope, shaking his head and trying to free himself. He gave two little bucks, going straight up in the air. But he didn't panic. It was as if he knew that struggling would get him nowhere.

"Clever boy," Issie said. "You know I've got you, don't you?"

The stallion gave a defiant toss of his head and pulled back against the rope once more, testing his limits. Then he stopped struggling against Blaze's weight and stood still. His body was quivering but he seemed almost resigned to being caught.

"Aidan!" Issie shouted out. "I've got him. Bring the halter."

Aidan rode up on Diablo, the halter in his hand. He headed towards the stallion but then decided against it and handed the halter over to Issie. "He trusts you and Blaze more than me. You do it!" Aidan instructed.

Issie nodded and rode Blaze forward, pulling up the slack on the rope in her hand as she went. When she finally reached the stallion, she managed to slip the halter quickly over his head.

"Steady boy, I've got you." She spoke softly to the horse as she refastened the rope from around his neck, attaching it to the halter instead. "All done. We've got him. I don't believe it!" She grinned over at Aidan who was watching the whole thing.

"I don't believe it either!" Aidan shook his head. "Well, well. Aren't you something, Issie Brown?"

Issie looked at the black horse, now standing peacefully beside her. "Did you see that, Aidan? He's so clever. He calmed right down as soon as he knew he was caught."

Aidan nodded. "He's a smart horse." Then he smiled at Issie. "I think it helps that he seems to be in love with your mare!"

"I know." Issie nodded. "He's happy when he's with

Blaze, isn't he? I'd better lead him home. Can you ride Diablo and lead Paris?"

"Sure," Aidan nodded, "whatever you say, horse-whisperer! Let's get him home."

As they set out along the Coast Road Issie took the lead on Blaze with the stallion trotting along beside her. Issie began to think that Aidan was right. Maybe the stallion was in love with her mare. He trotted along briskly beside her, his head held high, his tail erect.

"He's got a beautiful trot, hasn't he?" Issie shouted back over her shoulder at Aidan, who was riding a few lengths behind her, keeping Diablo and Paris well out of the stallion's reach in case he lashed out.

Aidan nodded. "Floating paces. A classic warmblood – just like Avignon. I can't wait until Hester sees him. I want to see the look on her face."

The look on Hester's face when they arrived was not at all what they had anticipated. Instead of the beaming smile they had been expecting, Hester turned white with shock. Her eyes welled with tears as she reached Issie's side. She looked up at the black horse and was very quiet for a moment. When she finally spoke her voice was shaky.

"Do you know," she said, "when I saw you all coming down the driveway just now it was like seeing a ghost. He's the spitting image of my darling Avignon!"

Hester stepped forward, reached out a hand and took the lead rope from Issie, untying it from the saddle. As Issie and Aidan watched, she cooed and clucked softly to the big, black horse. The stallion took a step towards her and Issie marvelled at her aunt's natural ease with the animal. Within moments she was stroking his nose and running her hands down his neck and over his back.

"Steady there, my lovely boy," she cooed. "You're not a bit wild, are you? Where did you come from?"

Hester smiled up at Issie now. "How clever you both are, catching him like that! Your mother would kill me of course, Isadora, if she knew I was allowing you to go out on a wild horse hunt! But how fabulous! And you were right: I have no doubt in my mind as I look at him now. He is Avignon's son. You have brought him home. Coming here was his destiny."

"Destiny! That's it!" Issie said. "Aunty Hess, you're a genius! I've been trying to think of a name for him all the way home. That's the perfect name for him. Destiny it is!"

Aunt Hester turned to the black stallion. "Do you

hear that, Destiny? You've got a new home and a new name all in one day." She smiled at Issie and Aidan. "Come on then, let's get Destiny settled in. He can go in the field next to the duck pond. It's too soon to expect him to be stabled. Besides, he would go bonkers if we kept him too near the mares!" she explained.

They all stood and watched as Destiny moved around the perimeter of the paddock, which had high fencing on every side. He trotted back and forth and let out a few high-pitched calls. Then he galloped the fence-line, charging down on the rails at the end of the paddock. For a moment it looked as if he might try to jump, but at the last moment he swerved and kept galloping. After a few laps of the field, punctuated by moments when he stopped to sniff the ground, looking for the smells of horses that had been there before, Destiny eventually settled down.

By the time Issie returned from the stables after putting Blaze away for the night, the stallion was grazing peacefully as if he had lived at Blackthorn Farm all his life.

Issie helped Aidan untack Paris and Diablo, feeding them and bedding them down for the night, then they headed back up to the manor where Aunt Hester was cooking dinner.

"What's she making us?" Issie said.

"Her famous lasagne," Aidan groaned.

"That doesn't sound so bad," Issie said optimistically.

"It's called famous lasagne because it's famous for giving you a stomach ache for three days afterwards." Aidan grinned.

As they chewed their way through the lasagne on their plates Aunt Hester quizzed them both about how they had caught Destiny. When Issie told her about the stunt-riding trick Hester whooped with delight. "I'm so glad all my trick-training got put to real use for once!" She beamed.

"Aunty Hess," Issie said as she put down her cutlery and stopped trying to hack into her lasagne crust, "please, I want to talk to you about the cull."

The table went quiet.

"Isadora, I know how you feel—" her aunt began. But Issie cut her off before she could say anything more.

"Aunty Hess, you feel the same way. I know you do! We have to stop it!"

Hester shook her head. "It can't be stopped, my dear. Don't you think I've already tried? My group, Save the Blackthorn Ponies, have been fighting Cameron on this for years now. We've won several legal wrangles, but the

Conservation Trust are very hot under the collar about the damage the ponies are doing. They've done their homework and their paperwork. They took it all the way to the high court and it has been decreed that the horses must go. Cameron is a good man, he's given us loads of second chances and we've exhausted all the options. I don't see what else we can do."

Issie was about to answer back when she heard Aidan's voice speaking up next to her. "We can catch them ourselves," he said.

"What?"

"The Conservation Trust doesn't care what happens to the horses, as long as we get them off the land, right?" Aidan shrugged. "So all we've got to do is catch them."

"That's all very well, Aidan, but Cameron and his men have tried that already," Hester sighed. "Those ponies are damn near impossible to muster and you know it."

"Maybe for Cameron and his boys, but we've never tried before, have we?" Aidan replied.

"Well," Hester said considering this, "what if we do catch them? What then? We can't keep thirty more horses on this farm! Besides, these are wild horses – they're unbroken."

"Ohmygod!" Issie yelped suddenly. "I've just had a

really great idea. Aunty Hess! We can do it. I know someone who can help us. We're going to save the horses! Not just Destiny – all of them!"

That night, around the kitchen table, Issie laid out her plan to Hester and Aidan. After much discussion, they all agreed that it just might work. Then phone calls were made, further plans were hatched and rooms were prepared with spare beds made up with fresh linen. After all, they needed to be ready. Tomorrow, the cavalry were coming.

Chapter 10

Issie looked anxiously at her watch. Unbelievable!
It was almost midday.

"They were supposed to be here by now. Why aren't
they here?" She complained to Aidan. They were sitting
together on the sofa on the upstairs balcony of the
manor overlooking the cherry-tree lawn.

"Issie, calm down," Aidan said gently. "They said
they'd be here by lunchtime and it's not even—"

"They're here!" Issie suddenly leapt up and left
Aidan in mid-sentence as she raced back into the house
and ran down the stairs.

Aidan listened to Issie's frantic footsteps on the staircase.
He heard the front door swinging open and slamming shut
again as Issie dashed outside. Coming towards her down the

long, leafy driveway was a dark green Range Rover. Issie waved, gesturing for it to circle the lawn and pull up in the parking bay right next to the front door of Blackthorn Manor. Dust flew up from beneath the tyres as it pulled to a stop. The driver's door flew open and out stepped Tom Avery.

"Well, Isadora, I wasn't expecting this. It's quite the grand country estate, isn't it?" Avery said, looking about.

"Tom!" Issie grinned. "Thanks so much for coming—"

She was interrupted by the sound of the other doors of the Range Rover opening.

"Issie!" Stella squealed, jumping down from the passenger seat and running round to give her best friend a hug.

"Ohmygod, it is amazing here!" Kate shrieked as she hopped out of the back and ran over to join her friends. Ben and Dan emerged now too, stretching dramatically and shaking out their arms and legs.

"I feel so cramped up after that long drive! We left at five in the morning to get here!" Ben groaned.

"Oh, stop complaining!" Dan snapped at him. "You slept most of the way. You were snoring and drooling on my shoulder."

"Hi, guys," Issie beamed at them. "Thanks for coming. I really, really appreciate it."

At that moment there was a sudden yelp and a chorus of barking as Strudel, Nanook and Taxi officially announced the arrival of the new guests. The three dogs bounded out the front door to greet everyone, followed by Aunt Hester and Aidan.

"Aunty Hess! Come and meet my friends. This is Stella, Kate, Dan and Ben," Issie began her introductions. "And this is my riding instructor, Tom Avery."

"Welcome to Blackthorn Manor, everyone!" Hester said brightly. "Lovely to meet you, Tom. Isadora has told me so much about you. You know, I used to watch you ride on TV. I once saw you do a clear round in the cross-country at Burghley on that enormous bay gelding of yours…"

"Lucky Jim?" Avery said. "He was a fabulous horse. Never slowed down for a fence, mind you. I rode him in a gag, but he was still impossible to stop."

"Oh!" Issie said, spotting Aidan quietly standing behind Aunt Hester. "I haven't finished my introductions. Everyone, this is Aidan. Aidan, this is Tom, Stella, Kate, Dan and Ben."

"Hello…" Aidan stepped out from behind Hester and gave them all a shy wave.

"Hi, Aidan!" they all replied.

Stella, who was boggling at Aidan, leant over and whispered rather too loudly in Issie's ear. "That's him? Issie, I told you so! I knew it. He's totally gorgeous!" Issie elbowed Stella roughly. "Ow! What did you do that for?" Stella said. Issie glared at her, willing Stella to shut up.

"Aidan helped me catch Destiny," Issie said. She kept an eye on Stella as she said this. She was terrified her friend might say something else. She would be so embarrassed if Aidan thought she had a silly crush on him or something.

"I'm dying to see him!" Kate said. "I've never even seen a stallion before. I bet he's beautiful."

"We'll show you to your rooms and then you can meet the horses." Hester smiled brightly. "Come on in – we're all ready for you."

While Aidan showed Avery and the boys to their rooms Issie took Stella and Kate on a whirlwind tour of Blackthorn Manor, showing them the vast ballrooms downstairs, the grand dining room and the wood-panelled billiards room.

"This must be what a princess' house looks like!" Stella gasped as she stroked the brilliant green feathers of one of the stuffed pheasants and stared up at the oil paintings of racehorses on the walls.

"This is most amazing room I've ever been in," Kate agreed as she cast her eyes around the ornate ceilings hung with sparkling crystal chandeliers.

"It's so good that you're here! I still can't believe it!" Issie beamed at her friends. "I'm really sorry for dragging you away like this. I know you were doing the summer dressage series and everything…"

"What? Are you nuts! We couldn't wait to leave," Stella said. "Natasha was driving us crazy. She was winning by like, a million miles on that new horse of hers. Which is fine, except after every competition she would go over the leader board in the clubroom with a highlighter pen and highlight her scores so that everyone could see how much she's winning by and—"

"Oh, just forget about it, Stella! We're here now!" Kate shut her up.

"Come on" Issie told them. "You can unpack your bags later. Let's go to the stables. I can't wait for you to meet Destiny."

Dan, Ben and Avery were already at the stables when the girls arrived. They were watching over the rails as Destiny paced and fretted along the fenceline. With an audience to watch him, Destiny broke out of his high-stepping trot into a canter, tossing his head as he circled the paddock.

"What do you think, Tom?" Issie said.

"He has terrific paces," Avery mused. "Hester might be right about Avignon. This horse certainly moves like a warmblood. Does he have a brand?"

Issie shook her head. "No, there are no markings on him. Hester thinks that Avignon might have escaped at some point and bred with a Blackthorn Pony."

"Perhaps…" Avery said. "But you say he's not as wild as the rest of them?"

"He let me put a halter on him and lead him back to the farm," Issie replied.

"It makes no sense," Avery said. "A horse like this, left to roam wild. How did he get there?"

Destiny stopped cantering now and stood at the end of the paddock nearest the stables. He let out a shrill, high whinny and a moment later another horse returned his call.

"That's Blaze!" Issie smiled. "Come on, I'd better go and check on her and then you can meet your horses."

"Today is Wednesday and the cull is due to happen on Friday. It's too late to ride out today, of course, so that only leaves tomorrow to muster the herd," Hester explained as they all walked together to the stables. "We thought if we allocated each of you a horse now then you'd be all set and ready to go first thing in the morning. We're aiming for a six a.m. start."

Issie pulled a crumpled piece of paper out of her pocket. "Right!" she said. "This is the list of horses and riders for tomorrow's muster. I'm on Blaze, obviously, and Aidan has Diablo – he's the piebald in the last stall. Stella and Kate – you're on Paris and Nicole – the twin palominos. Ben is on Scott – he's the skewbald in that stall over there to your left. Dan is riding Tornado – he's the dark bay hunter in the last stall. He's the one Aunty Hess usually rides…"

Issie looked back down at her list. "And Tom, you're on Titan," Issie said mischievously. "I think you'd better come over here and meet him."

Issie pulled a face over her shoulder at Stella and the others as she walked with Avery to the first stall in the row. They all gathered round as Avery opened the Dutch door. He looked puzzled. "I don't understand. There's no horse in here," he said.

"Yes there is!" Issie laughed. She unbolted the bottom half of the door and there was little Titan, all nine hands of him, looking up at them from underneath his enormous shaggy brown forelock.

Everyone started laughing as Avery strode over to the miniature pony and stood over him. Titan was so tiny that he barely reached Avery's hip. Everyone laughed even harder.

"I think you may have to find me a slightly larger mount, Isadora," Avery said, trying to keep a straight face.

"I've got just the thing right next door," Issie said. "You can ride Dolomite."

If the riders had been laughing hard before, they hooted and wailed now at the sight of the enormous eighteen hand Dolomite next to the tiny miniature pony.

"Haven't you got something somewhere in between these two?" Avery asked.

"Actually, no. I wasn't joking. I was hoping you'd ride Dolomite," Issie said. "I know he looks huge but Aunty Hess says he's very well schooled."

"Well, I'm certainly not riding Titan, so I guess I have no choice, do I?" Avery smiled.

With the horses all fed and the tack sorted for the next day they locked up the stables for the night and headed back up to Blackthorn Manor. Over dinner the riders looked at the map of Blackthorn Farm as Aunt Hester filled them in on the details of the impending cull.

"Cameron is assembling his team now. Friday is D-day," Hester said gravely. "It doesn't leave us much time… And then, of course, once we've got the herd back here that leaves us with an even bigger problem. What on earth are we going to do with them?"

"That's where you come in, Tom," Issie said. "When Aunty Hess told me that these horses were wild with no homes to go to I suddenly realised that I had the solution all along. You work for the International League for the Protection of Horses. You can take the wild horses and find them new homes – good homes where they'll be cared for properly by owners that love them. You can do it, can't you?"

Avery looked serious. "What you're asking is no small feat, Isadora. Your Aunt is right – these are wild ponies born and bred and they won't be easy to school. They'll be a handful for even an experienced horseman." Avery saw Issie's face fall at this news.

"Hey now! I never said it couldn't be done – just that it wouldn't be easy. Of course the ILPH will take these horses. I've been in touch with them and organised everything. The Blackthorn Ponies will be trucked to the ILPH fields after they're mustered. We'll keep them there and feed them up, break them in and give them a bit of basic schooling before we find them new homes. All the prospective owners will have to pass our checks before they can re-home a Blackthorn Pony, of course. These are very special ponies – you can be sure we'll be keeping an eye on them once they have new owners."

"Thanks, Tom," Issie smiled, "they're really amazing ponies. Wait until you see them."

"We should all get an early night," Aidan advised them as he headed back out the door and home to his cottage. "We'll need to be ready to mount up by six a.m. when it's light enough to ride."

"Who made him the boss?" Dan muttered as Aidan left.

"Aidan is the farm manager. He's a really good trick rider and he knows what he's doing," said Issie.

"Yeah, well, he's not that much older than us and he doesn't get to boss us around," Dan said sulkily. "Anyway, goodnight. I was going to bed anyway."

"What's up with him?" Issie asked Ben.

Ben rolled his eyes. "Duh, Issie! Think about it. Maybe he's jealous? You've been going on and on about Aidan this and Aidan that ever since we got here!"

Issie was shocked. "I don't know what you're talking about!"

"Yeah, right," Ben said. "I'd better get to bed now too. It's a big day tomorrow."

Could Dan really be jealous of Aidan? thought Issie.

"Of course he is!" Stella laughed when Issie asked her this. The girls were sitting on Issie's four-poster bed having hot chocolates with marshmallows as a pre-bedtime treat.

"I'm jealous too!" Kate said. "I mean, Aidan is so cool. Have you noticed how his hair kind of dangles over his eyes like that? How does he even see where he's going?"

Issie smiled at this. She had noticed Aidan's hair. It was kind of cute how it hung over his face, hiding his blue eyes. "But it's not like he likes me or anything," she protested.

"Issie! Haven't you noticed that he's always hanging around?"

"That's because he works here, Stella," Issie sighed.

"Anyway, we're supposed to be having an early night..." Issie started, then hesitated. She leapt to her feet and ran to the window.

"Issie, what are you—?" Stella began, but Issie hushed her.

"Listen!" Issie said. "Do you hear that?"

The three girls froze for a moment in silence. There was nothing to hear. The night air was completely quiet. And then, just when Issie thought she must have been imagining it, she heard the noise again. There it was! Even louder now. A deep rumbling, like the growl of a big cat.

The girls held their breath. There was silence again for a moment and then the feline rumble could be heard once more. Issie felt the hairs rise on the back of her neck. The growl sounded close. The animal must be right outside.

"Ohmygod!" Stella breathed. Her face was deathly pale, her eyes were wide with fear. "What is that?"

"That," said Issie, "is the Grimalkin."

Chapter 11

So much for an early night! Arming themselves with a torch, the girls had raced outside in search of the Grimalkin and they were now huddled together on the back veranda of the manor.

"Hurry up, Stella!" Issie hissed.

"I'm trying to make this work... ahh, got it!" Stella switched the torch on and shone the beam out into the inky blackness. The torchlight flickered over the lawn, the magnolia trees, the fishpond and then suddenly, caught in the beam were a pair of yellow eyes. Kate let out a scream and grabbed at Stella's arm.

The yellow eyes came closer. In the shadows a huge black animal loomed, bearing down on them.

"Wait a minute..." Issie took the torch off Stella and

shone it once more on the animal. She heaved a sigh of relief. It wasn't the Grimalkin.

"You guys – it's just Nanook!" Issie said.

Nanook bounded towards them now, wagging her tail happily.

"Nanook! You scared us half to death!" Stella growled at the dog.

"It's not her fault," Issie defended her. "That growling that we heard earlier – I'm sure that was the Grimalkin. Nanook probably heard it too; that's why she's out here."

"Well, it doesn't look like there's anything here now," Kate said, shining the torch over the garden and checking once more. As she shone the beam one more time across the lawn, though, there was something moving, coming towards them. A dark shape was moving swiftly across the grass, heading straight for the manor...

"Aidan!" Issie cried out with relief.

"What's going on?" Aidan asked as he ran up the stairs to join them. "What are you all doing outside?"

"We heard a noise," Stella said. "It sounded like a cat growling."

"Me too," Aidan said. "I was in bed when the horses in the stable block suddenly started kicking up a fuss. I went outside to check them and then I heard it.

I was just coming up to the house to make sure that everything was all right up here."

"Are the horses all OK?" Issie asked.

Aidan nodded. "They're locked in and there's nothing there. Whatever it was must have been scared off."

"So it's gone?" Stella sounded disappointed. "I wish we'd seen it!"

"No. You really don't," Issie said softly, remembering what the Grimalkin had done to poor Meadow.

"Issie's right," Aidan agreed. "You don't want to come face-to-face with this thing. We're just lucky it hasn't hurt any of the animals this time."

Aidan looked at the girls. "Listen, let me take the torch and I'll take the dogs and make one last round of the manor and the stables to make sure its gone. You guys go back to bed and get some sleep."

Kate reluctantly handed Aidan the torch and the three girls went back inside.

"I wish we'd gone with Aidan to check the grounds. I really wanted to actually see the Grimalkin," Stella grizzled as they walked back up the stairs to their bedrooms.

"Me too," Kate agreed.

"You guys, this is serious!" Issie said. "You don't know what this animal can do. The night when Meadow was killed I saw it on the fence in the moonlight, walking along the top of the rails. And then when I saw what it had done to Meadow. It ripped her throat open – it was horrible."

"Do you think it was the same animal that chased you on Blaze?" Stella asked.

"Uh-huh. It's really fast. Blaze was totally galloping and it nearly caught us," Issie said.

"This whole Grimalkin thing is starting to creep me out," Kate said with a shiver.

Sleep was a good idea. But it wasn't easy. Issie lay awake for a long time. When she did finally sleep she dreamt of Mystic. In her dream she was riding the little grey gelding down by Lake Deepwater. The cull had started and the gunmen were tracking the wild herd. She was looking for Blaze and Destiny, trying desperately to find them. There was confusion, horses running everywhere and then suddenly a shot rang out. She saw a horse fall as the gun fired and she began to gallop on Mystic towards the black shape lying on the ground. In her heart she knew the animal lying there was dead. But which horse was it? It was hard to see…

"Mystic?" Issie murmured. "Mystic, what's happening?"

The noise of her alarm clock woke her and she sat up in bed, her heart racing. She felt a wave of relief as she realised it had all been a dream. The bedside clock was flashing – 5:30 A.M. Issie rolled out of bed. It was dark outside but she could already see the faint blush of the sun as it crept up the horizon. She pulled on her jodhpurs and a jersey and headed downstairs for breakfast. Dream or no dream, this was mustering day and it was time to ride.

The riders barely spoke in the darkness of the stables as they prepared their horses. Once they were all saddled up, Aidan gathered everyone together outside near the gate for a team talk.

"We'll take it slowly along the ridge. No cantering – keep the horses to a trot," Aidan instructed. "We need them fresh for the muster, so let's not tire them out."

"Is this where the Grimalkin attacked you?" Stella whispered to Issie, looking up at the forest next to the ridge track. "Are you sure it's not still in there? Maybe we should go the other way along the Coast Road instead."

Issie shook her head. "It's much faster to the lake this way. Besides, the second time I got chased I was on the Coast Road anyway…" Issie realised as soon as she said this that she should have shut up. No one knew she had been chased by the Grimalkin twice now.

"What?" Stella looked at Issie. "You got chased twice? What happened?"

Issie hesitated, "Well… I'm not sure it was the Grimalkin that time. You know, I was out there on my own because Blaze had run away. I was probably just imagining things."

Stella nodded at this. "It must have been awful. Losing Blaze, I mean. You must have been so worried. And poor Blaze – out there all alone!"

Issie nodded and turned to her horse, putting an arm around Blaze's neck and stroking the crest of her honey-coloured mane. "It's so good to have you home again, girl. I don't want anything to ever happen to you. Not ever."

Issie's mind flashed back again to the dream she had last night. She had heard a shot and seen a horse fall to the ground. Had it been Blaze that had fallen? She was about to tell Stella about the dream, but she changed her mind. *It was just a dream,* she told herself, *forget about it.*

"Which horse am I on?" Stella whispered to Issie. "Is this one Paris or Nicole? How do you tell them apart? I'm—"

"Hello? Are you all listening up the back there?" Avery

called out rather pointedly to Stella. "Because Aidan is about to explain the plan for the muster before we set off."

Aidan took some sheets of paper out of his pocket and began to pass them around to each of the riders. "It's a map of Blackthorn Farm," he explained. "The herd have been seen at Lake Deepwater twice now so it looks like that's the best place to start. We'll track them down and then drive them back along the Coast Road to Blackthorn Manor. There's only seven of us and thirty horses so we'll have to spread out behind them and keep the herd moving."

"What if we don't find them?" Kate asked.

"It's Thursday now. Tomorrow they start the cull. We don't have a choice. We've got to find them," Aidan replied.

The horses and riders set off at a steady trot along the ridge track. Stella and Kate rode side by side on the two identical palominos. Aidan rode at the front on Diablo, with Avery next to him on the enormous Clydesdale, Dolomite.

As the horses all settled into a stride, Issie heard hoofbeats behind her and turned around to see Dan riding up next to her.

"Hi," he said uncomfortably.

"Hi," she replied.

"So… it's pretty cool, isn't it? Riding out to muster some wild horses. You don't get to do this kind of thing at pony club," Dan said.

"Uh-huh," Issie said. "Thanks for coming to help."

"No problem," Dan said. He paused for a moment and then he added, "When I heard you'd gone away to your aunt's I thought I'd have to go through the whole summer holidays without seeing you."

"Yeah, I figured I'd just see you again when I got back to pony club," Issie said.

"I know, I know…" Dan trailed off. Then he spoke again. "Hey, Issie. Can I ask you something?"

"Uh-huh. What?" Issie said.

"Is Aidan your boyfriend?"

Issie felt her heart begin to race. She looked at Dan. Was it true what Ben and Stella had said? Was Dan jealous of Aidan?

"I don't think so… I mean… no. No, he's not," Issie stuttered.

Dan's face broke into a huge grin. "Good," he said. And with that, he clucked his horse into a canter and rode off to catch up with Ben.

Issie spent the rest of the ride to the lake feeling confused. She was still puzzling over what Dan had said to her as the riders came over the green ridge of the hill and looked down into the valley of Lake Deepwater below. Issie's heart sank. The horses weren't there.

"Oh well, so much for plan A," Stella said as they scanned the lake. "Where to from here?"

"We'll ride around the lake and along the Coast Road to the very end, to Preacher's Cove." Aidan instructed as he rode Diablo down towards the lake. "This way!" he called over his shoulder for the rest of them to follow him.

"It's turning into a bit of a wild-horse chase," Ben said. Then he turned to the others and grinned at his own joke. Stella, Kate and Issie all groaned.

There was no sign of the herd on the ride to Preacher's Cove either.

"Needle in a haystack if you ask me!" Dan sulked as they reached the top of the hill. Below them was Preacher's Cove, a tiny beach wedged in between steep cliffs on either side. The sand was sparkling white, the sea was brilliant blue, there was kikuyu grass for the horses to graze on and low-hanging pohutukawa trees right down near the beach to tether the ponies underneath for shade while they ate.

"We're going to break here for lunch," Aidan said as he rode Diablo down the hill.

"I thought we were supposed to be mustering horses,

not having a picnic," Dan grumbled, following him.

At the bottom of the cove the riders dismounted and loosened their girths.

"Once we've eaten, we'll ride back along the Coast Road towards Blackthorn Manor," Aidan said. "If we stick to the road we'll have a good view. We might be able to see them from there—"

"And if we don't see them?" Dan interrupted him.

Aidan shrugged. "Then we keep looking."

"It doesn't sound like much of a plan," Dan said.

"Do you have a better one?" Aidan turned on him.

"Hey, listen, you two," Issie said.

"It wasn't me…" Dan began.

"No. I mean it. Listen," Issie said. "Shut up and listen!"

The riders realised what she meant now. They stopped talking and sat there for a moment in silence.

"Do you hear that?" Issie asked.

"Yup," Stella replied.

"Hear what?" said Dan.

"Hoofbeats," the girls replied.

They could all hear it now as the sound grew louder. They were coming closer.

"It looks like we won't have to find the Blackthorn Ponies," Issie said. "They've found us."

Chapter 12

As the sound of hoofbeats came closer the riders sprang into action.

"They're coming down into the cove." Aidan leapt up again and began tightening Diablo's girth, "We can corral them here and then drive them home." He turned to Avery. "If you take the girls and ride up the hill, you can take cover in the trees up there and then circle around behind the herd and trap them in the cove. I'll stay here with the boys and once they're trapped we'll try and herd them back up the hill again."

"Is there any other way out of the cove?" Avery asked.

Aidan shook his head. "The Coast Road is the only way in or out. If they come down here then we should have them trapped."

Avery took the lead on Dolomite as the horses galloped up the hill. Issie marvelled at just how fast the big draught horse could move. With each giant stride the Clydesdale swallowed up the ground, leaving Issie and the others galloping furiously just to keep up. They were halfway to the top when Avery directed them towards a massive fallen tree that was blocking one side of the road. The instructor pulled the draught horse up to a halt.

"This would be the best place to position ourselves. We can use this tree as a road block to help us pen the horses in," Avery said. "Those trees there should provide enough cover. We'll duck behind them, wait for the herd to go past and then we'll come out and form a road block – we'll have them trapped."

Unfortunately the clearing behind the trees wasn't big enough to fit four horses – especially when one of those horses was an eighteen-hand Clydesdale.

"Hey! I was going to go there! Move over – I don't have any room!" Stella squawked.

"I'm trying!" Issie snapped back.

"Just get your horses out of sight as much as possible and keep quiet!" Avery muttered. He had backed Dolomite in behind the biggest tree but the horse was so huge his rump stuck out one side and his neck stuck out the other.

"This is hopeless!" Stella groaned.

"Don't worry. Just stay still and keep quiet until the herd has gone past," Avery hissed.

The riders tried to hold their horses steady as the sound of hoofbeats thundered in their ears. Issie held her breath as she saw the first horse, the buckskin mare, enter the cove over the crest of the hill. She kept a tight grip on the reins, holding Blaze perfectly still as the mare galloped past without noticing the riders hidden behind the trees. Then the rest of the herd followed behind the buckskin down into the cove. Issie watched the blur of ponies pass by. There was the pretty grey mare with the black foal at her feet, and the chestnut skewbald mare with her matching foal, both tearing past at full gallop.

"Ohmygod! Look at those foals! Aren't they just the cutest things you've ever seen?" Stella whispered.

"I like the little black one," Kate said.

"Really? I think the chestnut and white one is the prettiest. Look at his little face, with that cute white blaze and that fluffy white and chestnut mane…"

"Girls! Get your heads back in the game. We've got a job to do," Avery growled at them.

"Is that the whole herd?" he asked Issie.

"I think so." Issie nodded.

"Right then, let's spread out and cover the road. We need to block their path out of the cove," Avery instructed.

The riders began to move back out from behind the trees with Avery directing them into position next to the fallen tree.

"Issie! Can you see what's going on down there?" Stella asked. "I can't see from where I am."

Issie looked down the hill. "They've stopped," she said. "They're settling down and grazing by the trees. I think I can see Aidan on Diablo… he's getting closer to them…"

"I can't stand it!" Stella said. She pushed Paris into a canter and left her position to join Issie so that she could see what was going on.

"Ohmygod!" Stella shrieked. "They've seen Aidan. They're off! They're coming back this way!"

Clouds of dust rose up from the dirt road as the herd headed back up the hill. The ponies were in full gallop, their eyes wild with fear. They were heading straight for Issie and the others.

"Move back into position NOW, Stella!" Avery yelled at her.

"It's no good, Tom, they're moving too fast. We'll get trampled!" Kate shouted.

Avery shook his head. "No. Just hold your ground. They'll stop," he said.

Issie was trying to hold her ground but as the horses got closer Blaze became more and more crazed. She gripped the reins as tightly as she could and held the mare steady.

"Easy, girl. Stand still. They're going to stop in a minute. Any minute now… I promise," Issie breathed.

"Tom?" Stella's voice was tense. "Tom? They're not stopping…"

"Trust me, Stella. Stay where you are," Avery said. He had positioned himself on Dolomite in the very centre of the road just beside the fallen tree. Dolomite was turned sideways so that his great bulk almost spanned the right-hand side of the road, cutting it off completely. The fallen tree blocked the road off to the left – the roots of the tree were pressed up hard against the banks of the cliff. The only way for the horses to escape was to the right of Avery and Dolomite, where Stella, Kate and Issie were all trying very hard not to panic as they manoeuvred their horses into the gap to form a barricade.

The Blackthorn Ponies were still in full gallop with the buckskin mare at the head of the herd, taking the lead.

Then suddenly the buckskin slowed to a canter.

She seemed to sense that she was penned in, that her path to freedom was blocked. Snorting and indignant, she swerved to the left towards Avery and Dolomite.

"She's going to turn around," Avery shouted to the others. "She's figured out that she's trapped and she'll lead the rest of the herd back down into the cove."

For a moment, it looked as if the little buckskin pony was going to do exactly that. Then, with a defiant shake of her head, she sped up again and gathered herself as she eyed up the fallen tree.

"She's going to jump the tree!" Stella yelled. "I don't believe it!"

The riders sat and watched, utterly gobsmacked, as the buckskin sized up the formidable tree trunk in front of her. Like all of the Blackthorn Ponies, the mare couldn't have been any more than fourteen hands. The tree, meanwhile, was enormous. It reminded Issie of the cross-country fences in the Badminton Horse Trials – it was at least a metre and a half high and almost two metres wide.

As the little mare approached the fence Issie winced in fright. The mare was so tiny in comparison to this tree, she was bound to injure herself. There was a sickening moment when the buckskin launched herself into the air. And then Issie and the others watched in total amazement as she soared over it easily with nearly half a metre to spare, landing neatly on the other side without breaking her stride.

"I do not believe what I have just seen." Avery was stunned.

"Watch out! Here comes the next one!" Stella shouted.

The riders stood by helplessly as one pony after another took the enormous log in their stride, all of them leaping it with ease.

"Incredible!" Avery said.

"Can't we stop them, Tom?" Issie said. "They're all getting away."

"Maybe not all of them," Avery said, gesturing towards the back of the herd. "The mares with the foals. We can still stop them."

He was right. The foals were far too young and too tiny to make such an enormous jump. And their mothers would never leave them.

"Aidan!" Issie shouted. "The mares with the foals. Get the mares with the foals!"

"Everyone close in!" Avery shouted. The last of the herd had just hurdled the fallen log and only the two mares and their foals were left behind now. "Does anyone have a halter handy?"

"I do!" Stella said.

"Focus on the skewbald mare," Avery instructed her. "If you can catch the mother then her foal will stick with her."

"I'll take the grey!" Aidan called out. "I've got my halter too."

"Everyone else, keep your horses tight together. Close up behind Stella and Aidan and form a barricade," Avery instructed.

The riders moved in slowly as Stella and Aidan rode on just ahead of them. Stella had her halter in her hand as she moved closer to the skewbald mare. When she was within an arm's length she threw the rope of the halter over the pony's neck. The skewbald flinched, but she didn't fight back. She stood quivering as Stella held her firm with the rope, dismounted and quickly but gently eased the halter on to her. At the mare's feet the chestnut and white foal stood nervously by its mother.

"I've got her!" Stella sounded shocked. "I've got her!"

As Stella moved out of the way, leading the skewbald and her foal, Aidan urged Diablo up close to the little grey and reached one hand out to grab a handful of mane near her ears. Then he leant over and quickly pulled the halter on.

"Got this one too!" he shouted to the others. A cheer rose up from the riders.

"I don't believe it!" Stella said, positively beaming as she tied the rope from the skewbald's halter to her own saddle. "Look, Issie! I caught a wild horse! Me! I caught her! Isn't that so cool?"

Issie beamed back at her. "Let's get them home," she said.

As the riders led the Blackthorn mares back along the Coast Road towards the manor, they relived their adventure at Preacher's Cove. The little foals both trotted along briskly at their side, determined not to be separated.

While Stella and Kate continued to *oohh* and *ahh* over the foals, trying to decide which one was the absolute cutest, Issie fell back silently behind the rest of the ride.

"Something wrong?" Avery asked, pulling Dolomite up so that he could join her.

Issie nodded. "Oh, Tom. I know it's great that we caught the mares and the foals – but, well, there are another twenty-five horses still out there and really, the whole plan didn't work at all, did it?"

Avery looked down at Issie – Dolomite was so huge

that he towered over her. Issie could see that his face mirrored her own concerns.

"No. You're right. It didn't work. And even if we had managed to corral those horses I still don't think we would have been able to drive them all the way back to Hester's. It's a long way back to Blackthorn Manor. We could never muster and control all those horses over such a long distance..."

Avery looked at the mares and their foals trotting alongside Aidan and Stella. "Still, at least we saved these ones, Issie. That must count for something."

They were almost at the manor now and as they trotted down the limestone driveway one of the Blackthorn mares, the little skewbald, let out a loud whinny. Her cry was immediately returned by an even louder call – the shrill, penetrating cry of a stallion calling for his mares.

"That's Destiny!" Issie said. "He must know that his mares are here."

When they heard the stallion's cry both the mares whinnied back in return. Their paces quickened as they set off down the driveway towards the stallion.

"Hey!" Stella yelped as the skewbald pulled hard on the lead rope, dragging her along. "Well, I guess it's a family reunion!" she giggled when she saw the stallion snorting and pacing the fence-line with excitement at the mares' arrival.

"You're back!" Hester grinned, emerging from the stables to greet them all. "I had got the stables ready for thirty, but four is a good start! Pop these mums and their little ones into the paddock next to Destiny, will you, Aidan?" she said. "Is this all you managed to bring home with you?"

"I'm afraid so," Stella said as she helped Aidan let the skewbald and her foal loose.

"Those foals don't look like Blackthorn ponies to me," Hester said, running her eyes over the two young colts cantering about on wobbly limbs, following their mums. "Look at those long legs! They both seem to have Destiny's lovely elevated paces too. Even that darling little skewbald lad seems to take after his dad…"

"Do you think Destiny is their sire?" Issie asked her aunt.

"I'd say so." Hester smiled. "Avignon's grandfoals. I'm quite sure of it."

As the riders watched, the pretty grey mare trotted up to the rails and poked her head over to greet Destiny. The stallion ran straight up to her and as their noses touched he gave a squeal, rearing up and racing impatiently up and down his side of the fence-line with the mare running alongside him on the other side.

"He wants to be with them. You can't keep a family apart," Hester said as they watched the stallion snorting his way along the fence-line.

"That's it!" Avery said.

"What? What's it?" Issie looked at her instructor

"That's our answer," Avery said.

"Umm… what was our question again?" Issie was confused.

"I think I've come up with a way to capture the rest of the wild ponies and bring them back to Blackthorn Manor." He turned to Issie now. "Issie, quick as you can – put Blaze away, and then ask Stella to do us a favour and groom her and bed her down for you. You won't have time for that now. I need you to meet me in the round pen. And bring your saddle and bridle and helmet. There's a girl – off you go!"

Issie stood rooted to the spot. "I don't understand, Tom. Why do I need my gear if I'm putting Blaze away for the night. Who am I going to be riding?"

Avery turned to her. "Isadora, I'm sorry, I'm not explaining myself clearly but time is of the essence so you'll have to trust me. I've come up with a way for us to lead the wild ponies home. And you and Destiny are the key."

Issie was still confused. "I'm sorry, Tom, I still don't understand..." she began.

"You saw how the mares reacted when they saw Destiny," Avery said. "Those ponies are a family. And we have the head of the family right here. They will follow him anywhere... you can lead them anywhere..."

"You mean, you want me to ride Destiny?" Issie was shocked.

Avery nodded. "He trusts you. I don't think any other rider would stand a chance, but with you riding him, maybe we can be ready in time. We still have the rest of the afternoon. The cull isn't until tomorrow..."

"You mean you want me to break Destiny in? In just one day?"

"Well, not so much a day as an afternoon," Avery said, looking at his watch. "Anyway, if it could be done and it was our only chance, wouldn't you say that we had to give it a go? Issie? What do you say?"

Issie looked across at her Aunt. "Aunty Hess?"

Hester nodded. "Tom is right, Issie. Destiny is our link to the wild herd. He trusts you. Plus you'll be light on his back; Destiny has never had a rider before."

Hester paused. "It has to be your choice. Your mother would kill me if she thought I was behind something like this. She'll probably kill me anyway. But I've watched you ride and I think you can do it. The question is, do you think you can do it?"

Issie looked at the big, black stallion. He was still pacing the fence-line and whinnying across the paddocks at his mares. The rest of his herd were still out there somewhere and tomorrow they would be killed in the cull.

"I'll ask Stella to put Blaze away for me," Issie said. "I'll get my gear and be right back!" And then she was off and running to the stables. Avery was right. There was no time to lose. Destiny was waiting for her.

Chapter 13

Issie's tummy churned with nerves as she walked into the round pen. She put her saddle and bridle down on the sawdust and looked around her. The last time she had been here, Aidan had tried to teach her how to trick-jump with Blaze and she had lost her nerve. If she wasn't brave enough to leap from Blaze's back on to Paris that day, there was no way she would ever be brave enough to ride Destiny. Maybe she should just give up right now – tell Avery that she couldn't do it. He would understand...

"Feeling nervous?" Avery's voice startled her.

"Uh-huh," Issie said.

"I need you to get rid of your doubts right now, Isadora," Avery said. "It's very important that you are confident, that you believe you can do this. A horse will always sense your fear. And there is no room for mistakes in this arena. It's vital that you feel strong and in control when Destiny comes in here."

"But, Tom, I'm not sure I can do this. He's a wild stallion and we don't have enough time…"

"Isadora, we have plenty of time. And you," he smiled at her, "you have more than enough courage."

"Now," Avery continued, "I'm going to explain the ropes to you before Aidan brings Destiny in."

"But, Tom," Issie interrupted him, "you'll be in there with me… won't you?"

Avery shook his head. "I can't come into the ring with you – this is something you need to do alone, Issie. You must make a bond with this horse."

"That's crazy!" Issie said. "I don't know how to break in a wild horse."

"You've been in my natural horsemanship classes before, haven't you? Well consider this your final lesson," Avery said. He pointed to the tiered seats that ran around the edge of the round pen. "I'll be watching you and calling instructions to you. Just do exactly as I tell you." Avery looked at her. "Now, can you do this?"

Issie took a deep breath. "OK, I mean yes, Tom, absolutely. I'm ready – let's do it."

As Avery explained how the training session would work, Issie sat listening intently. She was trying very hard to concentrate on absolutely everything that Avery was telling her, but there was so much to learn.

"Don't worry," Avery said as he left her alone in the arena. "I promise you, in less than an hour we're going to have you up on Destiny's back and riding him."

Avery left the round pen and Aidan came in leading Destiny. The black stallion was clearly spooked by his new surroundings. As Aidan led him past Issie the big, black horse shied at his own shadow, rearing up and jerking the lead rope almost out of Aidan's hand. "Easy boy," Aidan said. Issie could see the horse's nostrils quivering and there was sweat on his flanks.

He's afraid too, Issie realised, and at that moment her nerves completely vanished. If Destiny was scared, then it was up to her to be brave enough for both of them.

"You can let Destiny loose now," Avery called down to Aidan. Aidan nodded. He unclipped the lead rope from the halter. It took a moment for Destiny to realise that he was now free, and then he shook his head defiantly and cantered off to stand on the far side of the round pen, as far away as he could get from Issie and Aidan.

Aidan walked over to Issie and handed her the lead rope.

"Are you going to be OK in here by yourself?" he asked her.

"Uh-huh," she said. "I think so."

Aidan smiled. "I'm right outside that door if you need me." And with that, he headed back across the sawdust floor and out of the arena – shutting the door behind him, leaving Issie alone with the stallion.

"Right. We need to move fast here, Issie," Avery said. "Let's get started."

Issie nodded. Then she turned to face the stallion, her shoulders square to him, her gaze directly meeting his eyes. For a moment the horse looked back at her, holding her stare and challenging her.

"Use the rope now, Issie," Avery commanded from above.

Issie looked down at the long lead rope in her hand. She swung it around like a lasso and then let it fly. The rope flicked out and landed uselessly on the sawdust in front of her. Issie felt herself getting flustered – Aidan and Avery were watching from the seats above and she had no idea what she was doing.

"Don't worry about it. Try again," Avery said. "It will take you a few throws to get used to the weight of the rope."

Issie pulled the rope back, looping it loose in her hand and then threw it again. This time the rope flew out perfectly, tapping Destiny lightly across the rump. Destiny snorted with surprise and began to trot around the perimeter of the round pen. The rope fell away behind the stallion and Issie pulled it towards her, looping it back in her hands.

"That's it. Excellent. And again," Avery called to her.

Issie flicked the rope again and this time the stallion broke into a canter.

"Very good!" Avery said. "Those taps with the rope will keep him moving. Don't let him stop. We're going to keep him running for a while and pretty soon he'll get tired of going around this pen and he'll want to stop running. He's going to want to come to you instead, which means he's becoming submissive and acknowledging you as the 'alpha' horse, the boss of the herd. All you need to do now is keep him moving and look for the signs that I told you about."

Issie nodded at Avery's words but she didn't dare to take her eyes off the black horse and look up at her instructor. Avery had told her that she must never look away from Destiny, not even for a moment.

Destiny was cantering gracefully, his head held high, his nostrils flared. Issie found it impossible to believe that this proud, powerful, wild stallion would ever allow her to become the boss. Hadn't he always been the boss of his herd? She flicked the long rope at Destiny again to keep the horse cantering, waiting and watching like Avery had told her to, looking for a sign.

"There!" Avery called over the edge of the arena. "Do you see that, Issie?"

"Ummm, what?" Issie called up.

"He's listening to you. His ears are swivelling towards you, his head is turning towards you. He's paying attention now," Avery said excitedly. "In a moment he's going to make more signals – he'll lick his lips and lower his head. This is his way of saying, 'I accept that you are in charge – please let me stop running now'."

As Avery said this the black horse began to do exactly that. He lowered his head and licked his lips.

"You've got him!" Avery said. "OK, Issie, now look down at the ground and don't make eye contact. Look straight down at the ground. Do it now."

Issie did as Avery instructed. Almost immediately Destiny stopped running. Issie stayed perfectly still. The stallion took a step towards her and then another. He stretched out his nose to sniff at her. He took another step. He was so close to Issie that he was almost touching her.

"Don't make eye contact – just put your hand out, give him a pat," Avery said. The stallion didn't flinch as she reached out and stroked his face and neck. He even stood patient and relaxed as Issie stroked along his shoulders and rump. He seemed to be enjoying her touch.

"That's right, touch him along his back – that's where horses like to groom each other – he's letting you in now, you're the alpha." Avery's voice was calm and firm as he spoke to her. "Now turn away from him, Issie. Turn your back on him and walk away now," Avery told her.

Issie felt herself stiffen at this. Did she really have to turn her back on this wild horse? What if Destiny attacked her?

"It's OK," Avery said softly. "You can do it. He won't hurt you."

Issie kept her eyes down on the ground and turned her back on Destiny. She began to walk away, and as she walked she could hear the horse right there behind her.

"Don't look back," Avery said firmly.

"Tom! What's going on? Is he following me?" she hissed.

Avery laughed. "That's right. You're the alpha now. Go ahead and take him for a walk. He'll follow you."

Issie giggled and began to walk around the arena with Destiny following along right behind her like a puppy dog on a leash – except there was no leash. The horse was right there next to her, his nose nudging against her sleeve.

"This is cool!" Issie smiled up at Avery as she walked a whole circle around the arena with Destiny following at her side.

"OK, alpha girl. You can put the saddle and bridle on him now," Avery said. "It looks like you've got yourself a new partner."

Issie couldn't believe how easy it had been to win Destiny over. But the thrill of becoming the "alpha" quickly faded when she strapped the saddle on and Destiny began to buck uncontrollably.

"It's fine, let him buck," Avery reassured her. "He's never worn a saddle before. Just let him get it out of his system and he'll come back to you."

Avery was right. Destiny quickly calmed down and let Issie put on a bridle too.

"OK, Aidan, you can come back in now," Avery called. Aidan stepped into the arena. "Give Issie a leg up," Avery instructed.

"What?" Issie couldn't believe it. "But I've only just put the saddle on! It's been less than an hour! You can't break a horse in this fast!"

"Isadora. Do you trust me?" Avery said.

"Uh-huh," Issie replied.

"Then get on. He's ready. You'll be fine. Remember, you're the alpha."

"I'm the alpha, I'm the alpha," Issie chanted over and over under her breath as she put her knee in Aidan's cupped hand and sprang lightly into the saddle. Issie looked down. She had never been this high up on a horse before. Destiny was much bigger than either Blaze or Mystic. He was nearly sixteen hands. It felt like a million miles up in the air. Issie slipped her feet into the stirrups and grasped the reins in her hands. Beneath her she felt Destiny tremble, his muscles tensed as if he were ready to bolt.

"Do you want me to keep holding him?" Aidan asked. He had both hands firmly on Destiny's reins.

Issie shook her head. "No, Aidan. Let him go. It's the only way." She took a deep breath, braced her feet against the stirrups and held on.

As Destiny took a step and felt the weight of the rider on his back he gave a little half-buck. Issie hung on, her hands gripping tightly now to the front of the saddle. Destiny snorted, lowered his head and bucked again. It was a big buck this time and she felt herself lifting up and crashing back down into the saddle, but she didn't fall off.

"He's OK. He's just getting used to you," Avery said calmly. "Put your legs on him and ask him to move forward."

Issie took a deep breath and did as Avery asked. Nothing. Destiny held his ground against her, refusing to move. Frustrated, Issie gave the big, black horse a swift kick. "Get-up!" she demanded, growling under her breath nervously.

As Issie's heels dug into his sides Destiny gave a snort of defiance and reared straight up in the air and Issie, who hadn't been expecting it, flung herself at his neck, grasping desperately at his mane to hang on.

"Stop it!" she growled as the stallion thrashed the air with his hooves. By the time Destiny plunged back down again, Issie was white and shaking like a leaf.

"Are you OK?" Avery called to her.

"I think so," Issie said. "He was fine one minute and then I kicked him and he just went up without any warning at all."

"This is your first time on a stallion, isn't it, Issie?" Avery asked.

Issie nodded.

"In the past you've ridden geldings and mares," Avery continued. "A gelding, of course, is a castrated horse, which means he's pretty docile by nature. You can get as bossy as you like with a gelding. They're easygoing and they don't mind if you push them around and tell them what to do. Mares can be temperamental, but if you ask a mare like Blaze nicely enough then she'll do pretty much anything, yes?"

Issie nodded at this.

"Stallions are different," Avery said. "They're used to being in charge. They're strong-willed and they don't take orders." Avery looked serious. "You need to treat them with the utmost respect. If you try and force a stallion against his will like you did just then he'll turn against you, Issie. You must convince a stallion that he wants to work for you. Never, ever fight him – you won't win that way."

Issie nodded.

"OK," Avery said, "I think he's calmed down now. Talk to him, Issie. Ask him to move forward and take a lap around the arena…That's good! See how his ears are swivelling? He's listening. Now ask him to canter."

When Issie put her legs on the big, black horse he objected a little, but Issie didn't lose her cool. She softened her hands, whispered softly to the stallion and tried again. Destiny gave a snort, arched his neck, and instead of battling her, he flung his right leg out into a perfect smooth canter transition.

"Excellent, excellent. Now you're talking!" Avery said. "This is good progress. Are you ready to ask him for more? Here's where the lesson really begins…"

Over the next two hours Issie slowly gained Destiny's confidence. They began moving around the arena in perfect harmony, the stallion cantering on her command and then halting again with the lightest touch of the reins.

"Now ask him to turn left, now right…" Avery called to her from the seats up above the arena. "Good, good, excellent! That's enough for today. You can get off now – and take his saddle and bridle off too. We're done."

There was a clapping noise from the other side of the arena and Issie looked up to see Stella, Kate, Dan and Ben.

"That was amazing!" Stella said. "I totally held my breath when you were getting on him! And then when he reared up, I was sure you were going to fall off!"

Issie grinned up at her friends in the seats above her. "Have you guys been there the whole time?"

"Pretty much the whole time," Kate said. "Avery said we could watch as long as we didn't disturb you."

"Well, you're disturbing her now," Avery grumped at the girls. "Isadora, don't dawdle. You need to put Destiny away for the night."

Avery turned to the other riders who were now leaning over the sides of the round pen watching. "If you lot have all fed your horses then you can head back up to the house and help Hester. She's getting dinner ready. There'll be plenty of time for chit-chat when the food is on the table."

Everyone was so desperately hungry after the day's adventures that they wolfed down their meals before beginning to talk about the breaking-in of Destiny.

"I still can't believe I actually rode him!" Issie said, shaking her head.

"You two made great progress today," Avery agreed. "But I wish we had another day up our sleeves. We don't know how Destiny will behave outside the round pen in the open countryside, or what will happen when he meets the wild herd again."

Issie nodded. She had suddenly lost her appetite – and it wasn't because she had already eaten two helpings of roast chicken. Avery was right. It was easy to ride Destiny in the round pen. The real test would be riding him outside where there were no fences to stop him.

Although she guessed they would find out soon enough.

"I was wondering," Stella said as she heaped a third helping on to her plate, "do we have a plan yet? I mean, I know Issie is going to ride Destiny and he'll hopefully lead the herd. But is that it?"

Avery cocked an eyebrow at Stella. "You're right, of course, Stella. I think we all agree that a plan is needed." Avery paused. "And luckily for us, Aidan has one. A rather good one actually. We should talk about it now, since we'll need to leave early in the morning again. So gather round everyone. Here's what we're going to do…"

As Aunt Hester brought out dessert Avery and Aidan explained the plan to the others. There was much nodding and frowning as the riders talked it over. Then they began to use whatever was on the table – dessert spoons, pudding bowls and cream jugs – to mark out a strategy map so they could figure out the details.

"Just pretend I'm the sugar spoon…" Stella shouted out at one point, moving the spoon across the table. "What about if I go over here by the teapot…"

"No! No!" Kate said to her. "You need to be back here on the place mat with the rest of the dessert spoons…"

They carried on like this for quite some time until they all felt certain that the plan would work. Then, when Hester suggested they should all go to bed, ready for an early start, no one argued. As the riders headed for their rooms, there was a mood of optimism in the manor.

"Do you really think we can pull this off?" Issie asked Tom as she stood up from the kitchen table.

Avery looked down at the dishes sprawled about in front of him. "I don't think ponies are quite as easy to manoeuvre as teaspoons," he said, "but yes, yes, Issie, I think we have a very good chance indeed." He smiled at her. "Now, get some sleep. Tomorrow is a big day. I can't have my alpha horse exhausted before we even begin."

Issie smiled and climbed the stairs to her room. She washed her face, brushed her teeth and put on her pyjamas before climbing beneath the soft cotton sheets of the enormous four-poster bed. Then she lay there silently, taking one last, long look at the portrait of Avignon above her fireplace before she turned out the light.

Chapter 14

The crunch of car tyres on the limestone driveway woke Issie up. She could hear car doors slamming and the sounds of whispered conversations just outside the front door of the manor.

This was ridiculous! She knew Avery wanted to get an early start, but it wasn't even light outside. She didn't want to get up yet; she was still half asleep.

Issie sat bolt upright in bed. That wasn't Tom's voice she could hear downstairs. She listened again and felt a sudden chill as she realised who it was.

Flinging herself out of bed and wrapping a dressing gown quickly around her, Issie sprinted across the landing and down the stairs. She flew out the front door and crashed straight into Cameron, making him drop his clipboard.

"Good Morning," the ranger said stiffly as he bent down and picked his paperwork up.

"What are you doing here?" Issie blurted out. "It's not even light yet!"

"We're making an early start. My men are assembling here at the manor. We'll be out of your hair shortly."

"What do you mean you're meeting here?" Issie demanded.

"Your aunt agreed to it," Cameron shrugged, "take it up with her." He turned away and scribbled something down on his clipboard, making it clear that the conversation was over as far as he was concerned.

"Aunty Hess! Aunty Hess!" Issie raced frantically through the house.

"I'm out here!" Hester called from the back porch.

Issie found Hester out by the boot rack pulling a single pink Hunter wellington on to her foot, the one that didn't have a cast on it.

"Isadora, dear. Why are you still in your pyjamas? We need to get a move on, you know!" Hester said.

"Aunty Hess, did you tell Cameron that his men could all meet here before they began the cull?" Issie panted. She'd been hunting the whole manor for her aunt and she was clean out of breath.

"Yes, dear. I did," Hester said matter-of-factly.

"Aunty Hess! How could you? Why would you help them?" Issie was furious.

"Help them? I'm doing nothing of the kind. I just wanted to have one more chance to get them together and reason with them about this whole cull business," Hester said. "Now, where is Cameron – the front porch? Ask him to come into the kitchen, will you? I'll make us all some tea."

When Issie went back to the front of the house to find the ranger she saw another three cars had arrived in the driveway. Five men, all dressed in the same uniform as Cameron, were now gathered in conversation on the front porch. All of them were carrying guns.

"Aunt Hester would like to talk to you," Issie told Cameron. "She's made a pot of tea if you'd like to come in."

The ranger nodded, then he turned to his men. "Wait here for me. We'll set off as soon as it's light. This won't take long." And with that he followed Issie inside.

"Ah, Cameron!" Hester greeted the ranger. "Cup of tea?"

"Thanks, Hester," he replied gruffly, sitting down at the kitchen table.

"Cameron," Hester continued, "I know it's going to seem like a dreadful waste of time for you, now that you've got your men out so bright and early, but the thing is, we're going to bring the rest of the herd in today. It's very good news actually – we've come up with a way to find homes for them all. My niece's riding instructor is very well connected with the International League for the Protection of Horses and he's kindly going to help us find new owners for all the Blackthorn Ponies."

Hester sat down opposite Cameron and poured the tea before continuing, "We had planned to have the herd back here at the farm already, but we've had a few setbacks. Still, we're going to bring all the horses in today. So you needn't bother with the cull. If you want to go out now and tell your men they can go home, that would be lovely…" Hester paused. "Naturally they're welcome to come in and have a cup of tea before they go home. I've put the jug back on and—"

Cameron shook his head. "I'm sorry, Hester. I can't do that."

"Whatever do you mean?" Hester said. "If they'd

prefer coffee, of course, I can make a pot—"

"No, Hester. I mean, I can't call the cull off. It's going ahead as planned. You've already delayed us so many times now. We've had petitions and Conservation Trust meetings and lawyers meetings. Then your niece tries to sidetrack us with all this talk of a Grimalkin – some mythical creature that my men have been wasting their time over..."

Issie couldn't believe this. "I didn't make it up! The Grimalkin is real..." she began. But Cameron hushed her with a sullen glare and continued.

"So we don't find any trace of this 'Grimalkin'. And then you tell us you can catch the horses. You promised you'd catch the herd and bring them home to your farm if we just gave you more time. Friday was the deadline and today is Friday. There's a limit Hester and you've reached it. My men are here to do their job. None of us wanted this cull to happen, but it is going to happen. You can't stop it now; it's too late. We're taking our guns and we're going out there. I'm sorry, but it's got to be done."

Hester stared at the ranger. "Cameron. I'm asking you. As a friend. Please – give us just a little more time. What difference will one more day make? It means nothing to you but it may save these horses' lives. Isn't there anything you can do?"

Cameron looked down at the mug of tea in front of him and sat in silence for a moment. Then he looked up at Hester. "I can't give you the day," he said with a glint in his eye, "but I can give you a couple of hours to get a head start."

He turned to look at Issie. "I think my men could do with a big, hearty breakfast before we head out there to look for the herd. Issie, if your aunt wouldn't mind serving us up some farm eggs and bacon, and perhaps doing us a few of her famous griddle scones… and then after that we'll spend some time consulting our maps and doing a bit of a rifle check… well, it could take us a couple of hours before we're ready to set off."

He looked at his watch. "It's six a.m. now – all that should keep us busy until about eight a.m…"

"Thank you, Cameron," Hester said.

"Yes, thanks," Issie said.

"Are you still here?" Cameron looked sternly at Issie. "I thought you would have been out there saddling up your horses by now. You don't have that much time."

"I'm gone," Issie said as she raced for the door.

204

Dust clouds billowed up as the horse truck belted along the Coast Road heading for Preacher's Cove. Sitting in the front seat, Issie looked at the speedometer and then checked her watch. It was nearly seven a.m. "Come on, Aidan!"

"I'm driving as fast as I can. We'll be there in less than five minutes," Aidan snapped back at her.

Issie and her friends had made the most of the ranger's two-hour head start. Instead of setting out on horseback for the cove as the ranger had assumed they would, they had loaded their horses into the truck.

All the horses were on board except Dolomite. Since Issie was riding Destiny it had been decided that Stella would ride Blaze and Avery would ride Paris. "We need Blaze's speed and agility; it will come in handy for the muster," Avery reasoned. "Besides, it will keep Destiny happy in the horse truck if Blaze is at his side."

Issie looked back now through the window of the truck cab. She could see Blaze and Destiny standing side by side in their partitions, the stallion craning his neck around to get closer to the chestnut mare.

"How many of the Blackthorn Ponies do you think you can fit in here?" Issie asked.

"It's big enough to take seven horses the size of

Dolomite, so I dunno, about fifteen if we're lucky," Aidan said.

Issie looked worried. "It's not enough, Aidan," she sighed. "That still leaves maybe ten horses that won't make it on to the truck."

"We can herd the stragglers home," Aidan said. "There's six of us on horseback. We should be able to manage the ones who are left behind."

When they reached Preacher's Cove Aidan parked the horse truck at the top of the hill.

"Let's get them off quickly everyone," Avery said. Issie moved swiftly inside as soon as the ramp was lowered, hurrying to untie Destiny's ropes. "Easy, Destiny, good boy," she murmured. The black stallion was in surprisingly good shape after the journey. He seemed to take the truck ride in his stride.

"Good lad, Destiny. Come on, we're here now…" Issie said. Destiny picked his hooves up neatly and precisely as he marched down the ramp of the truck. At the end of the ramp the black horse lifted his head high and scanned the horizon. His nostrils were flared wide as he sniffed the air.

"Do you think he'll be able to find his herd?" Issie asked Aidan.

"His instincts are strong. He'll find them," Aidan said. "Let him go wherever he wants. All you have to do is get on him and hang on."

Is that all I have to do? Issie thought to herself. Aidan made it sound so easy. Had he forgotten that this was a wild stallion? Just yesterday she had ridden Destiny for the very first time. Now here she was, taking him out alone on to the open plains to reunite him with his herd.

"I'd better go saddle him up then," Issie said.

"Do you want help?" Aidan asked.

Issie shook her head. "It's better if I do this alone. You go and help the others."

Issie went to the truck and grabbed her saddle. Then she returned to Destiny's side. The stallion was shifting about nervously, his nose still high in the air. Was it the scent of his herd that had captured his attention? Issie wondered.

She moved very deliberately and slowly as she put the saddle on Destiny's back and did up the girth. The horse didn't flinch as the strap tightened around his belly. "Good lad," Issie breathed softly. She drew the bridle up gently over his face now and quickly did up the straps, then pulled on her helmet and fastened her chin strap. She checked the girth one last time.

"All ready?" Tom Avery appeared at her side. "Do you want a leg up?"

"Uh-huh, I guess so," Issie said.

Avery took Destiny's reins in one hand and offered the other hand to Issie for a leg up. She put her knee in Avery's hand and with a quick bounce she leapt up into the saddle. Avery was still holding the reins. He seemed reluctant to let go.

"When you find the herd, let him take control," Avery instructed. "He'll do what comes naturally to him. Then all you need to do is guide him back towards the cove. Get the herd to follow you down to the sea and then we'll do the rest."

Issie nodded. She straightened the peak on her helmet and took up the reins. She noticed that her hands were trembling a little.

Avery noticed too. "You know, Issie, you don't have to do this," he said gently.

"I know. I'm not scared, Tom, honest," she replied.

"Remember," Avery said, "you're the alpha."

"I'm the alpha." Issie smiled at him. Then she wheeled the stallion around to face the road.

"I'll see you soon. Be ready for me," Issie called back. And with that, she clucked the stallion into a canter, riding him swiftly up and over the crest of the hill, along the Coast Road that would lead her to Lake Deepwater.

As they cantered along the Coast Road Issie steeled her nerve and let the reins go slack so that the big, black horse was in control. *Give him his head*, she thought, *let him find his own way. He will lead me to the herd.*

Destiny immediately sensed his freedom and broke into a gallop. Issie wrapped her hands tight in his mane and clung on.

As the stallion veered off the Coast Road and began to skilfully pick his way across the rocky terrain at full gallop Issie fought the urge to snatch back the reins and slow him down. Destiny was going far too fast. *If he stops suddenly*, Issie thought, *I'll go flying over his head.*

At that very moment Destiny gave a sudden lurch to the left to avoid a large rock and Issie felt herself sliding uncontrollably to one side. For a moment she was sure she was going to fall. But she managed to hang on to the hank of mane that she had tangled in her hands and in a couple of strides she had righted herself again.

Hang on, she thought to herself. *No matter what, you have to hang on…*

Destiny slowed down to a canter as he rose up over the brow of a hill. He let out a loud, vigorous whinny as he surveyed the valley below. Issie scanned the fields in front of her but there was nothing to see except green pasture and a few blackthorn trees. Destiny whinnied again. Still nothing. The stallion stood alert, his ears pricked forward. He was listening, waiting. And then, from out of nowhere, came the whinny of a horse returning his call. Issie's heart raced. He had found the herd.

Issie was left behind in the saddle as Destiny lunged forward and began galloping headlong down the hill. From the other direction she heard the low thunder of hoofbeats as the herd approached.

When Issie had first met the Blackthorn Ponies they seemed to be one big faceless herd, but now, she realised, she was beginning to recognise each of them as distinct individuals. They were all so wild, so alive. Issie felt herself choking back her anger at the rangers and their stupid cull. How could anyone ever think of hurting these beautiful horses?

The herd slowed down to a trot as the stallion reached them. Issie had been worried that they would scatter when they saw her on Destiny's back, but the ponies seemed not to notice or care about her.

The stallion cantered a wide circle around the herd, establishing his territory. Then he moved closer, nipping and lunging at his mares to snap them into line, asserting his authority over the other horses. The buckskin mare wasn't easily subdued. She lashed out with her hind legs as he nipped at her and Issie had to hang on once again as Destiny swerved to avoid her flying hooves.

When the stallion seemed satisfied that his herd were all under control he began to move them back up the hill. Issie held on tight to his mane, resisting the temptation to touch the reins. Destiny was heading back towards the cove, exactly where they needed to go, and the ponies were following him. All she had to do was hang on.

When they reached the hill at the top of the valley she expected Destiny to trot on straight ahead, back down to the Coast Road and the cove. But the black horse seemed to suddenly change his mind. He broke into a canter, altered his direction and turned along the ridge in completely the wrong direction.

"Destiny, NO!" Issie pulled hard on the right rein to turn the stallion around. As soon as she had done it, she realised her mistake. *Never, ever fight him.* She remembered Tom Avery's words. *You won't win that way.*

As he felt the jarring of the metal bit pulling harshly in his mouth Destiny responded by fighting back. He reared up, his front legs thrashing the air in front of him. Then, as he came back down with Issie still on his back, he gave an almighty buck.

Issie had fallen off her horse loads of times, but this fall was different. Destiny's buck sent her flying up in the air in a dramatic arc. It all happened so fast there was nothing she could do to soften the fall. She hit the ground with such force, she immediately felt the wind being knocked out of her. Breathless and shocked Issie tried to push herself up on her elbows, coughing and heaving as her lungs struggled desperately for air. As she propped herself up on her arms she felt a shooting pain down her left arm and the thought flashed through her head that her wrist must be broken.

She stayed there on the ground a bit longer. She was too dizzy to stand up; the ground and the sky were spinning around her. What had just happened? Where was Destiny?

The nicker of a horse brought her back to reality. She took a deep breath and pulled herself together. She needed to stand up and look for her horse. Issie forced herself to her feet. The sun on the horizon was blinding her now but she could make out the shape of a horse. He was coming towards her.

"Destiny?" Issie croaked. And then there he was in front of her. Not a big, black stallion at all, but a little grey gelding. Weak and exhausted from her fall, Issie fell forward and wrapped her arms around the horse's neck, hugging him tightly, her face buried in his mane. It was Mystic.

Chapter 15

What a complete disaster! Right now Avery and the others would be waiting at the cove for Issie to return, leading the herd back to them. They had no way of knowing Destiny was gone and there was no sign of the wild ponies. The clock was ticking. The rangers would be here soon, tracking down the herd to begin their cull. She had to do something – and fast!

Issie scanned the horizon desperately. Then she turned to the little grey gelding. "Mystic! You found them before – you can do it again. We've got to get those horses back!"

She looked around for somewhere to mount up and spied a fallen tree just a few metres away. If she climbed up on that log, it would be easy to make a leap on to the little grey's back. Issie put a hand out to grasp Mystic's silvery mane, and let out a sudden squeal, doubling over in pain. She had forgotten about her injured wrist. She gave her fingers one more tentative wiggle and winced as the pain shot up her arm. She was pretty sure it wasn't broken but it was still really sore. She couldn't ride like this.

Issie felt tears of anger and frustration welling up. She had to get on Mystic's back if she was to stand any chance at all of finding the Blackthorn Ponies. But how could she do it with an injured wrist?

Calm down, she told herself sternly, *calm down and think, Issie.* She paused for a moment and then, very carefully so as not to hurt her wrist, she pulled off her jacket. It was one of those stretch velour tracksuit jackets, pale blue with white stripes. She took it and knotted one sleeve around the elbow of her injured arm, checking that it was firm but not too tight. Then she took the other sleeve and used her teeth once more to tie a knot with the end of the sleeve around her sore wrist. With the sleeves secured at her elbow and her wrist she pulled the rest of the jacket up and over her head, wriggling and squirming her head through so that the jacket was now strung over her shoulder with the sleeves stretched taut, holding her arm in a makeshift sling.

"If I can't use that arm, I'm just going to have to keep it out of the way," she said to Mystic. Grabbing a hank of his mane with her right hand she led the horse over to the log, trying to protect her injured wrist as she vaulted lightly on to his back. Steadying herself, she wrapped her good hand tightly in Mystic's mane. *As long as I can hold on and ride with just one hand,* Issie thought…

"Let's go, Mystic." She gave the grey gelding a light tap with her heels to let him know she was ready. "Go find them for me." The little grey immediately set off at a fast canter, following the trail of the Blackthorn herd.

Issie had ridden Mystic bareback many times before, but one-handed bareback added a whole new challenge. As the little pony galloped on she tried to keep her balance by staying low and gripping with her legs. She sat tight and didn't even try to guide him; Mystic seemed to know exactly where he was going.

"Oh, where are they, Mystic?" Issie said: They had to find the ponies fast. It must have been nearly two hours since Issie had left the farm. The rangers would be loading up their four-wheel-drives right now and heading this way.

Thankfully it didn't take Mystic long to track down

the herd. When the grey gelding galloped up to a plateau overlooking the Coast Road, Issie let out a cry of relief. There they were! Destiny and the ponies – and not more than a hundred metres away.

The black stallion still had his saddle and bridle on and he was grazing happily alongside the buckskin mare. When he saw Mystic he raised his head and stood, alert and watchful, as if deciding whether to spur his herd into action and run again.

Issie and Mystic froze too and Issie could feel her heart racing as she realised what she was about to do. Her plan was dangerous and she knew it. She wasn't in the best shape to take on a stallion – the throbbing pain in her arm reminded her of that.

She looked at the ponies. She had to act fast. This was her last chance – and their last chance too.

"Come on, Mystic!" she said decisively.

Mystic moved swiftly into a gallop as Issie turned the little grey around in a wide circle and then began bearing down on the black stallion, approaching him from the rear.

Destiny had been waiting, watching them and deciding what he would do next. Now, as Issie and Mystic got closer, the black horse began to run. Destiny had a bigger stride than Mystic. He should have been able to outrun the little grey gelding. But Mystic had the element of surprise on his side. The little pony had already gathered speed and was now in full gallop. He had gained too much ground for the stallion to get away from him that easily. Mystic swiftly caught up to the big, black horse. Issie could feel him grunting and heaving with the effort of keeping pace with the stallion. The two horses were racing now, and Mystic was giving his all to stay neck-and-neck alongside Destiny.

Galloping hard, Mystic moved closer and closer to the black stallion. When the horses were matching each other stride for stride, Issie, who had been leaning low over Mystic's neck, suddenly sat up straight. She untangled her hands from Mystic's mane and then let go so that she was riding with no hands at all, her right arm held outstretched, her left hand tucked into the sling. Only her natural balance now kept her on Mystic's back.

Issie thought back to that day in the round pen when Aidan had tried to teach her the Flying Angel. She hadn't been able to do it then. Could she really do it now? There was no round pen out here on the open plains. She was racing at a wild gallop against an unpredictable stallion, and she had an injured arm. Even if she made the leap, would she be able to hang on?

Issie took a deep breath. There was only one way to find out.

"Now, Mystic!" she shouted at the pony. The grey gelding lengthened his stride and got even closer to the black stallion so that the two horses were almost brushing up against one another. Issie looked over at Destiny, then her eyes lowered to the ground below her. She saw the hooves thrashing beneath her and for a moment she felt sick. She couldn't do this!

Yes, you can, she told herself firmly. *Just don't look down. In fact, don't look at anything!* Issie turned in the saddle to face Destiny. She put out her hands and began the countdown. Ah-one, ah-two, ah-three. She shut her eyes and screwed them tight. Everything went black and she held her breath and took a flying leap.

There was a split second as she left Mystic's back when she felt absolutely nothing underneath her except for a rush of air and the thunder of hooves dragging her down. Then she felt her right hand grasp the leather of Destiny's saddle. She opened her eyes and began pulling herself up, dragging herself on to the black horse. Forgetting about the pain in her arm she clung on desperately with both hands, hooking her left foot into the stirrup and swinging her right foot high over the back of the saddle. Her hands hurried to find the reins. There they were! She took them up very gently so she wouldn't spook Destiny. She wasn't making that mistake again. Slowly, carefully, she pulled the black stallion to a canter and then slowed to a trot.

It took her moment to realise that she had done it. And then there she was. She was back on Destiny! The black horse was hers again.

Issie steadied the stallion to a halt and looked around. Mystic was nowhere to be seen, but the Blackthorn Ponies were still with her. They had followed Destiny when he ran and now they stood there, all of them with their ears pricked and their expressions alert, watching the black stallion, waiting for him to decide what they would do next.

"Easy, Destiny," Issie spoke softly to the big, black horse. "We need them to follow us. You have to lead them. Do you think you can do it?"

Did the stallion understand her? Did he know that she was trying to save his herd? Issie didn't know, but Destiny did seem to listen to her voice this time as she coaxed him on. Issie circled wide around the herd, slowly edging Destiny closer towards them, driving the ponies forward.

Issie was pretty sure they were heading in the right direction. Still, when they rounded the corner and she saw the Coast Road and Preacher's Cove ahead of them her heart soared. They were almost there! She pushed Destiny on to quicken his pace now, overtaking the herd and sweeping around to the right, driving them down the road towards the sea.

"Not much further, Destiny," she breathed to the stallion. "We're almost there…" They were coming up to the brow of the hill that led to Preacher's Cove. They were going to make it.

As Issie and Destiny reached the hill she could see Avery, Kate, Stella, Dan and Ben all mounted on their horses. The riders were in position, their horses almost hidden by the bushes at the top of the ridge next to the fallen tree. The Blackthorn Ponies didn't blink at them as they galloped past. They thundered straight down the road, heading towards the green grass and shady trees at the bottom of the hill.

When the ponies were safely past the fallen tree Issie heard the low rumble of an engine starting up and the graunch of gears and crunch of tyres on the gravel road as Aidan reversed the truck down the hill. As Aidan backed the truck up, manoeuvring it deftly into position, Avery rode forward on Paris and waved directions. Aidan kept driving back until the truck was wedged right in between the steep cliff on one side and the fallen tree on the other. The tree and the truck together created a total road block. The cove was completely closed off now. The only way the Blackthorn Ponies could possibly escape was the same route they took last time – by jumping up and over the fallen tree trunk.

"Tom!" Issie shouted to her instructor. "The tree! They can still hurdle it and get out again."

"Don't worry. We're on it!" Dan yelled out as he and Ben quickly helped Aidan lower the back ramp of the horse truck. The two boys ran inside the truck and emerged carrying a large bundle of what looked like a fishing net. As they unwound the tangled heap and stretched it out, Issie realised it was the old net from the tennis court back at Blackthorn Manor.

Moving quickly, Dan, Ben and Aidan strung the net up – using ropes to attach it to the truck at one end and tying it to the tree roots at the other. The net ran all the way across the top of the fallen tree. It was at least a metre high and bordered by two huge green bands. The ponies would see it quite clearly and there was no way that even the cunning Blackthorn Ponies would manage to jump over this obstacle. They were trapped.

"What happened to you?" Avery had noticed Issie's makeshift sling.

"I'm OK, Tom, honest," Issie insisted. "I can still ride."

Avery looked at her uncertainly.

"Please, Tom. I'm fine. And we don't have time to argue. We still have to get the horses on to the truck."

"All right then," Avery conceded. He turned to the others. "We'll split into two groups. Issie will take Stella and Kate with her down the left-hand side of the cove. I'll ride down the other side with the boys. We'll close in on the herd from either direction, driving them back up the hill. With the tree blocked off now they'll have no choice. They'll have to go up the ramp and on to the truck."

Issie nodded at this and set off down the hill at a canter on Destiny, with Stella and Kate close behind her on Blaze and Nicole. They had almost reached the flat, grassy area at the foot of the hill when Destiny let out a shrill, commanding whinny, calling to his herd.

The buckskin mare responded to his call, nickering back in return.

"Issie, they'll follow Destiny back up the hill. Take

the lead and we'll ride behind you," Stella called to her.

Issie rode Destiny in a sweeping circle, breezing past the buckskin, and the mare instantly picked up the stallion's lead and fell into step behind him, with the other ponies in hot pursuit.

"Excellent! They're following you. Head for the truck!" Avery shouted.

Dust rose up as the ponies cantered back up the dirt road with Issie and Destiny in the lead. At first the noise of the thundering hooves was so loud that Issie didn't notice the four-wheel-drives pulling up at the brow of the hill behind the horse truck. It wasn't until she heard the slamming of car doors and saw Cameron and his men grabbing their rifles and manoeuvring into position along the steep banks of the cliff that she realised what was going on.

"Tom!" Issie cried back over her shoulder.

"I see them," Avery replied. "Don't worry about it; there's nothing they can do. Keep going."

They were just a few metres away from the truck now. Surely the rangers wouldn't shoot and risk hitting one of the riders? Cameron had no choice. He had to give them a chance to get the horses on to the truck.

Issie looked up at the uniformed men who had clambered over the tennis net and were arranging themselves with their guns on the fallen tree. She could see two more rangers climbing up the steep banks to the right, hanging on to tree roots to hoist themselves up with their guns strapped to their backs.

Not much longer now, not much further, Issie thought to herself.

As Issie approached the foot of the ramp she slowed Destiny down to a trot.

"Bring him over here," Aidan instructed, leaping forward to direct her to the side of the ramp.

The rest of the herd had slowed down too and were boggling nervously at the truck.

"Don't give them time to think!" Aidan yelled back at the riders. "Get in behind them now and herd them forward."

"Yee-hah!" There was a cowboy whoop as Ben and Dan rode up on Tornado and Scott, driving the herd forward. The buckskin mare snorted in shock and took a wild leap, cantering up the ramp and into the truck. As she did so, the others followed.

"Keep them moving!" Aidan commanded, bolting the ponies one by one into the partitioned booths in the truck as the boys herded more ponies onboard. Occasionally one would escape their clutches, leaping off the side of the ramp and cantering back down the hill to rejoin the others underneath the trees down by the sea. It was Stella and Kate's job to drive the stragglers up the hill once more to join the herd moving on to the horse truck.

"How many have we got in so far?" Issie shouted out to Aidan.

"Thirteen!" Aidan yelled back. "Do you think we should raise the ramp now?"

Issie nodded. "I guess so. At least that's half of them."

"The rangers are here. We need to move fast," Aidan said. "If we can round the others up and get them penned maybe we can…"

He was interrupted by the sound of screaming.

"What's going on down there?" Avery shouted.

Stella, who had been trying to herd the stragglers back up the hill, was underneath the trees at the far end of the cove. She was trying desperately to hang on to Blaze, but the chestnut mare was going crazy. Stella screamed as Blaze reared straight up in the air, throwing her backwards on to the ground.

"Stella!" Issie began to ride towards her. But instead of looking pleased to see her friend, Stella's face was white with fear as Issie approached.

"Don't!" Stella squealed. "Issie! Stay back!"

Issie was confused. What was wrong? Why didn't Stella want her help?

"In the trees!" Stella yelled. "It's in the trees!"

Issie looked up into the pohutukawa branches above her head. She saw a dark shadow moving, a black blur silhouetted against the blue sky. And then she heard it. The low rumble of the feline growl. So that was what had made Blaze rear!

Issie peered up nervously into the trees above, trying to see where the Grimalkin had gone. She could still hear its growl. She knew it was close.

"Where is it?" Stella said, her eyes flicking nervously over the trees above them. "I don't see it any more. Where is it?"

A bloodcurdling yowl drew their attention from the trees above, followed by the sickening squeal of a horse.

"Blaze!" Issie screamed. The chestnut mare squealed again and gave an enormous buck as a big, black cat the size of a mountain lion leapt on to her back and sunk its claw into her haunches.

Blaze let out a terrified whinny as she felt the claws sink in. She kicked out desperately, trying to free herself from the predator on her back.

"Blaze!" Issie screamed again. She rode Destiny towards the mare. She didn't know what she was going to do, but she did know that she had to try and save her horse.

She had almost reached Blaze when Aidan overtook her on Diablo. "I'll get her. You stay back!" he shouted at Issie as he rode straight at Blaze.

When he reached her he tried to grab the mare by the reins. But Blaze was terrified and bucking like a bronco to get the cat off her back.

With one huge final buck Blaze managed to throw the big cat loose. The Grimalkin turned immediately to new prey, his eyes on Aidan and Diablo. It drew back its lips in a deep, grumbling snarl, revealing a set of long, white fangs.

"Issie, get Stella and Blaze out of here!" Aidan yelled.

"But, Aidan…"

"Do it!" Aidan commanded.

Issie jumped down off Destiny and rushed forward. She had just enough time to pull Stella to her feet before the Grimalkin leapt to attack again. This time the black cat threw itself through the air at Diablo, its gleaming white teeth were bared as it lunged at the horse's neck.

Diablo went up in a half rear to meet the big cat and

just and he did so Issie heard the gun fire. Two shots rang out one after the other, echoing through the cove. Issie turned to see Ranger Cameron perched up on the hill behind them. His face was white with shock. The rifle was raised in his hands.

"Blaze?" Issie yelled, utterly terrified. She ran forward. Where was her horse? In the darkness underneath the trees she could see the body of a horse lying on the ground and as she got closer she felt an icy chill run up her spine.

It was just like her dream. Her heart raced as she reached the point where she saw the horse fall. She was shocked to see not one, but two bodies lying deathly still on the ground.

There was the enormous black shape of the Grimalkin sprawled in front of her, lying there with its deadly jaws spread wide in a rictus smile. Next to the Grimalkin, though, was another body. The body of a horse. It was just like her dream – except she could see now that the horse wasn't Blaze. It was Diablo.

Chapter 16

Diablo! Issie ran towards the piebald gelding lying motionless on the ground. She had almost reached the horse's side when she felt strong hands around her shoulders holding her back.

"No, Issie…" Avery said firmly. "It's no use. There's nothing we can do to help him…"

"Tom! Ohmygod! It all happened so fast. I heard the two shots and I thought it was Blaze… and where is Blaze?" Issie was suddenly gripped with panic.

"It's OK. She's here and she's fine. I've got her," Stella called out. "What happened?"

"Cameron shot the Grimalkin – and he shot Diablo too," Issie called back to her.

Dan and Ben had heard the gunshots and were already

off their horses at Issie's side. They stared at the two dark forms on the ground. Dan nervously prodded the limp body of the black cat. Issie could see a trickle of red blood matted into the black fur on its chest where the bullet had entered. The great cat's eyes were shut but its mouth lolled open, exposing two rows of white razor-sharp teeth.

A few metres away from the Grimalkin was the body of Diablo. The horse wasn't moving. Dan gave Diablo a nudge with his foot, but the horse didn't respond.

"Where's Aidan?" Issie suddenly panicked. "He was riding Diablo when he was shot. Where is he now?"

"I'm over here," Aidan called back. He was sitting on the ground under the big pohutukawa tree, looking vacant and dazed.

Issie and Stella ran over to him as Aidan tried to stand up. "I must have been knocked out for a moment," Aidan said, rubbing the back of his head. He still looked wobbly on his feet. "What happened?"

"Diablo's been shot," Issie told him.

"What? But how…"

"Here's Cameron. He knows what happened," Issie said.

"Are you all OK?" Cameron gasped for breath. "I was trying to get a clear shot when I fired at the cat, but there were people in the way and…" Cameron stopped in his tracks when he saw Diablo on the ground. "But… I don't see how… I wasn't aiming for the horse. I was aiming for the cat!" he said. There was a look of horror on his face. "I was aiming for the cat…"

Aidan wasn't listening. He left them standing there and ran over to the horse lying on the ground. His face was ashen as he crouched down beside Diablo and slowly put out his hand to stroke the horse's neck.

"Aidan, I'm so sorry—" Issie began.

Suddenly Aidan leapt back from the horse and stood up. When he turned around to look at the others he had a massive grin on his face.

"Aidan? What is it?" Issie asked.

Aidan looked down at Diablo. "Well done, boy," he said. "Very good!" Then he clapped his hands together twice. "Wake up, Diablo!" he commanded.

On his word, Diablo began to stir, shaking out his mane and snorting as if waking from a nap, pushing himself up on his front legs and then rising on all fours to stand there before them, perfectly and absolutely alive.

"I don't believe it!" Stella was stunned. "You mean he wasn't shot at all?"

"Nope." Aidan couldn't wipe the grin off his face. "He was just performing his favourite trick. He's been trained to pretend that he's dead whenever he hears a gun fire. When Cameron's rifle went off and he fell to the ground you thought he'd been shot, right? But he was just foxing. Weren't you, Diablo?"

"Ohmygod, Diablo!" Issie laughed. "You crazy horse! You scared us all half to death!"

Issie, Stella and Kate all took turns to hug the big piebald while Aidan stood by, stroking Diablo's nose and telling him how clever he was for playing dead.

"I know it gave us all the fright of our lives, but it's exactly what he was trained to do, so I can't tell him off, can I?" Aidan said, grinning. "I'd better go back to the truck and get him a carrot; he deserves a reward for being such a good, dead horse!"

While Aidan raced back to the truck to get Diablo his treat, Avery went to check Blaze's wounds and the riders gathered around the body of the Grimalkin.

"Is *he* really dead?" Stella asked nervously.

Cameron bent down to examine the black cat. He looked back up at Stella and nodded. "I'm afraid so. It looks like one of the bullets went straight through his heart. It would have killed him instantly." Cameron sighed. "It's a terrible shame. I wish I'd had a choice, but when he began to attack Diablo and Aidan I knew I had to shoot…"

Issie looked at the Grimalkin. "He's even bigger than I remember him, that night on the fence behind the stables…"

"He's huge!" Stella agreed. "What sort of animal do you think he is?"

"He looks a bit like a black panther," Ben said, leaning closer and giving the cat a nervous stroke to feel his soft black fur.

"Yes, I think that's exactly right," Cameron said. "Panthera Niger – that's the Latin name for them. They're a type of leopard really – see, underneath the black pigment if you look closely you can make out the spots or rosettes in the fur." Cameron shook his head. "Remarkable! I'd always heard that rumour about one escaping into the hills from that wildlife park a few years back, but I never thought it was true – until now."

"Why did he attack now? Stella asked.

Cameron looked over their heads at the pohutukawa trees.

"Panthers sleep in the trees during the day. He was probably taking a nap and we disturbed him."

"Blaze was so brave fighting him off like that," Stella said.

"Ohmygod, Blaze!" Issie looked over to where Avery was checking the mare's wounds. "I'd better go and see if she's OK."

Avery gave Issie the thumbs up as she headed towards him. "It looks like really good news, Issie," he called out. "A few superficial claw marks and puncture wounds where the cat clung on to her back, but not too bad considering."

Issie gave her pony a hug, wincing a bit as the pain in her arm reminded her of her injured wrist. "Good girl, Blaze! That cat should have known not to mess with you!"

"You see, here," Avery continued, "on her rump… there are a couple of deeper cuts that will need a few stitches. We'll get a vet to come and check on her, but it's nothing to worry about. Blaze is a fighter – she's proven that many times now and she showed it again today. She'll be fine."

"Hey!" Aidan called out to them, "there's still one space in the horse truck, Issie. Blaze is probably a bit too sore to walk all the way back to the manor. She can ride home with the Blackthorn Ponies."

"What about the rest of the ponies?" Kate asked. "We still have ten wild horses trapped in here with us. What are we going to do with them?"

"I think we can help you with that," Cameron said, looking grave as he unslung the gun that was strapped to his back.

"Cameron, please…" Issie began.

The ranger smiled at her. "Don't worry. I don't mean like that, Issie. The cull is cancelled. We have no plans to shoot any more animals today." He turned to his men. "But since we're all here now, I'm sure my rangers would be happy to give you a hand. Do you have a few spare halters in that truck of yours?"

Issie nodded.

"Tell Aidan to keep the truck parked there a little longer and we'll help you to corral the rest of the horses and get halters on them. It'll be easier to get them back to the manor if they're all on lead reins."

"Oh, Cameron, that would be amazing. Thank you!" Issie said.

"Let's get a move on then," Cameron said, "before those ponies in the truck get too restless."

With the help of the rangers it didn't take long at all to catch the stragglers. While the others put halters on the Blackthorn Ponies, Issie was busy loading Blaze into the horse truck.

"Don't worry. She'll be fine. I'll take care of her, I promise," Aidan said. Then he gave the riders a wave and revved the truck into gear, driving off up the Coast Road with the thirteen Blackthorn Ponies and Blaze onboard.

"Are you going to be OK to take it from here?"

Cameron asked Issie as the riders prepared to head home.

"Uh-huh, I think so," Issie said. "We've only got nine Blackthorn ponies left. And six of us. Which would be fine except I can't lead a pony with my wrist in a sling like this. I guess the others are going to have to lead two ponies each."

"I can manage two at once on Diablo," said Avery.

"I think I can take two as well," Kate said.

"So can we," Dan and Ben offered.

"Then I bagsy leading that pretty strawberry roan one if I'm only leading one!" Stella said.

"Ohhh. I was going to choose her," Kate sighed. "All right. I'm having that lovely dapple-grey and the silver roan."

"I'm taking the chestnut with the white star and the buckskin," Ben joined in.

"I'll take the two bays," Dan added.

Avery cocked an eyebrow at them. "I didn't realise we were all picking our favourites. I thought we were herding ponies – not choosing chocolates from a box!"

The riders all laughed. Then they laughed even harder when Avery picked the last two skewbalds in the herd to lead home. "Their patches kind of match yours, don't they, my lad?" he said to Diablo, giving him a slappy pat on his black and white neck.

As the riders tied the ponies' lead ropes to their saddles and prepared to ride out, Cameron strode back over to them. "We're all packed up ready to leave too," he said, gesturing over his shoulder towards his men who were waiting in the jeeps. "I'll call ahead to Hester on the car phone and let her know you're on your way home."

"Thanks, Cameron… for everything." Issie smiled at him.

Cameron smiled back. "You've got some beautiful ponies here, Issie. You did a good job here today."

He turned to Avery. "I hope you'll find good homes for them."

Avery nodded. "The ILPH are already talking to potential owners. We'll get the ponies broken in and schooled up. They're very clever and bold jumpers. The way those ponies jumped that tree the last time we were here, well, I wouldn't be surprised if some of them become eventing superstars one day."

With nine wild horses to manage, the journey home to Blackthorn Manor was a slow ride. By the time the riders came down the long, leafy driveway they were all exhausted. Still, their spirits lifted when they saw the huge banner Hester had painted and strung over the balcony. It read: WELCOME HOME BLACKTHORN PONIES – SAFE AT LAST!

Hester was there waiting for them of course. She was joined on the lawn by a welcoming committee that included Aidan, Nanook, Taxi and Strudel, several of Hester's neighbours and members of the Save the Blackthorn Ponies group, a reporter from the local Gisborne Gazette and a pretty blonde in jodhpurs with a photographer in tow.

The sight of the riders leading the wild ponies down the driveway caused an outbreak of spontaneous clapping from the crowd, and the photographer began to snap furiously like a red-carpet paparazzi trying to get the perfect shot.

"Isadora! Isadora!" the pretty blonde woman with the jodhpurs raced forward. "I'm Cinnamon Lane from *PONY Magazine*. Can I get an exclusive with you about the Blackthorn Ponies? How did you catch them? What will happen now?"

"Cinnamon, dear!" Hester beamed. "I'm sure my niece will be more than happy to give *PONY Magazine* the exclusive story. You're welcome to stay and interview her over dinner. Right now let's get these ponies into the field with the others, get these riders unsaddled and get the kettle on for a nice cup of hot tea. You must all be exhausted!"

It was the best homecoming the riders could have imagined. Down at the stables the riders went out to the paddock to let the new ponies loose and watched as they all happily greeted one another.

"A real family reunion at last!" Hester grinned.

"I can't believe we really saved all of them," Stella said as she leant over the rails to watch the ponies. "They're all together again!"

"Not for long, though," Kate added. "Tom and the ILPH are finding them new homes, remember – they'll have to be split up eventually."

"Well, at least a few of them will be staying together," Hester said. "I've been talking to Tom. He's agreed that Destiny and the two mares with their colts at foot will stay here at Blackthorn Manor with me."

"Really?" Issie said. "Aunty Hess! That's wonderful."

"Well, I couldn't let Avignon's son and his grandchildren go off and live somewhere else now, could I?" Hester said. "Destiny belongs here at Blackthorn

Manor and so do his children. Besides," she added, "I think Tom is right. Those two colts may be future superstars. If they have Avignon's bloodlines and that Blackthorn spirit then there will be no stopping them!"

Issie looked over at Destiny. The black stallion had been put in a separate paddock from the rest of the horses. He was high-stepping now in a swift trot along the fence-line, his head held high. He gave a shrill stallion's call and ran at the fence where Issie was standing, heading straight for her and then swerving at the very last minute with a playful buck.

"Show off!" Issie yelled at him, making Stella and Kate laugh.

"I still can't believe I actually rode him," Issie said softly under her breath.

"I can, my dear." Hester smiled at her. "You're quite the horsewoman. But then, you've got good bloodlines too, you know. I wouldn't expect anything less from my favourite niece." And with that, Hester threw her arms around Issie, smothering her once more in a tight, Chanel-scented hug.

Chapter 17

It turned out that Issie's arm was badly sprained, but thankfully not broken.

"Thank goodness! Your mother would have killed me if I'd sent you home in a cast," Hester said. "Still, I don't suppose she'll be any more pleased when you turn up wearing that bandage and a sling."

Issie was hoping that the last few days at the farm would have been enough time for her arm to heal before she had to face her mother. But the doctor said she needed to keep wearing the sling for another week – and it was time to go home.

"The holidays are over and my leg is on the mend. I'll be getting the cast off next week," said Aunt Hester. "I've called your mother and she's expecting you home tomorrow. Tom is going to borrow my horse float to take Blaze back with you too. You can leave as soon as she's had her vet check in the morning."

"I can't believe I'm going to be leaving," Issie said. "I love it here so much. And I'll miss you, Aunty Hess."

"Well of course you will, darling! But you'll come back again, won't you? Blackthorn Manor is your home too now."

Dinner that night was a celebration and a farewell. All the riders had helped in the kitchen so that Aunt Hester could have a night off cooking. "This is the best meal I've ever had at Blackthorn Manor!" Aidan said as he tucked into a perfect piece of roast beef and mashed potato.

That night, for the last time, Issie went to sleep staring at the painting of Avignon opposite her enormous four-poster bed. When she woke up the next morning Strudel was sniffing around her feet and the sun was streaming in through the windows.

Issie had already packed her bags the night before. Now, as she pulled on her jersey and jeans, she decided to say goodbye one last time to the manor menagerie before breakfast. In the kitchen she found a bag of carrots to take with her as a goodbye treat for Butch, Blossom and the rabbits, throwing in a few apples as well as a farewell gift for the ponies.

The early morning light was golden and warm as she walked across the lawn. The rest of the house was shrouded in sleep and the air was still. She stopped off to see Butch, feeding the greedy pig four big carrots, then walked on past the duck pond to Destiny's paddock.

Issie was surprised when the stallion didn't hesitate, but came straight up to the fence to greet her. As the horse poked his elegant neck over the rails of the fence to take a carrot Issie put out a hand to stroke his glossy, jet mane.

"We would never have saved the ponies without you, Destiny," she said softly. Destiny gave a nicker as if he understood. Issie was about to say something else when a low, feline growl behind her made her jump.

"Meow!" Aidan grinned. "I can't believe you're still falling for that old trick, Issie!"

"Aidan!" Issie scowled at him. "I knew you weren't the Grimalkin – you just startled me, that's all."

"Sorry," Aidan said. Although he didn't look sorry at all. He was still smiling as he came over to the fence, took a carrot out of Issie's bag and fed it to a buckskin mare who had finally summoned up the courage to come close enough to the railing.

"Do you think they'll be OK? The Blackthorn Ponies, I mean," Issie said to Aidan.

"Yeah, I do. They'll be just fine – thanks to you," Aidan said.

"Me? No… I didn't do anything…"

"Of course you did," Aidan said. "You were amazing, Issie…" Aidan went quiet and looked at his feet. "Listen, I've been trying to tell you something since the first day you got here." Aidan's bright blue eyes were almost hidden beneath his black fringe as he looked up at her.

"What is it?" Issie asked.

"This," Aidan said. And without another word he stepped forward and kissed her.

Issie felt her heart skip a beat as Aidan's lips brushed against her own. Then she jumped back in shock. "You kissed me!" she said.

"I know!" Aidan said. "I was hoping that, well, that you wouldn't mind."

"I don't… it's just, well, I'm just kind of surprised…" Issie felt the butterflies in her tummy fluttering like crazy. Aidan had just kissed her!

"I didn't mean to… I… I'd better go…" Aidan said, his face glowing with embarrassment.

"No! Don't!" Issie yelled after him. But it was too late.

Aidan was already racing off back across the lawn towards the manor. She was about to run after him when a voice from the stable doorway startled her.

"Isadora! There you are!" Tom Avery called to her. "I've been looking for you everywhere. The vet has some very important news about Blaze. You'd better come in here immediately."

The warmth of Aidan's kiss disappeared as if someone had poured ice water all over her. Issie broke into a run and followed Avery back in through the stable door to the very last stall in the row where Blaze's nameplate was now hung from the carved wooden horse head on the door. Inside the stall the vet was bending over the mare. He had a syringe of blood in his hand and a worried expression on his face.

"What's wrong with Blaze. What is that for?" Issie asked, looking at the vial of blood that the vet was now putting into a plastic bag in his hold-all.

"This must be the mare's owner, yes?" the vet said to Avery.

"Yes, Andrew, this is Isadora. You'd better tell her what you just told me."

Issie felt the blood drain from her face. "Tom? What is it? What's wrong with Blaze? What is all this about?

I thought you said her wounds weren't that bad. She just needed stitches…"

Issie was panicking now; she could feel her heart racing. She felt like she was going to be sick.

"Isadora, no! I'm sorry. I've gone and given you the wrong end of the stick here." Avery smiled. "Blaze is just fine, but, well, you'd better explain Andrew…"

The vet stepped forward. "I came in to treat your mare this morning and when I was checking her wounds I noticed a few things about her that seemed odd. I've given her a thorough check-up, and I'm pretty sure that I'm right. I've taken blood tests which will confirm it once I've got them back to the lab but in the meantime you just need to make sure she's well fed. Just treat her normally and she should be…"

"I'm sorry… you still haven't told me… what is wrong with my horse?" Issie couldn't stand it any longer. "What is the matter with Blaze?"

"Nothing's wrong with her," the vet said. "Your horse isn't sick, Issie, she's in foal."

"In foal? You mean Blaze is going to have a baby?"

"It certainly looks likely," the vet said, popping the last of his equipment into the hold-all and giving Blaze a pat. "Your mare is about to become a mummy."

"Blaze!" Issie squealed, throwing her arms around the mare's neck. "Ohmygod! That's wonderful!"

The news that Blaze was in foal came as such a shock to Issie that the drive home to Chevalier Point was a total blur. She was so overcome, she didn't know what to think. Blaze, her own special pony, was going to have a foal!

"Isn't this the most exciting news you've ever heard in your whole life!" Stella squealed in the back seat of the Range Rover where the three girls were crammed in together.

"Can you still ride her?" Ben asked. He and Dan were sitting up the front with Avery for the ride home.

"The vet said it was fine – at least until her tummy gets really big," Issie nodded.

"And Destiny is the father, right?" Kate said.

Issie shook her head. "The vet couldn't tell me that for sure. He needs to check the blood tests first. I guess we'll know in a day or two."

"Ohmygod! Imagine how beautiful the foal is going to be!" Kate beamed. "What do you think she'll have, Issie? A filly or a colt?"

"I hope it's a girl," Stella said. "A little baby Blaze running around. How cute would that be?"

For the whole trip they talked on and on about the foal, what it would look like and what they were going to name it. Issie was so excited, she almost forgot all the other events of the past few weeks: breaking in Destiny, making the Flying Angel leap from Mystic, saving the Blackthorn Ponies and her kiss with Aidan that morning...

It was late afternoon when the Range Rover pulled up at the pony club. Avery pulled the horse float to a stop underneath the magnolia trees in the first paddock and Stella jumped out to help Issie lower the tail flap.

"Here, you can't do that with your sore wrist. I'll help you put Blaze's rug on while you get the feed sorted," Stella told Issie.

"Thanks," Issie said.

"How much longer are you going to have that sling for anyway?"

"The doctor said maybe a week or so. It's starting to feel better already." She gave her wrist a wiggle.

When Issie emerged again from the tack room with Blaze's feed the mare was rugged up and ready for her.

"I'm going to check on Coco. I'll meet you back at the

car," Stella told Issie, leaving her alone with her pony.

Blaze shoved her head eagerly into the feed bucket, then lifted it up again and gave a happy nicker across the paddock, calling out to Coco and Toby.

"It's good to be home again, huh, girl?" Issie said.

She was just waiting for Blaze to chew up the last remnants of her chaff and pony nuts when she saw a rider striding towards her from the clubrooms. Even at a distance she recognised the stiff blonde plaits and haughty manner immediately.

"Hello, Natasha," Issie sighed as the rider approached her.

"Isadora! I thought it was you," Natasha said icily. "Mummy just brought me to the club to pick up my hard hat. I left it behind at training. And here you are! Well, I must say I'm so glad you're back!"

"Really?" Issie looked at her.

"Yes. I wanted you to be the first to congratulate me on my win," Natasha smirked.

"What?" Issie was confused.

"The summer dressage series. I completely won it. Fabergé and I annihilated the competition. Nobody else stood a chance!" Natasha's smirk had spread from ear to ear now. "Of course I know that technically you didn't compete because you weren't here, but I can tell you that Fabby was pretty unbeatable. I'm sure that we would have won anyway, even if you had been riding. So that makes us the best in the whole club. Anyway," Natasha looked over at the Range Rover where Stella and Kate were staring at her through the windows, "I see you're all back. How was your holiday? Did anything interesting happen?"

Issie looked back at Stella and Kate, who were now pulling faces at Natasha and mouthing at Issie to hurry up.

"Nope," Issie said with a grin on her face. "I mean, what can I say that could possibly beat your story, Natasha? Wow, huh? Good for you! It sounds like you've had quite the exciting time. I'd love to hear more about it, but I need to put Blaze in her paddock and get home now. It's been a long day."

Issie tried to suppress her giggles as she turned away from Natasha and led Blaze through the paddock gate. She didn't need to tell Stuck-up Tucker about what had happened. Natasha would no doubt hear all about it at the pony club soon enough.

Issie slipped the halter off Blaze's head and watched as the mare trotted off happily to join Coco and Toby. It was hard to believe that her pony was going to have a foal.

"I hope it's a girl. She'll be beautiful, Blaze – just like you," Issie said.

As Avery leant on the horn of the Range Rover, telling her to hurry up, Issie paused and took another look around the familiar fields of the Chevalier Point Pony Club. It was good to be home.

Stardust and the Daredevil Ponies

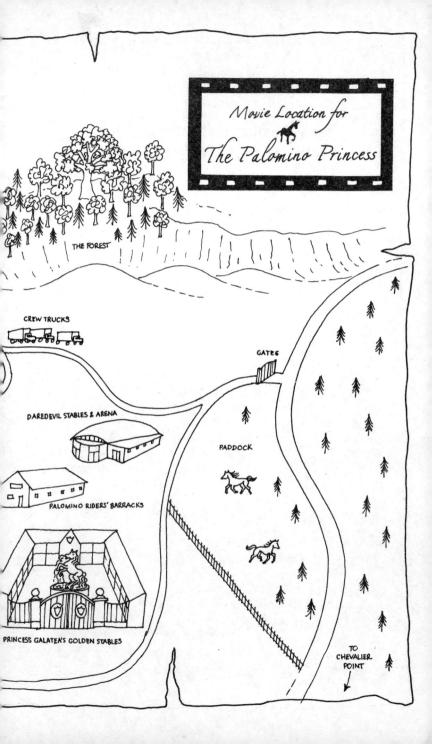

For my editor, Sally Martin, who
always makes everything better

Chapter 1

The dark castle gleamed in the rain, its stone turrets like blackened teeth against the moon. It had seen many storms like this one. Perched high on top of a rocky citadel, it was at the mercy of such grim weather. As the rain fell like a cloak, the huge iron portcullis that hung over the drawbridge creaked and groaned in the wind. A wolf howled at the cold moon. Then, louder than either of these, came another sound – the thunder of hoofbeats.

Far below the castle, at the foot of the mountain fortress, a horse and rider could be seen in the moonlight. The rider was a young woman with long blonde hair. She wore pale blue jodhpurs and her white cotton blouse was soaked from the lashing rain. The horse she was riding was impossibly beautiful, a golden palomino with a mane and tail so white they almost sparkled in the pale light.

The palomino's hooves flashed and clattered against the cobbled stones of the mountain path as the girl drove the horse on, up and up the terraced steps which wound like a corkscrew around the mountainside to the castle above.

As the girl and the horse galloped up to reach the second terrace it suddenly became clear that they were not alone. Seven riders on jet-black horses were quickly closing in on them. The riders looked enormous compared to the girl. They wore long black robes that billowed out behind them as they rode. Black hoods hid their faces, making them look like ghostly apparitions in the dark night.

The hooded horsemen were gaining on the girl and by the time she reached the third terrace they had surrounded her. Trapped, the palomino turned on the horsemen and reared in the air, lashing out with her front hooves, catching one of the black-robed riders with a glancing blow to the shoulder.

The hooded rider grabbed at his injured shoulder and cursed the palomino in a strange language. Then he gave instructions to the other horsemen and they obeyed him without question, forming a tight half-circle around the palomino. As the horses closed in, the palomino began snorting and stamping, turning this way and that, looking for a way to escape.

Up close, the black horses were monstrous and otherworldly. Their eyes gleamed red, their mouths frothed as they champed at their bits and their bridles were strung with strange talismen, carved symbols that hinted at the power of the ancient curse that bound them to their fate.

Suddenly the head horseman rode forward to face the girl. The other riders closed ranks behind him and stood, watching and waiting as their leader raised his pale, bony hand and drew back the hood of his cape.

The face that was revealed beneath the hood did not belong to any earthly man. The horseman had no hair at all and his bald head throbbed with pale, purplish-grey veins. His cruel, pale eyes and hooked nose gave him a crow-like appearance. His skin, which shone horribly in the moonlight, was as white as a corpse.

The palomino snorted in fear at the sight of him and the girl put her hand to the sword that lay on her hip, ready to unsheathe it.

"Leave her alone, Francis," the girl said bravely. "You cannot possibly think you will win like this."

"Oh, but that is exactly what I think, Princess," the black-robed rider hissed like a lizard. "Tonight we take Seraphine's life. She is the last of her kind. Your last hope. When she joins us and becomes one of the Horses of Darkness then you will have lost your kingdom forever."

The horseman jumped down from his black mount and stepped forward so that he was standing before the palomino. A smile played across his lips, which widened to reveal a set of long white fangs.

"Say good night, Seraphine," the vampire rider said softly as he opened his mouth wide and lunged forward to plunge his fangs deep into the palomino's golden neck...

"And... cut!" a voice shouted out. The rain suddenly stopped and the studio lights flashed on, bathing everyone in a golden glow.

"Terrific! Great scene, everyone! That's a wrap!"

There was a clapping and a whooping from the film crew at the news that the night's shooting was over. Issie jumped down off the palomino and looked up at the man who had shouted "cut!" He was sitting on an enormous camera crane erected high above the horses. "Hey, Rupert," she called out to the director, "is it all right if I take this off now?" She gestured to the long blonde wig that she was wearing over her own long dark hair.

"Absolutely. Hand it over to Helen in make-up and give your costume back to Amber, then get those horses back to the stables and you can go home. You did great work this evening, Isadora. You too, Aidan!"

The head vampire rider smiled at this, then stuck his fingers in his mouth to pull out a pair of shiny, white fake fangs. "What a relief to finally have those out! They're murder to wear when you're riding!" he said, smiling at Issie.

"Ohmygod, Aidan! You are so scary with those fangs; sometimes I almost forget that we're just making a movie and get all freaked out!" Issie grinned back.

Aidan, who was busy peeling off his latex bald cap to reveal the thick black hair hidden underneath, looked pleased at this. "Really? Thanks! You did some great stunt riding tonight, Issie. See you tomorrow on the set for breakfast, OK?"

"See you then," Issie beamed.

As Aidan set off back down the hill, leading his horse, Issie's best friends, Stella and Kate, rushed forward to help the black riders, each of them taking the reins of a pair of horses. With the lights on it was easy to see that these black horses weren't evil or strange at all, but perfectly normal horses dressed up in costume. The girls held the horses still and waited patiently as make-up artists clustered around to wipe the fake froth from the horses' mouths and remove the red glitter from around their eyes.

"That was so exciting!" Stella called out to Issie. "You did the best rear. Stardust wasn't naughty at all!"

Issie looked at the palomino mare standing next to her. "She was good, wasn't she?" Issie grinned.

"Good? She was brilliant!" Kate said, reaching forward to pat Stardust on her velvety nose. "I think you're finally getting through to her, Issie."

"I hope you're right, Kate, I really do," Issie said.

Stardust, the beautiful palomino mare, was the star of this movie and it was Issie's job as her stunt rider to make her perform for the cameras. But the mare seemed determined to misbehave and her naughty stunts had the whole film crew upset. Aunt Hester had been driven to despair by her dangerous tricks. It was Hester, of course, who was responsible for involving Issie and her friends in the whole movie business in the first place...

Issie hadn't heard from her aunt in months, since her last visit to Blackthorn Farm, so the phone call came as a bit of a surprise.

"Isadora! My favourite niece!" Hester had trilled down the phone. Her greeting made Issie laugh straightaway – Hester always called Issie her "favourite niece", when in fact she was her only niece so she didn't have much competition!

"Hi, Aunty Hess. How are things at the farm?"

Blackthorn Farm was a grand old country manor with hundreds of hectares of land, high in the hills outside Gisborne on the East Coast. It was there that Aunt Hester trained her mad menagerie of movie animals, including a team of stunt horses.

"Busy, busy, busy!" Hester told her. "We've got a big movie coming up – *The Palomino Princess* – have you heard of it?"

"Ohmygod!" Issie squealed. "Aunty Hess! I love that book! Are they making a film of it? How cool! And your horses are going to be in it?"

"Absolutely," Hester said. "Well, at least a few of them are – Paris and Nicole and Destiny and Diablo to be exact. They need quite a few stunt horses for the film, but as you'll know if you've already read the books, the

Horses of Darkness all need to be pitch black – plus we need five palominos for Galatea and her princesses. Paris and Nicole are perfect for princess horses and Diablo is having his piebald patches dyed so that he can play one of the black horses."

"That's so exciting!" Issie said.

"I'm glad you think so, dear," Hester said, "because I was hoping you might want to come and work with me on the movie."

"What? Me?"

"Well, yes. And your friends too. They're looking for riders and wranglers right now and you've got some school holidays coming up. I thought the timing was perfect," Hester said.

"I couldn't…" Issie began to protest, but Hester interrupted.

"I know Blaze is expecting her foal and you won't want to leave her alone," Hester said, "but the movie set isn't far away from Chevalier Point. You could still go home at weekends to check on her. How long is it now until she's due?"

"The vet says she has maybe a month to go," Issie said.

"Well, that's perfect then! They're doing most of the filming with the actors back at the studio on blue screen

– lots of special effects. That means the outdoor shooting at Chevalier Point is only scheduled to take a few weeks. Filming should be wrapped by the time your foal arrives."

"But I…" Issie began.

"The best part is that this will give you a chance to ride in your holidays. I mean, you can't possibly ride Blaze, can you? She must be so fat now, you won't be able to fit a girth around that tummy of hers!" Hester insisted. "Listen, my favourite niece, I could really do with your help. There are nearly two dozen horses in this film and Aidan and I are responsible for all of them. Which is fine except it's tricky to find riders who are the right size to play the palomino princesses. We need four girls who fit the costumes to double for the stars of the film, and they must be good riders. There's no problem finding stunt doubles for the black horsemen – we've got seven stunt riders who are all over six feet tall. But it's been a nightmare finding our four girls. They can't be too grown-up; Princess Galatea and her riders are all, well, actually they're about your size…" Hester paused. "We'll pay you all of course – film rates for stunt riders are really very good."

"It all sounds great, Aunty Hess!" Issie said. "And I'm sure Stella and Kate will be keen and we can find a fourth girl to ride with us…"

"Excellent!" Hester said. "So what's the best way to organise this? Do you want to put your mother on the phone? I think she's more likely to say yes if I ask her, don't you?"

"Actually, Aunty Hess, I wouldn't bet on it. She's still mad at you after last time," Issie said.

"Oh, I was hoping she would have forgotten about that by now."

The last time Issie had stayed with her aunt she had caught and ridden Destiny, a wild stallion that led a herd of wild ponies at Blackthorn Farm. Issie had returned home from her adventures with her arm in a sling – a fact that her mother was none too happy about.

"Your mum is such a fusspot," Hester sighed. "It was only a little sprain. Put her on the phone. I'm sure she'll say yes once I talk her round."

"Muuum!" Issie called with her hand over the receiver. "It's for you!"

As Mrs Brown took the phone out of her daughter's hands with a quizzical look, Issie held her breath and hoped Aunt Hester would be able to make her mother say yes.

Issie's mum and Aunt Hester were sisters, but the two women were the complete opposite of each other in every way. Hester was, as her mum put it, a "bit too bohemian for her own good". She had been an actress before she gave up the movies herself and started training animals to act instead. She had curly blonde hair that tumbled over her shoulders and always wore lots of jewellery and scarves, even when she was riding. Hester had been married three times – "All of them wonderful weddings!" as she told Issie – but she had no children of her own.

Issie's mum had only been married once – to Issie's dad – although they split up years ago and Issie hardly ever saw him. And Mrs Brown looked nothing like Hester – she looked just like Issie, with long, straight dark hair and tanned olive skin.

The most important difference between the two sisters though, as far as Issie was concerned, was horses.

Aunt Hester was horsy through and through. Right now she had twelve horses in her stables at Blackthorn Farm. Issie's mum, on the other hand, didn't like horses one bit. Issie had to beg and plead for years before her mum finally caved in and bought Mystic for her.

Issie could hear her mum on the phone now with Aunty Hess and it sounded like Hester was getting a telling-off. She could only catch snippets of the conversation but it clearly wasn't going well.

"You must be joking!" she heard her mum say. "…Yes, Hester, I know she's an excellent rider but she's also my daughter and after last time…"

Issie slunk away to the kitchen and waited for her mum to finish yelling at Hester and get off the phone. Finally, she heard the receiver being hung up and Mrs Brown appeared in the kitchen doorway, her arms crossed and her brow furrowed in a deep frown.

"I have a feeling that you already know what that phone call was about," she said.

"Uh-huh," Issie said.

"So you really want to help Hess with this movie?"

"Uh-huh."

Mrs Brown sighed. "I've told Hester that if I see so much as a sticky plaster on you when you come home this time I will hold her responsible. She insists that it's perfectly safe. There's a bit of riding apparently, but you'll mostly just be grooming the horses and mucking out the stalls."

"Wait a minute!" Issie said. "Does that mean you're going to let me go?"

Mrs Brown nodded. "Your Aunty Hess is very

convincing. You start work as a stunt rider on *The Palomino Princess* next Monday."

Issie whooped with delight. "Thanks, Mum! I'll be fine, honestly. Wow! This is so cool! I'm going straight over to see Stella. I'm sure her mum will say she can do it too! And Kate! Oh, this is going to be great!"

"Hey, hey wait!" said Mrs Brown as Issie tore off towards the front door. "Kate and Stella make three. Hester told me she needs four girl riders. She's relying on you to find her a fourth girl." Mrs Brown gave Issie a cheeky grin. "You know, I can think of one girl who would love to work on a film like this."

"Oh, very funny, Mum! I know exactly who you mean and don't you dare say her name. Don't even think it!" Issie groaned. "I'm sure we can find someone else. I'm not that desperate."

Her mum might think it was funny to lumber Issie with Natasha Tucker for the holidays but Issie couldn't think of anyone, or anything, worse. Mrs Brown didn't understand why Issie didn't like Natasha. After all, the girls were the same age – thirteen – and they were both members of the Chevalier Point Pony Club. But Natasha had it in for Issie and she was such a snob.

No, there had to be someone else that Issie could ask. There was no way she was asking awful Stuck-up Tucker. It was never going to happen. No matter what. Not in a million years.

Chapter 2

Stella's cheeks were as red as her hair. She looked like she was about to explode.

"You've done what?" she spluttered in disbelief.

"I've asked Natasha Tucker," Issie groaned.

"But why, Issie? It was going to be such fun – you, me and Kate. Why would you ask Natasha?"

"Because Aunty Hess really needed a fourth rider and it had to be a girl because we'll be stunt-doubling for the actresses in the film. Natasha is a good rider and she was the only other person I could think of."

"What about Morgan?" Kate offered. "Couldn't you have asked her instead?"

"She's away on the showjumping circuit right now with her mum," Issie said.

"This is a nightmare!" Stella fumed.

"I can't believe Natasha wants to come with us," Kate said. "She usually ignores us at pony club."

Issie shrugged. "I know." She had dreaded turning up at the River Paddock this morning to break the news to Kate and Stella. She knew they would take it badly.

"What a nightmare!" Stella groaned again.

"Oh, Stella, get over it. Don't be such a drama queen," Kate snapped.

"Natasha will have to behave herself," Issie pointed out. "Aunty Hess will be there running things and so will Aidan…"

"Aidan?" Stella said. "Ohmygod, Issie! You didn't tell me Aidan was going to be there. You haven't seen him since last summer."

"Yes, Stella, I know. I don't need reminding," Issie replied, trying to shut Stella up.

Aidan was Aunt Hester's stable manager. The last time Issie saw him was the morning they left Blackthorn Farm. She still remembered Aidan's kiss, the way his long dark fringe had brushed against her face and she had felt her heart race. She had been so shocked that she hadn't known what to say. Then Aidan had got all embarrassed and run off and they hadn't spoken since.

Only Stella and Kate knew about this – she had told them once they got home. Although Issie was beginning to wish she hadn't said anything about it to Stella at all. Stella was her best friend but she was also boy-mad and could be a bit of a twit sometimes – she was bound to blab to Aidan and embarrass her!

"Don't say anything to him about it, OK, Stella?" Issie begged her.

Stella grinned back. "About what?"

Issie blushed. "Anyway," she said, changing the subject back to Natasha, "I've already asked Natasha. Her mum says it's OK and she's coming and that's final. You need to be at my house tomorrow morning at 7 a.m. We're all trucking out to the film set together.

"How far is it?" Kate asked.

"It's only about an hour away, up past the lake," Issie said. "You know where the ruins of Chevalier Castle are, on that big hill? Well, that's why they're filming here. They're using the castle as part of their film set and they've built all these other sets and everything there. There are sleeping quarters for the stunt riders and wranglers too. We'll be working long hours and we need to take care of the horses so we'll stay there during the week, but we can come home at weekends."

"What about Blaze?" Kate asked. "You can't leave her here alone all week with the foal coming."

"I've already moved her to Winterflood Farm," Issie said. "Avery says he'll keep an eye on her. Besides, the vet says she's still not due for another month…"

"It's so exciting!" Stella blurted out. "I can't believe Blaze is actually going to have a foal!"

Issie still couldn't believe it herself. When the vet at Blackthorn Farm had told her the news she had been in shock. At first, Issie had assumed that the father must be the jet black wild stallion Destiny. Destiny had amazing bloodlines. He had been sired by Aunt Hester's own beloved Swedish Warmblood stallion, Avignon, so Issie had been very excited at the prospect of Blaze carrying the black stallion's foal.

Then, when Issie got home and her own vet examined Blaze, he dropped a bombshell. Blaze wasn't just a little bit pregnant. It seemed she was very pregnant indeed. The mare was more than three months gone already! That meant that Destiny couldn't possibly be the sire. Issie had been stunned. If Destiny wasn't the father of this foal, then who was? Finally, she figured it out. Marius! The great, grey Lipizzaner stallion was the star of the El Caballo Danza Magnifico

– the famed Spanish dancing horses. Blaze had once belonged to the troupe too, one of the El Caballo's seven Anglo-Arab mares, renowned for their beauty and balletic performances in the arena.

When Issie thought about it the timing made perfect sense. Blaze had been returned briefly to Francoise D'arth, the head trainer at the El Caballo Danza Magnifico. Issie remembered going to visit Blaze at the El Caballo stables. She had arrived to find Francoise busily ticking off the stable boys for allowing Marius to jump out of his paddock in with the mares. It took almost all day before the stable boys realised the stallion was in the wrong paddock.

Issie had immediately sent a letter to Francoise, telling her the exciting news, but she hadn't had a reply. Then Issie saw a big story in *PONY Magazine* about the El Caballo Danza Magnifico which said the troupe was still on its world tour. Perhaps Francoise hadn't been home and had never received Issie's letter. The French trainer would surely have got in touch if she knew that Blaze was going to have a foal.

There was still a month to go, but every day that Issie checked on Blaze she seemed to be more and more enormous. Her belly was now so huge that Issie couldn't fit a girth around her and the pony was eating twice as much hard feed as usual, as well as the lush spring grass in her paddock at Winterflood Farm.

Avery, meanwhile, was like an expectant father, fussing over the mare. He had set up the barn ready for the birth and organised the foaling monitor that would alert them the minute Blaze went into labour.

"The foaling monitor means we can leave her outdoors to graze naturally until she actually goes into labour. After that, things tend to happen very quickly," Avery warned Issie. "When my great showjumping mare Starlight was foaling, I popped off to grab a cup of tea and by the time I came back from the kitchen she'd had him and the little tyke was already trying to stand up!"

Everything was prepared and the vet had pronounced Blaze perfectly healthy. Still, Issie was nervous about going away with Aunt Hester and leaving her pony.

"She'll be fine," Avery reassured Issie. "You go and have fun. I'll keep an eye on her, don't you worry. You're only an hour away – I'll let you know the minute anything happens, I promise."

"Just don't make any cups of tea while I'm gone. I don't want Blaze to have her foal without me!" Issie had joked.

Even with Avery's reassurances, Issie didn't want to say

goodbye to Blaze. On the night before the truck was due to pick them up and take them to the film set, she stopped by Winterflood Farm and stood in the paddock for ages, giving the mare snuggles and feeding her at least six carrots.

"After all," she giggled as Blaze snuffled and munched a carrot from the palm of her hand, "you are eating for two, aren't you, girl?"

She ran her hands one last time through Blaze's long flaxen-blonde mane. The mare was so pretty with her dished Arabian face and her perfect white blaze. Issie loved Blaze so deeply now it seemed strange when she thought back to the day they first met.

It was Tom Avery who had brought Blaze to her. The chestnut Anglo-Arab had been so awfully mistreated, she was in a terrible state. Avery and the International League for the Protection of Horses had rescued her. Issie couldn't believe it when Avery told her he wanted Issie to be her guardian and take care of the mare.

It was a lot for him to ask. Until Blaze turned up, Issie had sworn off horses for good. She didn't want anything more to do with them after what had happened to Mystic.

Mystic had been Issie's first ever horse. A fourteen-hand, swaybacked grey gelding with faded dapples and a shaggy mane. Issie had loved Mystic deeply from the first day they met. When Mystic had been killed in a road accident at the pony club, Issie thought she would never get over it. She was sure she would never have another horse. But Avery knew better. He brought Blaze to her and together the broken-hearted girl and the broken-spirited pony healed each other and became a real team.

And Mystic? His death was just the beginning of a whole new adventure. Issie's bond with Mystic was more powerful than even she suspected. In fact Mystic wasn't truly gone at all. Whenever things got really bad, whenever Issie needed him most, he would be there at her side – not like a ghost or anything like that, but a real horse, flesh and blood.

Mystic was her guardian angel. He had saved her and Blaze countless times now. She hadn't seen the grey gelding in a long time, but she felt his presence more strongly than ever now that Blaze was close to foaling. Just knowing that the grey gelding was watching over Blaze and protecting her made Issie feel better about leaving the mare behind.

"I have to go, but Mystic will keep an eye on you, OK, girl?" Issie murmured as the mare nuzzled against her. Then she gave Blaze one more carrot for the road and left the mare in the paddock, heading home to pack her bags.

But when she got home, Issie was surprised to find her bags already packed and her sleeping bag rolled and ready at the front door.

"Mum?" Issie called out. Mrs Brown emerged from the kitchen.

"There you are!" she said breezily. "I figured you'd be running late so I went ahead and packed for you. I've washed and folded all that stuff you had in your laundry basket and put that in, and you've got three pairs of jodhpurs, your new hoodie and your *PONY Magazines*…"

"But Mum, I thought you didn't really want me to go," Issie said.

"Well, I was hoping you'd get a nice, safe, ordinary part-time job on the supermarket check-out for the holidays." Mrs Brown put her arms round Issie and gave her a hug. "But then I realised you wouldn't be my Issie if you did that, would you?"

Mrs Brown's hug got tighter. "I've told Hester to take good care of you this time, and I'll be there to pick you up and bring you home at the weekend." She let go of Issie and smiled. "Your dinner is ready – go and sit at the table. After that, you better get straight up to bed. You have an early start in the morning."

Issie did go straight to bed after dinner and she was so exhausted she had no trouble falling asleep. The last thing she remembered was setting her alarm clock for six. Then she was dreaming. In her dream she could hear Avery calling to her. He was telling her to hurry up because Blaze was having the foal. Issie could hear the foaling monitor going *parp! parp! parp!* telling her that she must go to her mare, but it was like her limbs were made of lead, it was so hard to move. Then, as she drowsily woke up out of her sleep, she realised the noise wasn't a foaling alarm at all. It was the sound of her alarm clock and there was her mother, sitting beside her on the bed and shaking her gently by the shoulder.

"Issie! It's time to get going. I came in and woke you up already, but you must have gone straight back to sleep," Mrs Brown said. "Come on. Everyone is here waiting for you."

"What time is it now?" Issie mumbled, rubbing her eyes.

"Seven o'clock."

"Ohmygod!"

Issie leapt out of bed. She pulled on her dressing gown and ran to the window on the other side of the hallway, the one that looked out to the main street. Aidan's horse truck was already parked outside. Issie could see Stella, Kate and Natasha waving madly through the truck windows at her. Stella was mouthing something at her but Issie couldn't hear her. "What?" she called back. Stella looked exasperated and wound down her window. "I said hurry up, sleepyhead!" she laughed. "We've been waiting for ages!"

"Yeah, come on!" Kate grinned at her.

Natasha glared at her balefully. "Typical," she said. "Making the rest of us wait for you."

"Sorry! I'm coming. Give me five minutes!" Issie called back.

There was barely time for a shower and no time for breakfast. Mrs Brown managed to thrust a piece of Marmite toast in Issie's hand and give her daughter a kiss goodbye as she raced out of the door.

Outside the horse truck was waiting. A boy stood by the door of the truck cab. He was wearing black jeans and a flannel shirt and his long dark hair fell in a floppy fringe over his face. "I've put your bags in the truck. The others are all sitting in the back, but I thought you might like to ride up in the cab with me," Aidan said.

Aidan! Issie could feel her heart beating fast in her chest and her mouth was so dry there was no way she could choke down the last bite of the Marmite toast. "Uh-huh," she managed.

Aidan looked pleased and gave her a shy smile, pushing his fringe back so that Issie could see his startling blue eyes. "Let's go then!"

The first five minutes of the drive were excruciatingly painful. Issie didn't know what to say so the pair of them sat there in silence looking out the window.

Finally Aidan spoke. "Do you know much about this movie?"

"I've read the book, like, a hundred times," Issie said. "There's this princess – her name is Galatea, but everyone calls her Gala. She's the ruler of a kingdom where the women are all princesses and brave warriors – but she's the strongest of them all and she has superpowers and stuff. Anyway, in Galatea's realm the horses are all palominos and they have magical powers too. Then there are all these really creepy guys called the Elerians. The Elerians have these black horses, and the really horrible part is that their horses were all once palominos too. They used to belong to Galatea's stables, but one by one the Elerians have captured them and turned them into the Horses of Darkness. The Elerians are actually vampires – except they bite horses, not people. They use their vampire fangs to suck all the life out of the palominos and turn them into these awful black horses, drained of all their pure strength and overcome by evil…"

Issie suddenly turned to look at Aidan. Why was he smiling at her? "What?" she said defensively. "What's so funny?"

"Nothing's funny!" Aidan said, still smiling. "It's just that I'd forgotten how excited you get about stuff – especially horses. I really like that about you."

Issie fumbled around in her bag. "Here," she said, handing Aidan a dog-eared paperback. "I brought my copy with me. You can borrow it if you like."

Aidan smiled. "I've already read it. It's one of my favourite books too."

After that, Issie and Aidan talked non-stop and the hour-long drive seemed to take no time at all. The horse truck thundered along the road past the pine forests north of Chevalier Point, through rolling green fields dotted with grazing cows. Finally they pulled off the main road down a gravel driveway and Issie was surprised when they were stopped by a burly security guard at the farm gate.

"There have been loads of paparazzi – tabloid newspaper photographers – trying to get on the set," Aidan explained to Issie as they drove on again through the paddocks. "Apparently the girl they've got playing Princess Galatea is really famous. There's been loads of rumours. They're trying to keep everything hush-hush. Even the crew haven't been told who it is…"

But Issie wasn't really listening to him. She was too busy looking out the front window of the truck.

"Ohmygod!" she breathed. "Aidan! This is incredible!"

As they came over the hill, there in front of them was a grand golden gate that led to a vast white cobbled courtyard and in the centre was a gold fountain, with life-size statues of rearing horses spouting brilliant turquoise water from their golden mouths. Surrounding the white courtyard were rows of white loose boxes with golden doors.

"The stables of Princess Galatea," Aidan grinned. He turned the horse truck past the golden gates. "And over there is the black castle of Eleria."

Issie looked to her left and saw the familiar sight of Chevalier Castle. Only the castle didn't look like it usually did. The ruins, which sat on top of a hill that looked out over farmland and forest, had been sprayed with black paint. The broad, cobblestone terraces that wound round and round like a corkscrew to the summit had also been painted black. The castle, with spikes on its turrets and a huge iron portcullis, would have been a terrifying vision if it weren't for the crew members and builders running about the place. Everywhere you looked there were set dressers lugging enormous black-varnished styrofoam boulders towards the castle or painting fake green slime on the drawbridge.

"Production has been under way for weeks now. These are just the finishing touches. They're nearly ready to start filming," Aidan said.

He turned the truck around and parked it near the golden gates of the stables, giving a cheery wave to one of the set dressers who was busily pouring more turquoise dye into the golden fountain.

"We brought all the horses here a month ago – Hester has done loads of desensitising work with them. They've filmed some of the vampire riders' scenes already – but the main stunts need palomino riders too and that's where you come in." He jumped out of the truck cab, followed by Issie.

"I'll give you a proper tour later, but first let's get

you all settled in. Your rooms are over there behind the stable block. We'll grab your bags. It's easier if we walk through from here."

As Aidan said this, the door swung open on the side of the truck and Stella, Kate and Natasha emerged.

"Whoa!" Stella said, looking at the golden stables. "Is this where we'll be staying?"
The others laughed.

"The golden stables!" Kate squealed. "They're just like I always imagined they'd look!"

"I know," Issie beamed. "Isn't it cool?"

Natasha was the last to climb out of the truck. She cast a disdainful glance at Aidan.

"Well? Where are our rooms?" she demanded, gesturing at the luggage lying on the ground. "Come on! Bring my bags, will you?"

Stella rounded on Natasha immediately. "Aidan's not your servant, you know. We all carry our own bags around here."

"Oh, really?" Natasha glared at her. "Mummy always told me that ladies never carry luggage. I'm not sure what your mother taught you..."

Before Stella could snap back, they were interrupted by the sight of the most enormous car they'd ever seen cruising towards them down the driveway.

"What is that?" Kate said as the chrome-yellow Hummer with black tinted windows pulled up next to them.

"You mean *who* is that, don't you?" Aidan said. "I have a feeling we're finally going to discover who's got the starring role in *The Palomino Princess*."

As the rest of the crew ran over to the Hummer and gathered round, the front doors of the vehicle swung open and two men in black suits wearing earpiece microphones jumped out.

"Who are they? I don't recognise them. Are they famous?" Issie whispered to Aidan.

"I think they're just the bodyguards," Aidan whispered back.

The bodyguards spoke into their earpieces and nodded to each other. Then one of the men stood guard while the other opened the back door of the Hummer. From behind the tinted glass a girl emerged, helped down by a third bodyguard.

"Ohmygod! I don't believe it! It's the Teen Drama Queen!" Stella squealed.

"Stella!" Issie hissed at her. "Don't! You'll embarrass her!"

The girl, who had clearly heard Stella's comment,

pushed her dark glasses back to reveal her violet eyes. "Don't worry," she said in a soft mid-west American accent. "People always call me that. I get it, like, all the time." She smiled, revealing her perfect white teeth. "Are y'all working on the movie?" she asked.

"Ummm, yes. We're stunt riders," Issie said. "My name is Isadora and this is Stella and Kate, Natasha and Aidan."

"Nice to meet y'all." The girl smiled again. "I'm Angelique Adams."

Chapter 3

Issie couldn't believe it. Angelique Adams! The girl that *Sixteen Magazine* called "the most famous teenager in the world" was standing right in front of her.

Angelique looked just like she did on all those magazine covers. Her long honey-blonde hair was ironed straight and she had a deep golden tan. Dressed in designer jeans, a leather vest and enormous sunglasses, she looked much smaller than she did in her movies. Issie was actually ever so slightly taller than the pint-sized celebrity.

Angelique clicked her fingers and two more people leapt out of the back of the Hummer – a dark-haired woman and a blond man.

"Her entourage," whispered Aidan under his breath

to Issie. Angelique gestured to the woman who scurried forward and handed her a coffee. Angelique took a quick sip and then thrust the cup back at her assistant as the blond man darted in and began to fuss around, fixing her hair, pulling make-up brushes out of his belt to add some blusher and a fresh coat of lip gloss.

"That's enough, Tony!" Angelique snapped, pushing the make-up man out of the way just in time as the gang of paparazzi photographers, who had been tailing the Hummer, all leapt out of their cars. They jostled each other to get close to Angelique and began to take her picture, their motor drives whirring, cameras flashing.

"Angelique!" the paparazzi shouted to her. "Over here! Look this way. Give us a smile, Angelique!"

Suddenly there was a noise at the back of the paparazzi pack. "Lemme through!" A little man in a khaki army jacket was leaping up and down like Rumpelstiltskin, elbowing his way past the photographers. "One side, comin' through!" he snapped as he barged his way forward. When the little man reached the front and found himself blocked by Angelique's bodyguards he began to shout even louder. "Hey! You big apes! Yes, you! Lemme through I tell ya!"

The little man was lugging an enormous video camera on his shoulder. He was accompanied by a pale thin man carrying what looked a bit like a fluffy grey cat pinned to the end of a long stick.

"I'm with Angelique!" the man insisted to the bodyguards. "I have an access-all-areas pass. She'll tell you, won't you, Angelique, baby? Tell them!" he pleaded.

Angelique looked over and gave a nod to the bodyguards to let the man and his skinny sidekick through. The other paparazzi began to complain loudly at this and the little man gave them a smirk. "A-list access!" he beamed. Then he turned to the teen starlet and smiled his oiliest grin.

"Angelique! Honey!" His voice took on a crawly tone. "Great entrance, baby! Right on! But… uhhh, the thing is, we've had a slight technical hitch and we're going to have to reshoot all of that."

Angelique's smile disappeared. The little man looked nervous. "It's all because of Bob here," he stammered. "He didn't get the sound recorded right. Isn't that right, Bob?" He shot a withering glare at his sidekick, who looked suitably guilty and didn't say anything.

"So… we need you to do it again from the top," the little man said. "Can you get back in the car and then drive up and do the whole arriving-on-set thing again? And make it really, you know, *real*."

Angelique rolled her eyes. "All right. But this better not take all day, Eugene!" she snapped at him. "I've got, like, a masseuse and three beauticians waiting for me back at my trailer."

She glared at Bob, who cowered a little, then she clicked her fingers at her assistants and climbed back into the Hummer. Her bodyguards quickly piled in after them, slamming the car into reverse as the paparazzi scrambled to get out of their way.

"Hey, you kids!" the man in the khaki jacket turned his attention to Issie and her friends.

"Who us?" Stella said.

"What? Yes, you! Of course you!" the man said. "You kids were great!" he enthused. "We'll go once more, just like last time. Are you ready?"

Stella looked at him blankly. "Ready for what?"

"The second take of course!" the little man said. There were more blank looks from Stella and Issie. The man sighed. He didn't have time for this.

"We're making a documentary here, kids! The name is Eugene – Eugene Sneadly – Hollywood's most hardworking documentary film-maker." Eugene gestured over his shoulder at the skinny man with the cat on a stick. "This here is Bob, my sound man. That stick of his is what we call a sound boom. Hey, watch it with that thing, Bob!"

Eugene cast a surly look at Bob and then continued, "Bob and I are here with Angelique Adams. She's given us A-list priority on the film set so that we can do this behind-the-scenes documentary about her. *Drama Queen – Behind the Scenes.* That's what we're calling it. Sounds exciting, right? And it is! It's gonna be big, big, big, baby, because everyone loves Angelique and, well, the girl just can't help herself. Like they say, she's a regular, real-life drama queen."

"You just got lucky, kids," Eugene went on, barely pausing for breath. "This is gonna be your big moment. You can all be in my documentary. So get ready to go wild because… Angelique Adams is about to arrive!"

"But she's already arrived," Stella protested. "We just met her."

The little man sighed. Then he raised his hands to the sky and began talking to himself. "Oh, Eugene, Eugene! Why are you working with amateurs here?" He looked back at Stella.

"I know she's already arrived, sweetheart," he said through gritted teeth. "What I'm saying is, let's pretend and do it again, shall we?"

The girls and Aidan all nodded at this. They weren't sure what Eugene was up to, but it seemed easiest to agree and go along with it.

"And… action!" Eugene shouted, waving his hand frantically at the Hummer in the distance.

The chrome-yellow car drove down the road and pulled up in front of the stables for a second time. The doors opened and Angelique appeared, looking every bit as fresh-faced and eager to meet everyone as she had the first time round.

"Hi!" she smiled sweetly. "Nice to meet y'all. I'm Angelique Adams!"

The girls and Aidan were dumbstruck as the paparazzi bounded after her and started snapping wildly once more and Angelique grinned and waved.

"Perfect! Perfect!" Eugene yelled out. "Got it! Great work, Angelique."

As soon as the cameras stopped rolling Angelique abruptly stopped smiling. "That's it, Eugene! I'm outta here."

"But, baby, Rupert ain't even here yet. He wants to meet you. They start shooting tomorrow," Eugene said.

"Y'all can wait for him if you want, Eugene. I'll be in my trailer gettin' a spray tan!" Angelique snapped. She hopped back in the Hummer, obediently followed by her assistants and bodyguards who slammed the door and promptly floored it.

"Angelique, cupcake! Wait! We're coming too!" Eugene cried. He and the paparazzi made a dash for their cars. Clouds of dust and gravel flew up from the road as the Hummer sped off with a line of cars following closely behind.

"I thought the security guard at the gate was supposed to keep the photographers out," Issie said to Aidan.

Aidan shrugged. "I guess Angelique let them in. Maybe she likes the paparazzi following her everywhere. You know, taking her picture for all those magazines."

"I still don't believe we just met Angelique Adams!" Stella said. "She is soooo famous!"

Natasha sighed. "Yeah, she seemed real thrilled to meet you too, Stella. She couldn't wait to get away! Didn't you notice how fast she got out of here?"

Natasha glanced around. "Not that I blame her for wanting to get away from this place," she muttered under her breath, just loud enough for everyone to hear.

Aidan ignored Natasha and picked up her bags. It was clear that he was going to have to carry her luggage since the snooty blonde still refused to do it herself.

"Grab your bags," he instructed the others. "I'll show you to the barracks."

"What do you mean 'barracks'?" Natasha said as she followed along behind him through the white courtyard of the stables. "Surely we all have our own private trailers? Aidan? Aidan!"

They walked straight through the golden stables and on the other side they found themselves standing in front of a row of makeshift wooden huts.

"These really were army barracks once," Aidan explained. "Rupert, the director, bought them cheap and had them moved on to the site to use as accommodation for the crew."

Aidan pointed to the left. "That building over there is where the props department and the set builders live. And over there are the sleeping quarters for the Elerian horsemen – that's where I'm staying." He pointed to the right. "Those two silver trailers are the costume department and make-up and that white building next to the trailers is the main dining hall where we all meet for meals."

"This is your barrack." Aidan gestured to the building directly in front of them. "Palomino wranglers' quarters!" he grinned. "Come on inside."

The wooden barracks turned out to be much

plusher inside than they looked. The lounge was really cosy with lots of colourful beanbags, plump sofas and a wide-screen TV. Beyond the main lounge was a hallway with three doors leading off. Each doorway opened on to a bunk room.

"The room at the end is Hester's," Aidan explained. "That leaves two rooms for you guys to share."

Stella stuck her head round the corner of the first bunk room. It had three single beds. "I bagsy this bed!" she cried, flinging herself on the best bunk underneath the window.

"I'll go here then!" Kate said, heaving her bags up on to the bed closest to the door.

That left one more bunk in the room. Issie looked at it. Then she looked over at Natasha. The snooty blonde was milling about out in the hallway, pretending she wasn't even slightly interested in the sleeping arrangements.

If Issie took the third bunk, she realised, she would be sharing a room with Stella and Kate, which was great. But that also meant Natasha would be left out, all by herself in the other room. Issie picked up her bag. "Hey, Natasha?" she said. "Do you want to come with me and check out our room?"

Natasha looked at Issie with grateful eyes. "OK," she said cheerfully. She grabbed her bags and began to walk ahead of Issie down the hall. Then she turned back and added, "But don't get any ideas because I'm having the bunk by the window."

As Issie unpacked her bags and filled the chest of drawers next to her bunk, Natasha opened the windows for some fresh air and fussed about the state of the bed linen, which was "cheap cotton, not proper Egyptian like at home" and the bunks, which were "like concrete and totally impossible to sleep on".

"You didn't have to come, you know!" Issie snapped, but as soon as she said it, she wished she hadn't.

Natasha stopped unpacking. She glared at Issie. "Why did you ask me then?"

"What do you mean?"

"Why did you ask me to come? Was it just because you needed another rider?" Natasha sneered. "You must have been desperate. I know you and Stella and Kate don't actually like me, so it's not like you asked me because I'm your friend or anything…"

"Natasha, no, it wasn't like that…" Issie began, but Natasha cut her off.

"I know what you all think of me, you know. I'm not

stupid. You think I'm stuck up just because I go to a private school."

"Well…" Issie began, uncertain what to say to this.

"I know you say horrible things about me," Natasha insisted. "Well, not you so much. You aren't so bad, I suppose, Issie. But Stella is always being mean to me."

"But, Natasha!" Issie protested, "you always say mean things to her too! You kind of bring it on yourself, you know."

Natasha shrugged at this. "Anyway, you don't have to share a room with me. I don't care. Go ahead if you'd rather be with your friends."

Issie shook her head. "No. It's OK, honest. I don't want to move," she said. "I like this room. I think it'll be fun to share together."

This seemed to cheer Natasha up a bit and she began to unpack her clothes, laying them carefully into the drawers.

"I'm glad your mum let you come," Issie said.

"Oh, Mummy was desperate for me to come!" Natasha said. "She couldn't wait to get rid of me."

"What do you mean?" Issie was confused.

"You mean you don't know?" Natasha looked shocked. "I thought everyone had heard about it." She began to pull random things out of her bag, throwing her T-shirts violently into the drawer. "My parents have split up. They're getting a divorce. They're so busy arguing with each other, they barely notice that I'm in the room." Natasha's face was flushed with embarrassment. "I thought that was why you asked me to come. I thought your mum made you ask me because of the divorce."

"No," Issie said. "No, I didn't know. Mum didn't make me ask you – I just thought, well, I thought we might have fun."

Natasha seemed to perk up a little at this. "You know," she said as she arranged her hairbrush and lip gloss on the dressing table, "it will be fun! It'll be like a sleepover." She was smiling. "I've got loads of treats like chocolate fudge in my bag for us to share. We can eat lollies and tell ghost stories and… ohmygod! Argghh!"

Natasha leapt up on to her bunk squealing with fear as three enormous dogs suddenly bowled into the room; their claws scratched against the wooden floorboards as they ran about panting, sniffing and slobbering.

"Ewww! Get them away from me!" Natasha howled.

"Strudel! Taxi! Nanook! Lie down!" Issie ordered. The dogs obeyed immediately and dropped down on the floor, lying perfectly still with their heads on their paws.

"Aunty Hess?" Issie called out. "Is that you? I'm in here!" Through the doorway behind the dogs came a glamorous woman with shoulder-length, curly blonde hair, dressed in black jodhpurs and a crisp white blouse.

"Isadora! My favourite niece!" Hester beamed as she grabbed Issie in an enormous hug. Issie found herself squished in her aunt's arms, drowning in the familiar scent of Chanel perfume.

"Aunty Hess! It's so good to see you again!" Issie said. She turned to Natasha. "Aunty Hess, I want you to meet my friend Natasha from pony club. She's a really good rider."

"Hello, Natasha. How terrific to have you here!" Hester smiled.

Natasha smiled back stiffly. "Thank you," she replied.

"And these are Hester's dogs," Issie said, finishing her introductions. "This is Nanook," she explained, pointing to the shaggy black Newfoundland, "and Strudel," she said, patting the golden retriever. "And this one is Taxi," Issie said, scratching the black and white cattle dog behind the ears.

Natasha looked nervously at the dogs and still didn't get down off the bunk.

"Good boys! Outside now!" Hester instructed the

dogs – and the three of them leapt up immediately, tearing off out the door.

"Are you girls unpacking? There's time for that later. Right now you're coming with me," Hester said firmly. "Go and get the others. It's time to meet the horses."

Chapter 4

Issie had been wondering about the horses. She hadn't seen any sign of them at the golden stables. "No, no," Hester laughed. "The golden stables are just a movie set. We don't actually keep the horses there!" She pointed down the road which ran in the opposite direction behind the barracks. "The stables are down the hill. Much less grand than the film set version, I'm afraid."

Hester was right. The real stables weren't trimmed with gold or anything flashy. Still, Issie thought they were totally amazing. The stable block was enormous, with a huge indoor arena in the middle of it where the riders could train. Two long rows of loose boxes ran down either side, where the horses were stabled.

"We arrived here and began training and preparing

the horses for filming last month," Hester explained as she beckoned them to follow her through the arena towards the stables. "We've already shot a few scenes with the vampire riders. Now, over the next two weeks, while you girls are here, we'll do the rest of the big stunt work."

"Two weeks!" Stella squeaked. "That's not much time, is it?"

"Most of the movie will be finished off back at the studio – they do all the special effects on blue screen," Hester said. "You girls are here to film the stunt double work. You'll all double for the princess riders. You'll be riding the scenes instead of the real actors; sometimes you'll even get to speak their lines. Then they'll use special effects back at the studio to replace your faces with the movie stars' and make it look like they were the ones riding the horses the whole time."

"But won't it look fake?" Stella asked.

"This is the movies, dear. Nothing is really real," Hester grinned. "Come on, I'll introduce you to the real stars of *The Palomino Princess*." She led them to a row of loose boxes.

"There are thirteen horses in total living here," Hester said. "Eight black horses and five palominos."

"But why do you need so many black horses?" Kate

asked. "In the book there are only seven vampire riders."

"We're using two different horses to play the role of Dante – the black horse ridden by Francis the vampire king," Hester said. "One horse will be Dante for all the action sequences and chase scenes. The other horse will do the close-up work. We'll make it look like the same horse of course, but it won't be."

She unbolted the top half of the Dutch door of the stall, swinging it back on its hinges, and a black and white piebald face came out to greet them.

"Diablo!" Issie cried, delighted to see the black and white Quarter Horse once more.

Kate looked confused. "But you said you were only using black horses! How come Diablo is here?"

"We'll put black dye on his white patches," Hester smiled. She ran her hand down Diablo's nose. "You'll never be able to tell that he's dyed when you see him at a distance." She stroked the big piebald on his soft muzzle. "Diablo will play Dante in the chase sequences, like the scene in the forest when Francis is after Galatea."

Hester opened the next stall. "Diablo is a good stunt horse, but he's not pretty enough for the close-ups. For those we need a really dramatic, handsome horse with a long mane," she said, "and that's what Destiny is here for."

Issie hardly recognised Destiny in his loose box. The stallion had changed so much since she saw him last. When she first met Destiny he had been running wild with the Blackthorn Ponies. She remembered his sun-bleached black coat, caked in mud and his mane and tail, ratty and tangled from his wild life. Aunt Hester had spent the past few months putting in long hours grooming the stallion and now he was completely changed. He gleamed like a show horse. His coat was like black satin and his mane and tail were long, glossy and jet-black. Issie noticed that even the white stripe on his elegant Swedish Warmblood face had been dyed so that he was totally black all over.

"Hey, boy, remember me?" Issie called to him over the stable door. Destiny pricked up his ears at Issie's voice and came over to her. He nickered softly as Issie stroked his nose, then rubbed his head against her jacket until she produced a carrot for him.

"Well!" Hester said. "Look at that! He won't give the stable hands the time of day. He's not even this affectionate with me or Aidan. He obviously remembers you, Isadora."

"You're such a beauty, aren't you, Destiny?" Issie said, running her hands down the stallion's glossy neck.

"He is looking marvellous, isn't he?" Hester beamed with pride. "I've been training him with Aidan, who's stunt-doubling for the actor who plays Francis. Aidan handles Destiny nicely. It's not easy with a stallion – as well you know, Isadora – after all, you were the one who broke him in."

Natasha let out an incredulous snort at this. "Yeah, right… sure she did!"

"She did, Natasha!" Stella leapt to Issie's defence. "We were all there. We saw it. Issie broke Destiny in all by herself – well, with a bit of help from Tom. And she did it in one day too!"

Natasha could see that she was outnumbered. "What-ever," she said, rolling her eyes at Stella. Then she turned to Aunt Hester. "I'm bored now. Is this tour going to take all day?"

Aunt Hester gave Natasha a steely look. "I expect you're keen to get down to work, are you, Natasha? These stables could really do with mucking out. You'll find your roster on the inside of the main stable door."

"What do you mean 'mucking out'?" Natasha said.

"Well, dear, surely you didn't think the horses would look after themselves?" Hester said. "It's part of the palomino wrangler's job to look after all the horses, doing the feeding and grooming and mucking out. As I said, the roster is on the door. In fact," Hester said to Natasha, "I believe you're rostered on for dung duty first. Would you like to get started now or would you like to come with the rest of us and meet the palominos?"

Natasha's face furrowed into a scowl, but she didn't say anything as Hester led them across the arena to another row of stalls.

"This is where my girls are stabled," Hester said. She moved along the row of stalls, opening the top of the first four Dutch doors. One by one, the golden palominos thrust their heads over the partitions of their loose boxes.

"Hey! I know those two," Stella said, pointing to the horses in the second and third stalls. "It's Paris and Nicole!"

"Well spotted!" Hester smiled. "My own two palominos from Blackthorn Farm. I am impressed that you could tell them apart from the others." She pointed to the palominos in stalls one and four. "These ones are my new girls, Rosie and Athena." Rosie and Athena were just as pretty as Paris and Nicole with white blazes down their palomino noses and dark sooty muzzles.

"Rosie is a great stunt pony. She's green but she learns fast. You'll be riding her, Natasha," Hester said. "Athena is my reserve – a back-up in case one of the other mares goes lame or something goes wrong. I don't want any problems with the horses to hold up the filming. Rupert, the director, is on a tight schedule."

"You mean just swap one horse for another?" Stella asked.

"Why not, dear? After all, they all look so alike, don't they?" Hester smiled. "Except for Stardust. She's got that X-factor that makes her special. You'll see what I mean. Come with me and I'll introduce you to my new superstar!" Hester moved down the stable aisle now to the last stall in the row and unbolted the door.

"Girls," she said grandly, "I'd like you to meet Galatica Supernova – or Stardust as she's known on the set."

As if on cue, Stardust poked her head over the stall. Hester was right – the mare was a true beauty. She was larger than the other palominos, nearly fifteen-two, and her coat was darker and glossier, the colour of warm treacle. Her mane was so white it was almost silver. "She looks like a Barbie doll!" Issie laughed. "She's so pretty and perfect it's almost like she's not real."

"She's real – and she's a real handful too!" Hester said. "Stardust is supposed to play Seraphine, Princess Galatea's horse." Hester shook her head. "It's the most important role in the film. But our training sessions haven't been going very well so far. Have they, Stardust?"

As she spoke, Hester reached out to give Stardust a friendly pat, but Stardust shook her head indignantly. Then, completely without warning, the mare lunged over the stable door. Her teeth were bared as she tried to land a nip on Aunt Hester's arm.

Hester was too fast for her. She had been working around horses for far too many years to be caught out so easily. Instead, she sidestepped quickly, avoiding Stardust's teeth, then turned round and grabbed the mare with a tight hold on her halter before she could try it again.

Stardust's ears were flat back against her head in anger as she fought to free herself from Hester's hands. The palomino's eyes had turned dark with fury.

"You see?" Hester sighed. "She's a naughty little madam. I'm at my wits' end trying to deal with her."

"Why don't you just use one of the other palominos instead," Natasha sniffed.

"It's not that simple," Hester said. "Stardust might be troublesome, but she's also very talented. She can rear on command, she can nod and shake her head on cue and she can perform all sorts of tricks that none of my other palominos have mastered. Plus she's gorgeous.

Rupert says that the camera loves her. He's the director and he's the one who cast Stardust to be his Seraphine."

"But why did he choose her if she's so badly behaved?" Kate asked.

Hester sighed. "That's the thing! Stardust wasn't always like this. She used to be one of the best horses in the movie business. When her owners offered to let me use her for this film, I jumped at the chance to cast her. I didn't realise what a drama I was in for."

Issie looked at the palomino. Stardust had her ears flat back still, as if she was waiting for her chance to strike again. Hester sighed and let go of the halter, and the mare threw her head up and reared back, immediately heading back into the stall, standing at a distance where no one could reach her. She stood there, pawing restlessly at the floor of the loose box, shaking her head as if to say, "Go away and leave me alone!"

"Her owners finally admitted to me that they knew she was having problems," Hester said. "They say it all went wrong on her last film. Bad handlers apparently. I suspect they didn't know what they were doing and so when Stardust wouldn't perform for them, they got quite rough with her."

"Poor Stardust," Stella said. She clucked over the stall

door at the palomino mare, but Stardust just glowered back at her from the corner, her ears still flat against her head. Stella looked at the expression on the mare's face and stepped away from the stable door.

"Her owners said they were hoping that working on this film with me would turn Stardust back into her old self again." Hester shook her head. "But I'm not so sure. She's a very sensitive mare. I've tried to put the extra time in with her, but she isn't responding. She's developed some frightful vices – she bites and kicks, she's unpredictable to ride."

Hester sighed. "I have thirteen horses here and I've had my hands full with the vampire riders. I simply don't have time for prima-donna palominos." She turned to Issie. "So I thought maybe you'd like to take over."

"What?" Issie squeaked.

"Issie, I'm at the end of my tether," Hester said, looking serious. "We're about to start filming Seraphine's scenes and we're no closer to sorting Stardust out than we were a whole month ago when she arrived on set." Hester shook her head. "At this rate Stardust is going to hold up filming. If filming is delayed because of my horses, it could cost millions. I haven't had the nerve to tell Rupert that we're having trouble with her. He's got enough on his plate keeping the actors in line without worrying about problem palominos. Seraphine, I mean Stardust, needs to be the perfect angel in front of those cameras when we start filming next week or Rupert will blow his top." Hester paused. "Isadora, I want you and Aidan to work with her. I'll take care of the other horses if you two knuckle down and focus on her training. You must get Stardust to behave like her old self again. I need my palomino princess back on form in time for filming to begin next week."

"Me?" Issie was stunned. "Well, I can try, I suppose…"

"You'll have to do better than that, Isadora," Hester said darkly. "This is Stardust's last chance."

Chapter 5

The mood was very gloomy at the palomino barracks the next morning.

"What do you think Hester meant?" Stella asked. "You know, when she said this was Stardust's last chance?"

"I heard her mutter something about 'glue factory'," said Natasha, who was lying on the sofa in front of the big-screen TV trying to get the remote to work.

"You didn't!" Stella snapped. "You're just making that up!"

Natasha glared at her. "That's what I heard," she said. "I don't care if you believe me or not."

"Well, she's not going to the glue factory anyway," Kate huffed. "Poor Stardust. She's been mistreated, that's all. She's not really bad natured."

"She looked pretty bad when she was trying to sink her teeth into Hester's arm if you ask me!" Natasha said.

"No one did ask you though, did they?" Stella said. "In fact, I can't figure out why anyone even asked you to come on this trip in the first place."

"Hey! Don't take it out on me, Stella!" Natasha shrugged. "It's not my fault that palomino is going to be petfood. There's no point in… Hey! This TV has cable!" Now that Natasha had figured out the remote control, she gave up on fighting with Stella as she channel-surfed. She flicked through until she struck the E! channel.

"Hey look, Stella!" Natasha smirked. "*The E! True Hollywood Story*. It's all about your NBF, Angelique Adams.*" Angelique was talking to an E! reporter about her new role in the upcoming movie, *The Palomino Princess*.

"It's a dream come true working on this film," Angelique gushed. "Rupert Conrad is the hottest director in Hollywood right now. I was desperate to work with him. It's so funny because when I heard Rupert wanted a real rider for the part of Galatea I was, like, that's totally me! I've been riding all my life since I was, like, a baby, and when this role came up everyone said it was perfect for me because I am such a great rider. I am, like, totally the Palomino Princess!"

Angelique gave the reporter a flash of her big white smile.

The reporter smiled back. "This film has a lot of great horse action in it, Angelique," he said, "but we hear that most of it will actually be done with stunt riders and special effects. Will you be using a stunt double?"

"No way, y'all!" Angelique smiled at him and flicked her long blonde hair. "Rupert says he wants me to really get into the role of Princess Galatea. I'm going to be doing all my own stunts."

"Wow! I didn't know she was a really good rider too!" Kate said, looking impressed.

Issie shrugged. "Me neither. That's pretty cool."

"Maybe she'll be able to handle Stardust then?" Stella said hopefully.

"If she's riding her own stunts, she should come down and join our training session," Issie said. "Aunty Hess wants us all at the arena first thing tomorrow to put the palominos through the desensitisation course."

"I wish we didn't have costume fittings today," Stella grumbled. "I really want to start riding."

"Ohmygod! The costume fitting!" Kate looked at her watch. "We're due there right now!"

"Are you coming, Natasha?" Issie asked. "They said we all had to be there."

Natasha groaned and reluctantly turned off the TV, dragging herself up off the sofa and following the other girls out of the barracks to the costume trailer.

The silver trailer was like a caravan only much longer and it had the words COSTUME DEPARTMENT written across the door in bright purple letters.

The girls had just reached the door and Stella had her hand out to grab the handle when it suddenly swung open. Standing in front of them was a woman in a brown hippy skirt and peasant blouse; she had curly hair down to her waist.

"Hi, I'm Amber," the woman said. "I'm Head of Costume. You guys are the stunt riders, right?" She smiled at them. "Come in! We're just finishing up. You're next."

Issie stepped up the silver stairs into the trailer. Inside it was like a gypsy tea room. The walls were draped with floral scarves and covered with mirrors trimmed with glowing lightbulbs. There were tea chests overflowing with clothes and prop boxes stuffed with swords and lances.

In the middle of the room stood a tall man, dressed in a black monk's robe with an enormous hood. As the girls all piled into the trailer, the man turned to face them, flicking back the hood to reveal his bulbous bald head which was covered with ugly purple veins.

"Hi!" The man smiled pleasantly at them. His voice sounded familiar somehow, Issie thought. "Did Hester introduce you to the horses? Isn't Stardust a stunner? Bit naughty though…"

"Aidan?" Issie was shocked. "Ohmygod! Aidan? Is that really you?"

Aidan nodded. "It's amazing what a latex bald wig and two hours in the make-up chair will do for my good looks."

Stella giggled at this and elbowed Issie. "You didn't recognise your own boyfriend!"

Issie blushed furiously, hoping that Aidan hadn't heard what Stella had just said.

"Hey, check this out!" Aidan said to the girls. He reached into the pocket of his black robe then hid his face for a moment beneath the hood of his cloak. Then he flipped the hood back and smiled again, revealing a pair of long white vampire fangs.

"Ohmygod!" Stella shrieked.

"Scary, huh?" Aidan said. "They look great but it's hard to ride in them. I keep biting my tongue."

"Hey, guess who else is riding?" Stella said. "We just found out that Angelique Adams is going to be doing all her own stunts. It turns out she's totally horse-mad!"

"Really?" Aidan raised an eyebrow at this news. "I didn't pick Angelique for a horsy girl. If she's riding, why haven't I even seen her on the set yet?"

"Maybe she's so good she doesn't need to practise," Stella said.

"All right then." Aidan flicked his black hood back up and bared his fangs. "I'd better get going. We've got dress rehearsals for the vampire horsemen… but first I might have a bite to eat…" He made a sudden lunge at Issie as if he were about to sink his fangs into her. Issie shrieked and leapt back and the other girls and Aidan began laughing.

"I'm not a real vampire, you know," Aidan grinned at her as he ducked out the trailer door. "I promise I won't bite."

As Aidan bounded out of the trailer, Amber the costume lady came back in with an armful of clothes. She put the clothes down on a chair in the corner and then looked Issie up and down. "You're a size ten, right? Here – take this blouse and these jodhpurs. You can go into that changing room over there to put them on."

Amber gestured to a row of four changing cubicles built into the wall of the trailer. She passed Issie a pile of silver, blue and white clothes and then turned her attention to Stella, Kate and Natasha.

"I'll get you all dressed and sorted and then you can go next door and do make-up try-outs after that," she said.

Issie walked into the changing room and held up her costume. There was a pair of sky-blue jodhpurs that looked about her size, and a flowing white blouse that fell down past her hips. The blouse had big billowy sleeves and it was trimmed at the neck with silver. Issie also had silver wristbands to wear.

There was a knock at the door and Amber passed in a pair of shiny black patent leather riding boots. "You're a size seven foot – right?" Issie nodded.

Amber looked at Issie with a stern expression. "It all looks good on you," she said. "I don't think it will need any adjustments at all. Put the boots on and I'll just grab one last thing…"

Issie pulled on the boots. The costume fitted her all right – but she still didn't feel like a Palomino Princess. She felt like Issie Brown in a silly costume. There was another knock at the door and Amber came back in. This time she held a long blonde wig in her hand.

"Let's slip this on you now and see how you look," Amber smiled. She wound Issie's long dark hair back into a twist and pinned it at the back of her head with hair grips. "We'll do this properly on the day of the shoot – this is just to see how it looks," Amber explained. She yanked the blonde wig firmly down on to Issie's head and tucked a couple of stray dark hairs back underneath the blonde fringe.

"Perfect!" Amber said. "Come out and take a look!" Issie walked out of the changing cubicle and stood in front of Amber's full-length mirror.

"Wow! I look amazing!" she gasped.

"You look great!" Amber agreed, fussing round Issie, straightening the hem of her blouse. She stood back and admired her work. "Maybe we'll go with a slightly longer wig? I'll see what we have in stock. Anyway, I'll just get the others to pop out and we can see what you all look like together."

One by one, Stella, Kate and Natasha all emerged from their changing cubicles. Amber had tucked Stella's red hair and Kate's short blonde bob underneath long blonde wigs just like Issie's. Natasha, who didn't need a wig, had undone her plaits so that her own long blonde hair was loose around her shoulders. The three girls were all wearing sky-blue jodhpurs too, but Stella wore a violet blouse, Kate emerald green and Natasha wore scarlet.

"Wow! You guys look incredible!" Issie said.

"I know!" Stella shrieked. "It's so cool!"

"You can take your costumes off now," Amber said, gesturing towards the changing cubicles. "I'm just going to pop out for a coffee. Head over to Helen next door in make-up when you're done."

Stella, Kate, Natasha and Issie all piled back into their cubicles and began carefully taking off their costumes.

"Hey!" Stella called out. "Do you think we'll get to keep our outfits after the movie is finished?"

"I don't think so!" Kate said.

"How about the wigs?" Stella continued. "They must let us keep the wigs. I'm going to ask if we can."

"Stella! Don't—" Issie stopped in mid-sentence as she heard the front door of the costume trailer swing open. The girls fell silent at the sound of a voice outside the trailer. It was a familiar voice. And so loud! Angelique Adams was positively screaming down her mobile phone as she walked into the costume trailer.

"Malcolm? Where the heck have y'all been?" Angelique shouted down the phone. "I've been trying to reach y'all for, like, a whole day! You're my agent!

Never, ever, ever switch off your phone!" There was silence for a moment as Angelique listened to the voice on the other end of the phone.

"Listen, Malcolm. I don't care about any of that. I want to talk about *The Palomino Princess*. It's a nightmare, Malcolm! You've got to get me off this film." There was more silence for a moment as Angelique listened again.

"Malcolm! I can't do this. I thought I could fake it, but I'm so scared. They're going to find out the truth sooner or later and when they do it will be a scandal! Malcolm, you have to get me out of here. I don't know how much longer I can keep this up. Malcolm?" Angelique sounded like she was going to cry.

"Malcolm, I can't talk any more right now. I'm relying on you. Get me off this film before they find out my secret. Do it or you're fired!" Angelique snapped the mobile phone shut just as Amber walked back in the door.

"Hi, Angelique!" she looked around. "Are the girls in here with you?"

Angelique looked puzzled. "What girls?"

"The stunt riders," Amber said. She looked around again and shrugged. "I guess they must have gone to make-up already."

"Yeah, what-ever," Angelique sighed.

Amber gave her a broad smile. "It's so great to be working with you. I've got your costumes all ready..."

Angelique shook her head. The phone call with her agent had left her frazzled. "Uh-uh, no way. I don't have time for this now. My masseuse is waiting for me back at my trailer. All this work is so exhausting!"

"But, Miss Adams!" Amber was panicking now. "I have to fit you for your gowns... Miss Adams?"

"OK then, you can bring them to my trailer. I'll try them on later." Angelique turned on her heels. "Well? Come on then! What are you waiting for?" she shouted at Amber. "And don't even think about bringing anything ugly. I can tell by what you're wearing that you have no taste!"

"Wow! What a brat!" Amber muttered under her breath as she grabbed an armful of dresses off the hanger by the door and raced off after Angelique. "Miss Adams!" she called out. "Miss Adams, wait! I've got the dresses... Miss Adams?" Amber chased after Angelique, leaving the trailer in total silence.

A whole minute later Stella finally stuck her head out, looking about nervously and checking if the coast was clear.

"Hey, you guys! It's safe!" she hissed to the others. "You can come back out now." One by one the other girls emerged from their changing rooms.

"What was that whole scene about?" Kate said, pulling off her blonde wig. "Why doesn't Angelique want to do the movie all of a sudden?"

"She said she was scared," Natasha shrugged. "Maybe someone is blackmailing her or something."

"Ohhh, ohhh! Yes!" Stella said excitedly. "I saw that in a movie once! I bet this sort of thing happens all the time to Hollywood stars. You heard what she said to that Malcolm guy on the phone. She said it would be a scandal if her secret got out!"

"OK, we don't really know what we heard, do we?" Issie began. "I mean maybe we got the wrong end of the stick. We couldn't even hear what he was saying to her on the other end of the phone."

"Maybe not," Stella said. "But I know what we heard. Angelique Adams wants to get off this movie. And she has a secret – a secret that no one knows about." Stella looked at the others. "No one… except us!"

Chapter 6

That night the girls got their chance to try and find out Angelique's secret. When they arrived at the dining hall for dinner Angelique was already there, and she was sitting at a table all by herself. "Well, almost by herself," Stella said, "if you don't count her bodyguard, her assistant and her make-up guy."

"We need to go and sit with her," Issie said decisively. "It's the only way to ask her questions and find out what's going on."

"Oh, really," sneered Natasha. "And what are you going to do? Just fill your plates up at the buffet and sit down with her? Cool."

"Come on, Natasha," Stella said. "Are you doing this with us or not?"

As they approached Angelique's dining table, their plates groaning with prawn risotto and salad, things were going smoothly. Until Angelique's massive bodyguard got up to block their path.

"Miss Adams don't wanna be disturbed," the guard said in a low growl.

"It's OK, Joe." Angelique waved him away with her hand. "They can sit with me." Joe sat back down reluctantly and Issie, Kate, Stella and Natasha all hurriedly grabbed a seat at the table before he changed his mind.

"Ummm, we're the palomino stunt riders. We met yesterday?" Issie said.

Angelique looked at her totally blankly. "What-ever," she said flatly.

"Ummm, yeah, well…" Issie stuttered, trying to stay cool. "Anyway, my Aunt Hester is the head trainer and tomorrow we're going to be riding the horses through a desensitising course…"

"We saw you on E! You know, talking about how you love horses?" Stella blurted out. "So we thought maybe you'd like to come to the stables with us tomorrow…"

Angelique gave a sigh. "Y'know, I really don't think so." Her voice was dripping with boredom. "I've got, like, a totally busy day." She looked at her hands.

"Like, I've totally, absolutely *got* to get a manicure."

"I know what you mean!" Natasha said brightly. "I am so over my nail colour right now!"

Natasha held out her hands for Angelique to see. The Teen Drama Queen peered at Natasha's fingers and for the first time since the girls had sat down she perked up a little. "Hey!" she said. "You're wearing Power Poppy Pink! That is so rad! It used to be totally my fave nail colour."

Natasha nodded. "I know, me too. But now I love Ultra…"

"Ultra-Violet by MAC!" Angelique finished her sentence for her. "That's what I always wear! Wow, you have great taste!"

Natasha looked at her chipped nails. "I know. I get a manicure every week, but horse riding always totally ruins it. I keep telling Mummy I should give up riding and then my nails would look good all the time, but she keeps buying me these expensive ponies…"

"That is so *awful* for you!" Angelique looked genuinely upset at this. She reached over and grabbed Natasha by the hand. "Hey, I know what we can do! I have two beauty therapists working for me back at my trailer. Why don't you come with me tomorrow after breakfast and we can both get a manicure at the same time? We can hang out and stuff."

"She can't!" Stella interrupted. "She has to come with us. We've got training to do."

Natasha glared at Stella. "I can get a manicure first!" she snapped. "Training isn't until the afternoon."

"But, Natasha, you're rostered on for dung duty, remember?" Stella objected.

Angelique smiled. "Hey, hey. I think y'all are forgettin' something, girlfriend," she said in a sarcastic tone. "I am the star here – and I decide." She turned to her assistant. "Debbie, go down to the arena right now and tell that trainer lady that Natasha is going to be too busy for her chores tomorrow. Tell her she's hanging out with me."

"Well!" Stella groaned as the girls walked back to the barracks after dinner. "That kind of backfired, didn't it? We're supposed to be finding out Angelique's secret – not her favourite nail colour!"

Natasha glared at Stella. "Oh, this is so typical! You're just jealous because Angelique wants to be my friend – not yours. I'm so over you and your attitude, Stella. I don't want anything to do with your stupid spying on Angelique anyway – find out her secret yourself if you're so smart!" She stomped off ahead in a huff leaving Stella, Kate and Issie behind.

"Jealous? As if I would be jealous of her!" Stella grumbled. "Just because she thinks Angelique Adams is her NBF! Stupid Stuck-up Tucker. I am so sick of her! Aren't you, Issie? Issie?"

Issie wasn't listening. She was deep in her own thoughts, thinking about their first riding session tomorrow. While Natasha was hanging out with Angelique, maybe it was time for her to make a new friend too. Tomorrow she was going to make a start with Stardust.

Issie woke up early the next morning and decided to skip breakfast and go straight to the stables.

"There is no better way to get to know a horse than with a body brush and a curry comb in your hand," Tom Avery always said. It was true. After all, hadn't Issie bonded with Blaze by grooming and caring for the chestnut mare? Issie loved grooming Blaze. She would spend hours and hours brushing her pony. Even now that Blaze was heavily pregnant she would still groom her every day, even if she wasn't riding her. Her favourite part was brushing out Blaze's gorgeous flaxen tail until it floated behind her like spun sugar candy. Blaze's favourite part was having the soft body brush used on her face just beneath her forelock. The mare would shut her eyes and go into a trance as Issie brushed her gently.

Issie looked at her grooming kit. She had packed everything neatly, including a rubber massage mitt which Blaze just loved. Hopefully Stardust would love it too. When she reached the stables, Stardust was standing with her head out over the top of the Dutch door. When she saw Issie coming though, she pulled her head back in and went to the furthest corner of her stall, making it clear that she wasn't keen on company.

"Hey, girl," Issie said softly as she opened the door to the loose box and walked in. She shouldered the halter she had brought with her, pulled a carrot out of her gilet pocket and offered it to the golden mare.

Stardust looked at the carrot, but she didn't move. Issie, too, stayed rooted to the spot. Finally, after a minute or so, Issie could see that Stardust wasn't going to budge. The game of wills had been played and Issie had lost. She stepped forward towards the mare and Stardust gave her a doleful look as she took the carrot out of Issie's hand.

"Good girl, Stardust, good girl," Issie cooed as she slipped the lead rope around Stardust's neck and began buckling up the halter over the mare's head. "I can see we're gonna get along just fine… owww!"

Stardust, who had finished her carrot, had made a sudden lunge forward as Issie was doing up the halter and managed to land a nasty nip on Issie's upper arm!

Issie squealed, letting go of the lead rope and grabbing at her sleeve. She instinctively stepped back from the palomino who was still glaring at her with her ears flat back.

"Stardust!" a voice over the Dutch door called out. Issie turned and saw Aidan standing there.

"Did she get you?" There was concern in Aidan's voice as he unbolted the door and dashed over to check on her.

"I, I don't think it's too bad," Issie said, trying desperately not to cry. "Aidan, I wasn't even doing anything! I was just trying to do up her halter and…"

"I know," Aidan said. "Believe me. It's not you. She's the same with everyone. She's tried to bite me loads of times." He rolled up the sleeve of Issie's shirt and checked her arm where Stardust had struck.

"You're lucky. She hasn't broken the skin. It's not a bad one," he said.

"It feels bad enough," Issie groaned.

"Come out of here for a minute and get your breath back," Aidan said, putting his arm round Issie and leading her out of the loose box. He sat down with her on a bale of hay. "She's been like that ever since she arrived at our stables," Aidan said. "I can't figure it out. Hester says she's a real star. She's done three movies already this year, but I can't get her to behave at all and I don't know what's wrong with her."

"Will Aunty Hess really get rid of her if she's no good?" Issie said. "Natasha said something. She was probably just being stupid but she said maybe Stardust would go to the glue factory."

Aidan shook his head. "I don't know. Hester doesn't own Stardust. It's up to her owners what happens to her." He looked at Issie. "You've got to remember that Stardust isn't a pony-club pony, she's a working horse. Movies are what she does and if she can't work as a stunt horse any more then I don't imagine that anyone is going to bother to pay for her upkeep."

Even though Stardust had just bitten her, Issie felt sick at the idea of something awful happening to the palomino.

"Hester is right then," she said. "You and me, we have to figure her out. We've got to get her to behave herself so she doesn't get kicked off this movie."

Aidan smiled at Issie. "What do you mean 'we'? You're the horse whisperer here. You'll figure her out, just like you did with Destiny."

"That was different!" Issie protested.

"He misses you, you know," Aidan said, looking at Destiny's stall. The big black horse had his head out over the top half of the door and was watching them.

"What do you mean?" Issie was confused.

"Destiny," Aidan said. "He misses you. After you left Blackthorn Farm, he kept trotting up and down the fenceline for days. He wouldn't settle down. It was as if he was waiting for you to come back again." Aidan looked at Issie. She was startled by how blue and intense his eyes were.

"Me too," he said softly.

"What?"

"I've missed you, Issie."

Issie felt her tummy doing flip-flops. "I, uhhh... ummm..." She felt Aidan's hand gently reaching out to take her own. He leant closer and Issie could feel his fringe against her cheek, tickling her skin.

"Hey!" Stella's voice shocked her back to reality. "There you both are! I've been looking for ages. Come on! Hester is here. We're ready to start the training session."

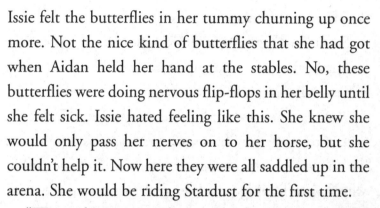

Issie felt the butterflies in her tummy churning up once more. Not the nice kind of butterflies that she had got when Aidan held her hand at the stables. No, these butterflies were doing nervous flip-flops in her belly until she felt sick. Issie hated feeling like this. She knew she would only pass her nerves on to her horse, but she couldn't help it. Now here they were all saddled up in the arena. She would be riding Stardust for the first time.

"We need to get straight into the desensitising work," Hester said to the girls as they walked across the sawdust floor of the arena. "Rupert, the director, wants us ready to be on the set with the palominos by next week. He's heard the rumours about the trouble we've been having with Stardust and I want to prove to him that the Daredevil Ponies are ready for action."

"Who are the Daredevil Ponies?" Issie looked confused.

"We are! That's the name of my stunt horse company – the Daredevil Ponies. Chase scenes, battle scenes, stampedes – there's no stunt that's too wild or too dangerous for my daredevils." Hester smiled. "Now let's get training, shall we?" She handed the girls helmets and back protectors. "Put these on please. When you're doing the stunts for the cameras you'll have to ride without any helmets. But at practice time we always wear them."

Stella wasn't paying attention though. She was busy staring at the curious set-up in the middle of the arena. "What's all that junk?" she asked.

"Stella, that's not junk," Hester grinned. "That is a crucial part of your film training. It's an obstacle course. These ponies will encounter many strange situations when we're filming and I've tried to recreate the same obstacles here in the training arena," Hester said. "They need to be bombproof – they must not bolt or shy or buck no matter what distractions we throw at them. We'll take them through the course here and see if they have any weaknesses that we need to work on."

Hester strode over to the middle of the arena. "At the start of the course, I want each of you to canter over to the centre of the arena and grab your sword out of the box here without getting off your horse." She pointed to the broadswords, which were facing blade downwards with their handles sticking out of the tea chest in the middle of the arena. "They're not real of course; they're made of hardwood," she said, picking one up and waving it about expertly.

"Then you ride back over here." Hester strode over to a big pile of black blankets. "This is obstacle number one. You must make your horses stand perfectly still while Aidan and I flap these at you. The vampire riders wear big black capes that billow in the breeze – so your horses need to become accustomed to black flappy things in their faces."

The second obstacle was a row of bending poles surrounded by big lights, which were set up at blinding angles and kept flashing on and off. "You have to wind your way through the poles, teaching the horses to ignore the lights," Hester said. "They must get used to the bright lighting on the film set."

The last obstacle was a row of straw dummies which had been strapped on to poles with bullseyes painted on their hessian-sack chests.

"Now this one is fun! You line up here, then ride straight at the dummy with your weapon held high and thrust it into his chest to hit the bullseye!" Hester looked at the girls. "We'll do it at a canter today and work up to a gallop by the end of the week."

"A gallop!" Stella squeaked. "So when we do this for real in the movie we'll be galloping with no helmets?"

"Well, yes, poppet." Hester smiled at her. "You're stunt riders. What did you think you'd be doing? This isn't a pony-club games day, sweetie. This is daredevil stuff!"

Stella's face turned pale. "But I've never even used a sword…"

Hester laughed. "Stella! You're on Paris. She knows exactly what to do. She's been well trained. She'll never put a hoof wrong, I promise you." Hester saw the uncertain looks on her riders' faces. "Right then! Issie, why don't you start? Go ahead on Stardust and show them how it's done."

Issie's butterflies were positively doing cartwheels now as she clucked Stardust forward and stood in front of everyone at the start of the course.

"Right then," Hester said, "canter Stardust to the tea chest and get your sword."

This was easier said than done. Stardust didn't seem to want to canter. The mare had her ears back in a grumpy mood and the most she would do was trot over to the tea chest. Then, when they reached the box, Stardust shivered and snorted and refused to get close enough for Issie to take a sword out.

"Stardust! What's wrong?" Issie gave the mare a tap with her heels, but instead of responding and moving forward, Stardust began to fret and pace about on the spot. She wasn't listening to Issie at all.

"Aidan," Hester said, "run over there, would you, and grab a sword out for Issie?" Aidan nodded and set off at a jog across the sawdust arena. He reached the box and pulled out one of the wooden broadswords. Then he walked over to Stardust, who was now backing away from him and trembling, and passed the sword up so that Issie could grasp the handle.

Issie had barely a moment to feel the weight of the sword in her hand before everything went bad. Suddenly, without any warning, Stardust went straight up on her hind legs and reared, flinging Issie backwards out of the saddle. Issie instantly dropped the sword and grabbed with both hands for Stardust's mane as the mare rose up on her hindquarters, thrashing her legs in the air.

"Hold on!" Aidan yelled as he came running back towards her to help.

Issie clung on for dear life. What else could she do? By the time Aidan reached her side, Stardust landed back down on the ground with Issie as white as a sheet.

"Ohmygod! Stardust!" Issie was shaking with shock.

But before she could gather her wits – and her reins – Stardust began to perform her next trick. The golden palomino dropped suddenly to her knees. "Stardust!" Issie shrieked. She had been ready for the mare to misbehave, but she hadn't been expecting anything like this. Stardust was still on her knees and was ignoring Issie's frantic kicks. "Get up, Stardust!" Issie growled.

"Hoi hoi! Up, girl!" Aunt Hester barked at the mare as she ran forward to help. But Stardust ignored Aidan and Hester and kept lowering herself so that she was now almost lying down on her side.

"Jump!" Hester yelled at Issie. "Isadora – jump! Do it now!"

Issie suddenly realised the danger she was in. Stardust was about to roll on top of her! If she didn't leap off now, she would be crushed beneath the weight of the enormous horse. Instinctively, she threw herself into the air, flying sideways out of the saddle. She managed to land clear of Stardust, falling hard to the ground and inhaling a mouthful of sawdust from the arena floor. Sputtering and coughing, she dragged herself up to her knees, quickly crawling on all fours to get out of the palomino's way. She was just in time before Stardust crashed to the ground right beside her and then began to roll.

"Stardust!" Issie squealed as she felt Hester's hands wrap around her waist and drag her out of harm's way.

"Nothing broken?" Hester asked.

"I'm OK," Issie nodded. "Aunty Hess – why did she do that? It was like she did it on purpose…" Issie looked at Stardust who was now rolling back and forth with her legs thrashing the air. There was an awful crack as she rolled right over on her saddle.

"That's the tree broken. That saddle is ruined!" Hester said as she helped Issie to stand up. "Still, thank God you're OK!" She dusted the sawdust off Issie's back. "I really don't know what has got into that mare—"

"Hello, Hester! Everything going well?" a voice suddenly boomed across the arena.

Issie and the others had been so busy with Stardust that they hadn't noticed a scruffy man with dark glasses and a beard walking towards them. The man was accompanied by a girl, also in dark glasses and jeans, with her hair tied back in a bandana.

"Rupert! Oh… ahh… What a surprise!" Hester faltered. "We weren't expecting you until tomorrow…"

"I know." The man took off his sunglasses as he came closer. "I wasn't going to be on set until then, but I ran into Angelique." He gestured to the girl next to him and

Issie finally realised that it was Angelique Adams – almost unrecognisable in her dark glasses and a scarf. She looked sulky, but she gave a reluctant smile when Rupert cast a glance in her direction.

"So, when I heard that you guys were rehearsing I thought, *Hey, why not drop by with Angelique?* It's a great chance for her to meet the palominos."

Hester tried to smile at this. "Uh-huh," she said weakly. "Well, we're right in the middle of rehearsals at the moment…"

"I can see that. And this is Stardust, right?"

"Yes."

"Well then – let's get started!" Rupert smiled. Then he turned to Issie. "You don't mind if Angelique takes Stardust for a ride, do you?"

Issie felt her heart race. What could she say? What could she do to stop this happening? If Angelique got on Stardust now, it would be a disaster!

"Ummm… uh…"

"Excellent!" Rupert said. "Angelique, my superstar rider, this is your moment. Let's get you up on this horse! We're all dying to see you ride!"

Chapter 7

What a disaster! Angelique mustn't ride Stardust! Not now. Issie had been lucky to escape without being injured – but what if the Hollywood superstar wasn't so lucky? They couldn't risk it. They had to stop her – but how?

Issie turned to Aunt Hester. She could see that her aunt was thinking the same thing, both of them desperately searching for a way to prevent disaster.

"I... the thing is..." Issie began. But before she could finish she was interrupted.

"Rupert! What a great idea!" Angelique smiled. "I would love to ride." She paused and pushed her sunglasses back on to her headscarf, locking her violet eyes on the director. "But I think the hair and make-up department are expecting me back for a make-up check. Can we do it tomorrow instead?"

Rupert smiled. "Hey, Angelique, of course! Whatever you say."

"Fabulous!" Angelique purred. "Really – I can't wait. I just love horses sooo much, I can't wait to get ridin'." She shot Stardust a nervous glance and then pushed her sunglasses back down again. "Alrighty," she said, heading for the arena entrance. "Well, I better get to make-up. I'll see y'all later, OK?"

"See you later, Angelique – come and see Hester for a training session tomorrow, OK?" Rupert said.

"For sure!" Angelique grinned as she headed out of the arena gate.

Rupert turned his attention to Issie. "I'm sorry, I don't believe we've met yet. I should have introduced myself earlier. I'm Rupert Conrad, the director of this movie. And you are?" He put out his hand for her to shake.

"Issie, ummm… I mean Isadora Brown," Issie said nervously. "I'm Hester's niece. I'm one of the stunt riders." Issie pointed to her friends standing beside her with their palominos. "And this is Stella, Natasha and Kate. They're all stunt riders too."

Rupert stood and looked Issie up and down. Then he held his hands together in front of his face and made a square with his fingers, closing one eye and squinting at Issie through the hole. He shook his head. "You're not one of the stunt riders," he said firmly.

"I'm not?" Issie said.

"No," Rupert said. "You are much more than that. You… are Angelique Adams's stunt double!"

"What?"

"Hester, your niece is perfect!" Rupert said. "With a blonde wig and a bit of make-up no one will be able to tell her and Angelique apart." He put his hand on Issie's shoulder. "Tell Amber in the costume department that you're the one. When you report to make-up tomorrow before the shoot, get her to dress you as Galatea, OK?"

"OK," Issie said. She was hoping Rupert would take his hand off her shoulder before he noticed that she was shaking with nerves. A few minutes ago she had been scrambling about on her belly in the sawdust trying not to get rolled on by a horse that could crush her to death, and now here she was being cast as a stunt double for the world's most famous teenager! Could this day get any crazier?

"Don't get too excited about this," Rupert added. "There may not be much riding in it for you. As you probably know, Angelique is a great rider – she'll be doing most of her own stunts. You'll probably just be watching from the sidelines."

Rupert clapped his hands together decisively. "Well, that's settled! Excellent."

He turned to Hester. "I was planning on hanging about a bit longer to see you all rehearse, but I'm already behind schedule. I've got a meeting with my special-effects team now. Would you mind if we left it at that for the day?"

"Of course!" Hester said, trying not to sound too relieved. "We wouldn't want to hold you up!"

"Nice to meet you, girls." Rupert waved to Stella, Kate and Natasha. "And you, my new stunt double!" He smiled at Issie.

As Rupert left the arena, Stella couldn't keep quiet any longer. "Ohmygod, Issie, are you OK? You could have been killed! Stardust went totally crazy on you!"

"Stella's right," Hester agreed. Her face was grave. "I'm sorry, Isadora. I knew this mare was trouble, but I had no idea she would do that. I taught her that rolling trick and now she's using it to get rid of her rider. You could have been crushed underneath her if you hadn't leapt off in time."

Issie looked at her aunt. "You mean you taught Stardust how to roll like that?"

Hester nodded. "Her owners had already schooled her in all the classic tricks. I showed her a few new ones, like the rolling. I use the same cues with Diablo to make him lie down and play dead. Stardust is a fast learner. She's so smart she can pick up a new trick like that almost instantly. But those tricks have become dangerous now she's acting like this."

"Aunty Hess, maybe it was my fault," Issie said. "Could it have been something I did that triggered Stardust's behaviour?"

"Yes, well… I suppose that's possible," Hester said. "Stardust's not as push-button as one of my own horses like Diablo or Paris. She's had other trainers and they may have used different cues to make her perform. Perhaps we're giving her the wrong signals."

Hester looked warily at the palomino mare. "Issie, I think we'd better call it a day for you. Why don't you take Stardust back to her loose box while I run the others quickly through the obstacle course?"

Issie was only too happy to agree. She'd had quite enough of Stardust's strange behaviour for one day. Even walking the mare back to the stall made Issie nervous. Stardust had her ears flat back the whole time and Issie had to keep an eye on her in case she tried to bite again.

As she put Stardust back in her stall and took off the crushed saddle with its broken tree, Issie felt sick; she could have been crushed beneath the palomino too. She felt so nervous around Stardust, she was tempted to leave her without even bothering to groom her. Reluctantly she picked up a body brush and began to brush the mare where her saddle had been. As Stardust met Issie's eyes with a cold stare she realised the truth. *I have no trust in her. We've got no bond.*

Issie shook her head. She was being negative. This was silly. Of course they didn't have a bond yet. She had only just met this horse. OK, Stardust may not have been exactly friendly so far, and OK, they hadn't got off to a great start. But surely the whole rearing and rolling incident had been a big misunderstanding? Stardust was a stunt horse after all. Issie had probably given her the wrong signals by mistake and that had caused her to act up. They would get used to each other. All they needed was time.

Issie had given Stardust her hard feed and was brushing the last of the sawdust out of the mare's mane when Natasha stuck her head over the Dutch door of the stall.

"What's taking you so long? We're all waiting for you, you know," Natasha sighed. "The rest of us are ready to go back up to the barracks now, but Stella said we have to wait for you."

"Yeah, just give me a minute," Issie said. She hurriedly put on Stardust's cover, aware that Natasha was glaring at her with contempt the whole time. As if she didn't have enough problems! Now Natasha was annoyed with her for some reason.

The walk home to the barracks was super-painful. Stella wouldn't shut up about how lucky Issie was to be picked as Angelique Adams's stunt double and Natasha wouldn't stop sulking.

"I can't believe Rupert asked you. You're so lucky, Issie!"

"Stella!" Issie groaned. "How am I lucky? If I'm Angelique's stunt double then I'll have to ride Stardust. And you saw what she just did to me! You were right! I could have been killed."

When they finally reached the barracks, Issie headed for her room. She was desperate to lie down, stick her head under her pillow and forget about everything. Unfortunately, Natasha had other plans. She followed Issie into their room and slammed the door behind her. Then she took off her riding boots and threw them noisily into the closet and began to stomp about the room, harrumphing and bristling as she rearranged her teddy bear and hot-water bottle on her bedspread. When Issie reached for the copy of *PONY Magazine* on their dressing table, Natasha shot her a filthy look.

"I was going to read that!" She grabbed it back.

"It's my magazine!" Issie said, snatching at it.

"You know what your problem is?" Natasha snapped at her. "You're not used to sharing anything. You're a spoilt only child who gets everything – and you always get your own way. And now…" Natasha fumed "…now you get to be Angelique Adams's stunt double when it should be me!"

"What?" Issie was stunned.

"It should be me!" Natasha yelled at her. "Angelique is my best friend, not yours! Besides, I look more like her than you do. I even have long blonde hair! I'm just as good a rider as you are, Isadora! Why do you always get to do everything?" She threw the copy of *PONY Magazine* across the room at Issie.

"Here!" she snapped. "You take it. You always get everything in the end anyway – so just go ahead and take it!"

"Natasha, I know you're having a hard time right now because of your mum and dad…" Issie began.

The look on Natasha's face turned to thunder. "I

knew I shouldn't have told you about that!" she shouted. "I suppose you've told Stella and Kate? I know you all talk about me. You're just horrible!" And with that, Natasha stormed out of the room and slammed the door behind her.

Issie sat down on her bed and reached for the crumpled copy of *PONY Magazine*. Her hands were shaking again after Natasha's little screaming session. She hadn't told Stella and Kate anything! And did Natasha really think that Issie had stolen away her chance to stunt-double for Angelique on purpose, just to make her miserable? Issie shook her head. Natasha was nuts. As if it wasn't bad enough having to ride psycho Stardust in this movie – now her room-mate hated her for it.

The door to Issie's room creaked open and Stella stuck her head around it. "Is it safe to come in?" she asked. Issie nodded and Stella came in, followed by Kate.

"What was that about? We heard her yelling from all the way down the hall," Kate said.

Issie told the girls what Natasha had said – minus all the stuff about her parents of course.

"Ohmygod, she is such a stuck-up brat!" Stella said. "Does she really think she's best friends with Angelique? As if! Natasha just wants everything her own way. That's why she can't stand it that you're going to be Angelique's stunt double instead of her."

Issie shook her head in disbelief. "She was just so angry at me. It's not my fault that Rupert picked me!"

"Of course it's not your fault!" Kate said. "Natasha just can't help herself. She doesn't know how to be nice. Forget about it." She gave Issie a hug. "Do you want to move into our room with us?"

Issie felt a hot tear making its way down her left cheek. She rubbed it away angrily with her sleeve. "No. I mean thanks and all that, but no. It'll just make things worse if she thinks I've moved out and we've all ganged up on her."

Kate nodded. "You're right. We'll just leave her alone and let her calm down. I'm sure she'll get over it."

Natasha, however, seemed in no hurry to get over things at all. She spent the rest of the evening ignoring everyone and watching TV, and when it was time to go to the dining hall for dinner she promptly left without them. The girls arrived at the buffet to find that Natasha had already filled her plate and was sitting at a table by herself.

"Should we sit with her?" Issie asked.

"Too late for that," Stella said as Angelique Adams and her entourage walked into the dining hall. Angelique waved at Natasha and made a beeline for her table with her assistant, Tony the make-up artist and Eugene and Bob all trailing along behind her. Issie watched as Eugene circled round Angelique and Natasha with his camera, filming them as they sat and ate together. Then she saw Natasha smile at Angelique and point over towards Issie and whisper. Angelique giggled and then said something to Eugene who nodded and immediately scurried over towards Issie, Kate and Stella.

"Sorry, girls," he said, "you're ruining my documentary. You'll have to leave."

"What do you mean?" Stella said. "We're just sitting here and eating our dinner."

"Exactly," Eugene said. "You're in the way. I can't film if you're sitting here making Angelique uncomfortable. She told me to ask you to leave."

"Oh, really!" Stella said. "Well, you tell Angelique and her friend Stuck-up Tucker that…"

"Hey, Stella, forget it," Issie said. She wasn't about to start a fight with Natasha and Angelique. She didn't need any more drama today. "We can take our plates back to the barracks and eat there." She picked up her plate to leave. "Let's go."

When they got back to the barracks, though, Issie didn't

bother to finish her dinner. She felt too sick to eat anyway. She couldn't believe she had to get back on Stardust again tomorrow. For the first time ever in her life, Issie found herself dreading the idea of getting on a horse.

"I know how you feel. You had a bad fall," Aunt Hester said when Issie told her about her fears the next morning. "But you know the magic rule when you fall off a horse. You have to get straight back on again."

Except, Issie couldn't help thinking, *except I didn't fall from this horse; she deliberately tried to crush me – that's kind of different.*

They were standing in the middle of the arena, with Stardust tacked up and ready to go. Issie watched as Aunt Hester walked over to the mare and attached a long webbing lunge rein, clipping it on to the bit and running it over the mare's poll and down the other side.

"Before you get on her, let's try putting Stardust through her paces on the lunge rein," Hester said. "Run the stirrups up the leathers, will you, dear?"

Issie slid the irons up on their leathers so that they didn't bounce against the mare's sides and then she stood back as Aunt Hester led Stardust into the centre of the arena.

"Tsk tsk, walk on!" Hester clucked at the palomino to get her moving, and Stardust obeyed her commands, stepping out on the lunge at a brisk walk. The lunge rein was about three metres long. Hester held the end of the rein and her eyes followed the mare as she circled around her.

"Trot on!" Hester called out and again Stardust immediately obliged, breaking into a trot on command.

"She's got the most lovely trot!" Issie called out to her aunt.

"That's nothing, wait until you see her canter," Hester grinned. "Come on, Stardust, canter on!"

Hester was right. Stardust had a canter that almost seemed to float above the ground – she was as graceful as a ballerina. Issie could see why Rupert had cast this mare in his movie. With her silver mane and tail flowing out behind her, she looked exactly like the sort of pony that belongs to a princess. Stardust shook her mane and arched her neck, as if she knew that she was the centre of attention as she circled round and round the arena.

"And steady… walk on! And… halt!" Hester instructed. Stardust did just as she was asked, pulling up on the lunge and stopping in front of Hester in a perfect square halt.

"Good girl, Stardust!" Hester said, walking forward and giving the mare a slappy pat on her glossy neck. "Ready to get on her now then?" she asked her niece.

"What, now?" Issie squeaked.

"It's OK," Hester said, running the stirrups back down the leathers. "I'll keep her on the lunge rein. She'll be under my control."

Issie nodded. "All right."

"I'll give you a leg up," Hester said, holding out a hand. Issie put her knee into Hester's palm and her aunt gave her a boost up on to Stardust's back.

"OK?" Hester said. "Let's go."

As Hester led Issie and Stardust back into the centre of the arena, Issie realised that something was missing. The tea chest full of wooden swords was gone.

"Yes, the props department needed it back apparently. You'll have to ride the obstacle course without a sword today, I'm afraid," Hester said.

"I'm going to do the obstacle course?" Issie felt the panic rising in her.

"Not yet. Don't worry, we'll make sure she's well warmed up on the lunge first," Hester said gently. She stood in the centre of the arena and Issie rode Stardust out so that she was at the full length of the lunge rein, walking in a circle round Aunt Hester.

"Trot on!" Hester called out. Issie didn't even need to do anything. She just sat in the saddle while the palomino responded to Hester's voice. Stardust stepped out in a floating trot, her neck arched and her tail swishing. "She seems very happy and you look perfect on her!" Hester called out to Issie with a grin. Issie realised she was grinning too. She felt her nerves melt away with each stride. Stardust was so lovely to ride; it was like being on a cloud.

"Canter!" Hester called, and Stardust obediently rose up into an easy canter. It felt as smooth as a rocking horse. They did a few more circles in each direction at the canter and the trot before Hester pulled Stardust to a halt in the centre of the ring.

"Good girl!" Issie said, giving the mare a hearty slap. "Good Stardust!" She had a smile from ear to ear.

"Well," Hester said, looking pleased, "that went very well. She seems to have settled down with you now. Maybe you're right, Issie, perhaps there was some trigger that made her misbehave yesterday."

Hester looked at her watch. "I was expecting Angelique to turn up for training," she shrugged. "Looks like she isn't coming – and it might be just as well! That gives us time to take Stardust through the obstacle course. We don't have to of course. We could leave it until tomorrow. Filming doesn't start until next Monday so we've still got a day or so to get her ready…"

"No, you haven't! Not any more. There's no time!" A voice across the other side of the arena startled them. Issie and her aunt looked up to see Aidan sprinting towards them across the arena. He had been running so hard he was short of breath and it took a moment for him to pull himself together and speak.

"I just saw Rupert at the dining hall," he panted. "He's posted up a new schedule. The crew are furious. He's changed everything. Apparently it's because they're worried about the weather turning bad. There's a storm forecast for next week and they can't afford to be delayed, so they've moved the whole shooting schedule forward instead." Aidan paused once more, crouching over his knees to catch his breath.

"What do you mean he's moved shooting forward?" Hester was confused.

"Rupert's rescheduled everything, including all the scenes with the horses," Aidan said. "He's going to be filming the forest chase scene tomorrow."

"What does that mean?" Issie asked.

"It means," said Aidan, "that Stardust has to be ready to film her big scene first thing in the morning."

Issie couldn't believe it. She had just started to make a breakthrough with Stardust, and now this! Would Stardust be ready to start filming by tomorrow? Issie felt the butterflies in her tummy returning. Stardust was still so unpredictable. Only one thing was certain: Issie had to be prepared for the worst.

Chapter 8

Stella squealed with excitement and threw herself down in the make-up chair.

"Ohmygod! This is so glamorous!" She beamed over at Issie, Kate and Natasha who were in the chairs next to her also having their make-up applied. "I can't believe we're actually on the set of a real movie!"

"Less giggling please, Stella," Hester said. "Don't forget, you're a Daredevil rider now, so act professional!"

"I *am* a professional! I'm a natural movie star!" Stella grinned. "Did you see our grand entrance, Hester?"

Hester groaned. "Trust me, Stella, *everyone* saw that."

The shooting location this morning was a ridge on the farm, not too far from the stables, and Aunt Hester had suggested that the four girls ride the palominos to the set.

She hadn't expected them to gallop up the hill together in a row, whooping and hollering like cowgirls, waving their hands in the air.

"We were just warming up and getting into character!" Stella had pouted when Hester told them off for being irresponsible.

Once they had tethered their palominos to one of the silver crew trucks, the girls were whisked off to have make-up and wigs applied before they got into their costumes. Meanwhile, the rest of the film crew were busily scurrying about the trucks. The girls watched as the men unloaded the lighting rigs, cameras and props.

"All this just for one scene?" Kate said.

"It's not just any scene!" Stella said. "This is the chase in the forest when the princess riders get away from the vampire horsemen. It's one of the most exciting bits in the whole book."

Hester looked over at Issie, who hadn't said anything since the girls had arrived on the set. "You're very quiet, Isadora. Are you OK?"

Issie smiled. "Sure, I'm fine, Aunty Hess."

The truth was she wasn't fine at all. Yesterday's training session had gone well. No, it had been better than that, Stardust hadn't made a single mistake. Issie had even ridden her through the obstacle course and Stardust hadn't put a hoof wrong. Still, even though the palomino seemed to be behaving herself, Issie couldn't help feeling there was something wrong with this horse – as if she was just waiting for the chance to try one of her tricks again.

Issie had really tried to make friends with Stardust. She had spent ages grooming her after their training session and had even smuggled extra carrots and some sugar cubes in her pocket for the mare. But sugar treats weren't going to win Stardust over and deep down in her horsy instincts Issie knew it. Sure, Stardust had stopped trying to bite her, but there was still no bond between them. It was as if Issie was an annoying fly buzzing around and Stardust was just waiting for her chance to flick her tail and swat her away.

"It's like she hates me or something," Issie had told Stella and Kate when she arrived back at the barracks that night.

"You're being ridiculous!" Kate said. "Stardust does not hate you. You know, Issie, you can't expect every horse to be like Blaze. Blaze is special. You saved her life and she loves you because of that, because of everything you've been through together. Stardust doesn't even know you yet. You just need to give her some time, that's all."

Maybe Kate was right, Issie thought. But it didn't matter. There was no time. This was it. They were on the film set and Stardust had to be ready for action. Issie felt a shiver run up her spine. Oh well, the chances were that she wasn't going to be in this scene anyway. Angelique was supposed to be riding Stardust today. Issie would just be standing on the sidelines in her blonde wig, watching along with everyone else.

"Can I have your attention, everyone?" Rupert shouted out. He was standing on top of a camera dolly next to one of the silver trucks and already a large crowd of cameramen and lighting operators, make-up artists and assistants had gathered round him. At the back of the crowd were the vampire riders, all of them mounted up on their black horses. Issie recognised Aidan on a dyed-black Diablo and gave him a wave. He waved back and smiled, revealing a set of fake white vampire fangs.

"Hurry up and come over to join us, please, palomino riders!" Rupert called to the girls. Issie, Stella, Kate and Natasha instantly did as Rupert said, riding their horses over to where the others were standing.

"Right!" he said once everyone was assembled. "Today we're shooting the scene where the vampire riders chase Galatea and her princesses through the forest of Eleria…"

"Where's Princess Galatea then?" Stella whispered to Issie.

The girls looked around. Angelique was nowhere to be seen.

"I think she's still in her trailer," Issie said, pointing to a long silver caravan with the name Angelique Adams on the door in large hot-pink letters.

At that moment, the door swung open and Angelique emerged from her trailer followed by a string of make-up artists, costume people, personal assistants carrying her coffee and mobile phone and, of course, Eugene and Bob, who were circling her like sharks with their camera.

"Good timing, Angelique!" Rupert called to his star. "Come on over! I was just explaining the scene."

Angelique was expressionless behind her dark glasses as she walked towards them. She snapped her fingers at one of her assistants who quickly handed over her coffee. When she saw Issie and the other girls all mounted on their horses, Angelique seemed to falter for a moment. She walked in a wide circle around them, positioning herself at the rear of the crowd as the director spoke.

"OK, as I was saying, here's what we'll be shooting today," Rupert explained. "We'll be doing the whole chase scene as one single take. Angelique, that means that when Francis and his vampires start to chase you and the princesses, you're going to ride right along the ridge ahead of us here, OK? Then the princesses will act as a decoy and lead the vampire riders off to the left. All the vampires will follow the princesses. Except for Francis. He'll stay on your tail. You just keep riding straight ahead along the ridge, weaving through the trees until you reach that large oak – straight past that tree and Aidan will follow you."

Aidan nodded at this and Rupert turned his attention to him. "Aidan, you'll be at the front of the vampire riders. I want you to stay close to Angelique, just a couple of horse lengths behind her. This is the scene where Galatea only just escapes Francis, so when you pass the oak tree and the trees start to get more dense, that's when you make your move. I need you to come right up next to her, so close that you actually touch her. Make a grab for her. We want it to look like she's in real trouble, OK?"

"No problem!" Aidan said cheerfully.

"Excellent. Can we have the camera crews in position and lighting technicians do your checks now, please? I want everybody ready in five minutes for our first run-through," Rupert said.

"You heard him!" the assistant director barked. "Come

on, everyone, let's go! Can the riders mount up, please?"

Rupert glanced over at Issie. "Isadora," he said, "you won't be riding. You can hand Stardust over to Angelique for this scene, thanks."

Issie dismounted from Stardust and began to lead her towards Angelique, ready to hand the reins over to the actress so that she could mount up. When Angelique saw Issie coming towards her, her expression turned sour. Issie smiled and gave a friendly wave as she led the palomino towards her, but Angelique just glared back at her.

Issie was still a few metres away from the Hollywood star when Angelique let out the most bloodcurdling scream.

"Oww! Ohh! Ohhhhhhh!" Angelique yelled.

"What?" Issie was panic-stricken. "What's wrong?"

Angelique flopped down dramatically on the ground, cradling her foot in her hands. Her face was screwed up with pain and she was whimpering pitifully.

"Owwww!" Angelique screamed again. "Rupert! Ohmygod! This… this… idiot here just made the horse stamp on my foot!"

Issie looked at Angelique in amazement. "What?" she said. "But I…"

"Don't say another word!" Angelique shouted at her. "You're a total incompetent. This is so unprofessional! I don't believe it!" She was still clutching her foot and rolling about on the ground.

"Get the doctor!" Rupert shouted at one of his assistants as he raced over to his star's side. "Angelique! Are you OK?"

"No, Rupert," Angelique was sobbing now, "I think… I think it's broken!"

"Quick! Ice packs!" Rupert shouted to another crew member.

"Oh, and can you get me another coffee?" Angelique asked her assistant, pausing suddenly between sobs to order a latte.

As she sat on the ground with the crew gathered around her, Eugene and Bob hovered like vultures with their camera whirring the whole time. "Angel sweetheart! This is great! We're getting terrific footage!" Eugene burbled.

"Eugene! My foot! Show some sympathy!" Angelique snapped. Then, when she realised the camera was still rolling, she looked directly down the lens with a pouty, pained expression. As Eugene came in for a close-up, Angelique allowed a single, solitary tear to trickle down her cheek. Issie couldn't believe what she was seeing.

"But, but I…" she began.

"Hey!" Eugene snapped over his shoulder at her. "Get

that horse out of here! I think you've done enough damage, don't you?"

Bewildered, Issie led Stardust back out of the way of the crowd, over to where Stella, Kate and Natasha were standing.

"What an idiot! I can't believe you let Stardust stand on her foot!" Natasha hissed at Issie.

"I didn't!" Issie hissed back. "I swear. We were nowhere near her! We were miles away and suddenly Angelique just collapsed on the ground and started wailing!"

Angelique's hysterics reached a peak just as the paramedics arrived. "Well," Stella said, "if Stardust didn't stand on her foot then she sure is a great actress!"

The crowd around Angelique had become even bigger now as the paramedics moved her on to a stretcher and began to carry her back to her trailer.

"Angel! No, Angel!" Eugene ran after her, his camera still rolling. Then the little man left Angelique's side and scurried over to Rupert. "This is no good! You gotta make her ride!" Eugene shouted at him. "Strap her foot up! Do what it takes. I need her to ride this scene! I need more drama!"

Rupert stared coolly at Eugene. "She's my star, Eugene, and she's been injured. If she rides now, she may make the injury worse and then she won't be able to work at all."

Eugene rubbed his hands together anxiously. "But, Rupert, you've got to—"

"I don't have to do anything, Eugene," Rupert frowned. "Angelique may have given you permission to get underfoot, trailing her around like a dog to make your behind-the-scenes special, but don't forget that I'm the one who makes the decisions on this movie. You're just a two-bit documentary maker." He turned to Issie.

"Mount up!" Rupert said gruffly. "You've injured my star and now it looks like you're getting rewarded for it – I need you to ride the scene."

"But I didn't…" Issie began to say. But it was too late. Rupert had already turned his back on her and was barking at his crew, yelling at them to get into position.

"Let's move!" he snapped. "Positions, everyone – now!"

"Are you OK, Isadora?" Aunt Hester asked.

"Aunty Hess!" Issie said. "I wasn't even near Angelique! Stardust didn't stand on her foot! I don't know what's happening – this is crazy!"

Hester looked concerned. "Really?" she said. "Well, we'll discuss it later. But right now, Issie, I need you to ride. Are you up for it?"

Issie looked at Stardust. She still didn't trust this horse. All of her horsy instincts screamed out that she shouldn't do this. But after Angelique's drama-queen moment just now, the whole crew was furious with her because they believed that she'd injured the star. If she refused to ride, well, she would get fired for sure, and Aunt Hester probably would be too. Everyone was relying on her. She had no choice.

"I'm fine, Aunty Hess." She gave her aunt a weak smile. "Let's go."

The vampire riders, Issie, Kate, Natasha and Stella all got into position at the start of the ridge track and Rupert ran them through the scene one more time.

"You, Galatea! Keep going at full gallop the entire time. The vampire riders will follow you all the way past those trees to the big oak on the ridge. That's your marker, OK? At the big tree, the rest of the princesses and palominos will turn to the left and lead the vampires away from you. You'll keep on riding into the woods and Aidan will follow at a gallop. That's when he'll gain on you and try to pull you off your horse. You have to swing at him with your sword while you're galloping. OK?"

Issie looked at the ridge they were going to ride along. It was dotted with enormous trees which the riders would need to weave in and out of as they rode. It was easy to tell which one was the big oak because it was twice the size of the others.

"So, I stay in front of the other riders?" Issie asked.

Rupert nodded. "But don't get too far in front or it won't look exciting enough. You must make it look as if it's a matter of life and death." He looked at the riders. "Right then. Everyone ready? Let's do the first take, shall we?"

The riders prepared to gallop on Rupert's command.

"Positions, everyone!" Rupert shouted to his crew.

"Ready to go!" the reply came back.

"All right. Riders ready? On my say-so… and…"

"Hey, hold on! Wait!" There was a shout as a man from the props department ran forward. He was waving a wooden broadsword in his hand. "Sorry, Rupert," he said. "My fault entirely. I almost forgot that Galatea is supposed to be carrying a sword in this scene."

Rupert nodded. "Hurry up and get in there, then, and give it to her."

The props man stepped forward with the broadsword and Issie felt Stardust tense underneath her. The mare stepped backwards nervously and Issie had to hold her tightly so that she could reach down and take the sword from the props man. As they took their positions again,

Issie realised something was wrong. Stardust was trembling, her muscles twitching, her tail swishing anxiously.

"Steady, girl, steady. What's wrong?" Issie's voice was low and soft as she spoke gently to the mare, trying to soothe her. But Stardust wasn't listening and there wasn't any time to calm the mare down.

"Lights!" Rupert called. "Camera and… action!"

The call took Issie by surprise. She had been busy fumbling with her reins trying to figure out how to grip the broadsword and hold back Stardust at the same time. Now, at Rupert's call, Stardust sprang forward like a racehorse from a starting gate, startling Issie so that she was left behind in the saddle. She made a desperate grab at Stardust's mane with one hand to keep her balance, still managing to hold on to the reins and her sword in the other.

"Steady, girl!" Stardust had broken so swiftly when Rupert called action that she was already too far out in front of the other horses. Issie needed to slow the mare down. If Stardust got too far away from Aidan and the vampire riders, it would totally ruin the scene.

Issie hauled back on the reins and for a moment Stardust seemed to slow her stride. Behind her, she could hear the thunder of hooves as Kate, Stella and Natasha galloped after her on their palominos. She turned round to check and saw the girls riding hard, with the black horses and the vampire riders following at their heels. Issie felt a chill run through her as she realised just how dangerous this stunt really was. The other horses were so close behind and galloping so fast that she couldn't afford to make a mistake. If she fell off Stardust right now, she would be directly in their path and they would trample her for sure.

Stardust was in full gallop, still nervous and tense and still fighting hard against Issie's hold on the reins as they galloped along the ridge, winding between the big trees, heading for the giant oak up ahead.

She's too fast, Issie thought. *I have to slow her down.* She pulled back hard on the reins and felt a wave of fear as Stardust completely failed to respond. The mare was bolting! She was bearing down on the bit and leaning hard so that all her strength was fighting against her rider. Issie heaved on the reins again. It felt like her shoulders were being wrenched out of their sockets.

Her hands were aching now, her fingers cramping from holding on to the sword and the reins. To make matters worse, the frothy sweat on the palomino's neck had rubbed into the leather of the reins, making them slick and wet. They were so slippery it was getting harder and harder for Issie to hold on.

Carefully Issie took her left hand off the reins, just for a moment, so that she could wipe her palm dry on her jodhpurs and get a better grip. She was still holding the sword in her other hand, while trying to keep her hold on the reins too, except the leather was just too slippery. As the palomino strained at the bit, Issie felt a sudden panic rising in her as both the leathers slipped clean out of her hands. She had completely lost her reins! Stardust was out of control.

Chapter 9

There is no feeling more terrifying in the whole world than being on a horse that is bolting. Issie made a frantic grab and managed to get the reins back, but by then Stardust had the bit between her teeth. Issie was struggling to hold her back. She could barely even keep a grip on the reins. She felt them sliding again back through her fingers and looked down at the broadsword clasped in her right hand. It would ruin the scene if she dropped it now, but she had no choice. If she was going to stop this runaway horse, she needed both hands to do it.

Issie opened the cramped, closed fingers of her right hand and felt the weight of the big wooden broadsword slip out of her hands. As the sword fell with a clatter to the ground, Stardust spooked, swerving violently to the left, and Issie let out a squeal as she struggled once more to hang on.

Stardust straightened up and Issie regained her balance and sat back in the saddle. She pulled back as hard as she could on both reins but Stardust didn't respond. The palomino was so strong and Issie's arms were so tired, they felt like jelly.

As another tree brushed against her, almost knocking her off her horse this time, Issie could feel the panic rising in her. They were about to reach the oak. Beyond the big tree the woods began to close in and become more dense. It would be harder to navigate her way through them. Riding like this, on a runaway horse at full gallop, there was no way she would be able to steer safely through the trees.

Then suddenly she remembered what Avery had said to her once about what to do when a horse bolts. *If a horse is too strong for you to fight them, the only way to stop is to make them turn.*

That was it! Issie had been fighting the mare by hauling on both reins at once. She couldn't beat Stardust like that. The mare was too powerful, leaning her full weight against Issie's hands with the bit in her teeth, making her virtually impossible to stop. But what would happen if Issie just tried pulling on one rein?

It would mean timing it right. The trees were thick now and she'd have to dodge and weave expertly between them. But what choice did she have? If Stardust kept galloping into the trees at this speed, Issie would be knocked off by a low branch for certain. She had to try something.

Issie ducked as Stardust swept beneath the branches of the giant oak. Then she sat upright and braced herself to turn, taking a deep breath, sitting back in the saddle and pushing her heels down low in the stirrups.

Tom had better be right about this, she thought as she let her right rein slide through her fingers and go completely slack. Then she put all of her strength into her left arm and pulled.

As she heaved on one single rein, the sudden sideways motion yanked the bit clean out from between Stardust's teeth. Surprised, Stardust lurched to the left, and then her stride slowed as she felt the bit against the bars of her mouth once more. Within a few strides, Issie had the horse back under control, slowing her down to a canter, then a trot, then a walk and finally, with relief, she had pulled up to a halt. It had worked!

Issie sat there, exhausted and shaking. Beneath her, Stardust was heaving after the exertion of her wild gallop.

Her flanks were working in and out like bellows and her neck was dripping wet with sweat.

"Issie! Issie! Are you OK?" Aidan, who had been galloping after her all this time, pulled Diablo up next to Stardust. "You were going so fast even Diablo couldn't keep up."

"She bolted, Aidan. She got the bit between her teeth and I tried, but I couldn't stop her," Issie said. She was shaking and her face was pale from shock.

Aidan jumped off Diablo, grasping Stardust's reins. Issie went to dismount too and felt her legs turn to rubber. They could barely hold her and she almost collapsed as she landed on the ground.

"Hey! Easy there, tiger!" Aidan put his arm around her to support her. "Are you OK?"

Issie collapsed in Aidan's arms and as soon as she felt safe the tears started. She was furious with herself for crying like this – and on the film set! She was supposed to be a stunt rider! If the others saw her like this, it would all be so embarrassing!

Suddenly there was the roar of an engine as a big black motorcycle came tearing towards them. Issie couldn't tell who the driver was because of the black visor on his helmet, but she recognised the passenger riding pillion on the back. It was Rupert and he didn't look pleased. His mouth was set in a grim line as he leapt off the back of the motorcycle and ran towards them.

"Hey, hey, what happened? Why did you stop? It was all going so brilliantly!" he said. As he said this, there was the high-pitched whine of another motorcycle belting along the track towards them. It was Bob and Eugene with their camera still whirring and filming.

"What happened?" Eugene demanded as Bob pulled the bike up. "Is anyone hurt?"

Aidan looked at Rupert with dark eyes. "No, we're OK."

"Oh!" Eugene sounded almost disappointed to hear this. He put his camera down. "Well, could you at least pretend you're hurt or something?" he said to Issie in a low voice. "You know, mug it up a bit for the cameras?"

"Leave her alone," Aidan said, pushing Eugene's camera away. "Can't you see she's been through enough?"

"Issie! Issie are you OK?"

Issie looked up to see the panic-stricken face of her Aunt Hester running towards her.

"I'm fine, Aunty Hess," Issie said. "Honestly."

"What on earth went wrong? Why did you drop your sword? Why didn't you follow your cues?" Hester asked.

Issie didn't want to get Stardust into trouble, but she

realised that she had no choice. She had to tell Aunt Hester the truth.

"Aunty Hess, Stardust bolted on me. It happened right at the start and I tried but I couldn't stop her. I was fighting her all the way and she wouldn't listen to me."

Hester gave Issie a hug. "You did very well to stay on and stop her."

"Problems with Stardust?" Rupert asked.

Hester nodded reluctantly.

"I told you, Hester, I don't have time for stunt horses that can't do the job. This little incident has cost us money and a whole day's filming. You're in charge here – I don't want another mistake like this happening again. I think I'm making myself clear?" Rupert's face was like thunder.

He called to his driver, who pulled up next to him so that he could climb back on to the motorcycle. "I'm going back to base. I'll get my assistant to let the crew know that we're wrapped. We can't continue today. We'll pick it up first thing in the morning. And your horses had better be ready next time." They watched as the director sped off on the motorcycle in a cloud of indignation and dust.

"He took that pretty well, didn't he?" Aidan groaned.

Hester sighed. "I'm afraid he's right. The horses are

my responsibility and this was the final straw. I should have made the decision sooner – now I've delayed filming and put lives at risk." Hester paused. "Stardust is just too dangerous and unpredictable to play Seraphine. She'll have to be replaced."

"But Aunty Hess!" Issie was shocked. "Stardust is the perfect Seraphine. Rupert chose her himself! Besides, what will happen to her if we get rid of her? What will her owners do to her if she can't work in the movies any more?"

Hester looked grim. "We can't afford to worry about that, Issie. I have to think of your safety and the safety of the whole cast and crew. Besides, if Stardust keeps acting like this she will ruin the movie. She's badly behaved and I don't know what to do with her. You heard what Rupert said. I'm afraid Stardust leaves us with no choice. She's got to go!"

The girls were already back at the stables waiting anxiously when Issie and Stardust arrived. "Ohmygod! Issie! Are you OK?" Stella didn't wait for her friend to speak. "We heard what Rupert said. Would Hester really get rid of Stardust? She wouldn't, would she? Oh, this is awful!"

"I know," Issie agreed. Even though Stardust had terrified her with her runaway antics, she still didn't want the palomino to get fired from the film. "I wish there was something we could do, but Aunty Hess has made her mind up."

"Do you know why Stardust bolted?" Kate asked.

"I don't know." Issie shook her head.

"It's like this whole film is cursed or something," Stella said, looking spooked.

"Don't be ridiculous, Stella! Stardust bolted, that's all!" Issie snapped.

"Oh yeah?" Stella said. "Well, what about Angelique's foot? Disasters like that don't usually happen on movie sets!"

"But that's just it!" Issie said. "Stardust and I weren't even close to Angelique and she just collapsed on the ground and started yelling about how we'd broken her foot. It was all an act. We didn't do it!"

"So why would Angelique pretend to be hurt?" Kate wondered.

"To get out of making the film of course!" Stella replied. "She said in the changing rooms that she wanted to get out of making this movie – no matter what!"

"So she's willing to pretend she's broken her foot? That sounds—" The girls stopped speaking abruptly as the tack-room door swung open and Natasha walked in.

"Oh," she said frostily, "I see. Another one of your secret meetings I suppose. All the gang together as usual – except me." She turned around to leave.

"Natasha!" Issie called after her. "It's not like that."

"Yes it is," Natasha turned on her. "You've got your little gang. You never include me in anything. It doesn't matter how much I try, I'll never be a part of it. Well, fine, I don't want to be anyway!" And with that she flounced back out of the door, slamming it behind her.

Issie groaned. "Should I go after her?"

"And say what?" Stella said. "She's right. We don't want her in the gang."

"Stella!" Issie said. "Did it ever occur to you that Natasha is such a total cow to us because she feels left out and wants to be our friend, but we never include her?"

"No," Stella said flatly. "No. It really didn't."

Natasha was in a huff with them – the best thing to do was to leave her until she calmed down. As for Angelique: "All we can do is keep an eye on her in case she does anything else suspicious," Hester told Issie when they talked about it a bit later. Issie tried to object but she knew her aunt was right. Rupert would never believe her word over Angelique's.

What would have happened, Issie wondered, if it had been Angelique on Stardust instead of her? Issie kept thinking back to that morning when Stardust bolted. OK, the mare could be super-naughty, but was it just naughtiness that made her bolt? There had to be some pattern to her bad behaviour. If only Issie could figure it out.

When she went to check on the palomino mare in her stall that afternoon, Stardust almost seemed glad to see Issie for once. She even put her head over the stall and nickered at the sight of her.

Issie reached out and stroked the palomino's pretty velvet muzzle and Stardust snuffled her palm, hoping for carrots. Then she rubbed her nose affectionately against Issie's sleeve as if to say, "I'm sorry I caused all that trouble today," which only made Issie feel even worse.

By the time she went to bed that night, Issie was sick with worry. She kept thinking about the chase scene and how she couldn't stop Stardust. The palomino wasn't at all like her beloved Blaze. Perhaps Stella was right – maybe Issie was expecting too much. She couldn't expect to bond with a horse like Stardust the way she had bonded with Blaze. All of this just made her miss Blaze more than ever. She was so homesick for her chestnut mare. Well, it was only one more day until the weekend and then she could go home and see her again.

Issie got her chance to go home for the weekend sooner than she thought. When she arrived at the dining hall for breakfast the next morning, she discovered that Friday's filming schedule had also been abandoned because of Angelique's injured foot.

"Angelique's doctor insists that she needs a week to heal and Rupert says there's no point in filming until Angelique is well again," Aidan told Issie as they sat down for breakfast together. "He's told everyone to go home for the weekend and we've all got next week off as well. Rupert's totally furious because it's costing a fortune to delay filming.

"On the plus side," he added, smiling, "that means you get to go home and see Blaze. I know you've been missing her lots."

"What about Stardust?" Issie said.

Aidan looked down at his plate. He didn't say anything.

"Aidan? What's going on?" Issie felt a chill run up her spine.

"Hester says she's got to go and there's no point in delaying it any longer. There's a horse truck coming for her this afternoon," Aidan said quietly.

"She can't do that!" Issie said.

"Issie…" Aidan began, but Issie didn't stop to listen. She had pushed her breakfast aside and was striding off out of the dining hall.

She found Aunt Hester down at the main arena training Destiny on the lunge rein. Hester saw her niece approaching and called the black stallion to a halt. "Good timing," she said. "I've just finished with him. You can help me put him away."

"Aunty Hess," Issie said as they walked, "Aidan just

told me you're getting rid of Stardust. What's going to happen to her?"

Hester was taken aback. "I was going to tell you before they came for her. I'm going to call her owners today and tell them to come and get her," Hester sighed. "I kept hoping that she'd improve. But she hasn't. And I can't keep a dangerous horse on the set, Issie. I've tried to change her, to understand her, but I can't do it any more. She's beyond my help."

Issie felt her heart quicken as her aunt said this. She suddenly realised there was still hope – she had an idea.

"Aunty Hess! Maybe you and I can't change her, but I think we both know someone who can."

Her aunt looked at her. "What are you talking about, Issie?"

"Tom Avery," Issie said. "Aunty Hess, what if Tom could fix her?"

"Tom? He's an excellent horseman, Isadora, but we simply don't have the time to—"

"Aunty Hess!" Issie objected. "We've got the whole weekend – and all of next week! Rupert has just called off filming until Angelique's foot gets better. That gives us loads of time! Don't phone her owners just yet. Let me take Stardust home to Winterflood Farm until filming starts again. I'll explain it all to Tom and ask him to help us."

Hester looked uncertain.

"Please, Aunty Hess? It's worth a shot," Issie said.

Hester nodded. "All right, Isadora. Tom has helped us out before. He has tricks up his sleeve that even I haven't seen, so maybe he *can* pull it off. You have a week until you're due back on set. Let's see what he comes up with!"

"Thanks, Aunty Hess! I'm going to call him right now!" Issie beamed. Then she turned on her heels and began to run back towards the barracks.

Of course! If anyone could help Stardust, it was Tom Avery. Issie felt her heart soar.

"Tell him he's got his work cut out," Hester called after her. "Stardust had better be a changed horse when she comes back or she's off the film!"

When Avery arrived to pick up Issie, Stella, Kate, Natasha and Stardust that afternoon, Issie was over the moon to see her instructor. The girls had so much to tell Tom, they didn't shut up for the entire drive home. Issie quickly filled Avery in on all the dramas, including Stardust and Angelique.

"She's impossible!" Issie said.

"Who is? Stardust?" Tom replied.

"No – Angelique! Stardust never stood on her foot! It's not my fault, but Rupert thinks I did it! I mean, just because she's a famous film star. And she's always rude to everyone and she has all these assistants racing after her."

"Well, celebrities are used to having people catering to their every whim—" Tom began, but Issie cut him off again.

"I don't know what to do with her. I've tried to work with her, but she ignores me and she's so arrogant. It's like she's a stuck-up girl who thinks she's better than everyone else."

"Who are we talking about now – Angelique?"

"No! Stardust!" Issie said. "I'm talking about Stardust now, Tom – keep up! I mean, I know she's a horse, but honestly she's worse than Angelique. She's like a bratty star or something!"

"Issie, that's it! You've hit the nail on the head," Tom said.
"What?"

"Stardust's been getting the star treatment – well, no more! If we're going to figure out what's making Stardust misbehave then we need to get her listening to us. The first thing we have to do is bring this mare back down to earth!"

Issie's eyes widened. "Tom! You're right. Stardust's been spoilt – and it's impossible to figure out what's wrong when she's being fussed over like a star on a film set!"

"Exactly. What she needs to straighten her out is to be treated like a normal horse again, like she's not anything special at all – like she's just one of the gang."

"How do we do that though?" Issie asked.

Avery smiled. "It's rather obvious when you think about it," he said. "If we want to make her act like a regular horse, we have to send her to a place where regular horses go." He looked at Issie.

"Tomorrow, Stardust is going to pony club."

Chapter 10

"Mum! Have you seen my pony-club jumper?" Issie called out as she ran down the stairs in her jodhpurs and white shirt. She found her mother in the kitchen making breakfast – and her pony-club jersey folded neatly over the back of the kitchen chair.

"It was buried under a huge pile of dirty clothing in your room and I figured you might need it. I washed it for you," Mrs Brown smiled, passing Issie the navy jumper. "Now sit down and eat a proper breakfast, please. No racing off hungry. You've got a big day."

It was 8 a.m. by the time Issie set off for Winterflood Farm on her bike. Pony-club rally didn't start until ten, which left plenty of time to prepare Stardust – and check on Blaze.

Avery stepped out of his front door as Issie parked her bike in the driveway. "Blaze is in the foaling stall," he said.

"Why?" Issie felt her heart race. "Tom… is she…"

"No, no," Avery said. "She's got three weeks to go until she's due to foal, Issie. I'm just getting her used to the stall. I bring her in for an hour or so each day now so that she'll feel comfortable in there when her foal finally arrives."

Issie ran round the side of the stable block to the foaling stall and stuck her head over the door. "Hey, girl," she called softly to her horse. Blaze raised her head from her hay net and nickered back in reply as she walked over to meet Issie.

"Wow!" Issie was shocked by the size of Blaze's tummy. "She's enormous! She's twice the size she was when I left a week ago."

Issie ran her hands over the mare's belly. "How can you tell when the foal is due?"

Her instructor gestured for her to bend down beside him and look between the mare's hind legs. "Look at her udders," he said. "You see how they haven't filled up yet?

At the moment Blaze's udders are full in the morning, but during the day the milk seems to go away again as she moves around. That will change and by the time the foal is due the udders will stay full all the time and you'll see little drops of colostrum, which is like a thick milk, coming out of the teats."

"What will happen when the foal comes out? How will it reach the milk?" Issie asked.

Avery smiled. "Foals aren't like human babies, you know. They're tough customers. Within the first half-hour of foaling, the mother will lick the foal dry and then the newborn will stand up all by itself and take its first drink."

"So the foal doesn't need our help?" Issie asked.

"I didn't say that," Avery said, looking serious. "There's still a lot that can go wrong, and Blaze will need our help to make sure that her foal is delivered safe and sound. That's why we have the foaling monitor." Avery picked up a small black box which he attached to Blaze's halter. "It should set off an alarm and let us know the minute she's in labour. Then we can bring her into the stall where it's safe and dry and warm for her to have her baby."

"Why don't we just keep her in here?" Issie asked.

"Mares get restless," Avery said, opening the stall door and leading Blaze out into the stable courtyard. "They like to move around and graze in the last few weeks. They hate being cooped up in the stall."

He looked at Issie. "Don't worry. I'll bring her in if the weather gets bad or if she's showing signs of foaling." He looked at his watch. "Come on. I'll put Blaze back in her paddock. You'd better catch Stardust and get her float bandages on so we can truck her to the club. It's nearly time to go."

Issie felt her stomach do a somersault as the horse truck turned down the gravel road to the Chevalier Point grounds.

"It feels like forever since I last rode here," she said.

"It has been a while, hasn't it?" agreed Avery, at the driver's wheel in the truck cab next to her. "I now declare winter officially over. The first rally of the season is here."

Chevalier Point Pony Club was bursting with signs of spring. The three pony-club paddocks were all bright green with new grass, dotted with the occasional cluster of snowdrops.

Everywhere you looked the club grounds were buzzing with activity. A long row of floats and trucks was already parked underneath the row of giant magnolia trees in the first paddock, and horses were being unloaded, groomed and saddled up. Riders in pristine white jodhpurs wearing the club colours were dashing in and out of the clubrooms. Meanwhile, in the far paddocks, Issie could see instructors and parents preparing the jumping courses and games for the day.

"Look! Stella and Kate are here already." Issie pointed under the far tree where Toby and Coco were tied up. The girls waved excitedly at Issie as Avery pulled the truck up next to them. As Issie and Avery jumped down out of the truck, Stella ran over to them.

"This is so cool!" she said. "I can't believe you've really brought Stardust to pony club with you!"

Avery gave Stella a stern look. "Stella, I need you to remember that the whole point of bringing Stardust along to pony-club rally day is to make her feel like a regular horse. Which won't happen if you stand around with your mouth hanging open gawping at her, will it?"

"But, Tom!" Stella grumbled. "Wait till everyone finds out that Stardust is really—"

"No, Stella!" Tom snapped. "You mustn't tell anyone that Stardust is really a movie horse. She's not to receive any special treatment or fuss. As far as you're concerned, she's just an ordinary pony-club mount. OK?"

Stella sniffed at this. "Well, Coco *is* just an ordinary pony-club mount and I make a fuss of her all the time!"

Avery sighed. "Stella, you know perfectly well what I mean. And I'm quite serious – this applies to all of you." He looked at the girls sternly.

"I still don't get it," Kate said. "Why did you bring her to the rally anyway?"

Avery went round to the back of the horse truck and began to undo the tail bolts. "Stardust has been treated like a celebrity," he said. "She's been spoilt and it's made her sour and bored. She's desperate for attention and she's willing to behave badly to get it." Avery lowered the ramp. "In the past her bad behaviour got her just what she wanted – more attention! It's become like a game, you see? What we need to do is ignore her when she's naughty and stop fussing over her. It's very important today that everyone should treat Stardust like a normal pony at a normal pony-club rally."

This proved to be easier said than done. Issie was leading Stardust out of the truck when her friends Dan and Ben arrived on their ponies.

"Look! It's the movie stars! Can I have your autograph?" Ben teased as he pulled his bay pony, Max, up alongside Avery's horse truck.

"Hey, I hope you haven't forgotten your friends now that you're all famous," Dan grinned. He was riding Kismit, his elegant, fleabitten grey.

When the two boys saw the graceful palomino, they were stunned. Dan ran his eyes over the mare's long silvery mane and her fine legs with their sparkling white socks. He was clearly impressed. "She's amazing!" he said.

"Is that one of the horses from the film?" Ben asked. "What's her name?"

"This is Stardust," Issie said as she tied the palomino up to Avery's truck. "She plays Seraphine – she's Angelique Adams's horse in the movie. But please, guys, don't make a fuss. No one is supposed to know." She turned to Stella and Kate. "Can you guys explain the whole deal to them? You know, what Avery said about treating her like a normal horse? I need to saddle Stardust up or I'll be late. You go on ahead and I'll meet you there."

As Issie tightened the girth the palomino tried to get in a vicious nip. Issie managed to dodge her the first time, but when the mare tried to nip her a second time, her teeth actually connected and tore a rip in Issie's best pony-club shirt.

"Stardust!" Issie squealed. She examined her arm. Thank goodness the mare had only got the shirt, not her arm!

Horse bites could really, really hurt. Issie took a deep breath. It wasn't just the shock of the bite that had shaken her. It was the disappointment of Stardust's bad behaviour. The other day at the stable she had thought the mare was beginning to like her. But Stardust was as unpredictable and nasty as ever.

Don't let her get to you. Just ignore her bad behaviour, Issie told herself and stuck her foot into the stirrup, bouncing up into the saddle. "C'mon, Little Miss Movie Star!" she muttered as they set off for the arena.

In the dressage arena Avery's class was already under way. Natasha was at the head of the ride, looking snooty on her gorgeous rose-grey gelding, Faberge.

"You're late," Natasha snapped at Issie as she trotted briskly past her. "Just because you're riding a movie star doesn't mean you can be late for the rally, you know."

Natasha was followed around the arena by Stella, Kate, Ben and Dan, Annabel Willets on her palomino gelding Eddie, and the Miller sisters, Pip and Catherine, who rode matching greys.

"Join in at the end of the ride, Issie," Avery called out to her. Issie trotted Stardust into the arena and joined up at the rear of the ride behind Pip Miller and her little grey, Mitzy. Pip turned round and gave Issie a shy smile. "Is this your new pony? She's beautiful," she whispered over her shoulder.

Yeah, beauty – and the beast! Issie thought to herself.

Stardust hadn't even managed to trot once round the arena before she began to act up. She would trot for a few strides and then stop dead and Issie would be jerked forward in the saddle each time.

"What's wrong?" Avery called out to Issie.

"She keeps being nappy. She won't listen to me," Issie said, trying not to sound frustrated. "Every time I ask her to trot she stops dead."

"Here," Avery said, walking over to her. He reached up to hand Issie his brown leather riding whip, which he always carried with him. "Take my whip. You don't have to use it on her, but if she knows you are carrying it, it may help to get her to respect your leg and move forward." Avery stepped forward and held the whip aloft for Issie to take.

"Stand still, Stardust!" Issie said gruffly as the mare tried to back away. "Stop it!" But Stardust wouldn't calm down. The mare was fretting and dancing about the arena, trying to back away from Avery. As he stepped forward again to try and give Issie the whip, the mare suddenly rose up on her hind legs, her hooves flailing wildly in the air.

"Stardust, no!" Issie screamed, grabbing on to the mare's neck with both hands. Then, as Stardust dropped back down to the ground, Issie instinctively knew what was coming next. She'd been here before. Quickly, she leapt out of the saddle and stood beside Stardust.

"Tom! It's just like that time in the arena on the film set," Issie shouted. "I think she's going to roll!" Issie was right. Stardust had dropped to her knees now and was about to lie down – and she was wearing Issie's favourite saddle! It was her Bates Maestro – the dressage saddle that Avery had given her. If Stardust rolled on it, she would break the tree and the saddle would be ruined!

"Hold her by the bridle. Don't let her roll!" Avery shouted. He rushed forward, still holding the riding crop and waved his arms at Stardust. "Get up!" he shouted at her.

Stardust seemed so spooked by this that instead of lying down to roll, she promptly leapt back up to her feet again and backed away from Avery, snorting and pawing the ground.

"Is she crazy or something?" Natasha said as she sat on Faberge and watched the whole commotion.

"Uh-uh," Avery said. "Quite the opposite. Stardust's a very bright horse and she's been trained to behave like this." He dropped the riding crop that he was still holding in his right hand and walked towards the trembling palomino.

"It's OK, Stardust," Avery said gently. "It's OK." This time the mare didn't back away as he took hold of the reins and led her out of the arena with Issie running at his side.

"You were right, Issie," Avery said as they walked Stardust back towards the horse trucks. "When you said that maybe something you had done had given Stardust her cue to rear and roll like that? You were dead right."

He turned to Issie. "When you were training in the arena that day and she reared and tried to roll on you, were you carrying a whip?"

Issie shook her head. "No, I wasn't," she said. Then she remembered. "But I was carrying a sword! A broadsword. I had just pulled one out of the props bin when Stardust started acting up!" Issie's mind began to race. "And the props guy, he handed me a sword too, just before Stardust bolted that day when we were filming the chase scene."

Avery nodded. "Issie, I think we've figured out what's wrong with Stardust. Hester was right. Those trainers on her last film must have done this."

"Done what?" Issie felt her heart sink – she knew what Avery was going to say.

"Issie, they beat her. With sticks and whips. They must have been trying to train her to do a trick – probably a trick where she needed to rear and roll – and they lost their temper and hit her hard. Look here! There's a freshly healed scar on her near shoulder. That must be from where the whip struck her."

Avery shook his head. "The wound has healed, but horses never forget. Now Stardust is terrified whenever she sees a whip, or a broadsword – any big stick. You were carrying a sword both times when she misbehaved on the film set. That's what set her off. In fact, I'd bet you that all of Stardust's bad behaviour, even the biting and the bad temper, began after they started to hit her. She's not really nasty, she's just acting in self-defence out of fear. She's scared of being hit again."

"Poor Stardust! How terrible!" Issie groaned.

"No," Avery said firmly. "This is good."

"Good?" Issie boggled at Avery.

Avery shook his head. "Don't you see, Issie? Now that we know what's worrying Stardust, that's half the battle won."

"But, Tom," Issie protested, "Stardust is a stunt

horse. If she can't be ridden with a sword then she'll still be kicked off the movie!"

Avery looked at the palomino. "Well then, we'll just have to retrain her, won't we? By this time next week, Stardust must be ready to rejoin the Daredevil Ponies – and we're going to make sure that she is."

Chapter 11

With hardly any time, every day was crucial in Stardust's retraining programme. The morning after the disastrous pony-club rally, Issie arrived at Winterflood Farm at seven a.m. and found Tom waiting for her in the kitchen with bacon, eggs and toast.

"This will be our routine for the next week," he said, dishing up grilled mushrooms on to her plate. "We'll be doing long days training. You need a good breakfast to get you started."

"Thanks," Issie nodded and asked nervously, "Tom? What is it exactly that we're going to do today?"

"Do you remember the desensitisation obstacle course that Hester put you through?" Avery asked.

"Uh-huh," Issie said. "Stardust was just fine about

everything – the blankets and the lights and that stuff, but she went crazy as soon as I tried to pick up a sword."

Avery nodded. "For a normal stunt horse a desensitisation course will solve any problems like that and make a horse bombproof – but Stardust isn't a normal horse. She's super-smart and she's been hurt, badly beaten, so she's got a very good reason to be scared of sticks, swords, whips – anything that she can be hit with."

"So how do we get rid of her fear?" Issie said.

"Same technique but more focused," Avery said, "for which we will need these…" He pulled a big leather bag out from beneath the kitchen table. It contained a broadsword, a riding crop, a big branch and a stock whip.

"…and also lots of these!" Avery pulled out another bag, which was full to the brim with fresh carrots.

"I'm not sure I get it." Issie was confused.

"Don't worry, it will all become clear," Avery said, grabbing a halter off the kitchen bench. "I'm going to go and catch Stardust while you finish up your brekkie. I'll meet you at the stables. It's time to get to work."

For the first stage of desensitisation, Avery put Stardust in a loose box. "She needs to be free to move around, but she mustn't be able to get too far away from you," he explained to Issie.

"We'll leave her loose in her halter without a lead rope. Don't tie her up," Avery instructed. "She needs to be able to back away if she wants to. You want her to feel comfortable." He passed Issie the bag of whips, swords and sticks. "We're going to get her used to these. I want you to go into her stall and rub them all over her body."

"But she's terrified of them…" Issie began to protest.

"Exactly," Avery said. "She needs to learn that a whip or a sword will not do her any harm as long as you are around. Slowly but firmly I want you to pick up the various sticks and use them like grooming brushes – walk around her and touch her firmly but gently with them. Stroke her with them as if they were an extension of your own hands. She's going to be nervous at first. Very nervous probably. Let her move away from you if she wants. Take it slowly. Then, when she's accepting your touch, give her a carrot because she's been good. After a while, she'll learn to associate being touched with the whips and swords with good feelings instead of bad – that's what the carrots are for."

Issie thought that Avery's plan made total sense – until she got into the stall with Stardust. The minute she took the first broadsword out of the bag, Stardust backed away from her, completely terrified, and cowered in the corner of the stall.

"Tom?" Issie said. "What now?" She didn't see how she could possibly rub the sword over Stardust's body when the mare wouldn't even let her get near.

"Keep the sword lowered and don't go to her," Avery advised calmly. "Sit down in the middle of the stall with your sword and your carrot and let her come to you."

And so Issie sat and waited. And waited. They only had one week to retrain Stardust and here she was, wasting time by sitting in a stall doing nothing!

"Stay there and don't move," Avery insisted.

Almost an hour later, just as Issie felt her patience completely ebbing away, the curious and hungry Stardust could stand it no longer. The palomino finally summoned up the courage to step forward. She took three tentative steps and then craned her neck, nuzzling the carrot out of Issie's hand.

"Good girl!" Issie said, letting Stardust eat the carrot which she held in her lap next to the sword. "Good girl!"

After that, Issie spent the rest of the morning slowly

coaxing Stardust to stand still in her stall while Issie fed her carrots with one hand, while stroking her with the sword in her other hand. By lunchtime, the mare would stand without flinching as Issie gently ran the sword over her neck and shoulders.

Issie wasn't at all happy with her progress. "It's not fast enough. We'll never have her ready at this rate!" she grumbled to Tom when she left Stardust in her stall and came inside for lunch.

"Nonsense!" Avery said sharply. "You've made huge strides today. You just don't know it yet. Remember, this is a horse that hates whips and swords more than anything and you had her eating a carrot while you stroked her with a broadsword! Trust me, this is big stuff, Issie. By the time you get in that stall tomorrow, she'll be a changed horse. Mark my words."

Avery was right. By the next morning, Stardust was letting Issie run the wooden broadsword all over her body, even under her belly and down her legs.

"I don't believe it!" Issie said. "Yesterday she was so strung out, I couldn't get near her."

"Once you build trust, anything is possible," Avery said. "She's getting more faith in you all the time, Issie."

It was true. Stardust seemed almost pleased to see Issie

now when she arrived each morning to lead her in from her paddock for her training session.

Issie's daily routine revolved entirely around rehabilitating the palomino. In the morning she would work in the loose box with the swords and the whips. Then in the afternoon she would put Stardust back in her paddock and Stella or Kate would come over and the girls would stage mock swordfights with each other right under Stardust's nose.

"She needs to get comfortable with the idea of the swords being banged about right next to her and know that they're not going to hurt her," Avery explained.

Each time Stardust stood still and didn't spook during their swordplay, Issie would pause to feed the mare a carrot and give her a pat before starting a fresh battle with Kate or Stella.

While they were doing this, Avery would walk around the paddock, sticking swords into the ground in odd places. There were even swords poking out of the ground next to Stardust's water trough and feed bin. "If she becomes familiar with them and knows they won't hurt her then there's no reason for her to be afraid any more," Tom replied when Issie asked him what he was doing.

After the mock swordfights each day, Issie would

saddle up Stardust for the final phase of her training, which Avery referred to as a "spoilt brat reality check". "Stardust has been stuck on film sets for so long. It will do her good to have a look at the real world and live like a regular horse for once!" Avery pointed out.

So Issie would saddle up and hack her out from Winterflood Farm to the River Paddock to meet up with Stella and Kate. As Stardust began to settle in and enjoy her outings with Toby and Coco, they would canter along the river bank and Issie would pretend it was a cross-country tournament and ride Stardust over fallen logs or ditches that they came across along the way. It turned out the mare loved to jump and would always pick up her feet nicely over a fence, never hesitating or baulking.

As each day went by, the palomino's newfound confidence in her rider showed. By the end of the week Issie could canter her along the grass riverbank between Winterflood Farm and the River Paddock on a loose rein without any fear of the horse bolting. On Friday, when Issie mounted up in the paddock and Avery passed her a sword, Stardust stood perfectly still and didn't flinch. By Saturday, Issie could sit on Stardust's back and swing her sword above her head without the mare batting an eyelid. And on Sunday, when they went back to pony club for the next rally day, Stardust didn't even seem to notice that Issie was riding her the whole time with a whip in her hand.

As she rode into the arena, with Stardust trotting along neatly, her neck arched and her ears pricked forward, Issie felt like they were ready for anything. But there was one obstacle she hadn't counted on.

"Isn't that sweet?" Natasha Tucker said as she saw Issie approaching. "Taking her for one last outing before she heads off to the glue factory."

"Very funny, Natasha," Issie sighed, "but for your information, Stardust is totally retrained and ready to go back to work."

Natasha pulled a face. "Are you planning on bolting again and ruining another day's shooting?"

"That wasn't Stardust's fault," Issie said, standing up for her horse.

"I didn't say it was her fault," Natasha smirked. "A good stunt rider would have stopped her. That's why Rupert should have picked me!"

Unfortunately it was games practice at pony club that morning and just when Issie thought she'd seen the last of Natasha, she found herself stuck with her again. The snooty blonde was racing against Issie in the bending race. Issie knew Natasha didn't really mean to be so horrible and it must be awful for her right now with her parents splitting up and everything. Still, she really could be a total cow! Issie couldn't help but feel a glow of satisfaction when Stardust aced the bending race and beat Natasha and Faberge by a whole two poles.

Things got even better after games practice. Avery had set up a jumping course and Stardust went totally clear on her first round, taking decent-sized fences with ease.

"Stardust is, like, a total pony-club superstar!" Stella said, shaking her head in amazement.

The biggest shock, though, came at lunchtime. Issie was untacking the mare when suddenly Stardust swung her head around. Issie panicked, thinking she was trying to bite her again. But instead of trying to nip, Stardust gave a friendly nicker. Then she reached over and nuzzled Issie gently on the arm.

"Oh, you're saying hello!" Issie giggled. "Well, hey there, girl! You startled me." She couldn't believe it. Something had changed in Stardust. The steely aggression was gone from her eyes. It turned out she loved being a regular pony-club horse!

It had been a great week, Issie decided. Her plan to bring Stardust home had really worked. The mare had improved so much each day. Not only that, the week at home had given Issie a chance to be with Blaze.

Every evening, after Issie had finished Stardust's training, she would take both her horses their hard feed. Then she would stay and watch as Blaze ate, talking softly to her mare and marvelling at how enormous her belly was.

Now that Blaze was so close to foaling, Avery had moved the mare into the sheltered paddock closest to the stables. One sunny evening, as Issie leant over the rails of the paddock watching the mare devour her bucket of hard feed, she heard Avery's voice behind her. "Filly or colt?"

"What do you mean?" Issie was confused.

"I mean Blaze's foal. What do you think it will be? A filly or a colt? What are you hoping for?"

"I don't know," Issie said, shaking her head. "I guess I really don't mind. Maybe a filly because then she'd look just like Blaze. She's so beautiful, isn't she, Tom?"

Blaze seemed to be enjoying all the adoration. She looked up from her feed bucket and seemed to shake her head up and down in agreement over her own beauty.

Issie smiled at the mare and then her face turned serious. "Tom, I don't think I can go back to the film set again. I can't leave Blaze behind. What if she starts to foal? I should stay here. She needs me."

"You heard what the vet said when he came out on

Wednesday," Tom replied. "It will be another three weeks at least. By the time Blaze is foaling, the film will be wrapped up and you'll be home again."

"I hope so, Tom," Issie said. "Blaze's foal is going to be special. I can feel it. I want to be there more than anything in the world."

Chapter 12

Hester was waiting anxiously with Aidan when Issie, Avery and the girls returned to the film set on Monday morning.

"Well?" Hester asked nervously as Issie clambered out of the truck cab. "What news? Have you reformed my star? Or do I need to saddle up Athena and tell Rupert the bad news?"

"Come and see for yourself," Issie grinned.

As Avery led Stardust down the truck ramp, Issie grabbed her riding helmet out of the truck. Before anyone could stop her, she had grabbed Stardust by the halter and vaulted lightly on to her bare back.

Issie clucked softly to the mare and steered her with the lead rope in one hand like a cowgirl. She gave Stardust a light tap with her legs and asked the mare to trot. Stardust responded immediately, prancing forward in a light, bouncy trot, circling around the grassy field outside the stables where the horse truck had pulled up.

"Meet the new improved Stardust!" Stella said to Hester as she and Kate joined her and Aidan to watch.

"New and improved?" Hester said. "She's like a totally different horse!"

Stardust had her ears pricked forward and Issie had a huge grin on her face as she urged Stardust on into a gallop and raced her in a loop around the field before pulling up to a sudden halt, spinning round on her hindquarters and cantering back towards Hester, Avery and the others. This time, when she came to a halt in front of the group, Issie tapped her toe lightly against the back of Stardust's right leg. Stardust dropped immediately down on to one knee and lowered her head in a circus bow. Then, as Stardust stood up on all four legs again, Issie vaulted off and ran over to her aunt.

"Well done!" Hester was overjoyed. She grabbed Issie in a huge hug and squeezed her so tight Issie thought she would stop breathing. "You are most definitely my absolutely, all-time favourite niece!"

"I taught her to bow," Issie grinned. "It's the same trick Blaze used to do when she was in the El Caballo Danza

Magnifico You were right, Aunty Hess – she learns tricks really easily. It only took me a day to teach her."

Hester shook her head. "She's a changed horse."

"That was Tom," Issie said. "He figured it out, Aunty Hess. You remember that first day when I rode her in the arena, when Stardust went completely bonkers? It was because she is scared of swords! Her trainers on the last movie must have hit her and she kept thinking that we would hit her too!"

Issie gave the mare a loving pat on her velvet muzzle. "Poor Stardust!" she said. "No wonder she'd turned sour."

"How did you retrain her?" Hester asked.

"We took her to Pony Club." Avery smiled and gave Stardust a firm pat on her glossy palomino neck. "Stardust got a taste of normal horsy life. It was just what she needed to bring her back down to earth again."

"Plus," Issie said, "we spent, like, hours and hours desensitising her so that she's not scared of whips and swords any more. Look! Watch this!" Issie nodded to Avery who picked up a broadsword out of the truck and threw it to her.

The sword sailed through the air and Issie caught it expertly. Stardust didn't move a muscle as Issie brandished the sword, waving it over her head before slipping it into the sword sheath at her hip.

"Brilliant!" Hester said as she watched her. Then she turned to Avery. "But how do I stop her from playing up again now she's back on the set?"

Avery smiled. "Don't train her," he said.

"What?"

"Just what I said. Stardust has been in dozens of movies – maybe too many for her own good. She knows all the tricks already and she's so used to swords and whips now – you'll have no problems with her any more. Just don't train her – that's my advice. If you spend too much time rehearsing in the arena, there's always the risk she'll start to play up again."

"So what do you suggest instead?" Hester arched a brow at him.

Avery smiled. "Let Issie ride her, Hester. But not in the arena – out there." Avery stared out at the farmland around them. "Let Stardust be a horse again. Give her and Issie the time and space to go wild together. Let them bond with each other."

Hester nodded at this. "Tom, I have a feeling I owe you big time for this one."

"Not at all," Avery smiled. "It was Issie who thought

of it really. She made me realise that sour, bratty movie stars and sour, bratty horses really aren't that different."

"Well then," Hester said, "maybe you can help us with our other little problem?"

"What's that?"

"It's Angelique Adams," Hester said. "She's locked herself in her trailer. She won't come out and she won't speak to anyone – not even Rupert."

"Angelique is throwing a tantrum!" Issie groaned as she threw herself down on one of the big sofas in the palomino barracks. "This is so crazy. We finally sort out Stardust's problems and now Angelique is being a total pain again!"

"Maybe this movie *is* cursed after all!" Kate groaned.

"Ohhh!" Stella squealed. "That's what I said and you all laughed at me!"

"Oh, don't be ridiculous, Stella!" Kate snapped. "I didn't mean it."

"Oh, really?" Stella sniffed. "Well, how do you explain Angelique's behaviour then?"

"Angelique is just a drama queen," Kate said. "You know

she doesn't want to do this movie, but we still haven't figured out why…"

"She won't even come out of her trailer or talk to anyone," Aidan said. "The only person she's letting in to see her is her make-up artist, her assistant and that guy Eugene – the one who's doing the documentary."

"What's going to happen?" Issie asked.

"There's a rumour going around that Rupert is fed up with her," Aidan said. "They say he wants to replace Angelique with some other up-and-coming new Hollywood actress, you know, Nevada Roberts? They say she was Rupert's first choice for the movie anyway and now he wishes he'd never given Angelique the role.

"That's it!" Stella said. "Maybe Angelique is trying to get herself kicked off this movie. We all heard her say that she doesn't want to do it. And now she's getting her wish."

Issie shook her head. "I don't think so. If Angelique gets kicked off the film, it will be so bad for her reputation. I don't see why she keeps embarrassing herself like this. There must be something more to it. Maybe Rupert wants to get rid of her and he's making her look bad?" Issie turned to Aidan. "You said he wants Nevada Roberts instead?"

Aidan nodded. "It makes sense. He probably does want to get rid of her."

"Get rid of who?"

The girls and Aidan turned round to see Natasha standing in the doorway. She must have just been dropped off by her mum because she was holding her bags and looking miserable.

"Hi, Natasha," Issie said. "Ummm, no one. Honest. It was nothing."

"Is someone trying to get rid of me?" Natasha looked at them all darkly. "Well, it wouldn't be the first time today," she said. Then she stormed past everyone. "I should have known you'd all be backstabbing me again!"

"But, Natasha, we really weren't…" Issie started.

"Oh, leave her, Issie!" Stella said. "We've got bigger problems to worry about without bothering with Natasha…"

By that afternoon, though, their problems were over. "Angelique has been talking to Rupert and everything is back on again," Aidan reported to the others. "Rupert has told the crew that we'll shoot tonight instead and do the castle chase scene. He's getting everything ready for it. Hopefully Angelique will have pulled herself together by then and be ready to ride."

"What do you mean we're shooting tonight?" Issie said.

"We're doing that scene, you know, where the vampire riders chase Seraphine and Galatea up the citadel to the black castle?" Aidan explained. "Angelique is supposed to ride it herself. Hester said to tell you to get Stardust ready for her to ride."

Issie had a sick feeling in her tummy that evening as she saddled up Stardust. The mare seemed to sense Issie's nerves and began to shift restlessly in her stall as Issie put on her saddle and bridle.

"Hey there. It's OK, girl," Issie cooed as she adjusted the mare's jewelled noseband. She knew her nerves were making Stardust anxious, but she couldn't help it. "There's nothing wrong. I'm just being silly, that's all," she told the palomino. "At least we're finally friends now, huh, girl?"

Issie had spent two whole hours grooming Stardust this afternoon so that she'd look her best for her big scene. The mare's golden palomino coat glistened and her mane, which was long and silvery white, seemed almost ghostly under the glare of the single bulb in her stable.

Issie ran her stirrups up the leathers and then led the mare out into the stable yard. She mounted up on the mounting block just as Hester came running over towards her. "They're ready for you now on the set," she said.

"Where's Angelique?"

Hester shook her head. "No one knows. She's gone missing. Rupert is looking for her. He's insisting that she has to ride this scene – but if we can't find her then, well, it's going to have to be you."

Hester switched on a torch so that the pair of them could see the track in front of them. Grass track ran between the stables to the film crew trucks and over to the base of the castle mountain. It was lit all the way along with hurricane lamps so that the crew could see where they were going in the dark. It was hard to tell in the gloom, but Issie guessed it was about a kilometre from the stables to the silver crew trucks and then another kilometre again down to the foot of the black mountain.

"Follow me," Hester said, "they're all waiting for you."

She wasn't kidding. When Issie reached the foot of the black mountain there must have been at least thirty crew members bustling about on the set. Lighting crew were setting up enormous scaffolding that ran out of sight down the terraces. The costume department people were running around with armfuls of black capes and the set designers were busily putting the finishing touches on the black castle. One of the crew was painting a strange liquid that looked like snail slime all over the black rocks surrounding the terraces that wound up the mountain.

Issie tied Stardust to one of the silver crew trucks and gazed up at the castle mountain ahead of her. A chill ran down her spine. Angelique hadn't turned up – she would have to ride. She would have to take the terraces at a flat-out gallop with the black horsemen behind her, and then turn to face the hooded vampire riders as their leader, Francis, tried to sink his fangs into Seraphine and suck out the mare's golden palomino blood so that she too became a black, soulless beast...

"Hi there!"

Issie just about jumped out of her skin as she caught a glimpse of a ghoulish white face looming towards her in the black night. She let out a high-pitched squeak.

"Whoaa! You're a bit jumpy tonight, aren't you?" It was Aidan and he was already dressed in his vampire rider costume.

"Yeah," Issie agreed, "I guess I am. It's scary shooting at night, don't you think?"

"Don't worry," Aidan reassured her, "it's perfectly safe. The crew have got all the lighting set up so you can see where you're going. You won't get lost in the dark and ride off the edge of the mountain or anything." His white vampire fangs shone in the light. "It looks like you'll be riding at this rate. I see Angelique hasn't turned up – as usual. What a drama queen! I heard one of the crew say that Angelique's totally living up to her reputation around Hollywood for being a brat. They're saying that Rupert has already approached Nevada Roberts and if Angelique drops out for any reason, Nevada will definitely take her place."

Voices could be heard coming through the darkness towards them. In the half-light of the hurricane lamps Issie recognised Tony, Angelique's personal make-up artist. He was waving a lip gloss in the air and bickering with another man who was also holding make-up brushes. "You've put too much blusher on her!" he was shouting. "She looks vermilion! I am her personal make-up artist – I should be in charge!"

Behind the bickering make-up artists came the rest of Angelique's entourage. There was her assistant carrying the coffee as usual, followed by two women, wearing headsets and carrying clipboards, who were busily ordering other crew members about. Finally, behind them, flanked by two bodyguards, was Angelique Adams.

"Angelique! Angel! Baby! That's it! Look at me! Now just act natural…" Eugene Sneadly was running around them all in circles, his camera lens trained on Angelique. Bob was trailing along behind him. "Great, baby! We're getting amazing footage here!"

Angelique, however, didn't look like she cared about Eugene's amazing footage. Her face was as white as a sheet and she looked completely petrified as she approached the set. As the make-up artist with the blusher brush darted in to fix her make-up again she swatted him away angrily.

"Angelique!" Rupert said, rushing towards her with his own entourage trailing behind him. Rupert embraced his star with a brisk air kiss. "Great to see you! You're looking fantastic! Are you ready to go then? Do you want to mount up and we'll get started? We've got everything in place waiting for you." He turned to his assistant. "Are the vampire horsemen ready to go?"

The assistant nodded. "We've got everyone on set, Rupert. They're waiting on your cue."

"Good, good!" Rupert rubbed his hands together. "Right! Time is money, as they say. So let's get cracking then, shall we?" He smiled at Angelique. The superstar returned his grin with a tense, tight-lipped smile.

"Ummm, the thing is, Rupert, maybe y'all should do this scene without me," Angelique muttered. "I tried to tell that doctor – my foot is still sore and…"

Rupert cut his star off with a glare. "Angelique, I have already delayed filming for a whole week for you. Do you know how much that has cost this production? I've had three different doctors look at your foot and they all say the same thing. You are fine."

Rupert leant forward and lowered his voice to a hiss so that only Angelique could hear. "Now, you spoilt brat, you listen to me. You have a contract with this film company. We can't keep making this movie without you. You are going to get on this horse right now and you are going to ride. Or you can quit right here and now and I will replace you with Nevada Roberts. I know you must have heard the rumour and I can tell you that it's quite true. I won't have you ruining my movie. So why don't you just grow up and get on the horse."

"The thing is—" Angelique began, but she was interrupted by Eugene.

"Angelique, baby!" he boomed. "Rupert is right. You have to do this scene." He grabbed the starlet by the elbow and pulled her roughly away from the crowd. "Honey, we need you to get in the picture! Here I am making a behind-the-scenes documentary and so far I have nothing!"

"But I—" Angelique tried to speak again but Eugene cut her off.

"Baby! This is an Angelique Adams movie, right? And who are you? You're Angelique Adams! You have to do this, sweetheart! This is your movie." Eugene flung his arms out. "All these people here are waiting just for you. This is your moment, baby! Now get on that horse over there and show them how it's done."

Angelique took a deep breath and then she turned to Issie. "You heard the man," she snipped. "Get off my horse. This is my movie and I'm riding this scene!"

"Way to go, Angel baby!" Eugene egged her on as he hoisted the video camera on to his shoulder again and began filming. He looked around him frantically. "Bob? Where the hell are you? Get over here, Bob! Now! I need sound!" Bob, who had been loitering at the back of the entourage, raced forward with his sound boom as Angelique marched right up to Issie and stood with her hands on her hips.

"Are you deaf or something?" Angelique pouted. "I told you to get off my horse."

Issie reluctantly dismounted from Stardust's back and handed Angelique the reins. Angelique reached out her hand to take them as if she were reaching out to touch an electric fence. It looked like she thought the reins were going to bite her. Then she turned to Issie again.

"Help me get up on him," she ordered.

"Her," Issie said.

"What?"

"Stardust isn't a 'him', she's a 'her'," Issie said.

"Oh, what-ever!" Angelique said, trying to sound tough. But Issie noticed there was a tremor in the starlet's voice as she spoke.

"Anyway," Angelique continued, "I said help me up."

Issie stood next to Stardust and cupped her hands so that Angelique could put her knee in Issie's palms for a leg-up. But the starlet just looked at her blankly. "What are you doing?" she growled.

"I'm giving you a leg-up," Issie said. "Put your knee in my hands and I'll push you up."

Angelique sniffed. "I knew that!" she said. "I know all about horses!" She put her knee in Issie's hands, but rather than bouncing up like riders naturally do,

Angelique sagged like a sack of potatoes. Issie found herself heaving her up like she was tossing a caber to throw her into the saddle. Angelique came down with a crash and Stardust lurched forward with shock.

As Stardust moved beneath her, Angelique squealed and made a frantic grab for the front of the saddle with both hands as if she were in danger and desperate to hang on. Issie instinctively grabbed the reins and held Stardust steady until Angelique picked the reins up. Issie couldn't help noticing that the actress held them in her clenched fists like a toddler gripping the steering wheel of a toy car.

"Where are the thingummys?" Angelique asked Issie as she looked down at her feet. Then she saw the stirrup irons dangling by her ankles. "Oh, there they are!" She shoved her feet into the stirrups then began flapping her arms and wiggling her feet around. It was like she was doing the chicken dance.

"Well!" she said to Issie. "Why won't she go?" Angelique gave Stardust a poke in the neck with her finger. "Come on then, horsy. What are you waiting for? Gee-up!"

And in that instant Issie realised the truth. The shock made her blood run cold. She had discovered Angelique's secret. There was no way that anyone who had ever ridden a horse before would hold the reins like that. Or flap their arms to make a horse go. *Ohmygod*, Issie thought, *it all makes sense*. The fake broken foot, the temper tantrums in her trailer, the way Angelique always made sure she wasn't standing too close to the horses. Even the fights with her agent and pretending she was injured so that Rupert had to stop filming for a week. Issie saw it all now. Of course! It was so obvious. And so awful! Angelique Adams, the star of The *Palomino Princess*, had a secret all right. She couldn't ride!

Chapter 13

Angelique flapped her arms wildly, jerking at Stardust's mouth. As Issie watched the mare getting more and more upset. She couldn't help herself; she rushed forward and made a lunge at Stardust's reins. "Stop it! You're going to spook her!" Issie shouted.

Angelique glared down at her. "Don't you dare tell me what to do!" she sneered at Issie. "I'm the star of this movie – nobody tells me what to do."

Issie didn't know what to say. Angelique was right. She was the star and Issie was a total nobody – a lowly stunt rider.

"Listen," Issie hissed under her breath, "Angelique, I know the truth. I know that you can't ride – it's OK, honest, I won't tell anyone. But please, trust me. You can't ride Stardust in this scene. She's a highly-strung, temperamental mare – she's not a beginner's pony. It's not safe. You'll hurt yourself. Please, let me ride her instead. I'll make an excuse for you. I'll tell Rupert that you've hurt your foot again or something. Please?"

Angelique fixed Issie with a cold stare. "I don't know what you're talking about!" she snapped. "I am a great rider. And I'm the star of this movie – you're not going to replace me. Now back off and leave me alone!"

"But…"

"You heard her. Back off – now!" A gruff voice behind Issie made her jump. She turned round to see Eugene looking menacingly at her.

"Eugene, please. Angelique can't—" Issie was cut off by Eugene who hissed at her in a low whisper.

"You think I don't know what's going on? I know exactly what's going on here, kid! You stay out of it and leave Angelique to me." Eugene turned to the trembling superstar and gave a broad grin.

"Angel baby, I'm telling you, you'll be fine. Don't listen to the kid here. Remember you're the star, baby! Look at you! You are a great rider – a natural! Now get out there and break a leg!"

Issie was shocked. "What?" Eugene shrugged. "That's

what we say in Hollywood – break a leg. It means good luck. You got a problem with that, kid? Now why don't you shut your trap before I shut it for you?"

"Hey, hey… what on earth is going on over here?" Issie saw Rupert striding over towards them. "Angelique? Eugene?" Rupert looked concerned. "Do we have some kind of problem here?"

"Rupert, baby!" Eugene's greasy charm went into overdrive at the arrival of the director. "Rupert, things are great! No problems at all. Angel was just giving this sweet little stunt rider here a few pointers on how to ride a horse. She's totally ready to go, aren't you, Angel?"

Angelique looked at Eugene. Then she gave Rupert a reluctant, forced smile. "Sure, Rupert. I'm ready."

"Excellent!" Rupert said. "If you'll head down to the marker at the foot of the hill where the vampire riders are gathered, please? Can we have lighting technicians ready on the set too? We need to have the lights shining on the terraces as the horses ride up the mountain. We'll do this first take with the crew set up at long distance and then we'll move in for the close-ups later."

Eugene elbowed his way past Issie and grabbed Stardust by the reins. "Beat it, kid," he growled at Issie. "I'll take it from here."

Angelique flapped her legs uselessly against Stardust's sides. "I still can't make him go, Eugene! Can you lead me?"

"I've already told you," Issie said through gritted teeth, "Stardust is a her, not a him, and you need to stop kicking her! She's sensitive."

"Hey, kid!" Eugene barked. "Are you deaf? Get out of here!" He took Stardust's reins and began to lead the mare over to where the vampire riders were standing, waiting to start shooting.

"Bob?" Eugene looked around behind him. "Bob! Get over here now! We're gonna get Angelique's big scene on film for the documentary! We don't want to miss this. Come on – let's hustle!"

Issie watched helplessly as Eugene led Stardust down to the foot of the mountain terraces with Bob trailing behind. She could feel her heart racing. Eugene was crazy! Didn't he realise that Angelique could get killed if she tried to ride a dangerous stunt like this? Issie didn't care what he said, she had to try and stop this. She needed help.

Aunty Hess! Her aunt was her best hope. She had to find her and explain everything. Rupert would have to listen to Hester. After all, she was his head trainer.

She looked about her frantically. Aunty Hess was

probably still at the trucks with the rest of the film crew, back up the track at least a kilometre away from the black castle. If Issie was going to get to her aunt in time, she would have to run.

She set off as fast as she could along the grassy track towards the trucks. Although the track was lit with hurricane lamps, it was still pretty dark in places, too dark to see where she was putting her feet. The grass on the track was thick and slippery with dew, which didn't help either, and she had to keep ducking past various runners and assistants who were all hurrying in the other direction, getting ready for shooting to begin. At one point, she nearly lost her footing, slipping over on the track and almost sliding down the steep bank to the ditch below.

By the time Issie finally reached the silver trucks, she was wet, muddy and exhausted.

"Ohmygod!" Stella said when she saw her. "What are you doing back here? I thought you were down on the set with Stardust and Angelique? What's wrong?"

Issie fought to get her breath back, sucking in great gulps of air. "No… time… to… explain… Must… find… Aunty Hess."

"But, Issie," Kate said, "Hester's not here. One of the

black horses threw a shoe and she's gone back to the stables to find the farrier."

Issie felt her heart sink. The stables were another kilometre at least from here. She would never make it. She was too tired to run that far. Besides, by the time she reached Hester, they would already have started filming and it would be too late.

"Issie," Stella said, "what is it? You have to tell us what's wrong."

Issie was still puffed. She took another deep breath and then managed to get the words out. "It's Angelique," she said. "She can't ride."

"What do you mean?" Stella said. "Of course Angelique can ride. She's a great rider. We heard her say so herself."

Issie nodded. "Yeah, but we've never actually seen her ride, have we? Until tonight. I just watched her get on to Stardust. She doesn't have a clue what she's doing. I'm pretty sure she's never even been on a horse before. In fact, I'd say she's terrified of them!"

"But, Issie!" Kate said. "If she can't ride, where is she now?"

"She's on Stardust! I told her not to ride. I told her I'd stunt-double for her, but Angelique said she was the star and then Eugene told me to beat it and…" Issie trailed off. "She wouldn't listen. She's going to ride the scene herself. She's going to get herself killed."

"We have to tell Hester," Kate agreed. "She can stop this."

Stella nodded. "Kate and I will go. Issie, you go back down the track and try and stall them until we get there."

Issie agreed. "Tell Aunty Hess she has to hurry. They're about to start shooting really soon. They were just getting the vampire horsemen sorted when I left. It can't be long now before they begin."

As Kate and Stella ran off together towards the stables, Issie bent over to catch her breath. She was exhausted. And what was the point in running all the way back again? Angelique and Rupert wouldn't listen to her.

She bent down, put her hands on her knees and took a deep breath. Even if she didn't care what happened to the spoilt brat movie star, she had to get back and try and help Stardust. If Angelique fell off, then Rupert was bound to blame the palomino and all of Issie's hard work rehabilitating the mare would be worthless.

Issie stood up and began to head back towards the path. Whether Rupert believed her or not, she decided she had to try.

There was no one else on the track now – all the crew were already down on the set, standing by, waiting for filming to begin. She was all alone, the hurricane lamps casting spooky shadows over the narrow grassy path in front of her as she ran. At certain points along the track the lamps had gone out completely. The moon had gone behind the clouds as well, so at times the path ahead was pitch-black. Issie could barely see where she was going.

Suddenly she let out a squeal as she felt the ground falling away beneath her feet. In the dark she had veered completely off the track and now she was sliding down the slippery grass bank, unable to regain her footing as she fell. As she plummeted, she reached out her hands, grabbing at the grass to stop herself and felt the vicious sting of blackberry prickles piercing her skin. Unable to hang on, Issie curled into a ball instead, with her hands over her head as she slid down the steep slope.

When she reached the bottom of the bank she hit the dirt with a thud. The fall had made her woozy and it took her a few seconds to stand up. Carefully, so as not to stick her hands into any more prickles, Issie gingerly pushed herself up off the ground and looked around. Above her, she could just about make out the track, lit by the dotted line of the hurricane lamps.

Behind her was pitch-blackness. The only way out was back up the steep blackberry bank.

This proved to be easier said than done. The grass was slippery and every time Issie found herself gaining some ground, she would mistakenly grab a hunk of blackberry vine and squeal in pain as the vicious prickles dug into her hands. She kept crawling on her hands and knees until she had got through the worst of it and was almost at the top – the steepest bit. Issie felt her heart sink as she tried to climb over the edge and found herself slipping back. It was impossible to get back up again! She clawed at the mud and grass, dragging herself towards the edge, before sliding back down once more.

I can't do it, Issie thought. *I can't get up. I'm too tired.* She clung on for a moment, her hands grasping the wet grass, her belly pressed against the mud, and felt hot tears welling in her eyes.

Then suddenly Issie found herself plunged into complete darkness as the hurricane lamp on the path ahead of her seemed to disappear. She strained her eyes against the blackness and it occurred to her that the lamp wasn't actually gone. It was still there, but there was something in front of it, a dark shape blocking out the light.

"Who's there?" she called out, panic rising in her voice. There was no reply. She could hear her heart beating loudly in her ears. What was that noise? Issie could hear something or someone moving towards her through the wet grass of the path above, coming closer and closer to the edge of the bank. She listened silently for a moment.

"Who's there?" she asked again. "Who is it?" Issie's heart was hammering in her ears, making it hard to think. There was the noise again! It wasn't footsteps at all! It was a horse, his hoofbeats making a soft thud on the grass above.

As the grey horse stepped forward to the edge of the path, a halo of light from the hurricane lamp surrounded him. Issie thought that he looked like an angel standing there above her. And he was an angel, her angel, come to save her when she needed him most. Issie felt her strength and determination returning. She wasn't alone any more. She had Mystic.

Still clinging on to the muddy bank with her left hand to stop herself from falling back down again, Issie reached out her other hand. She held her breath for a moment, almost afraid that if she actually tried to touch her pony, he would slip through her fingers like smoke.

But no. He was really there. Her aching fingers, covered in blood, blackberry prickles and mud, reached out and grasped on to the coarse strands of his shaggy mane.

The grey pony lowered his head so that Issie could reach out with her other hand. She knew what Mystic meant to do and she trusted him. She let go of the grass, but instead of falling backwards, she made a desperate grab with that hand too, hanging on to Mystic's neck. The pony took the strain of Issie's weight and backed up slowly on to the track, using the strength of his hindquarters to drag her with him, lifting Issie up, up, up until she was safely standing next to him on the track.

"Hey, Mystic," Issie murmured, throwing both arms around his neck, burying her face in his thick mane. "It's good to see you, boy."

Issie was so desperately pleased to see her horse, she wanted to just stay there like that, hugging him forever. But she had no time to waste. Hugs with her beloved pony would have to wait.

"We have to go now," she whispered. "Stardust needs us." Leading Mystic on to the track, she climbed up the other side, where the bank rose up a little. She was high up enough now to make a leap, throwing herself gracefully on to the pony's bare back. She felt the smoothness of Mystic's sleek dappled coat beneath her. She grabbed a hank of the gelding's thick mane. The bleeding from the blackberries had mostly stopped now and her hands didn't hurt so much any more. She grasped the mane tightly and tapped Mystic's sides with her heels.

"OK, Mystic, let's go!" she said, clucking him forward. Mystic gave a couple of trot strides and then began to canter down the track towards the film set. Issie felt the gentle rocking-horse motion of Mystic's canter and bent low over his neck as the pony picked his way along the darkened path through the inky blackness of the night.

On horseback at a canter it didn't take long to reach the bottom of the track. Straight ahead of her Issie could see the film crew crowded round. She felt sick. Was she too late? Her eyes searched frantically. Where were Angelique and Stardust?

Issie felt a surge of relief when she saw the vampire riders all gathered together on their black horses – and there was Stardust too! Eugene was still holding on to the palomino's bridle to stop her from bolting, which was just as well because Stardust looked completely spooked. So did Angelique. She was gripping the reins for dear life in two fists. She looked terrified. In front of her, Rupert was standing on a camera dolly and giving the riders their instructions.

"Right – we kick off here at the base of the mountain and we go all the way up the fortress to the castle in full gallop," Rupert said. "Angelique, let's give this scene lots of emotion. You are being chased by the vampires of Eleria. If they catch you, they're going to bite Seraphine and turn her against you. You are riding as if your life depends on it. OK?"

Angelique nodded, but Issie could see that she wasn't paying attention to anything Rupert was saying. She was too busy looking at the cobbled terrace steps that plateaued and then twisted and turned again, winding their way up the mountainside like a giant corkscrew towards the black castle. Even if Angelique had been a good rider, this was a dangerous stunt – the cobbles were slippery under the horses' hooves and the twisting track was bordered by a cold, hard stone wall on one side and a steep drop on the other. One step out of place and it would be all too easy to plummet in the darkness and fall to the rocks below.

"Rupert…" Angelique said with a shaky voice. "I have something I need to tell you…"

"What is it?" Rupert looked at the starlet. Angelique was about to speak when Eugene cut her off.

"Tell him later, Angel sweetheart! Rupert doesn't have time for this now, baby! Let's go!" And with that, Eugene gave Bob a quick nod and raised his camera into position on his shoulder. Issie saw Angelique's face turn deathly pale.

"No, wait! Stop! I don't want to—" She didn't get the chance to finish her sentence because, at that moment, Eugene pulled a sword out of the props chest next to him and lashed out, bringing the flat side of the blade down hard on Stardust's rump, letting go of the palomino's bridle at the same time.

Stardust, who was already wild-eyed with fear, felt the blow on her rump and immediately leapt forward as Angelique let out a terrified scream.

"Action!" Eugene shouted with a grin as Stardust bolted towards the first terrace. "Action!!"

Chapter 14

As Stardust galloped off with the screaming Angelique hanging on for dear life, Rupert rounded on Eugene. "You idiot! What do you think you're doing? We weren't ready! My cameras aren't even set up! It's not your job to shout action!"

Eugene ignored him and kept his own camera focused on the runaway palomino. "I'm getting great footage here, Rupert. Can we talk about this later?"

"Footage?!" Rupert fumed. "That horse is out of control! Angelique could be killed. That's it, Eugene! You will never work in Hollywood again. As of this moment you are banned from my set! Do you hear me? Banned!"

The men were so busy arguing that at first they didn't notice the second rider who had followed the runaway palomino up the citadel terraces at full gallop. Issie hadn't even stopped to think when she saw Stardust bolt. She had instantly kicked Mystic on, and the grey pony was already gaining on Angelique. They would reach the palomino before the first terrace, but would that be soon enough? How long could Angelique manage to stay on?

"Angelique! We're coming!" Issie shouted. A sudden gust of wind nearly drowned out her words, and then, as if from nowhere, the rain began to fall heavily.

What's going on? Issie wondered. The night sky above her was clear and starry. There hadn't even been so much as a breeze a few moments ago. W*here did this storm suddenly come from?*

The wind was howling around them now and the rain was so dense that Issie was already soaked to the skin. It all seemed so weird. *How come it isn't raining anywhere else?* Issie thought to herself. *It's only raining on us.*

She looked up. Above her, attached to the black stone walls of the mountain, out of view of the cameras, was the scaffolding that held the lights. Issie could see now that the scaffolding also held vast wind machines and sprinkler systems attached to enormous water pumps. This wasn't an ordinary storm – this was a movie storm! The film crew, who had been waiting in standby position, had seen the palomino coming up the mountain and must have thought they had missed their cue! They had leapt into action and cranked up the storm machines!

Not that it made any difference what was causing the storm. Issie was still soaked to the skin, and the cobblestones were slick with water and slippery beneath the horses' feet. Issie looked ahead and saw Stardust stumble. Angelique screamed again as she grabbed the mare's silver mane and hung on as the palomino miraculously regained her footing.

"Come on, Mystic," Issie clucked the grey pony on. "Now!" She had no time to lose. Angelique couldn't possibly hang on for much longer.

As they reached the cobblestoned plateau of the first terrace Mystic put on a burst of even greater speed. The little grey gelding came up alongside Stardust. Issie, crouched low like a jockey, kept one hand on Mystic's mane and reached over with the other to make a grab at Stardust's reins.

"What are you doing?" shrieked Angelique.

"Saving your life!" Issie snapped back. She grabbed at the reins again and this time she felt the leather in her hand. She closed her fingers and held on tight, making sure her other hand had a firm grip on Mystic's mane. This was a risky stunt. If Issie didn't get her timing right and Stardust pulled too hard, the mare could yank her right off Mystic's back and down on to the cobblestones below.

"Steady boy, whoa now," she called to the grey pony.

Mystic began to slow down, and as he did so Issie gave a hard tug on the reins to get Stardust's attention. The palomino seemed to understand immediately that Issie was in control, and didn't try to fight her. Issie had to be careful to slow Stardust down gently so that Angelique didn't get jolted out of the saddle. She spoke softly to the mare, making sure they stayed close to the safety of the high stone wall, away from the dangerous drop on the other side, as Stardust slowed down to a canter and then a trot. Finally, by the time they reached the second terrace, Issie had managed to steadily pull the palomino up to a total stop.

Issie leapt down from Mystic's back and held Stardust steady. The poor horse was shaking with fright. She had run purely out of fear when Eugene had hit her with the sword. Stardust had been just as terrified as Angelique.

"Easy, girl…" Issie cooed. Still clutching the saddle as if her life depended on it, Angelique looked pale and sick. Her knuckles were white from hanging on so tightly.

"Are you OK?" Issie asked.

Angelique nodded. She was trying not to cry.

"Do you want me to help you down?" Issie held out her hand to help and the starlet clambered down out of the saddle and fell to the ground, shaking and exhausted.

"Ohmygod, y'all!" she said as Issie helped her back up to her feet again. "That was the worst thing ever! I thought I was going to die!"

Tears were streaming down Angelique's cheeks and Issie could see that this time they were totally real. "Thank you," Angelique said, her voice still trembling. "That was amazing riding. I don't know what I'd have done if you hadn't—"

"Hey, hey, what's happening here?" Eugene suddenly emerged beside them out of the darkness. Bob, who was driving the motorcycle for him, was desperately trying to hang on to his sound boom and hold the handlebars at the same time. "Angelique! Baby, why did you stop?"

"Why did you hit Stardust?" Issie turned on Eugene, her face red with anger. "You spooked her! This is all your fault!"

"Hey, kid!" Eugene snapped back. "You stay out of this. That horse just needed a good whack to get her started, so I gave her one. I was helping!"

Suddenly the spotlights attached to the scaffolding above switched on, and Issie was blinded as the whole mountainside was bathed in a white glow. There was a dull whine like a plane engine dying as the motors that drove the wind machines began to slow down to a stop, and then she heard the sound of voices and footsteps coming up the hill towards them. Issie saw Rupert out in front of the others, running towards her and Angelique.

"Angelique! Are you OK?" he yelled out.

"I'm fine, Rupert!" Angelique called back, wiping her tears and pulling herself together. The director came running up the hill towards them.

"Are you sure you're OK?" he said, putting an arm around the shaking starlet.

"I'm OK," Angelique nodded.

Rupert looked around desperately. "Can I get a little help here? Now, please!"

Two of Angelique's assistants rushed forward with a blanket and some coffee and someone else brought out a chair which the starlet flopped down in.

"Angelique, you've been through quite enough for one night," Rupert said. "Why don't you go back to your trailer and get changed into some dry clothes?"

"Thanks, Rupert," Angelique said. She got unsteadily

to her feet as her assistants gathered around her and began to help her back down the mountainside.

Rupert turned to Eugene. "I thought I told you to get off my set!" he growled. Then he turned on Issie. "And what were you playing at?"

"Eugene hit Stardust so she bolted! I was trying to—" Issie began, but Rupert cut her off.

"Another night's filming ruined!" he fumed. "I don't really know what happened just now, but it seems pretty obvious. I've seen this before. You're a stunt double and you want attention. You want to be the star. Well, it's not going to happen, OK? So stop getting in the way."

"But... I was just..." Issie couldn't believe it! Why did Rupert always get the wrong end of the stick? It was like he deliberately wanted to blame Issie when all she was doing was helping. Rupert wasn't listening to Issie's explanation. He was looking around now with a puzzled expression on his face.

"Where is your horse?" he asked her.

"My horse?"

"The one you were riding when you stopped Angelique. The little grey. I didn't even know we had a grey on the set. The script doesn't call for one, does it?" Rupert began to leaf back through his director's notes, looking for the mention of a grey pony.

"Ummm…" Issie didn't know what to say. She had instinctively acted to save Angelique and Stardust. She hadn't even stopped to think about the fact that someone might see Mystic. In fact, she was kind of surprised that Rupert could see him.

Mystic was gone now of course. By the time Rupert and the crew had reached them, the little grey gelding was nowhere to be seen. He had disappeared up the mountain terrace as soon as Issie had dismounted to help Angelique.

"He's not actually in the script. The thing is I…" Issie began. But Rupert wasn't listening. He had lost interest in the whole Mystic matter. He was staring intently at the full moon above the castle. The clouds had cleared now and the night sky was sparkling with stars.

"Oh, brilliant!" Rupert shook his head. "A perfect full moon, everything is ready to go, the crew are all set, weather machines are working perfectly and now we don't have our star to ride the scene!" He looked at Issie, who was standing in front of him soaked to the skin and shivering in the chilly night air. "Will you do it?"

"Me?"

"Sure. You're Angelique's stunt double, aren't you? Well, this is her stunt. What do you say? Are you up for it?"

Issie looked at Stardust. The mare seemed to have calmed down now. Issie reached out her hand and stroked the palomino gently, running her hand down her velvety nose. "What do you say, girl? Want to go for a ride up to that castle?"

Stardust nickered back softly to her, and Issie knew then that the mare understood her. Stardust really trusted her.

"We're ready," Issie said to Rupert. "Let's do it."

The next thing Issie knew Rupert was barking orders and there was chaos on the set. Someone had thrust a script into Issie's hands. "You'll need to learn your lines," the assistant director told her. "But I'm not an actor!" Issie squeaked. "I'm just a stunt rider!"

"I know," the assistant director said. "You just need to speak the words to give us a marker. We'll redo the close-ups with Angelique in the studio against a blue screen later on." The assistant director grabbed the script back off Issie who was standing there staring blankly at it. "Here!" he said impatiently. "Page 126. This is your scene. Learn your lines. You've got five minutes!"

As Issie tried desperately to focus on the script, there was shouting and running as the props and lighting men got back into position and the weathermakers began to rev their engines. Then the costume and make-up department were swarming all over Issie, fitting a long blonde wig on her and pulling off her wet clothes to change her into a spare costume for Princess Galatea.

Meanwhile, at the base of the mountain terraces, the vampire riders were putting on their flowing robes and inserting their fake fangs once more in preparation for chasing her up the mountain.

"Isadora!" a voice called out to her. It was Aunt Hester running towards her with Stella and Kate close behind.

"Isadora! The girls told me what happened. Is Angelique all right?" Hester said.

"Uh-huh. I got to her in time and managed to stop Stardust. I think she's pretty shaken up," Issie said. "Aunty Hess, Angelique can't ride. That's what her big secret is. That's why she wouldn't get on Stardust the other day in the arena and that's why she pretended that Stardust stood on her foot. She's been doing anything she can to get off this movie because she's terrified of horses."

Hester looked shocked. "But she told Rupert that she was a great rider!"

"I know," Issie said, "but she's really not. Aunty Hess she doesn't know what she's doing. You mustn't let her ride Stardust again."

Suddenly a film crew runner appeared next to Issie. "Rupert is ready for you now, Miss Brown," the runner said. "Time to mount up."

"Wish me luck!" Issie smiled at her aunt as she swung herself up into Stardust's saddle.

"You're riding the castle chase?" Hester said. "Do you think Stardust is ready for this?"

Issie gave the palomino a firm pat on her glossy golden neck. "I know she is, Aunty Hess. Don't worry about us. Stardust is a star. Tonight we're going to prove it." And with that, Issie clucked the palomino into a canter and clattered off back down the cobblestoned path to the bottom of the hill where the rest of the riders were waiting to start the chase.

As the black hooded vampire riders gathered behind her ready to gallop up to the top of the citadel, Issie leant low and murmured to Stardust. "Hey, girl," she breathed softly. "Let's show them all what you can do."

"Take two… and… action!" Rupert shouted.

Issie and Stardust shot forward at a gallop, and as they did so the storm began to whirl around them. In the torrential rain, the vampire riders followed in their black, flowing robes. When they reached the third terrace, the black horses had surrounded the girl. The palomino tried to escape. She reared up, lashing out at the head vampire. The vampire drew back his hood to reveal his hideous white face. The palomino snorted in fear at the sight of him and the girl put her hand to the sword that lay on her hip, ready to unsheathe it.

"Leave her alone, Francis," Issie said. "You cannot possibly think you will win like this."

"Oh, but that is exactly what I think… Princess," Aidan replied with a lizard hiss in his voice. "Tonight we take Seraphine's life. She is the last of her kind. Your last hope. When she joins us and becomes one of the Horses of Darkness then you will have lost your kingdom forever."

Aidan jumped down from his black mount and stepped forward. He smiled, baring a set of long white fangs.

"Say goodnight, Seraphine," he said as he opened his mouth wide and lunged forward to plunge his fangs deep into the palomino's golden neck…

"And… cut!" Rupert shouted. The rain suddenly stopped and the studio lights flashed on, bathing everyone in a golden glow.

"Incredible! Nailed it in one take. That was terrific, everyone. It's a wrap!" There was a clapping and a whooping from the film crew at the news that the night's shooting was over. Issie jumped down off Stardust's back and gave her horse a huge hug. They had done it.

Later that night after they had put the horses away, the girls gathered together in Stella and Kate's room.

"I don't know why we're even having this meeting," Stella groaned. "I mean, it's all solved now, isn't it? So Angelique can't ride. Big deal. We know her big secret. She wanted to wriggle out of the movie so no one would know how useless she really is."

Issie shook her head. "I don't think it's that simple. I think someone has been trying to make a fool of Angelique all along." She paused. "I'm sure someone is deliberately causing trouble for Angelique. And that means Stardust is in danger – and so will I be if I have to ride Angelique's stunts from now on. I've thought of a way we can try and trap whoever is doing this, but we'll need help."

"Issie!" Stella said. "Of course we'll help."

"Thanks, Stella," Issie said, "but I didn't mean you. I mean we'll need help from someone else – and she's not going to like it…"

"I cannot believe you're asking me this!" Natasha glared at Issie. "After all this time, leaving me out of everything and being horrible to me, and now you want me to join your poxy little gang?"

Stella couldn't stand this. "Us being horrible? You're the one who's a complete—"

"Shhh, Stella! Let's not get into a fight about who did what." Issie tried to calm her down. Then she turned her attention to Natasha who was standing in front of the three girls with her arms crossed defiantly.

"Natasha," Issie said carefully, "I know that things haven't been great between us since we got here. But this isn't just about us. I think Stardust and Angelique are in danger. We need your help. I've told you my plan. Now what do you say?"

Natasha looked at Stella, Kate and Issie. She didn't say anything for a moment and then when she did finally speak her voice sounded high and nervous.

"If I do this, Stella is not allowed to make fun of me any more – ever. OK?" Stella bristled at this. She was about to say something, but Issie shot her a look.

"Yes, Natasha. Stella is OK with that. She promises."

"You know, it's not like I'm trying to be one of your dumb gang or anything…"

"Oh, what-ever!" Stella rolled her eyes. "Are you going to do it or not?"

"There!" Natasha pointed at Stella. "That's just what I mean! She is always being mean to me! Well, that's it! Forget it!" She stormed off towards her bedroom.

"What? I didn't do anything!" Stella protested.

"Stella!" Issie said. "Why do you always have to wind her up?"

"I don't!" Stella protested. "Anyway, do we really need Stuck-up Tucker for this? Can't we do it with just the three of us?"

"You know we can't, Stella. We need Natasha to make it look convincing," Issie sighed. "I'd better go in there and talk to her."

Issie found Natasha lying face down on the bed with her head in the pillows. "Go away!" she said without looking up.

"Natasha. Look, I'm really sorry. Stella is just like that. She didn't mean to upset you." Natasha pulled her face out of the pillows and Issie could see that she had been crying.

"You didn't tell her, did you? About my mum and dad splitting up? She'd be just awful to me if she knew. It's horrible at home at the moment – Mummy couldn't wait to drop me off here again to get rid of me. And then I get here and Stella is so awful to me…"

"I haven't told anyone," Issie said. "You asked me not to tell anyone and I haven't. And I'm sure your mum wasn't trying to get rid of you. And Stella, well, actually maybe Stella *is* trying to get rid of you…" Natasha almost smiled at this. "…but she can't, because we need you," Issie smiled back. "Come on, Natasha. Will you help us with our plan? Stardust really needs your help."

"OK," Natasha sniffled. "I guess I might as well help since I'm stuck here. After all, I'm not doing anything else, am I?"

"Thanks!" Issie grinned. "Tomorrow night then!"

Natasha nodded. "Tomorrow night."

"I can't believe you convinced Natasha!" Stella was amazed when Issie returned with the news.

"I know!" Issie said. "Now there's just one more person we need to get onboard if this is going to work."

"Issie, do you think she'll do it?"

"She has to," Issie said gravely. "Our plan depends on it."

Chapter 15

After a late night spent filming at the castle, Hester was surprised to find all her riders in the arena bright and early the next morning. Issie, Kate, Stella and Natasha were mounted up and kitted out in their back protectors and helmets, ready to start training.

"I didn't schedule a session for this morning, did I?" Hester was confused. "I thought I told you girls you could sleep in."

"You did," Kate said, "but we woke up early and thought we might as well get some extra practice."

"We want to try the obstacle course one more time," Stella said. "If that's OK?"

"Of course it is," Hester smiled. "Anything in particular that you want to practise?"

"Yes, actually," Natasha said. "We'd like to practise our swordfighting – you know, with the straw dummies?"

Hester nodded. "Good idea. We still have the big battle scene coming up. An extra rehearsal to practise your swordplay wouldn't hurt. You girls saddle up your palominos and I'll go and get the swords."

By the time the girls had tacked up and led their horses back into the arena, Hester had been to the props chest in the tack room and grabbed them each a broadsword. "Remember, just because these are only made of hardwood doesn't mean they aren't dangerous," Hester said as she handed out the swords. "They're not the real thing, obviously, but you could still do some damage with them."

"That's what we were thinking," Stella said.

"I beg your pardon, dear?" Hester said. "What did you say?"

"Ummm, she meant that they're dangerous and that's why we have to be careful," Issie said, giving Stella a look.

Stella shrugged and took her sword. "Well, come on then. Are we going to start fighting or are we just going to stand here all day?"

The girls rode over to the far side of the arena where Aunt Hester's obstacle course finished with the row of straw men tied to posts. The straw men all had red bullseyes on their chests.

"You girls have practised this at a trot and a canter already," Hester said. "I think you're ready to run through it at a gallop."

Issie, Natasha, Stella and Kate lined up on their horses about twenty metres away from their row of straw opponents. "Now, you carry your swords like this, with the blades pointed upwards as you ride," Hester explained, swinging the sword in broad strokes over her head. "Then use the flat of your blade like this to whack against the opponent, or if you want to go in for the kill, drive the point home like this!" She demonstrated by piercing the bullseye on the straw dummy with her own blade.

"Are you ready?" Hester asked. "Get set… charge!"

The four palominos leapt forward in full gallop, the girls waving their broadswords high above their heads. As they bore down on the straw men, each of them lowered their sword and struck a blow.

"I got him!" Stella squealed. "I totally got him."

"Me too!" Natasha said as she pulled Rosie up to a halt.

"I think I missed," Issie sighed as she turned Stardust around and trotted back towards the others.

"Well, we'd better try again then," Stella said.

"You can't afford to miss, Issie, not tonight."

"Tonight?" Hester looked confused. "What do you mean? We're not shooting tonight. The battle scene is being shot in the daylight, Stella – Rupert has scheduled it for tomorrow."

"Ummm," Stella said, "I guess I got mixed up." She smiled at the others. "Shall we go again? I want to get another bullseye!"

The girls had worked up quite an appetite by the time practice was over. They were the first in the queue at the dining hall for lunch.

"Look," Stella said as they were sitting down at their table. "There's Angelique." The starlet was over at the buffet, complaining loudly to her assistants. "I can't eat any of this! You know I'm only allowed a wheatgrass shot and mung beans! Get the chef to sort it out now!"

Issie stood up. "OK, wish me luck. I'm going to go talk to her."

"Wait!" Natasha said. "Maybe I should do it. Angelique is my friend. She'll listen to me."

Issie nodded. "OK. Let's both talk to her together."

"Good luck!" Stella and Kate said. They sat and watched as Issie and Natasha walked over to the blonde starlet.

"Can you hear what they're saying?" Stella asked.

"Uh-uh." Kate shook her head. "But they're talking to her. I can see Angelique nodding."

By the time Issie and Natasha returned to the table the girls were desperate. "What did she say? What did she say?" Stella was about to burst.

"It's done. She's in." Issie said.

The girls finished their meals, but they didn't leave the dining room. They continued to sit there in silence, their eyes glued on Angelique.

"Can I sit with you guys?" It was Aidan.

Stella gave him an anxious glance. "Yeah, yeah. Whatever. Hurry up and sit then! And don't say anything."

"What?" Aidan was confused. "Hey, what's going on here? Why aren't you guys talking to each other?"

"Shhhh, Aidan! Be quiet!" Issie hissed. "We're trying to listen to Angelique."

Over at the blonde starlet's table Angelique was holding court. Her entourage were all gathered around, attending to her needs and hanging off her every word. Suddenly the whole table fell silent as Rupert arrived in the dining hall.

"Rupert! Hi, y'all!" Angelique called out, waving frantically to the director. "Come over here and sit down and have some lunch with me!"

Rupert looked a little uncomfortable with this idea, but he nodded and sent his assistant over to the buffet to get him some food while he sat down at the table with Angelique. Angelique's entourage leapt up and moved out of the way to make a space for the director.

"Rupert." Angelique smiled her brightest, whitest smile at the director. "I was just telling everyone here that I feel simply dreadful about last night. You know, it gave me such a shock when that horse bolted. That's why my performance was so bad." Angelique batted her eyelashes at Rupert and smiled again. "I know I can make it up to you. I'm going to be, like, totally ready to ride my own stunts in the battle scene tomorrow. And to make sure I'm ready, I'm going to practise tonight."

"You are?" Rupert raised an eyebrow.

"Uh-huh," Angelique said. "No cameras or anything though, OK, Rupert? I just want to ride up to the castle by myself and practise. I need to get psyched. I think a little bit of time by myself with my horse will do the trick. I'm going to go up there alone when it gets dark."

Rupert nodded at this. "I think that's a really good

idea, Angelique. I'll tell the stables to get a horse ready for you this evening – and we can get the crew to leave the lighting rig switched on up at the castle. You go rehearse as much as you like—"

Rupert stopped in mid-sentence and turned around. There, behind him, was Eugene with his camera whirring and Bob holding the sound boom.

"What the… what are you two idiots still doing here?" Rupert's face was like thunder. "I thought I kicked you off my film set?"

"Rupert, baby, don't be like that—" Eugene began, but Rupert cut him down with an icy glare.

"I said leave my film set NOW!"

"Angelique?" Eugene pleaded. "Can you put in a good word for us? You want us to stay, don't you?"

"Sorry, y'all," Angelique said. "It's Rupert's decision." She made a telephone shape with her fingers. "I'll call you, OK? Bye bye now! Love your work!"

"All right, all right. We were just leaving," Eugene said flatly. "Come on, Bob. We're out of here."

Rupert turned to his assistant. "Tell security I want those two banned from the set. I don't want them bothering Angelique any more."

Angelique stood up. "Well, I'd better get going too! I

have a Pilates lesson with my trainer in my trailer," she said. There was a sudden shuffling of chairs as her entourage all stood up to follow her. Angelique flicked her hair back and blew Rupert a kiss over her shoulder as she left. "See y'all later!"

The girls all watched Angelique leave. And then, finally, Aidan spoke. "What's going on here, girls?"

Stella, Kate and Natasha all looked at Issie. "Should we tell him?" Stella asked her. Issie nodded.

"Tell me what?" Aidan was confused. "Issie, what is going on?"

"I can't talk about it here!" Issie hissed to him. "Meet us at the stables. Tonight."

That night, the moon was full once more. At the top of the black mountain, the castle made a grim silhouette against the night sky. As promised, Rupert had asked the crew to leave the lights on. The bulbs flickered like a thousand candles shining out of the tiny windows in the turrets and cast an eerie glow in the castle courtyard. While the courtyard and towers of the castle glowed, the cobbled path that circled up the mountainside was much more dimly lit. It was so dark on the mountain terraces that it took a moment to see the rider coming up the path in the moonlight.

Angelique Adams rode slowly up the cobbled tracks on her palomino. She was dressed in her Princess Galatea costume, a white gossamer shirt and sky-blue jodhpurs. Her long blonde hair tumbled loose over her shoulders and shone in the moonlight. Her sword hung at her hip.

When Angelique reached the first terrace she halted the horse and looked around, then set off again along the dark path that wound up and around to the peak of the mountain fortress to the castle gates. When she reached the gates, she hesitated once more, as if uncertain whether to enter. She stood at the drawbridge, holding her horse steady for what seemed like ages.

What was she waiting for?

Then, from the terraces below, came the clean chime of horseshoes on cobblestones as another rider approached the castle. Angelique was not alone. Someone had followed her.

Galloping up the terraced steps came a black horse. His rider, who was crouched low over the horse's neck, was hidden beneath the black hooded cloak of a vampire rider. The black rider rounded the third terrace and urged his horse to gallop faster as they closed in on their quarry, the horse's hoofbeats pounding their rhythm on the cobblestones. The palomino and her rider remained frozen, watching as the black horseman got closer and closer, waiting to see what would happen next.

When the hooded rider was just a few metres away from the girl and the palomino, he pulled the black horse to a sudden halt. He reached into the folds of his black cloak and grasped the broadsword that was hidden beneath his robes. In one swift movement he unsheathed the sword and held it high above his head so that it glinted in the moonlight.

The girl's face grew pale with horror as she realised what the hooded rider meant to do. He was going to attack her! In a sudden rush, the black rider charged down on Angelique with his sword aimed straight at her. As he did so, the girl wheeled the palomino swiftly around and urged her on at a gallop over the drawbridge and through the castle gate into the stone courtyard, with the black rider following hard on her heels.

The castle courtyard was vast and every corner was shrouded in shadows. The girl on the palomino had disappeared into the gloom and the black rider began to ride the perimeter of the courtyard, searching out the shadowy nooks, looking for his prey. Suddenly, from the opposite side of the courtyard, a girl on a palomino rode forward. Her blonde hair shone in the glow of the courtyard lights. She looked at the black rider and smiled as she put her hand to her hip and pulled out her own broadsword.

"Looking for me, y'all?" she asked.

"No!" came another voice from behind the black rider. "He's looking for me."

The rider in the black hood wheeled his horse around. Right behind him was another girl. She looked exactly the same – with long blonde hair and the clothes of Princess Galatea. This girl also rode a palomino and held a broadsword in her hand.

"Actually," a third voice came from the shadows at the other side of the courtyard, "I think you'll find that he's looking for me." Another rider, once again blonde and brandishing a broadsword, rode forward on her palomino.

The hooded rider began to yank his horse about viciously by the reins, circling this way and that, unsure of which way to turn as the three palominos closed in on him. Then, from behind him, he heard yet another voice.

"No. You're all wrong. It's me he's after." A fourth identical rider came forward, holding her sword high over her head so that its blade pointed straight up to the sky.

"I suppose you're wondering which one of us is Angelique?" the fourth rider said. Then she reached up and pulled off her blonde wig, exposing the long dark hair underneath. At the same time two of the other riders pulled off their own wigs and now it was plain to see that the riders were none other than Issie, Stella and Kate. The only blonde left was the girl the hooded rider had chased up the terraces to the castle gates, and he spun his horse around to face her.

"Sorry to disappoint you," Natasha shrugged. "My blonde hair might be real, but I'm not Angelique either." She drew out her broadsword.

"OK," Issie said, "that's enough. It's all over. You can't escape now, so you may as well give up."

The black rider sat perfectly still on his horse, neither speaking nor moving a muscle. Then, without any warning, he rode towards Issie, trying to get past her to escape through the castle gates.

Issie was ready for him. She kicked Stardust on and came back at the black rider, her sword propped at her hip like a jousting lance as she rode. As the horses met, the hooded rider swung his sword, but Issie pulled Stardust to one side, avoiding his blow, and the hooded rider's sword cut through thin air.

"Hey, leave her alone!" Stella called. She rode forward, swinging the blade at her side as if it were a cowgirl's lasso.

Before the hooded rider even had a chance to turn around she had struck him a glancing blow across his right arm. The black horseman cried out in pain. It was the first time the man had uttered a sound. Now he was silent once more as he turned his horse around and rode back into the middle of the courtyard, surveying his four foes.

"Look out, Natasha!" Stella shouted as the black rider rode desperately at her, barging past her and riding hard towards the castle gates.

"Aidan! Now!" Issie called out. There was the grinding and clanking of heavy metal chains as Aidan, who had been hiding behind the castle gates the whole time, turned the winch and released the huge iron portcullis. The vast rusty metal grille that hung suspended over the castle gates suddenly creaked into life and began to lower shut, blocking the castle entrance.

"He's going to make it in time!" Stella yelled.

"No, he's not!" Issie said.

She was right. The portcullis rattled down in front of the black rider, forcing his horse to stop. He turned to face the girls once more, raising his sword. Then he seemed to think better of it, dropped the sword instead and pulled back his hood. Sitting on the horse in front of them, looking rather embarrassed in his black robes, was Bob the sound man.

"Aw, for krissakes, Bob! What did you have to go and do that for? I was getting amazing footage and you ruined everything!" Eugene Sneadly ran forward out of the darkness with his video camera and glared up at Bob. Eugene still had his camera rolling as Bob dismounted from the horse.

"No, Eugene," he said. "You're the one who has ruined everything. You've always ruined it. You told me to get on the horse and ride after Angelique to give her a fright. Well, it's all backfired. Just like everything you do. Don't you get it? I quit. It's over."

Bob reached out and took the camera from Eugene's hands. In the dark outside the castle gates, footsteps could be heard approaching the huge gates of the castle's portcullis. He was right. It was over.

Chapter 16

At first when the others arrived Eugene had refused to admit to anything. "It didn't matter, though," Issie told Hester afterwards, "because Bob blabbed the whole story – he told them everything."

"You'd better explain this all to me again. I still don't understand," Aunt Hester said. The night's adventures were over now and they were all gathered together back at the barracks, the girls snuggled together under rugs on the sofa with mugs of hot chocolate.

"Eugene was deliberately causing trouble the whole time. He did it all for the sake of his stupid documentary," Issie said. "Angelique's supposed to be this big drama queen, but it turns out her real life just wasn't dramatic enough for Eugene. So he decided to make it a bit more exciting."

"That was why he wanted her to ride so desperately that day at the ridge," Stella added. "But then Angelique made all that fuss about Stardust standing on her foot…"

"So Eugene didn't know that she couldn't ride?" Hester asked.

"Uh-uh," Issie shook her head. "He couldn't figure out why his star kept disappearing and refusing to get on a horse. He wasn't trying to hurt Angelique. He just wanted a bit more action for his documentary. When Angelique kept coming up with excuses and refusing to do the stunts, Eugene got more and more desperate to create some drama. His last two films have been flops. This documentary was his last chance."

"How did you manage to set him up?" Hester asked Issie.

"Angelique helped us. She told everyone in the canteen that she'd be riding by herself tonight up at the castle. It worked – Eugene totally believed her. I guess after Rupert threw them off the set this was his last chance. So he made Bob pretend to be a vampire rider. He was never going to hurt Angelique or anything. He was only trying to spook her to get some controversial footage for his documentary."

"Bob thought he was following Angelique up to the

castle. Only it wasn't really her – it was me!" Natasha grinned. "It was Issie's idea. I look the most like Angelique. It wasn't until Bob got close and saw all four of us that he realised he'd made a mistake, and by then it was too late!"

"That was so cool when he chased you into the courtyard," Stella grinned. "He must have been so confused when he saw the rest of us in our wigs. Four Angeliques!"

"How about when you totally got him with your broadsword, Stella?" Kate giggled.

Hester raised an eyebrow. "So that's why you all wanted to practise your swordfighting! Riding about with swords in the middle of the night! What were you thinking? I wish you had let me in on this ridiculous plan," she said sternly.

"Would you have let us go through with it if we'd told you, Aunty Hess?" Issie said.

"Of course not!" Hester harrumphed.

"That's why we didn't tell you!" Issie grinned. The others all laughed.

"As for you!" Hester glared at Aidan. "I can't imagine what possessed you to go along with them."

"It's not his fault, Aunty Hess," Issie pleaded. "We

only told him at the last minute and he had to help us."

All this time, Strudel, Nanook and Taxi had been lying peacefully at Hester's feet. Suddenly they leapt up and began to head for the front door.

"Down! Stay!" Hester instructed the dogs.

"Is it OK to come in?" the voice outside the door asked nervously. Issie looked up and saw the last person she expected to lay eyes on.

Angelique Adams didn't have her usual entourage following her around. She was all alone. "Umm, are those dogs really safe?" she asked.

"They're perfectly safe. Come in, Angelique!" Hester smiled. Angelique smiled back and edged past the dogs over to the sofa where the girls were sitting.

"So," Stella said, "you're scared of dogs... and horses?"

Angelique nodded. She stood next to the sofa looking rather uncomfortable. "Hey, what's that y'all are drinking?" She peered into Stella's mug.

"Umm, hot chocolate?" Stella said.

Angelique eyed up the mug hungrily and sighed. "My nutritionist will only let me drink wheatgrass shots."

Hester smiled. "Well, your nutritionist isn't here now, dear. Would you like a nice cup of hot chocolate?"

"Yeah. Get me some," Angelique said. Then she

looked embarrassed as she realised she was being rude. "I mean, yes, *thanks*, Hester. That would be great."

"Sit down and make yourself comfy on the sofa next to the girls," Hester said. "I'll put the milk on."

Angelique smiled at Issie and Stella who both moved over to make room for her on the sofa. She sat quietly between them while Hester made her hot chocolate. Then, when she had the hot mug in her hands, she finally spoke.

"I never meant to lie, you know, about being able to ride. I never even wanted to do this stupid movie. I am, like, sooo scared of horses! But Rupert is the hottest director in Hollywood and Malcolm, my agent, said this film would be the big one. It might even win me an Oscar. He told me riding would be really easy. And then once I got here and I realised how scary it was, well, I tried to get out of doing the movie but by then it was too late. And Eugene kept harassing me. He said he wanted me to ride so that he'd have all this 'amazing footage' for his documentary."

Angelique stared at her mug. "I feel so stupid. I can't believe I trusted him. He didn't care if I got hurt or looked stupid, as long as I was a drama queen for his dumb ol' film…" she said miserably.

"It's so hard when you live like I do. I know it looks

like I have lots of friends because I'm, like, famous. But they're not my friends at all really – they're just people who work for me. I thought Eugene was my friend, and now I find out he was just using me."

Angelique paused as she looked around at the four girls sitting next to her. She smiled at them. "Y'all don't know how lucky you are. I wish I had friends like you, real friends that I could really depend on."

The girls were all silent for a moment. It was Natasha who finally spoke. "You do," she said, smiling back. "You've got us."

The news of what happened that night at the black castle spread fast. By the morning, when the girls turned up on set, the whole crew gave them a standing ovation. Leading the cheering was Rupert, who came straight up to Issie and shook her vigorously by the hand.

"Isadora, I'm afraid I've had the wrong end of the stick all along," he said. "I was a bit of an idiot really. I didn't know Angelique couldn't ride. And when Stardust stood on her foot, I had no reason not to believe her." Rupert sighed. "Angelique has explained everything to me and now it all makes sense. I can see that you were only trying to help…" He looked Issie in the eyes. "I misjudged you, Isadora, and I'm sorry. It won't happen again."

Issie smiled. "That's OK," she said.

"Well, it's over now!" Rupert said, resuming his normal brisk demeanour. He let go of Issie's hand and gave Stardust a firm pat on the neck. "Right! Shall we get started then?" He turned around to address the rest of his crew.

"All right, everyone!" he called out. "I think that's enough fuss. We've got a film to finish. Can I have everyone in their places, please?"

"Princess Galatea!" a deep voice growled. Issie turned around and saw a hooded rider coming up towards her on a black horse. "Are you ready to do battle?" The rider pulled back his black hood and revealed a bald head covered with purple veins.

"Ohmygod! Aidan!" Issie giggled.

"If you can do battle in the castle fortress in the middle of the night then this should be a piece of cake for you," Aidan grinned. "A battle scene at the castle in broad daylight."

Issie raised her sword in front of her and looked Aidan in the eye. "Bring it on!" she laughed.

"Everybody mount up!" Rupert called from his

director's chair on top of the camera crane. "I want the palomino riders with Galatea on standby outside the castle gates please!"

"I'll see you in battle!" Aidan smiled at her. "Try not to hit me too hard with your sword when we're fighting, OK?" He slipped his fake fangs into his mouth and gave her an evil grin. "Or I might be forced to bite you!"

Issie smiled back, then she wheeled her palomino mare around and cantered over to Stella, Kate and Natasha, who were already in position waiting at the castle gate.

"Vampire riders should all be in the courtyard now please! Final positions, everyone!" Rupert shouted through his loudhailer. The crew on the set went dead quiet as Rupert raised his hand and then pointed straight at Issie. "And... action!"

That was Issie's cue. She raised her sword to the sky and cantered Stardust forward to the middle of the drawbridge. Stardust, who had been waiting for Issie's signal, responded immediately when Issie tightened the reins, rearing straight up on her hind legs and letting out a loud whinny as she thrashed her hooves in the air. As Stardust came back down to the ground, Issie held the mare steady.

"You're through, Francis! I'm taking back my kingdom!" she said. Then she pointed her sword straight at the head vampire. "And I'm taking my horses back too!" And with those words, the golden palomino charged.

In the end, the battle would be swift and violent. Well, at least the final filmed version would be. But the truth of making movies is that nothing happens quickly. In fact, the battle scene took all day to film and by the time the girls arrived at the dining hall that evening they were all exhausted.

"My arm hurts from waving my sword over my head!" Kate groaned.

"I can't believe we had to shoot that same bit where I hit that vampire with my sword, like, ten times!" Stella grumbled.

"Sounds like my Daredevil riders need to toughen up!" Hester said, looking around the table at them.

"Not me!" Natasha said indignantly. "I wasn't even complaining."

"Well, dear," said Hester, grinning at her, "that just proves there's a first time for everything!"

As the girls went back to the buffet for second helpings of chocolate cake and whipped cream, Aidan came running into the dining hall.

"Issie!" He was trying to catch his breath to get the words out. "You've got to come… with me… we've got to go! Now!"

"But I was just going to have some more dessert!" Issie objected.

"No time!" Aidan wheezed. "I've got the truck outside. We need to leave straightaway!" Issie looked confused.

"Aidan? What's wrong?"

Aidan bent down with his hands on his knees, trying once and for all to get his breath back. Then he took a deep gulp of air and looked at Issie. "It's Blaze," he said. "She's having her foal."

Chapter 17

Issie's heart was pounding as she leapt out of the horse truck and ran across the gravel driveway to the front door of Avery's cottage.

"Tom?" she called out as she ran through the house. "Tom! Where are you?"

Issie tore through the kitchen and was heading for the back door when she ran straight into Avery who was bent over taking off his gumboots.

"Issie! You nearly ran me over," Tom grinned. "I wasn't expecting you to get here so quickly."

"Tom!" Issie's voice was strained with panic. "Where is she? Is she OK? I knew I shouldn't have left her. It's all my fault and now I've missed everything…"

"Hey, hey, calm down," Avery smiled. "It's OK. She hasn't had the foal yet, Issie."

Issie felt a wave of relief at this news. "Ohmygod, I was so worried! Aidan told me that you said to come straightaway and I thought…"

Avery shook his head. "I should have told Aidan not to worry you. I wanted you to come back because she's showing signs of foaling, but she's not in labour yet," Avery continued. "I've just checked her again now and I think it's probably going to be another forty-eight hours at least before anything happens."

He smiled at Issie. "Do you want to see her? She's in the paddock next to the house. I haven't moved her into the stable – the weather's been so lovely she's better off grazing outside."

Issie followed Avery out of the house. The paddocks behind his farm cottage were neatly fenced with dark-stained wooden rails. In the paddock closest to the house, standing under the shade of a magnolia tree, a chestnut mare with a flaxen mane and tail and a white blaze was grazing peacefully.

Issie gave a whistle and Blaze raised her head. Her ears pricked forward as Issie whistled again. Blaze nickered a greeting in return as she began to walk towards her owner. Issie watched her wobble along, her enormous belly swinging from side to side. The mare had grown so much in the past week. There was no doubt about it – she was ready to foal.

"She's been restless. She keeps lying down and then standing up again, but nothing is under way yet," Avery said.

"Hey, girl," Issie cooed softly to the mare. She gave Blaze a pat on her glossy neck and examined her. Issie peered at the little black box that was strapped on to the halter underneath Blaze's jaw.

"The foaling monitor's rigged to this pager," Avery said, gesturing to a second, smaller black box that was attached to his jacket pocket. "It will let us know the minute she goes into labour." He handed Issie the pager. "Now that you're back, why don't you hang on to it?"

Issie took the pager from Avery and held it in her hands as if it were a precious jewel. She looked up at her riding instructor. "Tom, I... I don't want to leave her again. I mean, I don't want to go home. I know my house isn't far from here, but what if she has the foal and I don't make it back here in time? What if I miss it?"

Avery nodded. "I'll call your mum and organise for

her to bring over a change of clothes. You'll stay here tonight in the spare room."

"Thanks, Tom," Issie said with relief.

"We'll phone her right now," Avery said, "and then I want to hear all about how things went with Stardust once you were back on the set. No more dramas, I hope?"

Issie laughed. "I wouldn't say that exactly. Actually, there was a lot of drama. It's a long story…" Issie told her instructor everything.

"Stardust was great, though, Tom. She wasn't scared of swords or anything and she acted like a real star."

"So filming has finished?" Avery asked.

"They've still got to film all the close-ups with the real actors. Hester has been coaching Angelique, giving her private lessons," Issie said. "Angelique won't be riding any stunts obviously, but at least she'll be brave enough to sit on Stardust while they film her close-ups and finish the movie."

At this point, Aidan, who had parked the horse truck and joined them, couldn't wait any longer. "Come on, Issie! Hurry up! You haven't told Avery the best bit yet. Tell him about Stardust."

"Oh yes!" Issie grinned. "I was really worried that Stardust would end up with some horrible trainers again on her next job, but Hester says she's spoken to Stardust's owners and they've agreed to sell her! Hester has bought her off them. Aidan will take Stardust back to Blackthorn Farm as soon as the film wraps. So now Blackthorn Farm has three palominos!"

The doorbell rang at that moment and Mrs Brown came in. "Ohhh, it's good to have you home in one piece!" she said, racing over and snuggling Issie up in a big bear hug.

"Muuum! Get off!" Issie said, shrugging off her mum, embarrassed to be getting made a fuss of in front of Avery and Aidan.

"Right then," said Mrs Brown as Avery brought out the scones and jam to go with the tea, and Aidan and Issie began to wolf them down. "I want to hear all the gossip! Did you get to meet any celebrities? What is Angelique Adams really like?"

"At first I thought she was a spoilt Hollywood brat," Issie said, "but once you get to know her she's OK..." She reached for another scone.

"I hear she's a very good rider!" Mrs Brown said.

Issie laughed. "Actually, Mum, I had to help her out with that bit."

"Well, at least you're back home without any slings or

bandages this time. You obviously managed to keep out of trouble for once," Mrs Brown said.

"Really?" Avery said as he plonked the teapot down on the table. "It sounds like there was quite a bit of trouble – especially that swordfight with Bob."

Issie shot Avery a look as if to say, "Be quiet!" but it was too late. Mrs Brown raised an eyebrow.

"Swordfight? What swordfight? Isadora, what is he talking about?!"

Issie spent the next hour trying to explain herself to her mum, a task which left her totally exhausted. At least it seemed to go OK and Mrs Brown calmed down in the end. Issie thought it was a good sign when her mother offered to stay and help Avery make dinner for them all. She even made Issie's favourite meal – cottage pie.

"Does this mean you're not angry with me?" Issie beamed between mouthfuls.

"It means you looked like you needed a good square meal," Mrs Brown said, frowning at her. "As for being angry with you, I haven't decided yet. The whole thing sounds so outrageous, I don't know what to think. I do know that your aunt will be getting an earful from me – but then what else is new?" she sighed, her frown thawing out into a smile.

After her mum had left, Issie went to bed early with grand plans to read the last chapter of the book Avery had bought for her, *The Care of the Mare and Foal*. But after just a couple of pages she found she couldn't keep her eyes open. As she drifted off to sleep she checked the pager which sat on the table beside her bed. The red light indicated that it was switched on, but nothing was happening, so Issie snuggled under the duvet and instantly fell into a deep sleep.

The night had been calm when Issie went to bed, but now a storm was coming. The wind had picked up and the rain was falling heavily. Issie felt herself getting soaked to the skin, goosebumps prickling all over as the drops of rain fell. What was she doing outside in the rain? What was going on? She was so wet and cold, she was shaking. Her body was chilled to the bone and the rain kept running into her eyes, blurring her vision and making it impossible to see. She tried to concentrate, to focus on the shapes in front of her – she could make out a black hooded figure in the rain, and a grey shadow moving about in Blaze's paddock.

"Who's there?" she shouted. "Mystic? Is that you? Where is Blaze? Is she in trouble, Mystic? Mystic!" she screamed out. "Where are you? What's happening?"

Mystic whinnied back to her. His cry was loud and shrill, so loud that it rose above the noise of the storm. So loud that it woke her up.

Issie sat bolt upright. She wasn't outside in the paddock at all! She was still in bed. She had been dreaming. But it didn't feel like a dream at all. It had been so real. She lay there shivering, her body cold and clammy with sweat, still half asleep, trying to figure out what her dream meant.

Her thoughts were shattered by the shrill whinny of a horse. It was the same chilling cry that had woken her from her sleep.

Mystic! She threw herself out of bed. If Mystic was here then there was no doubt that Blaze was in trouble. Issie looked at the bedside table where the pager was sitting. Nothing. The foaling alarm hadn't gone off. Never mind – she trusted Mystic more than some foaling alarm. Issie ran for the back door, pulling on her gumboots.

When she opened the door she could see that the storm had not been a dream after all. It was howling a gale and the rain was pelting down. She stepped back inside and grabbed Avery's huge black hooded jacket off the coat hook, pulling it on as she ran out into the darkness towards Blaze's paddock.

"Mystic!" Issie yelled out. Her voice was swept away by the storm. She was about to shout out again when Mystic suddenly appeared in the paddock right in front of her. The grey horse was dripping wet from the rain. Issie reached out over the rails and grabbed a handful of his coarse mane. It felt like damp rope in her fingers.

"Come on," she said, unbolting the gate to Blaze's paddock to join him. "We've got to get to Blaze."

Shutting the gate behind her, Issie climbed up the gate rungs and leapt on to Mystic's back. She hadn't counted on the rain making the grey horse so slippery. It was hard to stay on bareback and Issie found herself sliding as Mystic cantered across the paddock towards the magnolia tree at the far side. She knew that this was the fastest way to find Blaze, so she wrapped her hands in Mystic's mane, tightened her legs around the little grey and held on.

The rain was so heavy now and it was so dark that at first when they reached the tree, she couldn't see Blaze at all. Finally she could make out the shape of a pony sheltering up against the tree, her head hung low as she tried to avoid the worst of the weather.

As Issie slid down off Mystic's back and ran over to the mare she could see something was wrong. Blaze was turning her head back and forth as if she were sniffing at her flank with her nose.

She's in labour. The foal is coming, Issie thought. *Why hasn't the foaling alarm gone off?*

All she knew was that if Mystic hadn't woken Issie up, Blaze would have had her foal out here alone in the storm – and in this weather the foal could easily die. Issie shivered as she felt the rain soaking through her coat. The chill snapped her into action. Blaze was still in danger. She had to move quickly.

Issie looked back through the rain at the farmhouse. Should she run and get Avery and Aidan? There wasn't time. She would have to get the mare inside by herself.

"Come on, girl!" She grabbed Blaze's halter and pulled. But Blaze refused to move. The mare didn't want to leave the shelter of the magnolia tree and go out into the rain, and the pains in her belly were telling her to stay where she was.

"Blaze!" Issie cried, yanking on the halter. "Come on! We have to get you inside!" Issie could feel herself becoming more and more distressed as Blaze pulled back and refused to move. "Come on, girl!" she pleaded.

This wasn't going to work! Issie let go of the halter. She turned to the grey gelding standing next to her. "Mystic, I can't move her," she said. "You have to help me."

The grey pony seemed to understand. He walked behind Blaze and nudged at the mare with his nose. Blaze put her ears flat back and kicked out at him. Mystic nudged again, this time barging his own shoulder against Blaze's rump. The mare kicked out once more and almost caught the gelding, but Mystic stood his ground and Blaze reluctantly gave in and took a step forward… and then another, and another…

Issie grabbed hold of the mare's halter and pulled again. This time Blaze followed her slowly, gingerly stepping out into the muddy paddock towards the stable gate. It seemed to take forever to get there. The storm was getting worse too. Lightning crackled across the sky and the thunder rolled around them as she led Blaze through the gate and into the safety of the stable block.

Issie turned on the stable lights and led Blaze into her stall. Avery had everything ready. The straw had been packed warm and dry underfoot and there was fresh water for Blaze to drink, a hay net and towels and rugs for the mare. Issie grabbed a bundle of towels and began to dry Blaze off. Her first priority was to get her warm and dry. Then she would dash inside and grab Tom and Aidan to help deliver the foal.

Outside Blaze's stable door Issie could hear Mystic nickering and calling as he paced back and forth. The grey pony was anxious – he knew that the foal was coming. Blaze, on the other hand, didn't seem anxious at all. Now that she was inside, the mare seemed quite calm, even taking a nibble from her hay net. Issie had almost got her dried off and was rubbing a towel across Blaze's rump when suddenly the mare tensed up and a gush of water came out from underneath her tail.

Issie froze in fear. She had seen this in the foaling book. Blaze's waters had just broken. The foal was being born! There was no time now to get Tom. She would have to manage this by herself.

"Easy, girl," Issie said, trying to keep herself calm as she stroked Blaze's belly. She quickly grabbed a bandage out of the box in the stall and began to wrap the mare's tail to keep it out of the way.

She had just finished tying the bandage off when Blaze grunted and lay down. As the mare fell sideways on to the soft hay, Issie saw something poking out underneath her tail. She looked closer. There! There was the pale white membrane of the foal sac and a foreleg appearing. Issie watched as, a moment later, another foreleg and then a nose poked out. The foal was coming!

Issie felt the butterflies in her stomach churning. She hadn't finished reading the final chapter on foaling. She had fallen asleep! What was she supposed to do now?

Keep calm, she told herself, *you've read loads of books. You know this. Don't panic.*

As the foal's head emerged further, Issie took a deep breath and pulled herself together. She clasped the two front legs very gently, waited for Blaze to have another contraction and then she pulled downwards. The foal came even further out now, so that its head and shoulders were free. Issie ripped open the foal sac and cleared the foal's nostrils so that it could breathe. Then she stood back as Blaze pushed again. First the foal's tummy then its hindquarters came out, and then there was a sudden glorious rush as the hind legs slid out and the foal landed softly next to Issie on the straw. Issie couldn't believe it. She had done it. She had delivered Blaze's foal!

All three of them – Issie, Blaze and the newborn baby horse – lay there on the floor of the stable for a moment, catching their breath. Then Blaze nickered softly to her baby. The mare grunted, heaving herself slowly up to her feet, and the foal – all wobbly, long, gangly legs – tried to stand with her. At first it tumbled down and fell about on the straw, but eventually it got to its feet and began to drink its first milk.

Blaze licked her foal vigorously, cleaning up its wet coat, and Issie could finally see what her new baby looked like.

The foal was wet but Issie could already see that it was a bay with a black mane and russet body. It had the longest legs Issie had ever seen. It shared the powerful shoulders and haunches of its great sire, Marius. The foal's face, though, had the elegant dish of its dam's Arabian blood and a white blaze, too, just like it's mother.

Issie stroked Blaze's neck. "You did it, Blaze," she said with tears in her eyes as she looked at her beloved horse. "It's a boy. You've got a son."

There was a whinny behind her as Mystic appeared and stuck his head over the Dutch door to see what was going on.

Issie walked over to the grey gelding and hugged him. "It's a colt, Mystic," she whispered to him, "and he's beautiful." She looked at Mystic. "If it hadn't been for you, he wouldn't be here now. Not in weather like this." The little grey seemed agitated. She knew why.

She could hear voices through the noise of the storm. Avery and Aidan were coming.

"Goodbye, Mystic. Thank you, boy," Issie said, burying her face in his mane. Mystic nickered back his goodbye and then spun round and trotted off into the darkness. Issie peered out after him. She could see the glow of two torchlights bobbing about by the house. Avery and Aidan were on their way. Issie had just a few more moments alone with her precious Blaze and her new baby.

She looked at the rain outside the stable doors. The gale had turned even more treacherous now. She watched as the wind bent the trees and the lightning electrified the sky above them. "Born in a night storm," she murmured as she looked over at the little colt…

She had been thinking for months now about what to call Blaze's foal, but nothing had seemed right. Now, as the wind howled around them and the rain fell in sheets, Issie knew what this foal's name was. He was Nightstorm. At that moment, in her heart she knew that one day he would be the greatest horse of them all.

STACY GREGG

PONY  CLUB SECRETS

Book Five

Comet and the Champion's Cup

When Aunty Hess opens a riding school for the summer, Issie
and her pony-club friends go along to help out. Issie gets to
know Comet, a naughty but talented pony with real
showjumping promise. But can she train him in time to
compete at the Horse of the Year show?

HarperCollins *Children's Books*

Sneak preview...

The bay colt knew the girl was watching. He arched his neck proudly, delighting in her attention as he trotted by. When he passed the paddock railing where the girl was sitting, the colt came so close that he almost brushed against her knees. She giggled and reached out a hand to grab him, but the colt swerved away, putting on a sudden burst of speed, galloping away from her to the other side of the paddock.

When he reached the hedge at the end of the field his flanks were heaving and his muzzle was twitching with excitement. He wheeled about, his ears pricked forward, turning to face the girl who stared intently back at him.

The girl whistled. Her lips pursed together as she blew once, then a second time – a sharp, clear note that carried across the paddock. The colt heard her call, but at first he refused to obey, stamping at the ground and tossing his head defiantly. He held his ground briefly, his muscles quivering, before he leapt forward as if he were a racehorse, breaking from the gate. Thrilling in his own speed as his eager strides swallowed up the ground between them, the colt galloped back to her, wanting to start the whole game again.

"Good boy, Storm!" Issie giggled as the colt swept past again, once more managing to avoid her hand as she reached out to touch him.

They had played this game of tig many times, but Issie never got tired of it. She loved to watch Nightstorm move. His body still hadn't grown into those long, lanky legs – it was as if he were teetering about on stilts – and yet there was something so graceful about him.

Nightstorm was hardly recognisable as the tiny bay foal with the white blaze that had been born that stormy night in the stables here at Winterflood Farm. It was Issie who had named the colt Nightstorm as they sheltered together in the stables while the lightning flashed above their heads. Lately, though, she had taken to calling him by his nickname – Storm.

Storm was just three months old, but already Issie could see that he was the best possible combination of both of his magnificent bloodlines. His elegant head carriage and beautiful, dished Arabian face were derived from his Anglo-Arab dam, Blaze. Physically, though, the colt was much more solid than his mother. He bore a powerful resemblance to his sire, the great grey stallion Marius. You could see it in his well-rounded haunches, classical topline and strong, solid hocks, all true signs of the Lipizzaner breed.

As the colt cantered back once more, Issie leapt down off the rails, a signal that the game was over. Storm understood this. He trotted towards her and didn't try to swerve away this time. Instead, he came to a halt right next to her so that Issie could reach out and stroke his velvety muzzle. She ran her hand down the colt's neck. Storm was already moulting, losing the soft, downy layer of fur that all foals are born with, to reveal the shiny, smooth grown-up coat underneath. Issie could see bits of deep russet bay, the colour of warm mahogany, emerging from underneath the baby-fluff.

Storm was growing fast. Sometimes Issie felt it was too quick – she wanted him to be a foal forever. At other times, she felt it still wasn't fast enough. Horses take a long time to mature – and horses with Lipizzaner blood take longer than most. It would be three years before Storm was ready to be ridden. Such a long time! Issie had bitten her lip and tried not to say anything childish when Avery told her how long she must wait to ride the colt, but inside she felt bitterly disappointed. She didn't want to wait. She wanted to ride Storm now!

It had never occurred to Issie that when her beloved mare Blaze had a foal it would mean she would be left without a horse to ride for the whole of the summer holidays. She couldn't ride Storm – and Blaze couldn't be ridden yet either, not until the colt was weaned at six months. And that was ages away!

Never mind, Issie thought. She might not be able to ride, but she loved just being with her new baby. She was amazed at how quickly Storm seemed to put his trust in her. Perhaps it was because he had watched Issie and Blaze together and he was simply following his mother's cues. His mother was the centre of his universe and if his mum loved this girl with the long dark hair, well, then Storm loved her too. Issie could have happily spent her summer goofing around with the colt, playing silly games like the one they were playing today – if it weren't for Avery getting all serious on her.

"He's just a cute baby now," Avery pointed out. "But that foal of yours will be a sixteen-two hands high stallion one day. He's getting stronger every day, bigger too. That's why it's important to start his schooling now, while he's still small enough for you to be able to handle him. It's important to teach Nightstorm good manners and respect right from the start."

And so, under Avery's expert tuition, Issie began learning how to "imprint" her foal. She followed her instructor's advice to the letter, being firm but gentle with Storm as she taught him to accept a head collar and then a foal halter, how to walk politely beside her on a lead rein and how to stand perfectly still while she picked up his feet.

Issie would arrive at Winterflood Farm at dawn most mornings so she could spend time with the colt before school. She would bring Storm and Blaze into the stable block and spend the next hour grooming the colt while the mare ate her hard feed. The grooming sessions were a gradual process, part of the colt's training, teaching him to accept her touch as she ran the brushes over his body. The whole time she worked, Issie would talk softly to Storm, and he would occasionally nicker back to her, turning around to snuffle her softly with his velvety muzzle when she was brushing him, or closing his eyes in pleasure as she scratched him on that sweet spot on his rump.

The weekends were the best. Then she would cycle down to Winterflood Farm at dawn and wouldn't return home until dinner time. Issie couldn't really say exactly what she did at the farm all day. Sometimes she just lay in the long grass under the magnolia tree and watched Storm. She especially loved the way he would snort and quiver each time something new crossed his path. She could hardly wait until next week when the school holidays would finally be starting and she could spend all her time with the young horse.

Today, Issie had another new surprise for the colt. As she reached into her pocket and produced a carrot, she watched Storm boggle at it with wide eyes. He hadn't learnt to eat carrots yet – and he was uncertain what to do next.

"Here you go, Storm," Issie said softly, extending her hand, the carrot in her palm. Storm had watched his mother eat carrots before, but he'd never been offered one to try himself. He gave it a sniff and his ears pricked forward. It smelt good! He gave Issie's palm a snuffle, taking a tiny little bite, then he held the chunk of carrot in his mouth, unsure of what to do next. Issie giggled again at the expression on his face, those wide dark brown eyes filled with wonder.

"Here, Blaze, you show him how it's done!" Issie grinned, giving one to the colt's mother as well. The mare took the carrot eagerly, crunching it down. Issie was about to dig another carrot out of her jacket pocket and try to feed Storm again when she heard her name being called.

"Issie!" She turned around to see Tom Avery standing on the back porch of the cottage. "Your mum is on the phone. She wants to talk to you."

Issie sighed. "She probably wants me to come home and tidy my room. She's been on at me about getting it done before the holidays begin."

Avery smiled at her. "It is possible that your mother just wants to lay eyes on you for five minutes to make sure you actually exist. You've been spending all your time here with Storm."

Issie paused on the back porch to yank off her boots before padding along the hallway to pick up the phone. "Hi, Mum," she said brightly. "Listen, if it's about my room, I know I said I'd tidy it, but I couldn't find the vacuum cleaner nozzle and…"

Her mother interrupted her. "I've just had a phone call from Aidan." Mrs Brown's voice was taut and serious. "Issie, I'm afraid it's bad news. It's about your aunty Hess…"

To be continued…

STACY GREGG

PONY CLUB SECRETS

Book Six

Storm and the Silver Bridle

Issie is heartbroken when her foal, Nightstorm, is stolen in the middle of the night. Her journey to rescue Storm takes her to Spain where she enlists the help of El Caballo Danzo Magnifico.

But can Issie outwit Storm's kidnappers? And is she brave enough to compete in the ultimate riding race, the Silver Bridle?

HarperCollins *Children's Books*

STACY GREGG

PONY  CLUB SECRETS

Book Seven

Fortune and the Golden Trophy

This season Issie and friends are competing for a new prize – the Tucker Trophy. And Issie has to train the doziest Blackthorn Pony she's ever seen into a winner. That is if she can keep him awake!

Meanwhile, someone is sabotaging relations between riders and the nearby golf course... Could pony club itself be under threat?

HarperCollins *Children's Books*